## Harlequin Cowboy Christmas Collection

Family and friends gathered around the tree, exchanging gifts and good food, sharing the warmth of the season…there's no place like home for the holidays. Especially after spending their days tending the ranch and riding the range, the rugged men in this special 2-in-1 collection value the place they hang their hats.

And this Christmas, these cowboys could be coming home to a few surprises in their stockings! They may not be looking to find that special woman, but romance has a way of catching solitary men under the mistletoe.

So join us as we celebrate these cowboys and the women who lasso their hearts!

If you enjoy these two classic stories, be sure to check out more books featuring cowboy heroes in Harlequin Intrigue.

New York Times Bestselling Author

# B.J. Daniels
## and
# Joanna Wayne

# HOLIDAY RESCUE

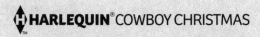

HARLEQUIN® COWBOY CHRISTMAS

Recycling programs
for this product may
not exist in your area.

ISBN-13: 978-0-373-60987-1

Holiday Rescue

Copyright © 2014 by Harlequin Books S.A.

The publisher acknowledges the copyright holders
of the individual works as follows:

One Hot Forty-Five
Copyright © 2009 by Barbara Heinlein

Miracle at Colts Run Cross
Copyright © 2008 by Jo Ann Vest

**Printed in U.S.A.**

HARLEQUIN®
www.Harlequin.com

# CONTENTS

# ONE HOT FORTY-FIVE

B.J. Daniels

This one is for Danni Hill
and her wonderful bookstore, Promises.

Thanks for letting me be a part of it.

# Chapter One

Every nerve in Dede Chamberlain's body was tense as she lay on the narrow bed in the barred, locked room. She listened to the late-night sounds: weeping, an occasional scream, the scrape of a chair leg at the nurses' station down the hall.

Dede knew better than to fall asleep. She'd heard that a new orderly had been hired, and she knew what that meant. She hadn't seen him yet, but she'd heard about him through the whispers of the other patients. A big guy with light gray eyes and a scar on his left cheek. Claude.

She didn't know his last name, doubted he would have used his real one for this job anyway. But she knew Claude would come for her tonight now that only minimal staff were on duty.

But there was no chance of escaping this place. After she'd escaped from the Texas facility, they hadn't taken any chances with her up here in Montana. They'd put her in the criminally insane ward under maximum security, assuring her she couldn't get out—and no one could get to her.

And they thought *she* was the one who was crazy?

The men after her *would* get to her. There was no escaping them—not while she was locked up.

The air around her seemed to change. She sensed it, the same way she had sensed her life coming unraveled just months before. No one had believed her then; no one believed her now.

Dede leaned up on one elbow, the metallic taste of fear in her mouth, a taste she'd become intimately familiar with since she'd discovered just how far her husband would go.

Battling back the fear, she vowed she wouldn't make it easy for Claude when he came to kill her. It was all she had left—she would give him one hell of a fight.

From down the hall, she heard a door open and close with the careful stealth of those who lived by secrets and lies. Dede sat all the way up, listening to the cautious squeak of shoe soles as someone crept down the hallway in her direction.

Another door opened with a soft click; another pair of shoe soles sneaked down the hallway.

Furtively Dede rose from the bed and padded to the door to peek out through the bars into the dimly lit hallway.

Two figures moved as quietly as cockroaches. She recognized them as patients and started to turn away. Whatever they were up to, she wanted no part of it.

But then one of them saw her.

From down the hall, Violet Evans shot her a warning look and touched her finger to her lips before dragging it dramatically across her throat.

Dede had seen her the day she'd been captured and brought in. Violet had watched her through the bars of her window. After spending the last month in a psych ward, Dede recognized madness. But when she'd met Violet's gaze that day, she'd known that she'd just seen true insanity.

"Who is that woman?" Dede had asked the armed orderly taking her to her room.

"Violet Evans. We all watch out for that one."

Violet was a raw-boned woman, late thirties, with straight brown hair and a plain face. The other patient beside her now in the hallway was a large buxom woman with a visage like a bulldog. Both seemed to be carrying what looked like a bright red blanket over one arm—only Violet had one over each arm.

As Violet motioned to someone down the hall at the nurses' station on the other side of the steel bars, Dede felt her stomach roil. She'd heard that Violet had tried to escape from here once before and it had gone badly. She was sure it would be worse tonight and wanted no part of it.

Dede started to step back as Violet came alongside her door. But before she could move, Violet stepped in front of the barred, open window. For the first time, Dede was glad that she was locked in.

She touched her finger to her lips to let Violet know she'd gotten the message loud and clear and wasn't about to give them away. Anyone with a brain could see that the woman was dangerous.

Violet nodded slowly, and Dede saw what she was carrying. Not a blanket. Two plush Santa Claus suits. Dede frowned. Were the costumes from the Christmas program she'd heard about that patients on the other side of the hospital were practicing for? But how did Violet—

The sudden blare of the fire alarm made Dede jump.

But it was the closer, quieter sound that sent her heart racing: the soft clunk of her cell door unlocking.

Through the bars of her window, Dede saw Violet smile and mouth, "You're coming with us."

The door swung up, and Violet reached in, grabbed her by the wrist and dragged her out into the hallway. Violet shoved a Santa costume at her before giving her a shove toward the confusion at the end of the hallway.

"Come on, Texas escape artist," Violet said. "Let's see if you can get out of *here* alive."

LANTRY CORBETT WASN'T used to the phone ringing in the wee hours of morning. Unlike his brother Shane, who was a deputy sheriff, Lantry's business didn't require middle-of-the-night calls.

That's why it took him a few minutes to realize what had awakened him.

"Yeah?" he said after fumbling around half-asleep and finally snatching up his cell phone.

"Lantry?" Shane's voice made him reach for the lamp beside the bed. The light came on, momentarily blinding him. His bedside clock read 3:22 a.m. His pulse took off, and he sat up, scaring himself fully awake.

"Sorry to call you so late, but one of your clients has been arrested and is demanding to see you."

*"What?"* He threw his legs over the side of the bed and dropped his head to his free hand. "You scared the hell out of me. I thought something had happened to…" He shook his head as he tried to shake off the fear that this call was about their father.

It had been a crazy thought, since the family had turned in early down at the ranch's main lodge, and none of them would have been out on a night like this.

Lantry padded barefoot to look out the front window of his cabin toward the main ranch house a good quarter mile away. Nothing moved, no lights shone, no sign of life. Everyone was in bed asleep—but him and his brother Shane.

Snow covered everything in sight, and more was falling, making the night glow with a white radiance. For a moment, he stared at the snowflakes suspended in the ranch yard light outside, wondering what he was still doing in Montana.

"Lantry, are you listening to me?"

He hadn't been. "There's some mistake. No client of mine is in your jail cell. All my former clients are in Texas." Which was where he should be—and would be, once Christmas was over.

"Not this one. She has the Texas accent to prove it," Shane said. "Look, this is kind of a special case, or I wouldn't have called you at this hour. They're coming for her at first light to take her back."

"Back to Texas?"

"Back to the state mental hospital here first, then back to the mental facility she escaped from in Texas."

Lantry let out a curse. "A *mental patient?* Why would you believe her when she said she was my client?"

"She asked for you by name."

He shook his head, still half-asleep he assumed, since this wasn't making any sense. "Who is this woman?"

"Dede Chamberlain."

Lantry let out a string of curses. "The woman's *crazy.* Why do you think she's been locked up? You call me in the middle of the night for this?" He started to hang up.

"She says it's a matter of life and death—yours. She

swears your life is in danger because you were involved in her divorce."

Lantry couldn't believe this. "I represented her *husband* in the divorce. I've never even laid eyes on this woman, and I can't imagine why *I* would be in danger. Frank Chamberlain was extremely happy with the job I did for him." Lantry thought of how well paid he'd been. "The only danger I might be in is from his lunatic ex-wife. Just keep her locked up until the hospital comes to take her back."

"She said you might need convincing. If you refused to see her, she said to tell you to have someone check the brake line on your wrecked Ferrari."

"My wrecked *Ferrari?*"

"I know, you don't have a Ferrari," Shane said.

No, but he *had* owned a Lamborghini. That was, until the accident just before he'd left Texas. His stomach lurched at the memory of losing control of the car. He'd been lucky to get out alive.

"I'll call her a court-appointed attorney," Shane was saying. "Sorry to have woken you for nothing. But she was so convincing, I felt I had to call."

"What time did you say they were coming to get her?"

JUST BEFORE FIVE O'CLOCK, Lantry walked into the White-horse, Montana, sheriff's department brushing snow from his coat. "Is Dede Chamberlain still here?"

Shane looked up in obvious surprise to see him standing in his office doorway. "Yes, but I didn't think you were interested in representing her. Something change your mind?"

"Can I see her or not?" Lantry asked.

"You might want to work on your bedside manner."

"I'm a divorce lawyer, not a doctor, and after being rudely awakened, I couldn't get back to sleep."

Shane picked up a large set of keys. "I had forgotten you get a little testy when you don't get your rest."

Lantry didn't take the bait as he followed his brother through the offices toward the attached jail. He nodded to a deputy who didn't look like he was out of high school, obviously a very recent hire given the fact that his uniform looked straight out of the box.

Shane led Lantry through a door and down a hallway between a half-dozen cells. All but one was empty. He noticed that Dede Chamberlain had been put in the last cell at the end of the row and guessed that was probably because she'd been disruptive and they hadn't wanted to hear it.

Lantry had dealt with his share of young wives married to rich older men. He knew the type. Privileged, spoiled, demanding, born with a sense of entitlement.

As he neared the former Mrs. Frank Chamberlain's cell, he saw a small curled-up ball under what looked like red fake fur. He cleared his throat, and she sat up looking sleepy-eyed for an instant before she became alert.

Lantry had never laid eyes on the woman before and was more than a little surprised. Dede Chamberlain had already been locked up in the Texas mental facility by that time so the only person Lantry had dealt with was her lawyer. When he'd handled her husband's side of the divorce, he'd assumed the fiftyish Frank Chamberlain hadn't been far off base when he'd claimed his younger wife was a gold-digging, vindictive, crazy bitch who was trying to take all of his money—if not his life.

Having seen his share of crazed trophy wives, Lantry had put Dede Chamberlain in the same category. He'd expected Botoxed, health-clubbed and hard as her designer salon acrylic nails.

That's why he was taken aback now. This woman looked nothing like the ex-wives he'd dealt with during his career.

Dede Chamberlain had the face of an angel, big blue eyes and a curly cap of reddish-blond hair that actually looked like her original color. There was a sweet freshness and innocence about her that he'd always associated with women from states that grew corn.

But if anyone knew that looks could be deceiving, it was a divorce lawyer.

She blinked at him as if surprised to see him, then rose to come to the bars. "Thank you so much for coming down here, Mr. Corbett," she said in a voice that was soft, hopeful and edged with maybe a little fear.

"I'm not here to represent you."

"You're not?" She lost the hopeful look.

"If you weren't already locked up and facing life in prison or worse, I would have you arrested for whatever you did to my *Lamborghini*." He stopped and frowned. "Why are you wearing a Santa Claus costume?"

She waved a hand through the air. No acrylic salon fingernails. Not even any polish on her neatly trimmed bare nails, he thought, distracted for a moment.

"The Santa suit? It's a long story," Dede said. "But you probably shouldn't hear about it since you aren't my lawyer. But for the record, I never touched your car. You can blame Frank for that."

Lantry shook his head. "Why would your ex-husband

and *my* client, who I might add I got a huge settlement for, want to destroy my car?"

"I can understand your confusion, Mr. Corbett. But that's why I had your brother call you. Your life is in danger because of something my ex-husband was involved in."

Lantry nodded, wishing he hadn't bothered to come down here. What had been the point? The woman had escaped from a mental institution. Two mental facilities, actually, and had shown a history of fanatical behavior on the verge of homicidal during the divorce. Had he expected reason from this woman?

He shook his head and turned to leave.

"Why do you think I'm in Whitehorse if not to warn you?" she said to his retreating back. "Why come all the way to Montana? Why not just take off to some place where no one could find me and save my own neck? Isn't that what you would have done?"

That stung, but he couldn't deny the truth of it. He stopped walking away and turned to look back at her, something in her words making him hesitate.

"I would be dead right now if it hadn't been for the two inmates who broke me out with them from the state hospital," Dede said.

"Instead, you came here to *save* my life."

She nodded, obviously missing the sarcasm in his tone—or ignoring it. "My motives weren't completely altruistic," she said. "I'm hoping you can save us both. But if they—"

He held up his hand to stop her. "Who's *they?*" he asked, waiting for her to say she didn't know so he could walk out without feeling the least bit guilty. "I thought you said *Frank* was behind this death wish for me?"

"Actually, it's two childhood friends of Frank's," she said. "I only know them as Ed and Claude. But when they showed up in Houston, that's when Frank began to change. I could tell he was afraid of them, but it was as if they had some kind of hold on him."

This all sounded like a bad B movie, and Dede Chamberlain was writing it from somewhere inside her demented brain.

Lantry had heard his share of pre-divorce stories over the years. He didn't want to hear Dede Chamberlain's, didn't want to feel any sympathy for her. Marriage was a choice, and she'd stupidly married Frank.

Those big blue eyes filled with tears. She bit her lower lip as if fighting to hold them back. "I know those men are why Frank turned on me—and why they're now trying to kill you."

He couldn't help but ask. "Didn't you question him about what was going on?"

"He said I was imagining things. But one night after he'd had a few drinks, he seemed to be the old Frank I'd fallen in love with. He said that he'd believed a man could change, could overcome his past, even his up-bringing. I said I believed that too, but he said we were both wrong. That his past had come back to drag him down, and there was no escaping it."

"What does any of this have to do with him trying to kill you or me?" Lantry asked impatiently.

"Didn't you ever ask yourself why it wasn't enough for Frank to just divorce me? He had me committed so no one would believe anything I said."

And it was working, Lantry thought.

"Last week Frank called me and warned me they

would try to kill me and that I had to get out of the hospital."

Lantry rubbed the back of his neck. His head hurt, and he needed sleep. "You do realize how crazy this all sounds, don't you?"

She nodded. "They're counting on you not believing me. That's why you have to get me out of here so—"

Lantry let out a laugh. "I don't think so. I'll take my chances with Frank and his boys. But thanks."

"They tried to kill you once when they rigged your Ferrari," she said grabbing the bars of her cell, calling after him as he started to turn away again.

*"Lamborghini,"* he said, turning back to her.

"Whatever. All those kinds of cars look alike to me," she said and glanced at her watch. "We don't have much time, Mr. Corbett. I'm your last hope. Once they kill me, there won't be anyone who can save you."

Why was he still listening to this woman? Because of an uneasy feeling that her story was just crazy enough to be true.

"How did you get to Montana anyway?" he demanded, wanting to trap her in a lie so he could wash his hands of this whole business and get back to bed. "Frank took all the money, the cars, the houses—"

"I have my own money, Mr. Corbett." There was a hard edge to her voice. "I didn't marry Frank for his, no matter what he led you to believe."

Lantry couldn't hide his surprise. He had wanted to believe she was a crazy gold digger. It made what Frank did to her easier to be a part of. "Even if I believed that Frank's buddies tampered with my car, they had other chances to kill me after that. So why haven't they tried?"

"I suspect they didn't know where to find you," she said. "Ed has got to be in Whitehorse by now. Claude is either still at the hospital or on his way here. If I have to go back in the mental hospital, he'll kill me. He came close in Texas. I'd be dead right now if Violet and Roberta hadn't broken me out. I know all this is hard for you to believe—"

The cell-block door opened, and his brother stuck his head in, motioning to him.

"Hold that thought," Lantry said to Dede, shaking his head at how foolish he was to buy into any of this. So the woman had her own money and she was no dummy, her story was still preposterous.

"We just got a call," Shane said. "A stolen vehicle believed driven by one of the patients Dede Chamberlain escaped with has been spotted. The patient, Violet Evans, is from here. The sheriff and I are going out there now. Are you about through with your client?"

"She's not my client," Lantry snapped irritably. His cell phone rang. He checked it. "I need to take this."

"Deputy Conners will be here in case you get any ideas about breaking her out," Shane joked.

Lantry mugged a face at his brother and took the call as the cell-block door clanged shut. "So, what did you find out?"

"How about 'Hello, James, sorry to wake you too damned early in the morning and ask you to track down my wrecked car.'"

"Sorry." James Ames was a close friend and a damned good mechanic. "You found it? And?"

"The brake lines weren't cut."

So it was just as he'd suspected. Dede Chamberlain was delusional.

"The steering mechanism was hinky, though."

*"Hinky?"* He glanced down the line of cells at Dede, then turned his back to her.

"I've never seen one torqued quite like that from an accident," James said. "What did you hit?"

"Nothing. I just suddenly lost control of the car. Are you saying it had been tampered with?" Lantry said, keeping his voice down.

"Only if someone was trying to kill you." James laughed as if he'd made a joke. "I guess in your profession that's always a possibility, though. Guess they missed you this time." He was still chuckling when Lantry hung up.

He glanced back at Dede again. She was holding on to the bars, watching him with that hopeful look on her angelic face again. Damn.

As he walked back to her cell, he pictured Frank Chamberlain, a handsome, well-to-do, powerful man in Houston who didn't need to resort to murder to get what he wanted. "You say Frank called to warn you. But if Frank wanted to protect you, why didn't he break you out himself?"

"How did Frank tell you he made his fortune?" she asked, the change of subject giving him whiplash.

"A killing on Wall Street."

She smiled ruefully. "He told me his grandmother left him the money."

Lantry had never cared how his clients made their money as long as he got paid. Frank Chamberlain had paid right away. The check had gone through, and Lantry had put the case behind him and gone to Montana for a family meeting on the Trails West Ranch, where his father and new wife had just settled. He hadn't planned to stay so long, but he'd gotten involved in some family legal business and then it was almost Christmas….

"Frank lied to both of us, and worse, involved us in his past." Dede met his gaze with a challenging look. "You're starting to believe me, aren't you?"

The woman didn't know a Lamborghini from a Ferrari. Did he really think she knew the brake line from the steering mechanism?

"Even if I bought into this, the state is sending someone to pick you up in—" he glanced at his watch "—less than—"

Her bloodcurdling scream made him jump back. She began to rattle the bars, screaming at the top of her lungs.

"What the hell are you doing?" he demanded and reached out to stop her.

She grabbed the front of his shirt and the strings from his bolo tie. He heard fabric rip as he tried to pull away, the bolo tie tightening around his neck. The door to the sheriff's office clanged open, and the still-wet-behind-the-ears deputy came running toward them.

It all happened so fast. Lantry made the mistake of trying to calm her, afraid he would hurt her if he pulled away too hard. Dede had wound her fingers into the fabric of his shirt and was hanging on to his bolo tie as if it were a lifeline.

The deputy jumped into the middle of the ruckus.

Lantry didn't see her get the deputy's gun. It just suddenly appeared in Dede's hand, pointed at the two of them at the same time the screaming stopped.

In the deafening silence that followed, all Lantry

could hear was the blood pounding in his ears as he stared at the woman with the gun.

Dede was so calm now he shuddered to see that she knew her way around weapons and probably the steering mechanisms on Lamborghinis as well. He couldn't believe how he'd been taken in by her. Probably the same way poor Frank Chamberlain had.

The deputy had turned a sickening shade of green.

"Take it easy," Lantry said, not sure if the words were meant for Dede or the deputy or himself. "Don't do anything rash." How could she do anything more rash than what she'd just done short of shooting them both now at point-blank range?

She barked out instructions to the green deputy, who did as he was told. "Now put the plastic cuffs on the lawyer. Loop them through that fancy belt of his."

"Like hell," Lantry said.

"I'm sure you don't want to see anyone get hurt here, do you, Mr. Corbett?"

He glared at her.

She pointed the deputy's pistol at the young man's heart. "Make sure they are good and tight."

Lantry had no option. He couldn't take the chance she would shoot the deputy.

"Now open the cell," she said, still holding the gun on the deputy. "Hurry up. We don't want to see any innocent people get hurt because you didn't move fast enough."

As instructed, the deputy opened the cell and traded places with her. Dede closed the cell door, keeping the pistol on Lantry, and took the keys.

"Come on, Mr. Corbett. We'll be leaving now. Cross

your fingers that no one tries to stop us. As crazy as I am, who knows what I might do?"

Lantry bit down on a reply and, with the gun barrel pressed into his back, let her lead him out of the sheriff's department and into the snowy, still-dark early morning.

## Chapter Two

There were no cars in the parking lot other than Lantry's pickup and the deputy's beat-up old Mazda, both covered with snow. The blizzard Lantry had been warned about on the news had finally blown in.

"Just a minute." Dede reached into his coat pocket and dug out his cell phone and keys. She hit the automatic lock release, the lights of the pickup flashing on.

As Dede walked him to his pickup, wind whirled the large, thick flakes around them as if they were in a snow globe.

He could imagine how ridiculous the two of them looked. Him in handcuffs tethered to his belt and a petite woman in a Santa costume holding a gun on him.

But unfortunately, there wasn't anyone around at this hour—and in the middle of a blizzard—to see them.

"You don't want to do this," Lantry said as they reached his pickup. "This is only making your situation worse."

"A hotshot lawyer like you? I'm sure you can get me off without even any jail time," Dede said, keeping the pistol pressed into his back.

"You can't possibly think that I can make all of this

go away. You pulled a gun on a sheriff's deputy and escaped from two mental hospitals and a jail cell."

"I did what I had to do," she said, pressing the gun barrel into his back. "When the time comes, I know you can make a judge understand that. Anyway, what would you have done under the same circumstances?"

He didn't know. He thought of his brother Dalton's criminally insane first wife. The law didn't always protect people. Oftentimes it was used against the person who needed and deserved protection the most.

Dede took him around to the driver's side and opened the door. "Get in and slide across the seat. If you think about doing anything stupid, just think about your part in helping Frank take everything—including my freedom from me—in the divorce."

He climbed in and slid across the seat, keeping what she had said in mind. He had helped put this woman away—just not well enough, apparently.

She followed, never taking the gun off him and leaving him little doubt that she really might shoot him if he tried to escape.

Shifting the weapon to her left hand, she inserted the key and started the pickup, then hit the child locks and reached over to buckle him in. "Just in case you're thinking about jumping out."

As if he could reach the door handle the way she had him hog-tied.

The wipers swept away the accumulated snow on the windshield. The glow of Christmas lights on the houses blurred through the falling snow, a surreal reminder that Christmas was just days away.

Dede turned on the heater, then shifted the truck into

gear and, resting the pistol on the seat next to her thigh, drove away from the sheriff's department.

Her composure unraveled him more than even the gun against her thigh. This woman must have nerves of steel. For just a moment, though, he thought he saw her hands trembling on the wheel, but he must have imagined it given the composed, unwavering way she had acted back in the jail.

They passed only one vehicle on the way out of town. A van with a state emblem on the side, but the driver was too busy trying to see through the falling and blowing snow to pay them any mind.

Lantry consoled himself that the deputy would soon be found in the cell and a manhunt would begin for the escaped prisoner and her hostage.

"You'll never get away with this," he said, his throat dry as she took one of the narrow back roads as if she knew where she was going.

He recalled that she'd spent the past twenty-four hours before her arrest with Violet Evans, a woman from the area. It was more than possible that Dede had gotten directions from the local woman.

"I suppose all this seems a little desperate to a man like you," she said quietly.

"A *little* desperate?" He looked over at her, then out at the storm. He could feel the temperature dropping.

The weatherman had forecasted below-zero temperatures and blizzard conditions. Residents had been warned to stay off the roads because of blowing and drifting snow and diminishing visibility.

Lantry had little doubt that the roads would be closed soon, as they had been earlier in the month during the last winter-storm warnings.

"You know, it's funny," Dede said as she drove. "Thanks to Frank, I've been forced to do things I wouldn't have even imagined just months ago. I suppose that *is* nuts, huh?"

Lantry studied her, not wanting to know what had pushed her over the edge. "Would you have really shot that deputy?"

"Of course not. What do you think I am? That deputy never did anything to me. Unlike you," she added. "You helped Frank get me locked up in a mental ward."

Lantry didn't want to go down that road. The wind rocked the pickup. Snow whipped across the road, forcing Dede to slow almost to a crawl before the visibility cleared enough that she could see the road ahead again.

The barrow pits had filled in with snow. Only the tops of a few wooden fence posts were still visible above the snowline.

"My brother will be combing the countryside searching for me," he said. Outside the pickup window he could see nothing but white. There were no other tracks in the road now. No one would be out on a night like this. *No one with a brain,* he amended silently.

"Shane will call in the FBI since kidnapping is a federal offense," he continued. "This time they'll lock you up and you'll never get out. Do you have any idea where you're headed?"

He glanced over at her when she didn't answer. Her angelic face was set in an expression of concentration and determination.

"The best thing you can do at this point is turn around and go back," he said. "If you turn yourself in, I'll do everything I can to make sure you get a fair hearing."

"I'm touched by your concern, Mr. Corbett. But I'm crazy, remember? *If* I get caught, they'll just put me back in the looney bin and throw away the key, and then the men after me will kill me. By then, they will have murdered you, so you'll be of little help."

She shifted down as a gust of wind rocked the pickup and sent snow swirling around them.

"But if we don't get caught," she continued, "I might be able to keep us both alive. So in the grand scale of things, kidnapping you seems pretty minor, don't you think?"

He hated that her logic made a bizarre kind of sense. She wasn't going to turn around and take him back, that much was a given.

In the rare openings between gusts, blurred Christmas lights could be seen along the eaves of ranch houses. But soon the ranch houses became fewer and farther between, as did the blur of Christmas lights, until there was nothing but white in the darkness ahead.

They were headed south on one of the lesser-used, narrow, unpaved roads. Between them and the Missouri Breaks was nothing but wild country.

"What now?" he asked as the wind blew in the cracks of the pickup cab and sent snow swirling across the road, obliterating everything.

"You're going to help me save our lives—once I convince you how much danger you're in."

It wasn't going to take much to convince him of that, Lantry thought as he noted the gun nestled between her thighs and the Montana blizzard raging outside the pickup.

DEDE GRIPPED THE WHEEL and fought to see the road ahead. Mostly what she did was aim the pickup between the fence posts—what little of them wasn't buried in snow on the other side of the snow-deep barrow pits.

Between the heavy snowfall and the blowing fallen snow, all she could see was white.

She didn't need Lantry Corbett to tell her how crazy this was. But given the alternative…

Nor did she want to admit that the lawyer's arguments weren't persuasive. There was a time she would have believed everything he said and been ready to turn her life over to him, thinking he would save her.

But this wasn't that time. Too much had happened to her. And too much was at stake. A part of her wished she'd been honest with Lantry back at the jail, although she doubted it would have swayed him anyway.

She couldn't let herself forget who this cowboy was or the part he'd played in bringing them both to this point in their lives.

This Lantry Corbett, though, looked nothing like the man she'd only seen on television. This blue-eyed cowboy hardly resembled the clean-shaven, three-piece designer-suited lawyer who she'd been told would eat his young.

She'd thought she had the wrong Lantry Corbett when she'd rolled over on her cot in jail earlier and had seen the cowboy standing outside her cell. This man wore a black Stetson, his dark hair now curled at the nape of his neck—not the corporate short haircut he'd sported in Texas—and he'd grown a thick black mustache that drooped at the corners and made him look as if he should have been from the Old West.

Maybe even more surprising, he looked at home in his worn Western attire. This was no urban cowboy, and the clothing only made him more appealing, accentuating his broad shoulders and slim hips. Even the way he moved was different. Tall and lanky, Lantry had walked into the jail with a slow, graceful gait in the work-worn cowboy boots and Wrangler jeans that hugged those long legs.

He had been nothing like that ultraexpensive lawyer she'd seen stalking across the commons of his office high-rise with a crowd of reporters after him.

No, for a moment in the jail, she'd been fooled into thinking she was wrong about the cutthroat divorce lawyer turned cowboy—until he opened his mouth.

Only then did she know she had the right man.

She kept her attention on the road—what she could see of it—and the blizzard raging outside the pickup, wishing there was another way.

VIOLET EVANS ALWAYS KNEW she'd come home one day. She'd thought about nothing but Whitehorse since she'd been locked up.

True, she had planned to come home vindicated. Or at least have everyone believe she was cured. But that hadn't happened.

In the passenger seat of the stolen SUV, Roberta began to snore loudly.

Violet knew everyone in four counties was looking for her. She'd become famous. Or infamous. Either way, she liked the idea of her name on everyone's lips. They'd all be locking their doors tonight.

She smiled at the thought, imagining the people who'd wronged her over the years. They would be terrified until she was caught. Once, they'd just made fun of her. But now they would have new respect for her.

Still, it bothered her that they all thought something

was wrong with her. No wonder they'd been quick to send her away to a mental hospital after that unfortunate incident with her mother. How different things would have been if they had believed her when she'd tried to explain why she'd tried to kill her mother that day.

She shoved away the disturbing images from the past. But one thought lingered. If Arlene loved her… If she'd saved her from her awful grandmother… If she'd tried to help her with the scary thoughts in her head…

A mother is supposed to save you. Arlene Evans had failed to save her oldest daughter, so what right did Arlene have to get married and be happy?

"No right at all," Violet's dead grandmother said from the backseat. "Her idea of saving you had been to marry you off."

Violet thought of the humiliation and embarrassment when no man had wanted her—and worse, the disappointment she'd seen in her mother's face.

"If Arlene hadn't tricked my son Floyd into marrying her and had you three kids—"

"Can you just shut up?" Violet said, wishing she could cover her ears. She'd heard this from her grandmother since she was a girl. Grandmother always causing trouble, stirring things up between them, then standing back and saying, "See? See what I mean about this family?"

Roberta stirred in the passenger seat. "What's going on?" She glanced in the backseat, then at Violet, frowning. "You aren't talking to your dead grandmother again, right?"

"I was talking to myself. I need you to run a little errand for me," Violet told her as she parked near Packys, a convenience store on the edge of town.

She had skirted Whitehorse, which wasn't difficult since the town was only ten blocks square and she knew all the back roads.

The first thing she needed to do, though, was find out everything she could about her mother's upcoming Christmas wedding. It wasn't like she'd gotten an invitation.

"You're going to run in and get me the local newspaper and the shopper—those are the area bibles when it comes to what's going on," Violet told her.

Roberta groaned and complained, but finally got out and went in. She was wearing a pair of blue overalls and a flannel shirt and looked enough like a local that she shouldn't have any trouble, Violet figured.

Getting a change of clothing had been easy since Violet knew which residents would be gone this time of year and which ones locked their doors. They'd tossed out the Santa costumes after tossing out Dede Chamberlain.

It had amused Roberta to dump Dede on the main street of Whitehorse wearing the Santa suit.

When Roberta returned from inside the convenience store with the newspaper and free shopper, Violet drove down the street the few blocks past town. She pulled over in front of Promises bookstore, gift shop and antique store—closed now—and took the papers from Roberta.

Snapping on the dome light, she scanned for what she knew had to be there. Whitehorse, Montana, was so small that weddings, baby and wedding showers, and birthday parties were advertised in the paper and open to everyone. Her grandmother had already said that Arlene would invite the whole town to show off the fact that she'd caught another man.

To her dismay, Violet didn't find anything about the wedding and was about to give up when she saw the wedding shower announcement.

There was no address as to where the shower was being held, since it was unnecessary. Instead all that was listed was the name of the person who was hosting the get-together. Pearl Cavanaugh. If you didn't know where the Cavanaughs lived, then you had no business at the shower.

"What the hell?" Violet said, thinking she must have read it wrong. "Pearl Cavanaugh is throwing a shower this afternoon for my mother? This has to be a misprint."

"I thought you said nobody in town liked your mother."

Violet shot Roberta a look that shut her up. Maybe it was a pity shower. Still, it seemed odd. Violet couldn't shake the uncomfortable feeling that everything had changed since she'd been gone.

She read it again and noticed something she hadn't seen before. It said in case of bad weather, the shower would be held at the Tin Cup, the restaurant out of town on the golf course.

Violet had heard about the winter-storm warning on the radio. She couldn't imagine worse weather.

Her thoughts returned to her mother and the shower. It was amazing enough that her mother had found another man when Violet hadn't even found one. And he was a man with money, from what she'd heard. She consoled herself with the assurance that Hank Monroe couldn't be much of a man.

"So, are we going to your mother's shower?" Roberta asked, reading over her shoulder.

"I wouldn't miss it for the world. But first there's somewhere we have to go."

ARLENE TOUCHED THE wedding dress hanging from her closet door.

She felt like Cinderella about to go to the ball. She closed the closet door as the phone rang. All morning she'd feared that Pearl would cancel the shower. After all, with this storm coming in… "Hello?"

"Hi, beautiful."

She melted at the sound of Hank's voice. That she'd been given a second chance was such a blessing. He'd changed her. Not that she didn't have a long way to go.

She still had to bite her tongue not to gossip or have uncharitable thoughts. Hank laughed at her attempts to be the perfect woman.

"Arlene, I love you exactly as you are." That alone amazed her. But she wanted to be better for Hank. His love had already made her a better person.

"I hope I didn't wake you," Hank said now.

"No, I was up admiring my wedding dress." Hank had bought it for her, saying she deserved her dream wedding. She and Floyd, her first husband and the father of her children, had gotten married by the justice of the peace. A shotgun wedding because she'd been pregnant with her first born, Violet.

Looking back, it was clear Floyd had never wanted the children. Nor did he care about them even now. He hadn't even been to see his own grandson.

Arlene was so thankful that Hank loved the baby

and had gone out of his way to help her daughter Charlotte and son-in-law, Lucas, make a home for their son.

"Then you haven't seen the news," Hank said, dragging her from her thoughts.

Arlene felt her heart drop. "No, why?" Her first thought was that the shower was cancelled. But from the sound of Hank's voice, she knew it was more serious than that.

Her worry intensified. Instinctively she knew it must have something to do with Bo. In the past, most news, especially bad news, was often about her son, Bo. But Bo was gone.

She still couldn't believe what he'd done to bring about his own death. For months now, she'd mourned his loss, knowing she had failed him by spoiling him, just as she'd failed her daughter Violet by not spoiling her enough.

"Honey, it's Violet. She's escaped from the state institution. There were three of them. One has already been caught, so I'm sure—"

"Ohh." She sat down hard in the middle of the floor, the phone clutched in her hand. *"Violet?"*

Her oldest daughter. The culmination of all her mistakes as a mother. Hank kept assuring her that she hadn't made Violet what she'd become. That there had been something wrong with Violet, something genetic. Just as she couldn't blame herself for the way Bo had turned out after growing up without a father present.

Arlene couldn't help but feel that if she'd been a better mother, if she'd insisted Floyd take more of a part in raising the kids, if she'd been able to stand up to Floyd's horrible mother and not let that old woman near her kids...

"I want you to come stay with me until Violet is caught," Hank was saying.

Caught? How was it possible to raise a child that would one day have to be caught like a rabid dog?

"Hank, what about Charlotte and the baby?" Little Luke was a year old now, but still Arlene thought of him as a baby.

"Violet won't hurt her sister or her nephew, and Lucas will be home from his ranch job up north. You don't have to worry about them."

"You don't know what Violet's like. She's so angry. She blames everyone for her unhappiness." She realized she was crying.

"If you're that worried, I'll have Lucas, Charlotte and Luke move in here with us. There's plenty of room."

Arlene felt sick. "You know why she escaped *now,* right before the wedding. She—"

"I won't let her stop the wedding."

She loved Hank more than life and knew how capable he was of taking care of her. But he didn't know Violet and what *she* was capable of. Arlene did. "Maybe we should put off the wedding."

"No," Hank said. "If she isn't caught before the wedding, then I'll see that security is stepped up. I just want to make sure that you're safe until then. I'll be down to pick you up. Pack just what you need until the wedding. Has the storm hit there yet? It's snowing really hard up here. I think it's moving south in your direction, so bundle up."

"Hank—"

"Arlene, I'm not taking no for an answer. I'm on my way there now." He hung up.

Not that it would have made a difference to argue

with him. She knew she couldn't talk him out of it, and maybe it would be best if she and Violet didn't cross paths right now. If Violet was upset about the wedding, there was no telling what she might do.

Arlene prayed that one day Violet could get well and live a normal life. But if she kept getting into trouble, she would never be released.

Going into the living room, Arlene walked over to the drapes and drew them back so she could look across the prairie as the sun crested the horizon—just as she had done for almost forty years.

As DEDE DROVE through the swirling snow, Lantry realized they were following the brunt of the storm south. The wind had kicked up, the temperature on the thermometer between the visors showing five below zero. He could no longer tell if it was snowing or if the snow in the air was being kicked up by the wind.

He hadn't seen a light for miles, and the secondary road she'd taken was getting progressively worse. The pickup was bucking drifts. If it wasn't for catching sight of the top of an occasional fence post on each side of the barrow pit along the narrow, unpaved road, he would have doubted they were even still on a road.

"I'm curious," Dede said, breaking the silence. "What made you become a divorce lawyer?"

"Excuse me?"

"Don't you feel guilty taking advantage of two devastated people who are fighting for their lives?"

He growled under his breath, but settled back into the seat. "Don't you mean trying to kill each other over their *assets?* Not exactly their lives."

She shot him a scowl.

"Watch the road!" he said as the pickup hit a drift, snow cascading over the windshield.

"You've never been married, have you?" she said as visibility improved a little. "So you don't know what it's like to get divorced."

"Do we have to talk about this now? You really should be keeping your attention on the road." She had shifted into four-wheel low, the pickup slowly plowing its way through the snow. All he could figure was that she planned to cut across to Highway 191 once she was far enough south.

"Divorce is heartbreaking—even if you're the one who wants out of the marriage," she said as if he hadn't spoken. "When you get married, you have all these hopes and dreams—"

"Oh, please," Lantry snapped. "You married Frank because he was rich and powerful."

The moment the words were out, he regretted them— and not just because she touched the gun resting between her thighs. He had seen the wounded look on her face. He didn't want to be cruel, but he also couldn't take much more of this.

"I married Frank because I *loved* him," she said quietly.

"My mistake." He was glad when she put both hands back on the wheel.

"I guess I shouldn't be surprised you don't believe in love," Dede said, still sounding hurt.

Lantry warned himself to treat this woman with kid gloves. Who knew what she'd do next? And yet, she was so annoying. This whole situation was damned infuriating.

"It isn't love I don't believe in, it's marriage," he said

into the hurt silence that had filled the pickup cab. "Any reasonable person who's seen the statistics would think twice before getting married, except that people in love always think they're going to be the ones who make it."

"But if you never gamble on love—"

"Marriage isn't a *gamble*. It's like playing Russian roulette with all but one of the chambers full of lead. Do you realize how many marriages end in divorce? Fifty percent of first marriages, sixty-seven percent of second marriages and seventy-four percent of third marriages."

"Have you always been this pessimistic?"

"Statistics don't lie," he said. "Most first marriages end after seven years. So do second marriages. Only thirty-three percent reach their twenty-fifth wedding anniversary. Half of all married people never reach their fifteenth anniversary. Only five percent make fifty years."

"I believed I was in that five percent."

"Even after what you'd been through?" He looked over at her as if she'd lost her mind, then remembered she had. "You thought Frank was the right person, which proves how blind love is. That's the reason why I am never getting married. My life is much safer without a spouse, and so are my assets."

She shot him a sympathetic look. "That's pitiful."

"I consider it intelligent."

"I still believe in marriage," she said stubbornly. "I've always loved those stories about married couples who die of old age within days of each other because the spouse can't stand to let the other one go without him or her."

He stared at her profile in the dash lights. "I'm astounded after your marriage to Frank that you can still wax romantic about marriage."

"When he put that gold band on my finger, I planned to wear it to my deathbed, the ring wearing thinner and thinner with the years." She shook her head. "I was wrong. But that doesn't mean that the institution of marriage is doomed."

He couldn't believe her, given what Frank had put her through. She actually had tears in her eyes.

"Come on, tell the truth. You pawned your engagement and wedding ring as quick as you could after the divorce without a second thought."

"I never even considered the monetary value."

"So where're the rings?" He saw her expression and burst out laughing. "You *did* pawn them."

"I had to use the rings to get out of the mental hospital in Texas. It was all I had to offer at the time." She glanced over at him, then back at the road. "Why can't you believe that I loved Frank?"

That was the problem. He *did* believe it. What amazed him more than anything was that she *still* loved the man.

THROUGH THE FALLING and blowing snow Violet could barely make out Old Town Whitehorse. The wind whipped the fallen snow into sculpted drifts, and the air outside the stolen SUV had an icy-cold weight to it that made it hard to breathe.

Violet cut the engine and stared down the hill at her mother's house. The day had turned bright with the earlier dawn and the falling snow.

"I don't understand what we're doing here," Roberta

said. "Aren't the roads going to blow in? Maybe we should find some place to stay for a while."

"I'm going down to my house to get us some warmer clothes, food and money."

"What if your mother is home?" Roberta asked. "Maybe it's a trap."

That was the problem with hanging out with a schizophrenic.

Violet watched a large SUV pull into the drive. She picked up the binoculars she'd stolen along with clothing from one of the houses they'd visited earlier.

She watched a large man climb out and go into the house. A few minutes later, he came out with a suitcase, went back in and came out with a long garment bag and carefully put that into the backseat. Her mother's wedding gown?

A few moments later, her mother came out. She saw Arlene look around as if she knew Violet was close by. Maybe her mother knew her better than she'd thought.

Arlene seemed to hesitate as if she didn't want to leave. Finally, she got into the SUV and the two drove away. Violet had seen the man driving. The fiancé, no doubt. He looked…nice. Bigger and better looking than she'd expected.

Violet started to get out.

"You sure no one's home?" Roberta asked, looking down at the house through dim winter light. The temperature had dropped quickly inside the SUV while they'd been waiting.

Violet rolled her eyes. "Didn't you just see them drive off?"

"Still…"

"All the lights are off. They're gone, okay?" she

snapped. She'd come to regret bringing Roberta along. "Stay here."

"What should I do if you don't come back?" Roberta asked.

"I *will* be back." Violet pulled the key from the ignition and climbed out. She was going home.

LANTRY WATCHED THE road ahead—what little he could see of it—and listened to Dede talk about her marriage, trying to distract himself from thinking about what this woman might have planned for him.

"Frank changed," Dede was saying. "One day I just woke up, and I was lying next to a stranger."

"If I had a dollar for every time I've heard that," he said.

"I'm sure you got more than a dollar every time you heard it." The pickup broke through another large drift that had blown across the road. Fortunately, the roads out here were fairly straight since it was getting harder and harder to see where the roadbed lay between the fences.

"It made me wonder why Frank married me," she said.

*That sexy body,* Lantry thought but was smart enough not to say anything as she drove deeper into the storm and farther from civilization.

The snow was piling up. At least a foot had fallen and was still falling. The weather conditions were worsening to the point that he was becoming even more anxious. Where the hell was she taking him?

"You're going to love this," she said, "but I think Frank married me because I was so normal."

"Funny," he said. "You know you really don't seem like a woman who is running from killers."

"Because I made one little joke?"

"*Little* is right."

"Oh, I would have bet you had no sense of humor in your line of work."

"I'm a lawyer, not an undertaker."

"Right, you bury people alive."

"Could we discuss the reason you've kidnapped me instead of my chosen profession, please." He was having a hard time concentrating on the conversation. Snowflakes thick as cotton were blowing horizontally across the road, obliterating everything.

Dede had slowed the pickup to a crawl and now leaned over the steering wheel, straining to see.

"This is insane," he muttered under his breath. "You don't even know where you are."

He'd been watching the compass and temperature gauge in the pickup. The temperature outside had been steadily dropping as she drove south toward the Missouri Breaks—into no-man's-land—and the road was nearly drifted in.

If she planned to hook back up with Highway 191 south, she'd missed the turn.

"Dede—" He'd barely gotten the word out when a gust of wind hit the side of the pickup as the front of the truck broke through a large drift. The drift pulled the tires hard to the right.

Lantry felt the front tire sink into the soft snow at the edge of the road. Dede was fighting to keep the snow from pulling the pickup into the deeper snow of the barrow pit, but it was a losing battle.

Snow flew up over the hood and windshield as the truck plowed into the snow-filled ditch.

Lantry had seen it coming and braced himself. The pickup crashed through the deep snow, coming to an abrupt stop buried between the road and a line of fence posts and barbed wire.

He heard Dede smack her head on the side window since the pickup didn't have side air bags.

The only other sound was that of the gun clattering to the floorboard at his feet.

## Chapter Three

Violet wasn't surprised to find the front door of the farm house unlocked. No one in these parts locked their doors—except when she was on the loose. Had her mother left the door open on purpose?

She gripped the knob as she pushed gently and the door swung in, the scents of her childhood rushing at her like ghosts from the darkness.

The brightness of the falling snow beyond the open curtains cast the interior of the house in an eerie pale light, making it seem even creepier, the memories all that more horrendous.

She stood for a moment, breathing hard in the dim light, then fumbled for the light switch. The overhead lamp came on, chasing away the shadows, forcing the ghosts to scurry back into their holes.

Violet moved quickly down the hall toward her old room and turned on the light. She hadn't expected her mother would keep her room exactly as it had been. She'd anticipated that Arlene might have boxed up her stuff and pushed it into a corner.

The room had been turned into a playroom for a child. Violet stared. She could tell that her mother had decorated the room. As she caught the scent of baby powder, she felt tears flood her eyes.

The realization hit her hard. Her mother had gotten rid of her—and her things. Arlene had never planned for her oldest daughter to come home again.

Violet swallowed the large lump in her throat only to have it lodge in her chest. There was nothing here for her.


"DEDE?"

She was slumped over, hands still gripping the wheel.

"Dede?"

She lifted her head slowly, looking a little dazed as she shifted her gaze from the snow-packed windshield to him. "What happened?"

"We went in the ditch. Shut off the engine. The tail-pipe's probably under the snow. The cab will be filling with carbon monoxide."

She took a hand off the wheel to rub her temple. It was red where she'd smacked it on the side window. Fumbling, she turned off the engine, pitching them into cold silence.

"Dede, you need to get these handcuffs off me."

She didn't move.

"We can't stay here. I saw a mailbox back up the road There must be a farmhouse nearby. If we stay here, we'll freeze to death. Do you understand what I'm saying?"

Her gaze went to her lap. He saw recognition cross her expression as she realized the gun was gone. She raised her eyes to him and saw that he'd managed to free the plastic cuffs from his belt, unsnap his seat belt and retrieve the gun from where it had fallen on the floor-board. He'd stuck the gun in the waist band of his jeans.

"I wouldn't have shot you," she said quietly.

"I guess we're about to find out." He held out his cuffed wrists to her. "There's a hunting knife under the seat. I need you to cut these off. Unless you want to die right here in this barrow pit."

She met his gaze, held it for a moment, then reached under the seat, pulled the knife from its leather sheath and cut the plastic cuffs. Lantry rubbed his wrists, watching her as she put the knife back. She looked defeated, but he'd seen that look before and knew better than to believe it.

He tried his door. Just as he suspected, it wouldn't move. Snow was packed in around the truck. Dede's side, he saw, would be worse since snow was packed clear up past her window.

"We're going to have to climb out my side through the window. But first…" He turned to dig through the space behind the seats for what little spare clothing he carried. This was his first winter in Montana.

His stepmother, Kate, had lived here her first twenty-two years and knew about Montana winters. She'd told him numerous times to take extra clothing, water, a blanket and food each time he ventured off the ranch.

He wished now that he'd listened to her. All he had was a pair of snow pacs that he kept in the car in case he went off the road and a shovel in the bed of the truck in case he had to dig himself out.

There was no digging the pickup out of this ditch, especially in this blizzard. But at least his feet would be warmer in the pacs than in his cowboy boots.

He tugged off his boots and put on his pacs. All the time, he could feel Dede watching him, that desolate look in her eyes.

"You're going to turn me in," she finally said.

He looked up at her from tying the laces on the pacs. "We can figure things out once we get to the house back up the road."

He dug around behind the seat again and found an old hat with earflaps and a pair of worn work gloves. "Here, wear these. I'm afraid that's the best I can do." He glanced at her Santa suit. The feet on it were plush black fake fur with plastic soles.

"Give me your feet," he said. She eyed him with suspicion but did as she was told. Even with the thick fabric of the costume, he was able to slip his boots over it, making the cowboy boots fit well enough to get her to the house back up the road.

"Ready?" He pulled on his gloves, reached over and turned the key to put down his window. Snow cascaded in. He dug through the snow until he could see daylight and falling snow. "Come on."

"Is everything all right?" Roberta asked as Violet tossed an armload of clothing into the backseat, handed her a couple boxes of crackers and some salami and cheese, and slid behind the wheel.

"Perfect."

"Are those *your* clothes?"

"They're my mother's, if you must know. I had to borrow a few of her things." Violet gave her a look, daring her to ask what had happened to her own clothes.

Roberta eyed her but was smart enough not to cross that line. "So what now?"

"We hang out until it's time to go to my mother's wedding shower, what else?" Violet snapped.

"Cool," Roberta said. "I love wedding showers."

Violet cut her eyes to her fellow escapee and questioned her own sanity for bringing Roberta along. True, Roberta had helped get the Santa costumes, since they weren't allowed real clothing on the criminally insane ward, and she had stood guard while Violet had stolen the SUV.

It had been Roberta's idea that they steal the Santa costumes for the upcoming Christmas show. "They will be warmer than our regulation hospital scrubs, and who is going to pull over three women dressed as Santas?" But Violet was beginning to think it was about time to ditch Roberta. All that kept her from it as she drove away from her former home was the fact that she might need Roberta in the near future.

"They say you're the company you keep," her dead grandmother said from the backseat with a chuckle. "In this case, two crazy peas in a pod."

"Shut up," Violet snapped.

Roberta looked over at her. "Your dead grandmother again?"

"That Roberta's a sharp one, all right," Grandma said. "Sharper than you, since going to your mother's shower is one of the dumbest things you've ever come up with. What's the point?"

Violet glared into the rearview mirror at her grandmother for a moment, then concentrated on the road. The snow was coming down so hard now that if she hadn't known the road, she would have ended up in the ditch.

She drove back to Whitehorse and turned onto the road to the Tin Cup. It surprised her how many cars were parked in the lot. She parked on the highway side on a small hill facing the large pond just off the road and cut the lights.

In the restaurant, she could see decorations hanging in front of the windows and people moving around behind the thin drapes.

"I thought we were going to a shower?" Roberta said.

Violet shot her a look. "We wait here for my mother."

"Then we follow her and run her off the road, drag her out of her car and beat her senseless," Roberta said with a smile. "How does that sound?"

Violet didn't answer as she helped herself to some of the neatly cut cheese and salami. It had been wrapped in the refrigerator, the boxes of crackers on the table with the note propped up against one of the boxes.

*I'm sorry. The cheese and salami was all I had on hand.*

Her mother had left her food, knowing she would come by the house. Knowing she would be hungry.

"Don't get all sentimental," her grandmother said from the backseat. "You should be in there at that party, eating that good food, not out here eating cheese and crackers."

The bite in her mouth turned to sawdust. Violet swallowed, hating that her grandmother was right. The unfairness of it all made her want to strike out at someone. That someone would have to be her mother.

DEDE DIDN'T TRUST LANTRY, but she didn't want to freeze to death in his pickup in a snowbank, either. She had little choice but to follow him. Lantry had the gun and, for the time being, she would have to go along with whatever he said.

She slithered out the window, crawling across the

top of the wind-crusted drift to the edge of the road, where Lantry lifted her up onto the more solid ground of the roadbed.

It was snowing harder than ever. The wind whipped the stinging icy flakes around her, freezing air biting at any bare flesh it could find.

"Cover your face and stay close," Lantry yelled over the wind as he motioned for her to follow him.

She squinted into the falling snow, then drew the costume up so only her eyes were uncovered. The cold and wind made her eyes tear. The boots on her feet made walking difficult.

Keeping to the tracks the pickup had made, she followed Lantry. But within a dozen yards, the wind had blown in the tracks and she found herself plowing through the drifts behind him, thankful for the moment that she wasn't alone out here in this storm.

Ducking her head against the bite of the snow and wind, she was at least glad for the thickness of the plush Santa suit and her hospital-issued cotton scrubs underneath. Following him, she put one foot in front of the other, trying not to think about the cold or her fear of what would happen once they reached the house he'd said would be back up the road.

Just as she'd done as a young girl, she counted her blessings to keep her mind off the cold and exhaustion that made each step a trial. At least she wasn't locked in a cage, and the men after her hadn't caught her. Yet.

That was as far as she could get on blessings. She was cold, tired, hungry, thirsty and scared. As badly as she couldn't wait to reach the house and get out of the bitter cold and snow, she dreaded getting anywhere that had a phone.

She didn't know how far they'd walked. She'd lost track of time, concentrating only on putting one foot in front of the other. The cold had numbed her senses, and she was beginning to believe Lantry had lied about seeing a mailbox, when he touched her arm, startling her since she hadn't realized he'd stopped.

He motioned for her to follow as he held two strands of barbed wire apart so she could climb through the fence. Then he broke a trail through the snow. Ahead, she caught a glimpse of a house through the driving snow and thought she might burst into tears with relief.

No lights glowed behind the windows of the two-story house. No Christmas decorations adorned the front yard or hung from the eaves. Was it possible the house was deserted? Just as she started to latch on to that hope, she heard a horse snort and saw three ghost-like shapes appear out of the storm next to a wooden corral fence.

The horses had a layer of snow on the quilted blankets covering their backs. As they trotted off, she saw that the road into the house was drifted in and didn't look as if it had been used for a while. Maybe the home-owners had only gone away for the holidays, leaving enough water and hay for the horses until they returned.

She slogged through the snow, the drifts to her thighs, the cold seeping into her bones. Just a little farther. She stumbled, her legs no longer willing to take another step.

As she felt herself start to sink down into the snow, her mind telling her she should sit down for a while and rest, Lantry picked her up and carried her the last two dozen yards to the porch. She leaned limply against him, her head on his shoulder, too exhausted to pick it up. She couldn't remember the last time she'd slept.

He set her down on the porch, but kept an arm around her. She hugged herself, shivering so hard that her teeth chattered. The sound of glass shattering made her jump. To her shock, Lantry had put his gloved fist through one of the small windows in the door and was now reaching in to unlock the door.

*"You're breaking in?"*

He shot her a look. "This from a woman who just pulled a gun on an officer of the law and left him locked in a jail cell?"

Had she not been so tired, she might have laughed at the incongruity of that. All thoughts evaporated as she felt a warm draft of air as Lantry opened the door and ushered her inside the wonderfully heated house.

She slumped down into a chair just inside as he closed the door behind them and tried the lights. "Good, we have electricity," he said as the reassuring glow of a lamp flashed on.

Her mind rallied long enough to form one clear thought: Did that mean they also had a phone? She still had his cell phone in the pocket of the costume. Had he forgotten about that?

She watched Lantry pick up a pillow from a nearby sofa and stuff it in the broken window before turning back to her.

She tried to still her trembling, but the effort was wasted. She could no longer feel her feet or fingers.

Without a word, he knelt down in front of her and pulled off the cowboy boots. Tossing them aside, he said, "Come on."

He pulled her to her feet and led her down the hall to

a bathroom. She plopped down on the closed toilet seat as he turned on the shower. "It's not quite hot yet. I'm going to go find you something else to wear."

She nodded and didn't move.

He disappeared. She managed to get the cell phone out of her pocket and tried it. No signal. She'd barely gotten it back into the costume pocket before he returned with a stack of clothing.

"See if any of these fit you. Looks like the water's hot now. You can get in." As he started to leave the bathroom, he hesitated. She'd been trying to unzip the costume, only to find that her fingers no longer worked.

"Here, let me." He unzipped the Santa suit and helped her step out of it. Her feet were beet red, the same color as her hands. Under the suit she wore the blue scrubs required in her part of the mental hospital.

Lantry seemed to hesitate for a moment. "Can you manage the rest?"

She nodded and waited until he closed the door behind him. Steam rose from the shower, and she felt her brain starting to work again. She looked from the clothing he'd brought her to the bathroom window.

Even though her mind wasn't working to capacity, she knew that she couldn't make a run for it. Not in this storm. Not without proper warm clothing. Even if she knew the country well enough to find her way in the blizzard, she doubted she would survive.

But none of those reasons were why she couldn't make a run for her life. She had to convince Lantry. That's why she'd come here. Without his help...

She choked back a sob, feeling defeated and afraid as she slipped out of the scrubs. The heat from the shower had steamed up the bathroom, making it warm and close as she stepped in under the spray.

The water made her hands and feet ache, but she didn't care. Tears coursing down her cheeks, she turned her face up to the spray. The heat felt so good, she wished she could stay under the soothing water and never come out.

She knew she would have to tell Lantry the truth. She no longer had any other option. And what if she couldn't convince him?

She stood under the water a little longer, then shut it off and reached for a towel. By now Lantry would have called his brother. Time was running out—and not just for her.

LANTRY WAITED UNTIL he heard the shower running before he checked the cell phone he'd taken from the Santa costume. Just as he'd feared. No service this far south of Whitehorse. This whole part of Montana had only pockets of cell-phone service around the towns.

He found a landline in the kitchen, but the moment he picked it up and heard the buzzing, he knew the storm had taken out the line. Happened all the time out here. He was surprised the electricity was still on.

No way to call for help. Not that help could probably get to them until the plows ran. He checked the time, shocked at how many hours had gone by. It was afternoon already, the light beginning to fade.

When he turned on the radio, all he could get was the static-filled local station. A Christmas carol ended, and the announcer broke in to say that all roads out of Whitehorse were closed due to the storm. Everyone was advised to stay inside. Only emergency travel was advised in Whitehorse because of poor visibility and dangerous road conditions.

"In other news, residents are to be on the lookout for three state mental-hospital inmates who have escaped and are believed to be in the area. At least one of the inmates, Violet Evans, is considered dangerous. Anyone who should see the escapees is advised to call the sheriff's department at once. Do not try to apprehend any of three."

Another Christmas carol came on. The announcer apparently didn't have the updated news about Dede and the hostage situation.

The wind howled at the windows, sending a shower of snow off the eaves, reminding him how far they were from Whitehorse. This country was so isolated, its own form of wilderness. They'd been lucky that a ranch house had been only a couple of miles back up the road. If they'd gone off a little farther to the south...

He shoved that thought away and stepped to the fireplace to build a fire from the stack of wood piled next to it. The house had felt warm at first, but now there was a chill in the room. He wondered if it was from the temperature dropping further—or from his own chilling thoughts.

Had either phone been working, he would have turned Dede in. He told himself it wasn't a question of whether he believed her or not. He was an officer of the court. She was wanted by the authorities. Of course, he would turn her over to them.

So why was he wasting time even thinking about it?

On the radio, there was another bulletin about the roads and the escapees. "The police believe they will try to seek shelter. Residents are advised to keep their houses and cars locked and stay inside."

The dry wood in the stone fireplace began to crackle, flames leaping warmly. He started at a sound and turned to find Dede standing behind him.

She looked so small, so vulnerable, so scared. But amazingly, she also looked softer, sweeter, if that were possible, her cheeks glowing from the hot shower.

From the look on her face, she'd heard the announcement.

"The phone's out, there's no cell coverage out this way and all the roads out of Whitehorse are closed," he said, wondering why he was so quick to reassure her of her safety—at least for the moment.

Her relief was palpable.

"The clothes fit all right?"

She nodded, and he tried not to notice the way the jeans hugged her bottom or the rust-colored sweater accentuated her curves as she stepped to the fire.

"The people who live here must have gone away for the holidays," Lantry said to her back. "I noticed when we came in that they left hay and plenty of water for the horses."

Her stomach growled loudly.

He couldn't help but grin. "Hungry?"

Her stomach growled again in answer. "Is there food?"

"This is rural Montana. There is always food. Why don't you check the kitchen while I see about bringing in more wood."

She nodded with a self-conscious smile. "I *am* a little hungry."

He watched her head for the kitchen, shuffling in the too-large slippers he'd found for her.

He listened to her opening and closing cabinets as he pulled on his coat. As he slogged out to the wood-pile through the drifts, the wind whipped snow around him. He bent his head to it, grabbed up an armload of wood and headed back toward the house.

As he caught a glimpse of Dede through the kitchen window, it hit him. They were stranded—at least until a snowplow could get down this road. Primary roads would get plowed first, and with all the roads out of Whitehorse closed, it could be days before this road was open.

He was trapped here with a woman who both scared and fascinated him. A woman he couldn't trust—and yet wanted to. He was in dangerous territory, he thought, glancing again toward the kitchen window and Dede.

# Chapter Four

Dede heard the front door bang open, felt the cold draft of air rush in as Lantry stomped his snow boots, slammed the door and dropped the armload of wood next to the fire.

She glanced toward the living room and saw him warming his hands in front of the fireplace. He looked so pensive. So deep in thought. She didn't kid herself that had the phones been working, he would have sold her down the river in a heartbeat.

She couldn't trust this man. No matter how considerate he'd been to her.

"Did you find something for us to eat?" Lantry called without looking in her direction.

The cupboards were filled with canned goods, and the freezer was full of beef. "Yes," she called back. She had taken two T-bone steaks from the freezer and put them in the microwave to defrost and was now considering which of many home-canned vegetables to prepare with the steaks when she heard him come into the kitchen.

She could feel him studying her as she heard him pull out a chair and sit down at the big oak table.

"I thought we'd have steak and baked potatoes. I

found some butter and sour cream in the fridge. But I can't decide between canned green beans and canned corn," she said, turning to look at him.

His smile softened the hard lines of his face. He really was an amazingly attractive man. "How about both? I'm starved." He stretched out his long legs.

"Me, too," she said as her stomach growled again. She glanced at the clock, and realized why she was so hungry. She hadn't had anything to eat since supper the day before at the hospital—almost twenty-four hours ago.

She took the steaks from the microwave and popped in two large potatoes to cook. The cast-iron skillet she'd put on the stove with butter melting in it was hot enough that she dropped in the steaks.

"I wouldn't have taken you for a woman who cooked," Lantry said behind her.

She bristled at the remark. "That's because you don't know anything about me," she said without turning around. "You made a lot of erroneous assumptions about me based on what your client told you, and since you weren't interested in the truth—"

His laugh made her break off in midsentence.

She turned to find him grinning at her.

"You're right," he said and held up his hands in surrender.

"What does that mean?" she asked suspiciously as the steaks sizzled in the skillet.

"You're right, and since we have nothing but time, after dinner I want you to tell me everything about you and what's really going on."

She narrowed her gaze at him, studying him. "And you'll listen with an open mind?"

He pushed himself to his feet. "You have my word," he said as he moved to the cupboards. He opened one, then another, before he found the dishes. He began to set the table. In the other room, the radio played "Deck the Halls."

They ate at the table to the glow of the fire in the next room. Music played softly on the radio. The house felt warmer. Or maybe it was just sitting across from this man, Dede thought as she devoured the food.

"I can't remember anything tasting this good," she said as she finished.

"I know what you mean. I didn't realize how hungry I was. Good job on the steaks."

"You make me nervous when you're nice to me," she said, studying him. She'd expected him to laugh. Or at least grin. But he did neither.

He looked at her with compassion. "I'm sorry you feel that way. I never wanted to be unkind to you."

The food had helped fight off some of her exhaustion, but she knew it wouldn't last. She had to convince him to help her before the snowplows opened the road.

After they'd cleaned up the kitchen, Lantry threw more logs on the fire and they sat down at separate ends of the couch in front of the blaze. He felt full and strangely content—all things considered. Dede seemed lost in her own thoughts.

He wanted to give her the benefit of the doubt. Now more than ever, he felt he owed her that. He'd helped Frank push her to this breaking point. And while all of that was true, he knew the main reason he wanted to hear her out was because he was beginning to like her.

The woman had a strength that amazed him. She'd

been through so much, and yet there was still a whole lot of fight in her. He thought about her trudging through the snowdrifts in that damned Santa suit and smiled to himself. He'd seen the exhaustion on her face. The cold had weakened even him.

She'd been facing ultimate defeat, but she'd kept going, knowing that if the phone had worked once they reached the ranch house, he'd have turned her in.

He felt guilty about that now. He'd been ready to throw her to the wolves without even hearing her out. Of course, she had taken him from the jail at gunpoint, he reminded himself as the fire crackled softly.

Dede sat for a moment, staring into the fire, before she said, "I haven't been completely honest with you."

Lantry looked over, saw Dede's face and felt sick. Hadn't he had a feeling that Dede wasn't telling him everything?

"I told you that Frank called me at the hospital in Texas. He told me things had gotten out of his control and that my life was in danger. He told me to do whatever I had to, but to get out of there and run."

"Why didn't you take his advice?"

"Because I knew my husband." She looked at him with those big blue innocent eyes, and he felt the pull of this woman, stronger than the fiercest tides. "I knew his secret. I overhead him on the phone one night before the divorce. I hadn't meant to be eavesdropping." She hesitated. "I feel disloyal telling this even now."

Dede took a breath and let it out slowly. "I heard Frank say he wanted out. Whoever was on the other end of the line was arguing with him. Frank said, 'There has to be a price for my freedom, dammit.' Then he fell silent. I could see his shadow on the wall. He had his head in his hand. After he hung up, I heard him crying." Her voice broke, and she got up to stand with her back to him in front of the fire.

"After that, Frank was a different man—cold, hateful. I tried to talk to him…" Her voice trailed off, and for a while, there was only the crackle of the fire and her fragile dark silhouette against the flames.

"You said you knew Frank's secret. Is that why these men are after you?" Lantry asked, rising to put more wood on the fire.

"Frank had something they wanted." She raised her gaze to his, the two of them standing inches apart as the fire roared softly in the chilly room.

"What would make you think that?" he asked, feeling a little light-headed. It was hard not to be completely entranced by that angelic face and those eyes of hers. This close, he could smell the fresh scent of the soap on her skin, in her hair.

"Look what they did to the house. You didn't really think I would destroy a seven-thousand-dollar couch like that, did you?"

He recalled the photographs Frank had shown him. Photographs of the house torn apart as if by a madman. Or a furious, crazed wife. He'd been shocked by the destruction. So had the doctor who'd signed Dede's commitment papers at Frank's urging.

"Insane or simply angry, who has the energy to ransack every room of a twelve-thousand-square-foot house?" she asked.

"Frank must have known who destroyed your house," Lantry said. "Why would he lie and say you did?"

"I told you. Frank *loved* me. He thought I would be

safe locked up where no one would believe anything I said. He was trying to protect me."

Lantry would have argued that, but one look in the depths of those blue eyes of hers and he couldn't bring himself to raise a word of protest. "You don't have to pretend with me."

"Pretend what?"

"That he didn't break your heart."

DEDE WAITED FOR that awful ache to form in her chest. To her surprise, she felt only a slight flutter, nothing more. She should have been relieved that it didn't hurt as much as it had, but instead she was filled with an odd sense of regret.

Frank was gone. Not just from her life, but from her heart. That made her sad. She'd planned to spend the rest of her life with him. Maybe Lantry was right about love and marriage. Maybe nothing lasted, not love, not even the pain of a broken heart.

"Dede, I can see how hard even talking about this is for you," Lantry said quietly. "I'm sorry. I hate the part I played in what's happened to you."

She stared at Lantry, unable to hide her surprise. He continued to keep her off balance.

She'd despised Lantry Corbett from the moment Frank had hired him and she'd heard how ruthless he was.

She'd heard he was an amazing lawyer but a man without a conscience, a poor excuse for a human being. She'd told herself there had to be more to Lantry Corbett than what she'd heard about him.

But on meeting him, she'd been devastated to discover that apparently what she'd heard about him was true. He seemed cold, calculating and with no regard for truth or justice.

So how did she explain what appeared to be this change in him? Or had there been this man inside the divorce lawyer all along? More to the point, could she trust him?

"I suspect you like letting people believe you're a heartless bastard," she said, not unkindly.

He smiled at that. "I suppose I do. But I don't like myself as I see me reflected in your eyes."

She wished he wasn't so devastatingly handsome, especially on those rare occasions when his smile reached his eyes.

"It *is* hard for me to talk about this, but you have to know everything," she said. "I'm ashamed to say that I didn't just eavesdrop on Frank. After the change in him, I listened in on his phone calls, I checked his pockets, went through his wallet, hired a private detective. That's when I found out his secret."

VIOLET FELT SOMETIMES as if her skin were too tight. As if her own body had turned against her like everyone else had. As if she were killing herself slowly.

"Crazy thought," she warned herself silently.

"Not so crazy," her dead grandmother said from the backseat as they waited for the wedding shower to let out. "I told your mother again and again that there was something wrong with you. Did she listen? Of course not. No one ever listens to me. Just like you. You don't listen to me, do you, Violet? If you'd have listened to me, all this would be over. But no, you just had to do things your way."

Violet covered her ears, but she could still hear her grandmother's voice. "Shut up! SHUT UP!"

Roberta's curly head popped up from the passenger seat, where she'd been sleeping as the blizzard raged around the stolen SUV. She blinked, looking around in confusion. "What's going on?" she demanded hoarsely.

Violet took her hands from her ears and glanced in the rearview mirror to where her grandmother had been sitting only moments before. "Nothing."

"Then who the hell were you yelling at?" Roberta wanted to know.

"No one. It was just—"

"Not your grandmother again," Roberta said, glancing around the interior of the stolen SUV. "You should have driven a stake through her heart when she died. Otherwise they come back, you know."

Violet knew only too well. Her grandmother had been coming back for some time now. In fact, it was her grandmother who'd kept Violet from getting out of the mental hospital. She'd been so close to being released. She'd convinced the doctor that she was well, that she could make it on the outside—until her grandmother started nagging at her, just as she had in life.

"Go back to sleep," she told Roberta. Not that it was necessary. The woman had already curled up and was snoring softly.

Violet wished she could sleep like that. The SUV rocked in the wind, and snow swirled around it. Violet had started the engine and turned the heater on high as she waited for her mother's wedding shower to end. It should be soon, given the storm.

She'd always hated winter and used to dream of moving to somewhere warm. Maybe that's what she'd do once she was free of the past. Before she went, she should go up to the cemetery in Old Town Whitehorse, where her grandmother was buried, and dig up the old biddy and put a stake through her heart.

As if listening in on her thoughts, her grandmother leaned forward and began to whisper horrible things in her ear.

Violet tried desperately not to listen. But in the end, she couldn't keep the words from gnawing their way in.

*Stop being that poor old-maid daughter of Arlene Evans and show them what you can do. Make it so no one in the county ever forgets the name Violet Evans.*

LANTRY LIFTED AN EYEBROW as if he realized what it had taken Dede to hire a private investigator to spy on her husband.

"There was another woman," Lantry guessed.

Dede nodded. "Frank had been meeting with a woman named Tamara Fallon. They were clearly close, probably having an affair, although the only photographs the private investigator was able to get was of them arguing and later hugging outside a restaurant.

"I know that doesn't prove anything," she said, hurrying on before Lantry could point out the obvious. "Clearly the two were involved in some way, and that was enough for me."

"Don't tell me you didn't try to fight for your marriage and your husband."

"You think you know me." She smiled ruefully and shook her head. "No sexy nightgown or romantic dinner was going to get my husband back. I needed information. The name Fallon had sounded familiar. I realized I'd seen it somewhere recently—but not in any of Frank's emails or correspondence. I found the name in the newspaper. Tamara Fallon and her husband, Dr. Eric Fallon, had recently been burglarized."

Lantry let out a low curse. She had his attention now. "Some very expensive jewelry had been taken. I remember the story in the newspaper, now that you mention it. A diamond necklace was taken that was said to be worth over a million dollars."

"What wasn't in the newspapers was that the Fallons were in the process of having a new security system installed. The P.I. had discovered that Frank had been in the security-system business before he met me. A woman named Tammy Lundgren had been his bookkeeper."

"Tamara Fallon is Tammy Lundgren."

She nodded. "Even more interesting, the reason Frank's business had folded was that he was being investigated because of a string of burglaries in houses where they'd either put in the security systems or had bid on the projects."

"Let me guess. You confronted Frank with what you'd learned."

"He denied everything." The memory still hurt her. "He told me I was crazy for even suspecting he might be involved with another woman—or in anything illegal."

"And, of course, you told him about the private investigator and showed him the photos of him and Tammy."

It annoyed her that she'd obviously done what other women faced with divorce had done.

"I wanted to help him, and as long as he kept denying there wasn't a problem…" She shrugged. "A mistake in retrospect."

"He had to have tried to explain the incriminating snapshots of him and Tammy Fallon."

"Frank said Tammy had called him out of the blue. She was having marital problems and needed a shoulder to cry on. Frank swore he told her he couldn't help her. Which could explain why they appeared to be arguing in the photos. He was furious that I'd spied on him and, worse, thought he was having an affair. He said he hadn't heard from her since."

"Did you believe him?"

Dede shrugged. "Things only got worse between us after that. Frank would get calls from either Ed or Claude. I would hear him arguing with them. And sometimes I would answer the phone and the party on the other end would hang up."

"You think Frank had something to do with the Fallon burglary?"

"Why would he risk everything? He was successful. He had a reputation to uphold in Houston. He didn't need the money."

"Unless these people from his past had some kind of leverage over him."

She nodded slowly. "But if that was the case, then I fear Frank double-crossed them."

A loud noise outside the ranch house made them both start.

## *Chapter Five*

Violet turned on the wipers and leaned forward in the driver's seat, her dead grandmother forgotten as she watched people come out of the Tin Cup.

The snow wasn't as deep, the storm as strong, here in the Milk River Valley as it had been farther to the south nearer the Little Rockies. But of the several dozen vehicles parked around the restaurant on the hill, all covered with snow and virtually indistinguishable, which one was her mother's? Maybe the rich fiancé had lent Arlene that big SUV he'd picked her up in earlier.

She gripped the wheel as she saw the figure of her mother, arms full of presents and flanked by other women carrying even more gifts, hurrying out. Arlene Evans hadn't gone far when one of the SUVs parked on the edge of the road started up and drove toward her.

"The fiancé?" Violet barely got the words out of her mouth when the driver flashed his headlights and Arlene was caught in the glare. A thought struck Violet like a punch: her mother looked happy. She couldn't ever remember her mother being happy.

Violet swore as she watched the man get out and help Arlene load all her presents into the car. Seeing how happy her mother was, seeing this man come to rescue his woman, all of it filled Violet with conflicting emotions that roiled inside her.

"Something wrong?" Roberta asked, blinking as she sat up and looked down at all the lights from the vehicles leaving the party.

"I should have known he'd pick her up," Violet said as she shifted into gear but didn't turn on the headlights. "This is even better than I planned. We'll take out both of them."

Roberta shrugged her disinterest. "I thought we were going to chase her down and pull her out of her car and—"

"You might want to buckle up," Violet interrupted as she slammed her foot down on the gas. She had positioned the stolen SUV in just the right spot. Ahead she had a clear view of the road out to the highway.

"This is another one of your bad ideas," Grandma said from the backseat. "Pure self-indulgence, and what is it going to accomplish, huh?"

"Satisfaction, you old hag," Violet snapped and hit the gas, anticipating the moment her mother saw her behind the wheel—the moment of impact.

AT THE SOUND OUTSIDE, Lantry moved to the front window to part the curtains and look out. A large plastic garbage container cartwheeled through the snow to disappear over a rise.

Just for a moment, all Dede's gloom and doom about their lives being in danger had seemed real. Too real.

Lantry realized he was tired and irritable from lack of sleep, worn thin from the cold and this situation.

"While all this is fascinating, Dede," he said as he turned from the window, his heart still jumping a little, "it doesn't explain why anyone would want either of us dead."

"I told you Frank called me at the mental hospital in Texas. What I didn't tell you was that Frank told me he was in serious trouble. He'd left a package with someone he had to get back. If he didn't, they were going to kill him. If Frank had something to leave for safekeeping, he would have left it with someone he trusted."

Lantry realized where she was going with this. "If you're thinking he left this package with me—"

"Frank trusted you. You'd done well for him. He had to have given it to you. I'm not the only one who believes that. What other reason could there be for these men to want you dead?"

Lantry shook his head, remembering the last time he'd seen Frank Chamberlain. Frank had kept looking at his watch, complaining about the air-conditioning being too low and mopping his brow. He'd been nervous as hell and had made a point of sitting facing the door.

He'd thought Frank was worried Dede would show up and make a scene or, worse, shoot him.

Maybe that's all it had been.

Or maybe Dede was right. Frank had been between a rock and a hard place because of Tammy Fallon— and because his wife had found out about his past. A man with secrets, some of which were coming to light. Did that explain why he'd had Dede put in a mental institution?

"If Frank had left some package with someone, why didn't he just go get it himself?"

She shook her head. "I've tried reaching him, but there hasn't been any answer, and his voice mail is full."

Lantry didn't like the sound of this and could tell that

Dede was worried about her ex. Had Frank tried to call him? When Lantry had taken his leave of absence from the business, he'd had his secretary, Shirley, shield him from all the day-to-day business.

Shirley was a bulldog when it came to protecting him from stressed-out, erratic clients, since almost all divorce clients were on the emotional edge.

"I'm sorry, but Frank didn't give me anything." That in itself was a little odd now that Lantry thought about it.

His clients often gave him "thank-you" gifts. Usually a bottle of rare Scotch or bourbon or a box of expensive chocolates. Frank Chamberlain hadn't even thanked him.

"Frank wouldn't have just *given* it to you. He would have hid it in a gift or—"

"He didn't give me *anything*," Lantry said, seeing that she had pinned all her hopes on this.

Dede looked crestfallen and uncertain. "I was so sure…"

Lantry couldn't say what made him do it—even later when he had too much time to think about it. She'd just looked so crushed he hadn't been able to help himself. He had smelled the scent of the soap, her hair still damp, the cap of curls framing that angelic face and those big blue eyes filled with pleading.… He'd weakened.

He hooked a hand around her slim neck and pulled her to him. Her blue eyes widened in surprise. His gaze went to her mouth, the full lips trembling slightly as he dropped his mouth to hers.

The kiss was gentle and soft, tender, the taste of her as sweet as he'd imagined it would be.

THE VEHICLE CAME out of the storm running full bore, no headlights, no chance to avoid it.

Arlene saw the cloud of snow an instant before the SUV came flying out at her. She screamed. Hank sped up. The vehicle missed Arlene's door and instead glanced off the back rear panel of Hank's bigger SUV, the impact jolting Arlene into silence.

The force of the crash spun them around and into the deep snow at the edge of the frozen pond. The big SUV came to a rest at an odd angle.

"Hank?" Arlene cried as she looked over at her fiancé. He unsnapped his seat belt and reached under the seat, coming out with a pistol as the vehicle that had hit them sped off down the road to the highway.

"Hank! No!" she cried, grabbing his arm as he started to open his door and get out.

He met her gaze, held it for a moment, then put the gun back under the seat and slid over to take her in his arms.

"Are you all right?" he whispered against her hair.

"I'm fine." She shuddered. Her world felt as if it had fallen away, leaving her teetering with no solid ground. "It was Violet." Her eldest daughter. The daughter that had resembled her. The daughter she'd failed.

She began to cry. Hank unsnapped her seat belt and took her in his arms, the only place she'd ever felt safe.

"It's going to be all right," Hank whispered. "I promise you. It's going to be all right."

But Arlene knew better.

"I should have taken more precautions," Hank was saying.

"We have to postpone the wedding."

"No. No one is going to keep me from marrying

you. You have my word on that. Violet isn't going to spoil this for us."

Arlene felt the lights of the other vehicles coming from the party wash over them.

"Do you believe me?" Hank asked.

"You don't know Violet. She won't stop until—"

He looked into her eyes, forcing her to meet the intensity of his gaze. "You and I are getting married Saturday."

She stared into his handsome face and felt his strength in the arms around her. She nodded as she heard car doors slam and people calling to them. Everyone would know soon enough that Violet was on the loose again. God help them all.

LANTRY SEEMED TO come to his senses almost at once.

"We should get some sleep," he said to Dede as he drew back from the kiss, his thumb skimming over her porcelain cheek.

She nodded slowly but said nothing. Her tongue touched her upper lip. She couldn't believe he'd just kissed her.

Dede shivered, hugging herself, chilled by the surge of emotions coursing through her.

She'd *wanted* him to kiss her. Wanted him to take her in his arms and hold her. She silently cursed herself. She'd been ready to fall into Lantry Corbett's arms.

That just proved how desperate she felt. How afraid. Lantry Corbett was still the divorce lawyer who everyone said would eat his own young.

It was just hard to remember that since it had been a good-looking, lanky cowboy who'd just kissed her. And worse, she'd always had a weakness for cowboys.

And when Lantry was kind and compassionate toward her, she had let down all her defenses. Worse, she'd welcomed the comfort of his kiss, his arms around her.

He tossed more wood on the fire and straightened, looking uneasy. "We're both exhausted and not thinking straight."

She nodded, but she knew it was over. Even if the phone lines stayed down for another day or so, the plows would come through in the morning and see Lantry's pickup in the ditch. It was just a matter of time before she was behind bars—or, worse, on her way back to the mental hospital, where Claude would be waiting for her.

She'd been so sure Frank had given whatever it was he'd been hiding to Lantry. The worst part was that Ed and Claude also believed Lantry had it. Just as they believed she knew something and had become a threat they weren't willing to live with.

As she looked at Lantry, she realized that she'd failed not only Frank, but now this cowboy.

LANTRY FELT A CHILL at the defeated look on Dede's face. "We'll figure something out in the morning."

A rueful smile curled her lips as her gaze met his.

"I'm not going to turn you in."

She shook her head. "I heard the weather report on the radio."

He had wondered if she'd heard it earlier. Apparently she had.

"In the morning, the blizzard will have stopped. A plow will come down that road and see your pickup. I'm sure your brother already has everyone in the county looking for you—just like you said." She sighed. "We both know I'll be on my way back to the mental hospital before the sun sets."

She started to turn away, but he touched her arm to turn her back to him.

He tried to find some words of comfort for her, but was at a loss. All of this had him feeling confused and unsure. He could see how much she was counting on him having whatever package Frank might have left behind. Her worry for Frank still amazed him.

"We'll figure something out in the morning," he repeated and saw disappointment well in her eyes before she turned away again.

She was right about all of it. He was counting on them being found in the morning. At first he'd told himself that all of this was merely the fictional fabric of Dede Chamberlain's demented mind.

He no longer believed that. Dede needed help all right, but not the kind she would get at the mental hospital. He would do everything in his power to get her out of there. Once he'd told Shane everything Dede had told him about Frank and the Fallon burglary...

It wouldn't be easy without some kind of proof, though, and unfortunately Lantry knew only too well how slowly the legal system's wheels turned. If he believed Dede, that her life was in danger—maybe especially in the mental hospital—then how could he let her be taken back there?

He should never have kissed her. He questioned his judgment. Had he bought in to all of this because of that face of hers? Those eyes? The way she looked at him with all that hope?

Frank hadn't given him anything for safekeeping.

Dede was mistaken. How much more was she mistaken about?

He heard her moving around upstairs in the bedroom he'd told her she could use. He heard the creak of the bedsprings, then silence. She wasn't crazy enough to try to make a run for it in this weather, was she?

But maybe freezing to death in the storm was the least of Dede Chamberlain's worries.

If she wasn't delusional, if someone really was trying to kill her, then sending her back to the mental hospital was a death sentence.

So how could he send her back there? And if she was right, then he'd better start worrying about his own hide, he thought with a curse as he remembered what his friend had told him about the steering mechanism on the Lamborghini.

Frowning, he moved to the window and pulled back the curtains to stare out at the storm.

*You were his lawyer. You got him everything he wanted in the divorce. He trusted you.*

Dede had asked him if Frank had given him something. He realized it had been a lie when he'd said no.

Frank *had* given him something. A wake-up call. Now, after all these years of living up to his reputation as a cold-blooded, merciless lawyer, it had come back to haunt him.

Snow blew past the window horizontally to pile in drifts along the road. An even bigger storm raged inside him.

Dede was right. A snowplow would be coming through sometime tomorrow. The driver would see the pickup in the ditch. It would be just a matter of time before the sheriff's department would be notified and he and Dede would be found.

Even with a lot of legal maneuvering, he wouldn't be able to keep Dede from being sent back to the mental hospital—at least temporarily. A mental evaluation would be required to decide if she should be charged with the incident at the jail.

He shook his head as he dropped the curtain and went back to the fire to curl up on the couch. As exhausted as he was, he knew he wouldn't be getting any sleep, not with his thoughts as wild as the weather raging outside the farmhouse.

What the hell was he going to do come morning?

DEPUTY SHERIFF SHANE CORBETT found everyone in the family waiting for him the next morning at the main house on Trails West Ranch. Everyone except his brother Lantry.

"Any word?" his father asked the moment he walked in.

Shane shook his head. "I came as soon as the road opened. All I know is what I told you on the phone earlier. Lantry was last seen with the wife of one of his clients from Texas."

"We heard on the radio that she is one of the three women who escaped from the state mental hospital— the criminally insane ward," his father's wife, Kate, said.

Shane cursed the media and its need to know and report everything. "She was only being held in that ward because she'd escaped from a mental hospital in Texas. She apparently had a breakdown during her divorce from one of Lantry's clients."

"If Lantry was her husband's lawyer..." Kate's voice broke.

"We have no reason to believe she will harm him," Shane said, wishing that were true.

Juanita pressed a mug of hot coffee into his hands. He took it, smiling his thanks at the family cook. He cradled the mug in his two large hands, trying to soak up the warmth—and hide how worried he was about his brother.

"I can't stay. We have all our deputies out looking for the escapees and Lantry," he said. "They couldn't have gotten far, not in that blizzard last night. More than likely they holed up somewhere to wait out the storm and will pay hell getting out with the roads blown in the way they are. We'll find them."

"Wouldn't Lantry have called if he'd got in out of the storm?" Russell asked. He was the oldest of the Corbett brothers and known as the most levelheaded.

"The phone lines were down for most of the county," Shane said. He didn't say that Dede Chamberlain was armed and might not have let Lantry make a call. If he was still alive.

He shook off that thought and took a sip of the hot coffee, burning his tongue.

"Lantry can take care of himself," the youngest of the brothers said. Jud, like his twin, Dalton, had been quiet since Shane's arrival. He'd seen the worry in all of his brothers' faces. The details of Lantry's abduction from the jail hadn't been released, but Shane had learned that nothing stayed a secret long in this small town.

"Jud's right. Lantry can take care of himself," Shane agreed. While no one had mentioned it, Shane suspected they all knew that Dede had taken the new deputy's weapon and abducted Lantry at gunpoint last night. That suspicion was verified a moment later.

"The man's a *divorce* lawyer. I'm sure this isn't the first time someone's held a gun on him," Jud joked, clearly trying to lighten the mood in the room. "He can certainly handle a woman."

"I should get going," Shane said and drank a little more of the coffee.

As he started to leave, the lights of the Christmas tree caught his eye. It was a huge ponderosa pine. The entire family had taken the hay wagon into the Breaks to cut it down, then come back to the ranch to decorate it.

Shane thought of the laughter and that safe feeling he'd felt being a part of this family. Especially with his fiancée, Maddie, at his side.

They'd been through so much this year. Three weddings, some close calls, the revelation of a long-held secret.

This Christmas was to be a celebration as well as a time to give thanks for all their blessings and being together.

But now Lantry was somewhere with a mentally deranged woman with a gun and a grudge. He feared for Lantry's life and the devastation of his family if something tragic should happen to his brother.

His father walked him to the door. Grayson looked older and grayer, worry etched in his face. "Be careful, son. I heard this morning about that one escapee running her mother and her mother's fiancé off the road last night."

"Violet Evans," Shane said like a curse. Violet had gotten away, but fortunately neither Arlene Evans or

Hank Monroe had been hurt. Now, though, everyone knew Violet was in town—and dangerous.

"It sounds like you've got too many nuts out there just looking for trouble," Grayson said.

Shane smiled at his father's concern. "I'll watch out for them, don't worry." He put a hand on his father's still-broad shoulder. "I'll call as soon as I find Lantry."

LANTRY DOZED OFF just before dawn and woke with a start. For a moment he didn't know where he was. He listened, the quiet so intense it was oppressive. Sitting up, he looked toward the window. Through a crack in the curtains, he could see that the storm had stopped. Snow was piled high against the window.

It came back in a rush. His gaze shot to the spot on the couch where the gun had been next to him.

Gone.

Lantry shot to his feet and rushed up the stairs, afraid he knew what had awakened him. At the second-floor landing, he slowed, trying to still his racing fear as well.

She wouldn't take off on her own.

She wasn't that stupid. Or that crazy.

Also, she'd begged for his help.

If she was telling the truth, she'd stick around and see if he could save her.

Even as he thought it, he knew. Once it got light and the storm ended, she had known what was going to happen. He'd told her he wouldn't turn her in, but she'd known that wouldn't matter. Once his pickup was spotted, it was only a matter of time before they'd be found and her butt was in the back of a van headed for the mental-hospital lockdown and...

He'd reached the closed door to her room and

stopped. Even as he grabbed the knob, cautiously turned it and pushed open the door, he knew she was gone before he saw the empty bed.

Still he called "Dede?" as he stepped in. The bathroom door was open. No Dede.

Swearing, he turned and raced back down the stairs, thinking she might be in the kitchen. Yeah, right—armed and cooking breakfast for him.

The kitchen was empty. No big surprise. Dede Chamberlain was long gone.

## Chapter Six

Lantry hurried to the front door and looked out, figuring she would head for the road but wouldn't be able to get far.

There would be tracks in the fresh snow. She would be easy to follow, and he had no doubt he could catch up to her.

He was sure he had only dozed off for a short while early this morning before the storm had stopped. Dede wouldn't have left until the storm was over, because she wasn't a fool. In fact, she seemed a hell of a lot smarter than him right now.

He opened the front door and looked out, surprised to see there were no tracks in the perfect, marblelike sculpted snow. The morning light glistened off the wind-crusted surface. Dede hadn't gone out this way.

At the back door, he found her footprints and followed them. They led right to the barn. Beyond it, he saw the horses and remembered Dede's reaction last night at dinner when he'd asked "Do you ride?" after seeing her watching the horses through the window.

"No." She'd shuddered. "I don't ride." He'd glimpsed what he'd thought was her fear of horses.

She'd lied.

He thought about catching one of the horses and going after her, but he knew she would have too much of a lead on him on horseback. As he listened, he could hear the sound of a snowplow in the distance.

As he trudged back through the snow, he couldn't help but wonder how much more of Dede's story had been a lie. He was furious with her. But mostly with himself.

After all these years of being a lawyer, a divorce lawyer who knew from the jump that there was always another side to any story in a marriage, he'd bought into her sad tale.

He cursed himself as he entered the house, questioning why she would make up such a story. On impulse, he tried the phone and, to his amazement, got a dial tone. He punched in his brother Shane's cell-phone number. It was answered on the second ring.

"Lantry?" There was both relief and fear in Shane's voice.

"I'm okay."

"Is she holding a gun on you?"

"No, she's gone."

*"Gone?"*

"We went off the road yesterday and ended up spending the night in a ranch house. When I woke up this morning, she'd taken off on one of the horses." He hesitated. "She has the gun."

Shane swore again. "But you're all right?"

"Just fine," Lantry groused.

"She can't have gone far. Not as deep as the snow is," Shane said. "Where are you?"

He'd noticed the address on some old mail in the kitchen. "Apparently, I'm in Joe and Mabel Thompson's place south of town." Lantry didn't have a clue where that was. Or where Dede Chamberlain was right at this moment.

But he sure would have liked to get his hands on her.

DEDE RODE THROUGH the snowdrifts, the horse sending the light snow into the cold air around them. She could see her breath, steam blowing from the horse's nostrils as the animal busted through the snow, the mountains rising from out of the horizon in the distance.

The blizzard had left the landscape looking like glistening white sensuous waves, the snow almost blinding once the sun came up. The land looked glazed smooth. There was nothing but white as far as the eye could see. It lay under a crystalline blue sky that was so intense it hurt to look at.

Dede had gulped at the sight of the huge horses and had been forced to tamp down her fear this morning before daylight.

"You can do this," she'd whispered to herself as she approached one of the horses.

She hadn't lied to Lantry last night when he'd asked her if she rode. She didn't. Not anymore.

As she slipped a halter onto the friendliest of the horses, the one who hadn't shied at her approach, she told herself that riding a horse again was nothing compared to what she'd already been through. This was the real lie.

She'd been deathly afraid of horses since an accident in her early twenties. Her horse had lost its footing on the side of a mountain and fallen. They'd both tumbled down the mountainside. While her injuries hadn't been life threatening, her horse hadn't been as lucky.

Just the barn scents had her shaking. "It's from the cold," she'd told herself as she'd swung up on the horse. The horse shuddered under her, and, for one terrified moment, Dede had thought he might buck her off.

She had thought she'd never get on another horse after her accident. This day, sitting astride this horse, reminded her of that other place, that other life and the pain. She was still terrified, and the horse sensed it, making it even more dangerous.

But danger was relative. The horse might throw her. Or take off and end up trampling her. The alternative, staying behind to go back to the hospital, was certain death. But try as she might, she couldn't relax and feared she had lost her original love of horses forever.

She slowed and glanced over her shoulder, half expecting to see Lantry coming after her on one of the other horses. Common sense told her that he was just glad to be rid of her. He hadn't believed her. That would be his worst and last mistake, she thought with no small regret.

If Frank had given his lawyer something for safe-keeping, then maybe she could have helped save Frank, Lantry and herself. But if she was wrong about that, then she was wrong in thinking she could save any of them.

She told herself she had no choice. Lantry would be safer without her. In fact, leaving him was probably the best thing she could have done. Now she would be the focus of Ed and Claude's deadly hunt.

Dede stared at the mountains ahead of her. She had no real plan. Just reach the highway and take her chances getting a ride. Maybe not everyone had heard about the escapees. At least she wasn't still wearing a Santa costume. Thanks to the clothing Lantry had found for her, she was dressed like everyone else in the county now.

As she rode, the cold stinging her cheeks, she tried to convince herself that it was time she looked after Dede and quit worrying about everyone else.

But Lantry Corbett wasn't a man easily forgotten. Not the ruthless divorce lawyer—the cowboy who'd kissed her last night in front of the fire.

At a fence, she slid from the horse, relieved to get off the beast at least for a few moments. She opened the barbed-wire gate and, after walking her horse through, closed it again. That's when she saw the single set of pickup tracks and realized she'd reached a road.

As she debated which direction to head, she heard a sound. An instant later, a vehicle appeared from over a rise. As the rig bore down on her, Dede realized she had nowhere to run. She couldn't outrun the vehicle on horseback nor was there time to reopen the gate and take off across the pasture.

Better not to run anyway. Better to hope the driver just thought she was out for a ride and kept on going.

Sunlight glared off the windshield, obscuring driver and passenger as the SUV roared toward her.

She shielded her eyes from the glare as the driver hit the brakes, noticing the smashed front end as the SUV came to a stop just feet from her and the horse. Dede already had her story ready about her early morning ride when both doors of the SUV swung open.

She had only an instant before she was tackled to the ground, her head pushed deep into the snow as her wrists were bound behind her and she was dragged to the back of the SUV and tossed inside.

LANTRY STORMED AROUND the ranch house, wearing a path between the fire and the front window. He'd made himself some breakfast, just to keep busy.

Too bad he couldn't corral his thoughts. They ran wild, rehashing every conversation he'd had with Dede Chamberlain, looking for other lies. He knew it was futile. The woman was sick. Deranged. How could he expect anything she said to make sense?

But it nagged at him anyway, driving him up the wall. He couldn't get Dede off his mind. Or how she'd fooled him. Or how he'd kissed her. He was still mentally kicking himself.

Shouldn't he have been able to spot deceit?

Except that he hadn't cared if his clients lied to him or not. It was all the same to him since with divorce it really didn't matter. It went without saying that there were two sides to every story. The only side he needed to know was his client's.

With that thought, he went to the phone, put in a call to the newspaper in Houston and asked a reporter to look for a story on a jewelry burglary. He recalled something about the case, but not enough to verify if Dede had been telling him the truth.

Lantry figured that if he could prove Dede had lied about that, then he could just assume all the rest of it was hogwash, as well.

"It would have been in late March or early April," he told the reporter. Right before Lantry left for Montana. "One of the necklaces was supposedly worth a million dollars."

"More like one point six million dollars," the reporter said. "Sure, I remember that story."

"Do you recall the name of the woman who was burglarized?"

"Give me just a minute." The reporter returned a few moments later. "Fallon. Dr. Eric and Tamara Fallon."

"Has the necklace been recovered?" Lantry asked, his heart in his throat.

"Nope. No arrests have been made, either, but a body was found in a canal last week that the police are saying might be Tamara Fallon. Some identification was found nearby. She and her husband were reportedly going through an ugly divorce. I understand he's been taken in for questioning several times, but no arrest has been made."

Lantry thanked the reporter and hung up as he heard the sound of vehicles coming up the road not long after the plow had gone through. Tammy Fallon dead. A woman from Frank's mysterious past. Add to that Ed and Claude, and what did you have?

Lantry shook his aching head. This all just kept getting crazier—and scarier, since at least some of Dede's story was true.

The first vehicle to arrive at the house was a wrecker, no doubt his brother's doing. The second vehicle was a sheriff's department SUV with his brother behind the wheel. The wrecker drove up the road and Shane and Lantry followed in the patrol SUV.

Lantry filled Shane in on everything Dede had told him while the wrecker operator worked to get the pickup out of the snowbank.

When he finished his story, he could see that his brother was as skeptical as he'd been. "I verified her story about the stolen necklace and the woman named Tamara Fallon. Apparently, Tamara Fallon's body was found floating in a canal last week. Her husband is a suspect, since they were in the middle of a divorce."

"This is all tenuous at best," Shane said. "Dede doesn't even know for sure that her ex-husband was involved in this burglary. She was also wrong about Frank giving you a gift. That should tell you something."

It told Lantry that they needed proof. "I should have asked her for the name of the private investigator she hired. Can't you at least see if you can find Frank Chamberlain? Do some digging into his past?"

Shane sighed. "I kind of have my hands full right now with three escaped mental patients on the loose and you to worry about. Looks like the wrecker's got your pickup out. Let's go see if it runs."

"Just a minute," Lantry said, grabbing his brother's coat sleeve to stop him. "What aren't you telling me?"

"Frank Chamberlain. He was found murdered."

Lantry couldn't hide his shock. "Then this proves—"

"Dede Chamberlain is wanted for questioning in his death. Frank was killed after she escaped the Texas mental hospital. The police have an eyewitness who places her in the neighborhood at the time the coroner estimates Frank's death."

"No way," Lantry said, shaking his head. He thought of Dede's face when she was talking about Frank, about her marriage. Those tears had been real, that pain and heartache genuine.

"She loved him. Still loves him after everything he did to her. There's no way she killed him."

"Frank was beaten with a lamp base. It has the earmarks of a crime of passion, and Dede's fingerprints were found on the lamp."

Lantry swore. "She lived in that house. Of course her

fingerprints—" He saw that he was wasting his time with this tack. "Won't you at least check into Frank Chamberlain's background? Find out if he really was involved with Tamara Fallon in the security business and if there were other burglaries as Dede says. Would you at least do that for me?"

"If you promise me you'll go straight to the ranch," Shane said. "The folks are worried sick about you. They won't be satisfied until they see for themselves that you're all right. And if you should hear from Dede—I hope I don't have to warn you how much trouble you'd be in if you help a woman who is not only wanted for questioning in her ex-husband's murder but an escapee with a growing criminal record."

"No," Lantry said with a brusque shake of his head. "You don't have to warn me."

"Get some sleep. You look like hell and you're cranky," his brother said as he squeezed Lantry's shoulder.

He knew how much he'd worried his family and his brother—even more since Shane, the former Texas Ranger, knew just how dangerous these types of situations could be.

"So there hasn't been any word on Dede?" he asked, before getting out of the patrol car.

Shane shook his head. "We have law enforcement and border patrol looking for all three of them. If they're still in this part of the county, we'll find them."

That's what worried Lantry. It would be just like Dede to resist arrest. With everybody so worked up and her armed, she could get herself killed.

The irony wasn't lost on him. Dede was convinced that if she went back to the state hospital she'd be dead.

Now she could be facing the death penalty for murder in Texas.

Lantry racked his brain as to what to do next as he drove back toward the Trails West Ranch. He couldn't just sit back and not look for Dede. She hadn't killed her husband. The eyewitness was mistaken. Or lying.

If Frank was involved in that burglary and that necklace was still missing, then wasn't it more likely that his buddies Ed and Claude had killed him?

A thought struck him.

At the top of a rise, Lantry stopped the pickup and reached for his cell phone. Good, he had service.

Dede had been so damned sure that Frank had given him something for safekeeping. What Lantry couldn't get past was that all her reasoning made sense. Frank would have trusted him. If the man really had something he wanted kept safe, why not give it to his lawyer?

Dede might have lied about riding a horse, but as he hit the number on his speed dial, he thought of his wrecked Lamborghini. He couldn't discount everything she'd told him.

"WHAT A NICE SURPRISE," Violet said from behind the wheel of the SUV as she gunned the engine, shooting down the narrow track of road. "Been enjoying your stay in our pleasant little community?"

"Not particularly," Dede said from the backseat.

"Oh?" Violet was studying her in the rearview mirror. "Didn't find that man you were looking for? Corbett, wasn't that his name?"

Dede met Violet's crazy eyes in the mirror. How had Violet known that? Dede hadn't told her, and it was doubtful Violet could have heard through the Whitehorse grapevine.

She felt her pulse jump. Violet had been carrying two Santa suits the night they escaped, Roberta only one. Violet had been planning on taking a third person out with her and Roberta all along.

Dede had thought taking her along on the escape had been impulsive on Violet's part. Now she doubted that. Hadn't she been surprised how easy it had been for them to escape? She'd known it had to have been an inside job.

She'd just never considered Claude had been behind it. But Violet had known she was on her way to Whitehorse. Known she had been going there to talk to Lantry Corbett.

"A large man with gray hair and a scar was behind my escaping from the hospital here in Montana, wasn't he?" she asked now. "Calls himself Claude. Or at least he did. What else did he tell you?"

Violet met her gaze in the rearview mirror. "I don't know what you're talking about."

"Don't you?" Dede challenged. "Well, consider this. Everyone at the hospital will be under suspicion because of the escape. Claude really wouldn't want the truth coming out. So how do you think he plans to keep the three of us from telling on him, hmm?"

Violet's gaze narrowed. She shot a look at Roberta, who was also looking worried.

The only question that remained was why Claude would help her escape. Because he thought it would be easier to kill her outside the hospital? He knew she couldn't possibly have whatever he and Ed were looking for.

Her blood turned to ice. Was it possible they'd hoped she would lead them to Lantry Corbett—just as she'd done?

THE PHONE RANG TWICE, and Lantry was starting to wonder if the office was closed for the rest of the week because of the Christmas holiday.

"Mr. Corbett's office."

Of course the office was open just days before Christmas. Divorce never took a day off—*especially* during the holidays, when there were always more domestic disputes than any other time.

"Shirley, it's Lantry."

"Merry Christmas," she said pleasantly. He could imagine his elderly secretarial assistant in her prim business suit sitting, back ramrod straight, behind her immaculate desk. "How is everything in Montana, or are you back in Texas?"

"I'm still in Montana." He told himself this was a fool's errand. "I need to ask a favor."

"Of course, Mr. Corbett."

"I need you to send me everything you have from the Frank Chamberlain case, anything he might have given me." He heard her hesitate and felt his pulse jump.

*"Everything?"* she asked uncertainly. "Does that include the large box he left for you?"

Lantry's heart pounded so hard he had trouble hearing, let alone breathing. "What box is that?"

"I was sure I mentioned it...."

"It's all right, Shirley. I'm sure you did. I just forgot." Or he hadn't been paying attention because the case was over and he couldn't have cared less about some gift Frank had given him.

Usually he told Shirley to open the boxes that were clearly gifts. If the box contained chocolates, he told her to keep them. Or share them around the office.

The booze found its way to the partners' lounge, since it was usually the really good stuff. Lantry never kept any of the gifts.

He was just thankful he hadn't told Shirley to get rid of the gift. "Would you mind opening the box?"

"I'd be happy to."

"It's not ticking, is it?" he asked belatedly, but Shirley was already off the phone. He could hear her in the background opening the box. He held his breath, suddenly afraid that the box didn't contain evidence—but some form of detonation device. All the packages coming into the building were screened, but what if somehow this one had gotten in another way?

"Shirley? *Shirley!*"


ED INGRAM SAT in the Great Northern Café sipping his coffee and listening to the group of local men talking at the table in the back. Regulars, from the way the waitress had greeted them as they came in.

The talk in Whitehorse was Violet Evans, one of the women who had escaped from the state mental hospital. Apparently, no one knew the other two.

From his table, Ed could see all the commotion at the sheriff's office. Cars had been coming and going all morning. He watched as a nondescript van with the state emblem on the side parked across the street.

Claude got out, looked both ways, then crossed the street toward the café. Ed noticed that Claude had put on a little weight, hadn't been taking care of himself like he should. A big man like that needed to watch his diet and get more exercise.

Ed turned his attention back to his coffee as Claude came in and took a seat at the counter close by, then turned on his stool to glance around the small space.

"Gonna be another cold one," Claude said in Ed's direction. "This normal weather for here?"

"Sorry, I'm just passing through on my way to Canada," Ed said.

"Canada, huh? I've never been up there," Claude said, getting up and coming over to the table. "I heard it's even colder up there. Are the roads open?"

"Last I heard, but there's another storm coming in tonight," Ed said. As his food arrived, he added, "Would you like to join me?"

"You don't mind? I do hate to eat alone." Claude took the chair across from him and glanced at the men in the back. One of them had been watching but turned back to the others, his interest spent.

Claude smiled, then turned his attention to the waitress, who'd just asked, "What can I get you?"

"Biscuits and gravy, two eggs sunny-side up and a side of bacon," Claude said.

Ed sprinkled berries over his oatmeal, watching Claude doctor his coffee with three packets of sugar and top it off with cream.

"What?" Claude asked quietly.

"Eating like that is going to kill you," Ed warned.

"Yeah? But what a way to go."

The locals wandered out, leaving the small café empty.

"Any news?" Claude asked after checking to make sure the waitress was in the kitchen out of earshot.

"According to the locals who were sitting in the back, so far no word."

"Nothing from your end?" Ed asked Claude.

"Just waitin'."

Ed knew Claude wasn't good at just waitin.' And it worried him. Claude made mistakes when he got antsy. They all did.

The waitress slid a huge plate of biscuits and gravy onto the table along with a plate of bacon and eggs. Claude unwrapped his silverware, tossed the napkin to the side and dove into the food.

Between bites, he said, "You got to hand it to Dede. She really is something else. I suppose you heard what she did over here at the jail." He chuckled. "Took the deputy's weapon and Corbett at gunpoint."

"Dede is much smarter than Frank ever gave her credit for," Ed agreed as he watched Claude devour the food as if he hadn't eaten in a week.

"You know she'll warn him."

"Yes, but how likely is he to believe her? The woman is clearly unbalanced. After all, she took him hostage at gunpoint." Ed shook his head. "I'm not worried about that."

"What if they don't catch her?"

Ed scoffed. "With every law-enforcement officer in Montana looking for them?" He grimaced as he watched Claude clean his plate, sopping up the last of the gravy with a chunk of biscuit.

"You eat like an animal," Ed said with distaste as he finished his oatmeal and blotted his lips with his neatly folded napkin.

Claude laughed. "I'm just a man with a good appetite." His cell phone rang. He dropped his fork to check it. His gaze shot up to Ed's as he took the call. "Claude here." He listened. "Uh-huh. Okay. Got it." He snapped off the phone and looked over at Ed. "Lantry Corbett's been found. Dede got away again. Looks like you're going to have to revise your plan."

## Chapter Seven

"Mr. Corbett? It's a boat."

*"What?"* Lantry felt weak with relief.

"The box held a small wooden boat."

"The package was screened downstairs, right?"

"Of course," Shirley said. "The boat looks like a collector's item. Unless I miss my guess, it's homemade and quite old. Even...valuable, if you don't mind me saying it."

He smiled, his heart rate dropping a little. "Shirley, I need the boat and Chamberlain's file overnighted to me. It's important that you do it immediately. Would that be possible?"

"I will see to it myself. You know you can depend on me."

He had for years. "I know. Thank you. Also, let's keep this between the two of us."

"Confidentially as always."

Lantry realized that he'd offended her. "Shirley, have I ever thanked you for being such a loyal and competent assistant?"

"With a nice bonus every year, Mr. Corbett."

"But have I ever said it before?"

She sounded flustered. "Well, no, not exactly, but—"

"I'm sorry I haven't done that before now. I apologize. I don't know what I would have done without you."

"That is very kind of you. Is everything all right, Mr. Corbett?"

"Fine." He made a mental note to make sure Shirley was taken care of financially when she retired, which he guessed wasn't far off. He'd always dreaded that day. Now he realized she would retire only if he ever quit.

"I'll get that package off as soon as I hang up," Shirley said. "You want it sent to Trails West Ranch?"

"Yes. Thank you." The moment he disconnected the call, he punched in his brother Shane's number.

"Shane, I need you to call off the cavalry. Just give me some time to find Dede and—"

"Lantry—"

"I think she might be telling the truth. I just need you to—"

"Lantry! I've got news."

He braced himself for the worst—that the men after Dede had found her.

"The three escapees have been spotted," Shane said. "We just got a call from a rancher who saw them drive by."

*"Three?"* Dede was with the other two? How was that possible? "That can't be right. The rancher has to be wrong."

"I have to go," Shane said.

"You'll let me know when you find her."

"You aren't thinking about representing her, are you? You're a divorce lawyer. She's going to need the best criminal lawyer money can buy."

Lantry didn't need to be told that. Frank Chamberlain had been a well-respected businessman who wielded a lot of power in Houston. Unless Lantry could prove that Dede's allegations about him were true and that she hadn't killed him… "Just let me know when you find her."

"I THINK YOU'RE JUST mad about the last time we saw you," Violet said as she drove along the narrow, plowed road through the wintry landscape. "I see you finally got out of your costume. You must have done all right by yourself."

Dede said nothing, turning to look out at the drifted snow that swept to the horizon. She knew now that everything about her escape and getting dumped on the main street of Whitehorse had been choreographed, and not by Violet Evans.

Violet had stolen clothing for herself and Roberta, forcing Dede to remain in her Santa suit. No wonder she'd been picked up so quickly by the sheriff's department.

All part of the plan? She'd been manipulated, maybe from the beginning. From the moment Frank called her, begging for her help. Her heart ached at the thought that Frank had been in on this. She realized with a jolt that *Frank* was the one who told her about Lantry's car.

*They already tried to kill my lawyer by rigging something on his sports car.*

Tears of anger and hurt burned her eyes. Frank *could* have protected her *and* Lantry. All he had to do was give Ed and Claude what they wanted.

"I hope that necklace is worth it," she said under her breath. That's all it could be. Frank had helped with the burglary and somehow had gotten away with the million-dollar-plus necklace.

He'd doubled-crossed his cohorts, and now he must be hiding out while Ed and Claude came after her and Lantry. Had they hoped to use her and Lantry as leverage against Frank to make him come out of hiding?

Well, it wasn't working. And Lantry swore that Frank hadn't given him anything to keep for him.

"So did you find him and kill him?" Roberta asked.

"Who?" Dede had to ask since her mind had been on Frank.

"Corbett," Violet said. "Lantry Corbett. Your ex-husband's lawyer."

"No," Dede said, meeting the woman's gaze in the rearview mirror. "I only made things worse."

"I know what you mean," Roberta said. "Everyone's looking for us after what happened last night."

Dede felt herself start. She recalled how Violet said she was going to Whitehorse to make sure her mother never walked down the aisle. "What happened?"

"Shut up," Violet snapped. Her gaze in the rearview mirror wasn't aimed at Dede though—but to a spot on the seat next to her. "My mother got away last night, but she won't again. So stop nagging me. You hear me?"

Roberta made a circle with her finger next to her head when Violet wasn't looking. "Violet ran her mother off the road last night," she said. "Guess she's shaken up pretty good. Now her mother at least knows she's back in town."

"She'll know a lot more than that when I'm through with her," Violet said, glaring in the rearview mirror at the spot next to Dede. Roberta was watching her, looking a little worried.

"Where are we going?" Roberta asked.

"To hell," Violet said. "In the meantime, we're going

to pay my mother another visit. But first we need to make a stop, and you, Texas, are going along for the ride in case we need your help. I'd say 'buckle up,' but I guess you can't, can you?"

Dede looked down from the hill they'd just topped to what appeared to be a ghost town. There were a few houses separated by empty, snow-filled lots. At least one of the houses was clearly abandoned.

Only one building had steam rising from it—a large barnlike place next to what could only be the one-room schoolhouse. Most of the playground equipment was buried in snow and looked as if it hadn't been used for a while.

Dede reminded herself that it was only days from Christmas. Of course the school would be closed.

"Welcome to Old Town Whitehorse," Violet said with the flurry of her hand as she pulled down a narrow road that had only recently been plowed, and stopped. "That is where I grew up."

"I thought you lived out of town," Roberta said.

"Just up the road."

Dede heard the irritation in Violet's voice and saw her frown at the other woman. She'd felt the tension between them the moment they'd abducted her from the mental hospital.

"See that building," Violet said, pointing at a large structure next to the schoolhouse. "That's the Whitehorse Community Center."

"I thought Whitehorse was to the north," Roberta piped in.

"This was the original Whitehorse. Then the railroad came through and everyone moved north to be next to it," Violet said, scowling at Roberta. "My family settled this land."

"Fascinating," Roberta said and yawned.

Violet seemed to clamp down on her temper, but Dede could tell it took a lot of effort. "We're going to wait until those people decorating for the wedding are finished, and then we are going down there to redecorate."

"That seems a little childish," Roberta pointed out. "I thought we were going to stop the wedding. That doesn't sound like it will do—"

"Shut up!" Violet screamed, making Dede jump. "Do you believe this bitch?" she asked, turning to look back at Dede. "This is *my* show. You're just along for the ride. So shut the hell up."

Roberta pouted, and the inside of the SUV fell silent. Dede didn't dare move for fear Violet would turn on her.

The vehicles that had been parked in front of the community center began to leave.

But Violet didn't move. She sat staring down at the town her ancestors had helped found. When she finally did start the SUV, she didn't head for Old Town Whitehorse, and Dede had a bad feeling that this might be the end of the ride for both herself *and* Roberta.

"LANTRY!" JUANITA WAS the first to see him when he walked into the main house at Trails West Ranch. As usual, there was something cooking in Juanita's big kitchen.

She clasped both of his hands. "I am so glad you're all right. We have been so worried."

"Thank you." He followed her down the hall to the large living room with huge windows that looked out over the ranch. He hadn't even stopped at his cabin, some distance from the main house, to clean up. He knew Shane had called the family and they were waiting for him.

They were. Everyone turned as he came in. His brothers Russell, Dalton and Jud and their wives, as well as his father and his father's wife, Kate. The relief he saw in their faces made him feel guilty for making them worry. He felt responsible for at least some of this, given his chosen profession—and how callous he'd been about his clients and their exes.

"I'm fine," he said to the crowd, his gaze settling on his father. Grayson smiled and nodded.

"We heard you'd been taken at gunpoint by a crazy woman," Kate said and rushed to hug him. "We were so worried."

"I'm fine, and Dede Chamberlain wouldn't have harmed me." His words surprised him in that he believed them to be true. Even as angry as she'd been at him.

"You'll join us for dinner, won't you?" Grayson asked. His father loved having his entire family at the ranch's large dining-room table. That's when he seemed the happiest.

But eating with his rambunctious family was the last thing Lantry could do right now. "Thank you, but I need to get a shower, a change of clothes and take care of some things."

"Of course," Grayson said amicably as he looped an arm around his son's shoulders. "You probably need some time alone to take all this in. Juanita will save you some dinner. It's just good to have you home."

Home. Lantry didn't think of Trails West Ranch or

Montana as home. And yet he didn't think of his condo in Houston as home, either. The only place he'd ever really felt at home had been the family ranch in Texas. But Grayson had sold that after marrying Kate and moved lock, stock and barrel to Montana.

"I just wanted you all to see that I'm fine," he said, excusing himself. As he left, he heard his brothers horsing around and their wives trying to intercede. Everything was back to normal with the Corbetts.

*All of them except me,* he thought as he drove down to his cabin by the creek. His father had ordered a half-dozen cabins built for his sons for when they visited Montana.

Now, with three of them married, houses were in various stages of construction on the ranch, with everyone still living in the cabins spread out in a half-moon shape some distance from the main house.

Lantry knew that even when his brothers' houses were completed, they would spend most of their time at the main house. Just as Grayson had hoped. Just as the brothers' deceased mother had wanted and specified in a letter she'd written before dying.

That letter, and the five letters she'd left for each of her sons to be read on their wedding days, had come as such a shock that Lantry and the others had drawn straws to see which of them honored their mother's memory by marrying first.

Lantry had gone along with it just to keep peace in the family. His brothers knew he was never getting married, so it would come as no surprise when he reneged on the pact. He figured by that time the others would be married and too busy to care.

At his cabin, he stripped, showered and changed.

Shane still hadn't called. Did that mean they hadn't found Dede and the others? If there had been a shooting, it would take his brother longer to call him.

Shane had told him to stay at the ranch, but he couldn't do that. Lantry grabbed his pickup keys. As he stepped out on the small cabin porch, he realized he'd left his cell phone inside and started to turn back when he heard the thwack of something striking the log next to his head. Bark and bits of wood flew into the air, several splinters embedding in his cheek.

He dove back into the house, but not before two more shots were fired—one hitting the door, another taking out the lamp on the table behind him. He slammed the door and belly-crawled over to his cell phone.

"Someone just tried to kill me," he said the moment his brother Shane answered.

VIOLET DROVE ONLY a short way before she stopped again. The area looked desolate, but this whole country did. For miles there was nothing but snow, broken occasionally by a house or tree.

"You aren't going down there," Roberta said from the front passenger seat.

Dede looked to see what Roberta was referring to. An old farmhouse sat among some outbuildings in a gully nearby.

"I need to see my mother," Violet said in a strange, little-girl voice that made both Dede and Roberta look over at her in alarm. "I know she's down there."

"Your mother will call the cops, and we'll all be caught," Roberta said, getting angry. "I thought we were going to—"

Violet pulled the keys out of the ignition and opened

her door. "You don't like it, take a hike," she said as she got out.

"That woman is crazy," Roberta said as Violet slammed the door and headed off down the hill toward the house where apparently she'd grown up.

Roberta slid down in her seat and closed her eyes as if planning to take a nap.

Dede saw her opportunity and began to work at freeing her hands. Violet had tied her with cotton rope that was now cutting off her circulation. With both her wrists bound, she had no chance of getting away from these two, and she hated to think what would happen if she stayed with them much longer.

She had to agree with Roberta. It was crazy, Violet going down there. No matter how it went, Dede worried it would go badly for Violet's mother. Or Violet.

And if Violet's mother called the cops, Dede and Roberta would be caught, as well.

"You know she talks to her grandmother who's been dead for years," Roberta said sleepily.

Dede knew Violet talked to someone who wasn't there. "She must have loved her grandmother."

Roberta laughed so hard the SUV shook as she sat up a little. "Her grandmother is the one she really wants to kill, but it's tough to kill someone who's already dead, you know? That old hag must have been a real piece of work. Violet's still scared of her."

Through the frost-rimmed window, Dede watched Violet approach the house. "What do you think her mother will do?"

Roberta shrugged. "What would you do if the daughter who'd tried to kill you came calling?"

*Run like the devil,* Dede thought.

Roberta seemed to realize that Dede was up to something. She glanced back at her.

"Could you untie me? This is really uncomfortable."

Roberta frowned. "I don't think so."

"We're all in this together."

"Not even close. I'm not sure how you ended up in the loony bin, but you're not one of us."

"Please. I'm not going anywhere."

"Uh-oh," Roberta said, turning her attention back to the farmhouse below them. "Did Violet just walk in the house?"

Violet was nowhere in sight, and Dede could make out movement behind the curtains. She listened for the sound of a gunshot, closing her eyes, wishing she was anywhere but here.

Lantry popped into her thoughts, bringing with him the memory of the kiss. She'd made a mistake not staying with him and taking her chances.

Sure. By now she'd be locked up at the local jail or on her way back to the hospital.

No, as crazy as it seemed, she had a better chance with Violet and Roberta than she did with Lantry Corbett. But that didn't stop her from working at the rope binding her wrists.

"I THOUGHT I told you to stay back at the cabin," Shane snapped at his brother as Lantry joined him on the small hill overlooking the cabin.

Lantry stared at the spot where the shooter had hunkered down. There were indentations in the snow where the marksman had used a tripod to steady his rifle.

"He settled in to wait for me to come out of the

cabin," Lantry said more to himself than his brother. "So he knew I'd returned to the ranch."

"It's this damned local grapevine," Shane said angrily.

Lantry looked over at his brother. "This proves that Dede was telling the truth."

"Unless Dede is the one who took the potshots at you."

"Right. She just picked up a rifle somewhere."

"Are you sure there wasn't one at the farmhouse you broke into?" Shane asked and nodded as he saw Lantry's expression. "That's what I thought."

"It wasn't Dede. You said yourself she was seen with the other two escapees," Lantry pointed out, ignoring the fact that he hadn't believed that sighting.

"They were seen in this *area*. Her friends could have dropped her off and picked her up down the road."

Lantry shook his head.

"You've put your trust in a woman who seems pretty capable of taking care of herself."

"If she wasn't capable of taking care of herself, she'd be dead right now," Lantry snapped. "She had plenty of opportunities to kill me back at the farmhouse. She didn't."

"Yeah, well, consider this. How many killers use a tripod to steady the gun and then miss three times? If someone wanted to convince you that your life was in danger, they did one hell of a good job of it, didn't they?"

Lantry hated that Shane had a point. Even a hunter could have made that shot without any trouble given the short distance he'd set up from the cabin.

"Did you check on the things I told you about the

Fallon robbery or Frank's old associates?" Lantry demanded.

Shane sighed. "Dr. Eric Fallon reported his wife missing four days ago—the same time Frank was murdered. Her body was found floating in a canal not far from where Frank and Dede lived. Texas is waiting on a positive ID from the crime lab. She was beaten beyond recognition—much like Frank. So not only is Dede's ex dead, but her ex's girlfriend. It looks really bad for Dede, Lantry. I think it's time for you to face the fact that this woman can't be saved. Not even by you."

He didn't give Lantry a chance to answer.

"I've got to go talk to the folks," Shane said. "I think the shooter made his point and won't be coming back, but just to be safe, keep your head down. Maybe you should move up to the main house."

"Sure, and put the family in the line of fire?" Lantry shook his head. "I think the best thing I can do is get as far away from the ranch as possible."

"Don't be a damned fool. Just because you didn't get yourself killed this time doesn't mean that your life isn't in danger. This woman wants something from you. You'd best consider what will happen if she doesn't get it. Or, maybe worse, what happens if she does and no longer needs you."

## Chapter Eight

Violet felt her heart lodge in her throat as she stepped into the house and saw her mother.

Arlene didn't move. Didn't speak. She just stood there, her eyes brimming with tears. And Violet knew that her mother had seen her coming. Had expected her.

Why hadn't she locked the door? Or gone to her fiancé's house to stay where she'd be safe?

Was her mother insane? Probably. Didn't it run in families, this mental-illness stuff she'd read so much about?

"I—I—" Violet's voice broke, and she felt her own eyes fill with tears.

"I was hoping to see you," Arlene said quickly. "It's been too long." Her mother was acting as if this was just a visit from her oldest daughter.

"You haven't seen me because you haven't come up to the hospital," Violet said, even though she knew that wasn't true.

"You always refused to see me," Arlene said quietly.

"I've been dealing with some things." She looked around the house for a moment, her throat tight, that old pain in her chest making it hard to breathe. "You got rid of my room, my things...." She cleared her throat, the dam of hot tears breaking and rolling down her cheeks.

"I packed up all your things and put them in storage. I didn't think you'd ever want to come back to your room," Arlene said. "You can get them out anytime you want. I have a key for you."

"You've changed," Violet said, making a swipe at her tears and trying to steady herself. "You cut your long hair." Her mother had always worn her hair long and tightly pulled back from her face. Floyd, Violet's father, didn't believe in wasting money at the beauty shop. Neither did his mother, she thought bitterly, remembering arguing with her grandmother—and losing— for a salon cut.

Arlene touched the soft curls and looked embarrassed. "I've been trying to change."

"Obviously it's working. You're getting *married*." The unfairness of that formed a jealous, resentful bile in her stomach.

"You'd like Hank," Arlene said. "He's a good man."

This whole conversation had taken on a surreal feel, and Violet wondered if she'd only imagined it—until she heard her dead grandmother speak up from where she was sitting on the couch.

"Enough of this inane chitchat. Shoot her and get it over with," Grandma snapped.

Something in Violet snapped as well. She pulled the gun from the pocket of her coat and pointed it at her mother.

Arlene didn't react. If anything, she seemed calm, resigned.

"You didn't protect me from that old woman."

"She was your father's mother. I was young. I..." Arlene shook her head. "I have no excuse. I should have protected you from her. I didn't."

"Both of you are sniveling whiners," Grandma said from the couch. "I tried to give you some backbone. But you can't make a silk purse out of a sow's ear."

DEDE'S EYES FLEW OPEN at the sound of gunshots. Her stomach clenched with fear as Violet came racing out of the farmhouse on the hill below them, running through the snow, a gun clutched in her hand.

"I hate to say I told you so," Roberta said.

"I'm not sure that would be a good idea right now," Dede said tactfully, even though her heart was racing and she felt sick. "Violet seems a little upset."

A feeling of impending doom had settled like a rock in Dede's chest as she watched Violet fall in the snow just yards from the SUV. Gut-wrenching sobs were coming out of her as she got to her feet and stumbled the rest of the way to them.

Jerking open the driver's side door, Violet practically fell into the driver's seat. She was covered with snow but seemed oblivious to the cold as she stuffed the gun into her coat pocket and fumbled to insert the key into the ignition.

Dede, fearing more bloodshed, prayed that Roberta kept her mouth shut.

The moment the engine caught, Violet stomped on the gas. The SUV fishtailed through the deep snow and back onto the road.

Violet glanced in the rearview mirror. But not at Dede. Then she just drove. For a mile or so no one spoke.

"So, did you kill her?" Roberta asked.

"Yes." Violet's voice sounded hoarse.

"Good," Roberta said. "Now you can get well."

Dede felt as if she might throw up. Violet looked over at her fellow inmate and actually smiled. "Yeah, maybe you're right." But when she glanced in the rearview mirror, Dede saw her haunted, lost look. Violet didn't believe it any more than Dede did.

"Have you ever been to Mexico?" Violet asked Roberta. "I've been thinking I'd like to go there."

"I like Mexican food," Roberta said. "In fact, I could use some right now."

"You can eat all the Mexican food you want once we get there," Violet said, sounding dreamy. "It's warm down there. We'll never have to wear a coat again. Imagine that."

Roberta had opened the glove box and pulled out a couple of candy bars. She was busy unwrapping one. Neither she nor Violet seemed to be paying attention to the road ahead.

Dede could see a stop sign ahead. They were coming to a four-way stop. Violet wasn't slowing down. She seemed lost, as if in a daydream on some warm, sunny Mexican beach.

Nor did either appear aware of the sheriff's department cruiser racing toward them from the left. Or the other from the right on the crossroad.

"Violet," Dede said, but it was too late. Violet didn't have time to react before one of the sheriff cars reached the intersection and skidded across the snowy road, blocking it. The second car came flying in, and suddenly Violet was standing on the brakes.

Dede tumbled to the backseat floorboard as the SUV skidded on the snowy road. All she saw from where she lay was snow flying through the air. There was a sudden thud that slammed her into the backseats as the SUV came to a stop.

The air seemed to suddenly fill with the wail of sirens as Dede let out the breath she'd been holding and red and blue lights rotated against the backdrop of the brilliant blue winter sky.

Before she could move, the SUV's doors were thrown open and she was hauled out with the others. She was finally untied, only to find herself in the back of a patrol car on her way to jail. Or, worse, back to the mental hospital.

"I DON'T UNDERSTAND why you didn't just kill Corbett when you had the chance," Claude said, sounding disgusted as he bit into a large piece of pizza.

"Do you have to eat that in here?" Ed demanded.

"Where would you like me to eat it? Outside?"

Ed would have preferred that. "You could have eaten before you came by my motel. As for Corbett, we need him alive, remember?"

Claude chewed for a few moments, then said, "But we don't even know for sure that Frank left it with the lawyer."

"Exactly. So we need to give him the incentive to save himself and Dede. Corbett is more motivated if he thinks someone wants him dead. Get it?"

Claude looked up, and Ed could tell that he hadn't been listening. Ed couldn't hide his disgust and marveled how much he and Claude had changed since high school.

Ed had grown, matured, was now civilized. Claude, well, Claude had just gotten older. He was still unfocused, immature, impulsive, uncouth and a slob. Nor was he particularly bright.

Claude would always need someone to look after him. That someone would always be Ed.

Claude's cell phone rang. Ed watched him gobble the last of the pizza, then wipe his hands on his jeans before answering it.

He nodded a few times, grunted, then said, "Got it." As he snapped the cell phone shut, he said, "They got our girl."

LANTRY DROVE HIS TRUCK up to the county road to meet the UPS driver. He had to see for himself what Frank had given him. He prayed it would be proof to clear Dede, to keep them both safe—once he'd turned it over to his brother.

With relief he saw the UPS truck come barreling up the road.

"You got something for me?" Lantry asked as the truck came to a stop, half afraid there'd been a mistake. That the boat had been from another client.

"Sure do," the man said congenially. "You must be anxious if you are out here waiting for me."

"I thought I would save you the drive into the ranch. You've got enough bad roads to fight today."

The UPS driver began to hum along with the Christmas carol playing on Lantry's pickup radio. He'd left the truck running, the radio on and the window down a little so he could listen for any word on Dede. So far, nothing.

The driver got out to help Lantry carry two good-size boxes to the pickup, sliding them into the extended cab behind the seats.

"Some kind of crazy weather we're having, huh?" the man said. "I was wondering if I'd even be able to get out here today. Glad to see the road was plowed. Just hope the wind doesn't kick up and drift it in before I can finish my route."

Lantry was distracted by the larger box he knew must hold the boat. "Let's hope the roads stay open for a while," he said, thinking about Dede, worrying about where she was and what kind of trouble she might have gotten into.

The moment the delivery man left, Lantry pulled out his pocket knife to cut open the larger box. The Christmas carol on the radio ended and the announcer came on.

"The Sheriff's Department has informed us that all three escapees have been caught."

Lantry pocketed the knife and grabbed his cell phone, cursing under his breath. Shane hadn't called to tell him.

"I have to see Dede," he said the moment his brother answered. "You have to hold her there at the jail until I can get the paperwork to stop the mental hospital from—"

"It's too late," Shane broke in. "The van driver already picked them up to take them back to the state mental hospital. Dede will be evaluated to see if she is competent enough to face criminal charges."

Lantry cursed. "She was all right, though?" He heard his brother hesitate in answering just a little too long. His heart dropped. "What happened to her?"

"She's fine. They had her tied up in the back."

Lantry let out a curse. He tried to reassure himself

that Dede would be safe—until she reached the hospital. "How long ago did the driver leave?"

"Look, I don't know what—"

"Shane, how long ago did they leave?"

His brother sighed. "About twenty minutes ago. But Lantry, you have no legal—"

Lantry hung up. The van driver wouldn't have that much of a lead, not with the roads being as bad as they were. If Lantry could reach the main road from where he was, he could cut off at least ten minutes, maybe more.

"ARLENE, YOU COULD have been killed." Hank Monroe paced her kitchen, his initial fear receding. Now he was just upset. "When I found your note—"

"I needed to see my daughter. I knew she would come back to the house. I would have told you, but I knew you wouldn't approve."

"Damn right. How could you take a chance like that?"

"She's my daughter."

He looked at this woman he'd fallen so madly in love with and couldn't decide whether to kiss her or wring her neck. "What am I going to do with you?"

She smiled through her tears. "Hold me."

He saw then that she was trembling and quickly pulled her into his arms. At least Arlene had called after Violet left. He was thankful for that. Because he would have had heart failure if the sheriff's department had called first. One of the other escapees, a woman named Dede Chamberlain, had told the deputies that she believed Violet had shot and killed her mother.

"Violet needs my help, Hank. She came to me because she needs me. You didn't see her, didn't hear her—" Her own voice broke.

"Arlene, she could have shot you instead of shooting up your couch."

"She and her grandmother used to sit on that couch, Hank. I would see the old woman clutching Violet's arm and whispering things in her ear. She blames me for not protecting her from her grandmother. I blame myself."

"Arlene," he said, holding her at arm's length to look into her eyes. "You told me about your mother-in-law. You were as much a victim of that woman as your daughter was."

"Still, I should have—"

"You have to stop this. It isn't helping Violet. What can I do?"

"We need to get her help, maybe a private hospital closer to Whitehorse so I can see her more." Arlene's eyes filled with tears. "Can we do that?"

He smiled. "Of course. I will make arrangements right away to have her moved to a private facility."

"Do you think they'll allow that after what she's done?"

"I might have to pull a few strings," Hank said. Maybe all those years with the secret undercover government agency might come in handy after all. They owed him, and he was about to call in one of those favors.

He cupped her face in his hands. "I love you, Arlene." He smiled and brushed a rough thumb pad over the tears on her cheek. "I've spent my life looking for someone like you. I just don't want to lose you."

"You aren't going to. A herd of buffalo couldn't keep

me away from the community center Saturday. I can't wait to be your wife."

He kissed her, and she felt that wonderful stirring that she still found a miracle. That she was given a chance of love at this age was beyond remarkable, especially after the mess she'd made of her life. And Violet's.

"I love you, Hank Monroe, because you've never asked me to be someone I'm not."

THE HIGHWAY LOOKED like a deserted wasteland. For miles, all Lantry could see was snow. Drifts had blown in across the road even since the plows had been through. Where there wasn't snow spines across the pavement, there was black ice.

The state driver wouldn't be able to make good time on the highway, which meant Lantry should be able to catch the van before it reached the mental hospital. That is, if he drove faster than he should.

He hadn't seen another vehicle, not another soul, since he'd left Whitehorse. A brisk breeze stirred the top of the drifts, sending snow showering over the pickup.

The day was clear but cold, the sky a brilliant blue and the sun too low on the horizon to do much more than warm the inside of the truck cab as he drove.

Anxious and upset with himself for his part in all this, he sped up. The rear tires lost traction, and he felt the pickup shift and slide on the ice. He hit a drift, got the truck under control again and slowed down.

His cell phone rang. It was his brother Shane. He had ignored the other three attempts Shane had made to reach him, not up for a lecture.

But worried now that Shane might have some news, he snapped open his phone. "Yeah?"

"Where are you?" his brother demanded. His tone was officious—the deputy sheriff, not the loving brother.

"I might have something that proves Dede was telling the truth. I have to get her out of that van so we can figure this out."

"You stop that van and you will be obstructing justice." Shane swore. "Once she's back at the hospital—"

"It will be too late. Damn it, Shane, I helped her husband do this to her. Did you check on Frank Chamberlain's past?"

"I made a couple of calls. I'm waiting to hear. That's why I need you to—"

Lantry cut him off. "I haven't had a chance to check what Frank left me for safekeeping. But if I'm right, it will prove why he had Dede put in the hospital—and why someone killed him. Not Dede. I have to go." He disconnected before his brother could argue further.

As Lantry topped the hill, he saw a vehicle in the ditch ahead. It wasn't until he drew nearer that he recognized the rig—the state mental-hospital van.

It sat at an angle in the snow-deep ditch, both front doors ajar. He felt his skin crawl, a sick lump in the pit of his stomach.

He touched his brakes and rolled to a spot on the highway a dozen yards back from the van. He looked down the long, empty highway and saw nothing but snow and ice.

Slowly, he climbed out of the pickup, leaving the engine running, and made his way along the edge of the highway as he came alongside the van. The driver was slumped in his seat, his cell phone clutched in his hand, his shoulder holster empty and a pool of frozen blood around him.

Heart hammering, Lantry stepped off the edge of the plowed highway into the deep snow of the ditch to reach in. No pulse. He peered into the back of the van. Another body lay crumpled on the floor, eyes vacant, clearly dead.

Not Dede. But for just an instant…

Lantry tried to catch his breath as he moved along the side of the van and, cupping his hands, looked in the far back. Empty. Dede wasn't in the van. Neither was the other escapee, Violet Evans.

What had happened here?

Had the driver been shot before the van left the road? Or after? Lantry couldn't tell. But it appeared from the way the bodies lay that the driver and the dead escapee might have gotten into some kind of struggle. The metal mesh gate between the driver and the rear seats was hanging open.

Lantry cursed under his breath as he studied the footprints in the snow next to the van. His heart pounded. Two people had gotten out of the van alive: Dede and Violet.

But as he checked the footprints in the snow along the edge of the road, he found only one set.

He felt his insides buckle as he looked back at the van. The only place he hadn't looked was the far side of the vehicle. One of the escapees now had the weapon from the driver's empty holster. Which one?

And where was the other one?

Dede was desperate, but still he couldn't see her killing anyone. Not her ex-husband. Not the driver of the van.

*What if you're wrong about that?*

He shook his head. It had to have been Violet. Which meant…

His blood pumping wildly, he bounded down into the deep snow of the ditch and around the front of the van, expecting to find Dede lying dead in the snow.

He rounded the open passenger-side door of the van and stopped. No body. No blood trail in the snow.

The rush of relief forced him to bend down, hands on his knees, until his head quit spinning. This was his fault. If he'd only believed Dede. If he'd gained her trust she would never have left the farmhouse this morning.

If he hadn't been so damned cynical when it came to marriage, divorce—hell, women. She'd been right about that, too.

What now? Dede was gone. Out there somewhere. And with at least one killer on the loose.

He lifted his head, saw the lone set of footprints in the snow. He let his gaze follow the path the person had taken and realized that one of the passengers from the van had gone down the road. The other had climbed over the nearly buried barbed-wire fence and crossed the pasture.

He blinked. Why would…? He saw them. Horses in the distance. Dede was headed for the hills on horseback. Again.

VIOLET EVANS FELT LIKE a new person as she walked down the highway. Killing her dead grandmother had finally freed her and apparently changed her luck because, unless she was seeing things, there was a car coming up the highway. It was the first vehicle she'd seen on this deserted highway since she'd started walking a good half hour ago. The car slowed.

As the car came to a stop just feet from her, the passenger-side window whirred down. She stepped over and leaned in.

Violet had walked a good five miles down the road before a car had even come along on the snow-covered highway. By then she was freezing. Her hands and feet ached, and the air coming from inside the car felt so wonderfully warm that even if this guy was a serial killer, she was getting in.

"Need a lift?" the man asked unnecessarily.

Violet gave him her best smile. She knew she was no beauty. Far from it. She'd been told, though, that she was almost pretty when she smiled. The person who told her that had probably lied, but right now she would do just about anything for a ride.

"Car went off the road," she said, wondering if he'd seen the van back up the highway. Not likely. He must have come from the west and only connected with Highway 191 about a mile back.

Otherwise he would have seen the van, and if he'd stopped to check, he would have found the bodies and he would be hightailing it for the cops—not stopping to pick up a hitchhiker.

"The roads are terrible," he agreed. "Where are you headed?"

*Mexico,* she thought. She'd had a year of Spanish in high school, and she figured she could pick up the language easy enough as smart as she was.

"What about your mother's wedding?"

She flinched at the sound of her grandmother's voice beside her, mortified to realize even emptying her gun into the woman hadn't exorcised her.

"Stay out of this, you old bat," she said in her mind.

Still, this car proved that her luck had changed and Grandma would just have to get used to the new Violet.

"Billings," Violet said to the driver of the car. She'd noticed the plates on the man's car. They began with a three, which indicated the Billings area, a couple of hours to the south.

"Well, that seems to be the direction I'm headed," the man said. "Hop in."

Violet didn't wait for him to ask twice. She opened the door and got in, closing the door quickly. "It's cold out there." She whirred up her window and rubbed her hands together, glancing in the side mirror. No cars coming up the road.

She was anxious to get going, but he made no move to get the car rolling again.

"You sure you don't want to go back to Whitehorse?" the man asked. "It's closer."

"No, I already made arrangements to get my car towed and my boyfriend is waiting for me down in Billings." She reached for her seat belt, thinking that must be what he was waiting for.

For the first time, she gave him a good look. Definitely not a local. He had a Southern accent and looked like someone passing through. Neatly dressed, he was short but solid, like someone who worked out and kept in good shape.

She recalled the plate number on the car and realized it must be a rental.

What in blazes was he doing on the Hi-Line, that no-man's part of Montana, in the dead of winter? Not that she cared enough to ask.

Slowly, too slowly, the man finally shifted the car into gear and started down the snow-packed highway.

Violet let out a sigh of relief and settled back for the ride, thinking about a new life in Mexico.

"You never finish anything you start," her grandmother said from the backseat. "You've always been like that. Make a mess of things and then leave it for someone else to clean up."

Violet hated the truth in her grandmother's words. She *had* made a mess of this. She hadn't exorcised the old crone, hadn't solved anything with her mother—who was still getting married—and now she was all alone and on the run.

"So you're just going to let your mother get married?"

*Yeah,* Violet thought. She was. She thought of her mother. Arlene *had* changed. Violet wanted to change, too.

Some days she didn't want to punish her mother, didn't have the energy. And wasn't it enough that her mother wouldn't have another sleep-filled night as long as her criminally insane daughter was on the loose? Wasn't that punishment enough?

"You just want to go to Mexico," Grandma said. "Stop making excuses."

"Well, one way or another, you're not going with me," she said under her breath.

"Sorry, did you say something?" the man asked. He was studying her. She prayed he wouldn't make her get out. Her hands and feet were only just starting to warm up. She couldn't face being out there in the cold again.

"Your accent. I was just trying to place it. Where in the South are you from?" Could the man drive any slower?

"Texas. I'm up here on business. In fact, I think you

can help me. I'm looking for someone. Her name's Dede Chamberlain, and I have a feeling you know where she's gone off to."

Violet's dead grandmother was the only one who wasn't surprised when the man pulled the gun.

# *Chapter Nine*

Lantry started to reach for his cell phone, then glanced back at the van, hesitating. There was nothing now that could be done for the driver of the van or the other escapee.

Who knew where Violet Evans was?

But if he made the call right now to his brother at the sheriff's department, he knew that Dede could be too easily tracked down. He had to find her first, get her to some place safe where they could open the box from Frank and figure this out.

Which meant he had to move fast. While there was little traffic because of the slick roads and the storm, he couldn't chance that someone would come along soon, discover the van, call it in.

He stared at the tracks in the snow. Deep shadows filled in the trail she'd left. He squinted in the direction the tracks led, seeing the path she'd taken. First to the horses, then clearly riding one of them bareback toward the foothills of the Little Rockies and the ponderosa pines.

It still grated at him that she'd lied about being able to ride—not that he didn't understand why she'd done it. He'd lied to her, as well—and to himself. He would have let Shane take her this morning if she hadn't taken off—and apparently they'd both known it.

There was really no debate. Both the driver and Roberta were dead. Dede was still alive. At least, he prayed she was.

He had to find her. She would be cold and wet. She'd have to find shelter. There were cabins up in the pines. That's where she would head—just long enough to warm up, rest…and then what?

She didn't know the area, didn't have anyone she could contact for help. She was alone and afraid. And he was the last person she would want to see.

Lantry busted his way through the snow back to his pickup and drove up the highway looking for a secondary road that would lead him to the cabins up in the mountains.

He took the first side road. It had been plowed sometime during the storm so the snow wasn't but a few inches deep. Still, Lantry had to buck a few drifts as he watched for Dede's tracks. She would have to cross this road to reach the shelter of the pines and eventually one of the cabins.

He hadn't gone far when he saw where she'd reached the road and rode up it. He followed the tracks into the foothills until they left the road. Pulling over, he glanced back toward the highway. He couldn't see the van from here.

Which meant whoever discovered the van wouldn't be able to see his pickup.

Getting out, he kept to the trees as he followed horse and rider up the mountain. Snowflakes floated in the cold mountain air, glittering in the sun like crystals. The snowcapped pines groaned under the weight of their white burden. He busted through the deep snow, following her tracks, glad when he finally caught sight of a cabin through the pines.

He'd been betting Dede would have been so cold and tired that she would look for shelter in the first cabin she came to. Apparently she had, since the tracks snaked up the hillside toward the cabin.

Lantry felt his cell phone vibrate in his coat pocket. He didn't need to check. His brother had been trying to reach him ever since their last call. Had someone reported the van and the gruesome scene below?

He'd gone only a few yards farther when he smelled it. Smoke. Of course, Dede would have made a fire to warm up. She would have felt safe enough and been desperate to dry her clothing before she could go on.

As he followed the scent of wood smoke through the trees, he worried what kind of reception he would get when he found her.

"WHO THE HELL are you?" Violet asked the man holding the gun on her.

"You can call me Ed. I'm a friend of Dede's. So where is she?"

Any other time, Violet might have found this funny as she watched the man pull off in a plowed, wide spot next to a stand of ponderosa pines.

"How should I know where she is?"

"Because you were in the van with her back there," he snapped and thrust the gun at her. "You had to have seen where she went."

Violet had watched Dede wading through the deep snow as she crossed the pasture, thinking how stupid the woman was.

But Violet hadn't tried to stop her. She'd been more interested in saving her own neck. As far as she'd been concerned, Dede was on her own. They all were.

"What's it worth to you?" she asked the man with the gun.

He blinked in surprise. "What's it worth to *you?* If you don't start talking, I'm going to blow your brains out."

"I really doubt that," Violet said and brushed a lock of her straight, mousy-brown hair behind her ear. "In the first place, you don't want blood all over your rental car. In the second place, killing me won't help you find Dede. So what's it worth to you?"

The man looked furious, but he put the gun back in the shoulder holster and pulled out his wallet. "I've got two hundred dollars," he said, counting as he thumbed through the bills.

When she didn't say anything, he looked up, realization dawning in his eyes as he saw the gun. Apparently, he hadn't realized that whoever had shot those people back in the van might be armed. Or had he thought Dede had the gun—wherever she was? Clearly he didn't know Violet Evans, didn't have a clue whom he'd picked up beside the road, she thought. His mistake.

"Now," Violet said as she reached over and took the wallet from him. "I'll take that gun, as well. Lift it out carefully. I would really hate to have to shoot you and get blood all over this nice car—and keep in mind I'm one of the crazy ones."

He did as she told him, but she could tell she would have to make sure she never ran across this man again. Had she told him where she'd last seen Dede, she was sure he would have disposed of her at the next wide spot in the road.

The car engine was still running. She whirred down her side window and threw his gun out into the deep snow.

"Now put down your window."

He frowned but did it.

"Now get out," she said.

He hesitated, just as she knew he would. His second mistake.

The gun blast inside the car was deafening even with her side window down. His scream of pain lasted longer.

"Out," she ordered, waving the gun at him.

This time he didn't hesitate. She noticed with annoyance that his arm was bleeding all over the car as he fumbled to get the door open before stumbling out into the deep snow, falling and then staggering up again.

Violet put up her window, then slid over under the wheel. She slammed the driver's side door that he'd left open.

He was standing a few feet away in the snow, holding his upper arm where the bullet had grazed it. She whirred up the window, waved and drove off.

In her rearview mirror, she saw him scrambling to find his gun, and laughed, enjoying this more than she knew she should. Maybe she really was crazy. She shrugged. There was no way he could find the gun in time to stop her, so what did it hurt?

She was free. Again. Now she had a car and two hundred dollars in cash and some credit cards. Nothing could stop her.

"You know you have to go back to Whitehorse, don't you?" asked her grandmother from the backseat.

As LANTRY NEARED the cabin, he heard the snort of a horse and saw the thin trail of smoke rising from the chimney.

He slowed, reminding himself that Dede might be armed. Whoever had killed the van driver and Roberta had a gun—no doubt the driver's weapon.

Cautiously he followed the tracks in the snow around to the back of the cabin. The horse was tied with clothesline to a tree. Dede's footprints led to the backdoor.

Creeping up to the backdoor, Lantry listened for any sound inside. He was pretty sure he hadn't been spotted. Dede would have been watching the hillside, ready to run if she saw anyone. She would have taken the horse.

No sound came from inside the cabin. He noted the shattered glass where she'd broken the windowpane to gain entry. She was using some of his techniques, apparently.

He tried the knob. She hadn't bothered to lock the door. He pushed, and the door swung inward, creaking just enough that he knew he had to move fast.

He charged in, hoping to take her by surprise. But she must have heard him. She'd picked up the poker from beside the woodstove and now brandished it, making him glad it wasn't a gun.

"Take it easy," he said, holding up his hands in surrender. "I'm here to help you."

"Sure you are," she said, narrowing her gaze at him and tightening her hold on the poker. "Just like you helped me earlier?"

"I had nothing to do with you getting caught."

"And you wouldn't have turned me in first chance you got?"

"Why do you think I'm here? I heard from my

brother that you'd been picked up and were on your way back to the hospital," he said as he took a step closer. "I couldn't let that happen."

He saw indecision cross her features and plunged on. "I called my secretary in Texas. I was wrong. Frank *did* leave me something."

Her eyes widened. He could see that she wanted to believe him, but she was afraid to. "You were so certain he hadn't, and now you find out he has?" she asked suspiciously. She took a step back at his approach, keeping the poker ready.

"Apparently he left it at my office after I came to Montana."

"Isn't that convenient."

Lantry supposed he couldn't blame her for not trusting him. "It's a small wooden boat, possibly a replica."

Her face crumbled. "He gave you the boat?" she asked in a whisper.

"You know about the boat?"

She looked up at him, a painful sadness in all that blue. "I should. My grandfather made it when he was stationed in Panama during World War Two. He was a boatbuilder. He and *his* father before him." She lowered the poker, and he stepped to her, taking it from her.

She slumped against him for a moment before she stumbled back and sat down hard on a wooden bench by the woodstove.

There were a dozen questions he wanted to ask, but he knew they didn't have time for that now.

"Claude, the driver of the van..." Her voice broke. "He told me that Frank is dead."

Lantry nodded. "I'm sorry."

"They killed him because of me."

"No. They killed him because of whatever he was involved in. You couldn't have saved him. He was dead before you left Texas." He pulled her to him. "We have to get out of here."

She looked numb. "Tell me why I should trust you."

"Because I'm here. Now let's go."

ED DUG IN THE snow until he found his gun, but by then his rental car was just a speck on the empty, snow-covered horizon.

He stood, breathing hard from the fury and the cold and the pain. His blood had left bright red splotches on the snow. His shirtsleeve was soaked, the blood freezing against his skin.

He looked up and down the long highway. Not another car in sight. He couldn't just stand here and wait.

In the first place, who was going to stop for a man standing beside the road, coatless and bleeding, wearing a shoulder holster and holding a gun?

He tucked the gun into the shoulder holster and checked his wound. It hurt like hell, but the bullet had only creased the flesh. She hadn't hit the bone. He should be thankful for that.

Up the highway, he saw what looked like a building in the distance. He started walking, knowing he had to keep moving. The cold was already starting to settle. To keep warm, he thought of Violet Evans.

Just the thought of the woman made him burn with fury again. For the moment, Dede Chamberlain was forgotten. He would deal with her after he dealt with Violet Evans. Violet had made this personal. He would find her, and she would deeply regret what she'd done to him.

Ed hadn't gone far up the highway when he spotted a

car coming toward him. He squinted against the bright sun reflecting off the fallen snow. The vehicle looked familiar. His heart skyrocketed.

He told himself he must be hallucinating from the pain. Why would Violet Evans be headed back toward Whitehorse when she'd been so anxious to go south?

Unless she'd come back to finish him off.

He smiled as he pulled the pistol from his holster. He didn't bother trying to hide. Where would he have hidden anyway? On both sides of the highway, there were high snowbanks from snow and ice thrown there from the plows. Beyond that was nothing but more cold white. Both lanes were glazed, as well.

He stood in the middle of her lane. Even if there had been somewhere to hide and ambush her, he was sure she'd already seen him—just as he'd seen her.

He waited, the pistol ready as the car sped toward him.

FROM SNOW-COVERED sagebrush and scrub juniper to towering ponderosa pines, the land rose into the Little Rockies before falling as it dropped to the Missouri Breaks.

"Where are we going?" Dede asked, worried as Lantry turned onto the main highway and headed south. Back up the road toward Whitehorse, she could just make out the van in the ditch. She shivered and turned away.

"We're going to Landusky. It's a small town down the road. I know someone who has a cabin on the edge of town. We can stay there for the time being."

"Landusky," she repeated.

"It's an old mining town, has a great history. At one

time it was as wild as any town there was. Smart men who wanted to keep breathing avoided Landusky, Montana."

He looked over at her when she said nothing. "I don't blame you for not feeling you can trust me. I thought a lot about the things you told me. When I talked to my secretary and found out Frank had sent me a present…"

"The boat." She shook her head. She couldn't believe Frank. "I wondered what he'd done with it."

The highway ahead ran straight south, snow piled deep on each side, the pines on the hillside laden in white. "I'm surprised it wasn't destroyed when your house was ransacked."

"I was so upset I didn't even notice that the boat wasn't there," she said. "Frank must have already gotten it out and hid it until he sent it to you. That means he'd been planning this for some time."

"You're that sure he hid something in the boat for safekeeping?"

"It has to be in the boat," she said. "If not, then you will go back to thinking I'm lying to you. Worse, that maybe I am as unstable as Frank led you to believe."

"You did lie about being able to ride a horse," he said after a few moments.

"I didn't lie. You asked if I rode. I said I didn't. Not anymore. I take it Frank never told you anything about me." She could only guess how Frank had portrayed her. "Never mind. I can imagine what he told you. I'm not originally from Houston. I was born and raised on a ranch in Wyoming."

Lantry tried to hide his surprise.

She smiled, anticipating his reaction. "I grew up drinking cowboy coffee and eating fresh-killed meat over an open campfire and riding horses." She took a breath and let it out slowly. "I had an accident on a horse before I left Wyoming. I hadn't gotten back on one until, well, not until this morning, when I had no choice. But if I never ride another horse, I'll be glad."

He didn't seem to know what to say. "What ranch?"

"The T Bar Double Deuce."

"I've heard of it. That's a big spread."

"I grew up hauling hay, slopping out barns and helping with branding and calving."

"So you've driven a four-wheel-drive truck in a blizzard before," he said, nodding.

"Just not in a blizzard like last night."

"You sound as if you liked ranching," he remarked with a look that said she continued to surprise him. "What made you leave?"

"I *loved* it. I would still be there if…" She looked up, hesitating. How much did she really want to tell him?

"Your horseback accident?"

"That was definitely part of it," she said noncommittally.

He nodded. "A man was involved, right?"

She smiled. "The first man I ever loved. My father. He sold the ranch after my accident."

"Oh. I thought—"

"I know what you thought."

He'd thought that her father was a ranch hand or maybe the ranch manager. Even when she'd said she had her own money, he hadn't really believed her. Just as it had never dawned on him that her father had owned the T Bar Double Deuce Ranch or that she'd been telling the truth about coming from money.

"I knew Frank let you believe I married him for his

money." Her chuckle had a bite to it. "But I told you I had my own money. My father gave me my inheritance when he sold."

"I…" Lantry shook his head. "I'm sorry. I did have preconceived notions about you, apparently most of them wrong."

"Most?" she asked and felt his gaze go to her mouth. For a wild moment she thought he would lean over and kiss her—and run off the road.

"The road…" she said.

He turned back to his driving as the pickup got a little too close to the snowbank on the edge of the highway.

Lantry swerved, the rear end of the pickup fishtailing a little before righting itself. She heard him swear. She'd gotten to him, and what made it worse for him was that she knew it.

FARTHER SOUTH ON Highway 191, Ed stood on the snow-packed pavement, waiting. As the car rushed toward him, he raised the handgun and pointed it at the spot just behind the steering wheel. His finger brushed lightly over the trigger.

He was going to kill this crazy bitch. Blow her away and take his car back.

The roar of the engine carried across the Arctic landscape.

He would have only one chance. Fire the gun. Dive for cover.

Well, not exactly cover—just a frozen snowbank. And if he didn't clear the top of it, he could be caught between the hard-as-concrete bank and the grill of the car.

At the speed she was coming… He would just have

to make sure he cleared the bank. Either way, Violet Evans was going down.

He took a breath, held it, finger resting on the trigger as the car bore down on him as seconds ticked off. He could smell the car's exhaust, feel the rush of cold air coming at him in front of the car.

He focused on the woman behind the wheel, counting off the seconds, the sight on the handgun aimed just inches below her chin. The gun would kick a little, just enough that the bullet should hit right between her eyes.

She was so close now that he could see the whites of her eyes. And then she did something so totally unexpected…

She swerved and hit her brakes, and he had an instant when he thought, *Hell, maybe she isn't as crazy as I thought.*

The car fishtailed and struck the unforgiving snowbank only feet from him, then pinged off to do a three-sixty in the middle of the snow-packed highway before smacking the opposite snowbank and bouncing off, disappearing behind him.

For a moment, Ed couldn't move. The car had come so close to him that he'd felt the back bumper brush his pant leg as it slid past. He began to shake as he realized how close she'd come to taking him out.

Had he moved a fraction of an inch, she would have gotten him. His skin went clammy, then ice cold as he realized that at this very moment she was probably putting the bead of her gun on his back.

He swung around, leading with the handgun in time to see the car come to a stop against the snowbank on the other side of the highway a good twenty yards away.

The car had come to a stop facing his direction, but

unmoving. At least for the moment. He rushed toward it, gun aimed in the vicinity of where the driver should be, since he couldn't see her because of the angle of the sun reflecting off the windshield.

It wasn't until he came alongside and grabbed the door handle that he saw Violet. Her head was tilted at an odd angle. He jerked open the door. Violet groaned and lifted her head. Apparently dazed, she stared stupidly at him, then made a grab for something on the passenger seat.

Before she could close her fingers over the weapon on the seat, he knocked her into next week.

Then he just stood there for a few moments, breathing hard. He was getting too old for this crap, he thought as he holstered his gun and reached across Violet for her pistol. Tucking the gun into his waistband, he considered what to do with her.

Leaving her beside the road was almost too tempting. But he doubted he could lift her up onto the high snowbank, and if he left her in the middle of the road, she would be found too quickly. Then the authorities would be able to put all their resources into finding Dede. He didn't want that.

With Claude dead, Ed didn't kid himself that he might not get the chance at Dede if she was picked up again and sent to the hospital. He had to find her. She was his bait to get what he needed from Lantry Corbett.

Ed looked up and down the highway. Someone was coming from the direction of Whitehorse, the vehicle still only a speck on the horizon. Hurriedly, he popped open the trunk and dragged Violet out of the car.

Violet was heavier than she looked. *Dead weight, so to speak,* Ed thought as he dragged her back to the trunk, thankful he'd gone for the full-sized car—and trunk.

He had to strain to pick her up. She tumbled in, banging her head. He started to slam the trunk lid, but realized he couldn't have her coming to and causing a ruckus.

He'd bought duct tape and a coil of rope in case he needed it for dealing with Dede and the lawyer. He ripped off a length of duct tape, wrapping it around Violet's wrists behind her back, then taped her ankles, working quickly.

As he ripped off a strip to cover her mouth, he thought to check her pulse. Hell, he might be tying up a dead woman. Nope, she was still alive. He slapped the tape over her mouth and slammed the trunk lid.

As he started toward the open driver's side door, he saw that the vehicle was almost to him.

Hurriedly, he climbed behind the wheel and got the car going, glad the engine was still running. The solid ice snowbanks on each side of the highway had played hell with the body of the rental, but fortunately hadn't disabled the engine.

As the other vehicle grew closer, Ed saw that it was a pickup. He felt his pulse jump. It was the same color as the one Lantry Corbett had parked in front of his cabin.

In the rearview mirror, Ed saw the driver. Lantry Corbett. As the pickup passed him, Ed turned his face away but not before he'd seen the woman in the passenger seat. Dede Chamberlain. It seemed they were all on Highway 191 headed south.

Ed couldn't believe his luck. Lantry had taken the bait. Since he'd come from Whitehorse, he would have seen the van and the bodies inside it. But instead of taking Dede back to town and the authorities, he must be taking her some place where the two of them could be safe.

He watched the pickup keep going and continued at his slower speed, keeping the truck in sight as he followed at a safe distance.

## Chapter Ten

Distractedly, Lantry glanced back at the car he'd just passed, then over at Dede. The woman just continued to surprise him—and worry him.

"Dede, I need to know what happened back at the van," he asked finally.

Her eyes filmed over for a moment. She took a deep breath and let it out. He listened without saying anything until she was finished. "That's pretty much what I figured."

He could feel her gaze. "You believe me?"

"Why shouldn't I?" he asked, glancing over at her as he drove.

Dede was studying him. "What changed your mind about me?"

What exactly *had* changed his mind? Not her angelic face. Or those innocent big blue eyes. Or the sweet taste of her when he'd kissed her back at the farmhouse. But he had to admit, some of that had played a part.

"I don't know. I wanted to believe you at some point. Then when I found out Frank had given me a gift just as you'd suspected and someone took a potshot at me…" He frowned. "You don't seem surprised."

"I told you Ed would try to kill you again."

"Except he didn't *try* to kill me. Unless he's a really bad shot, he purposely missed."

That seemed to surprise her. "You think he was just trying to scare you?"

*Hell, he did scare me.* "No, I think he wants something he thinks I have, and he just wanted to let me know he'll be coming for it."

"What Frank hid in the boat?"

Lantry nodded.

"And you have the boat with you?" she asked, glancing behind the seat into the extended cab and the two boxes there.

He found himself staring at her again. Only this time it had nothing to do with kissing her. "You know what's in the boat, don't you?"

"I told you—"

"I know what you told me. How about the truth?"

Those blue eyes narrowed into deadly daggers. "I am telling you the truth. I'm afraid the necklace is in the boat."

"From the burglary."

She nodded, then turned to look out her side window as the road climbed into the foothills of the Little Rockies.

He couldn't shake the feeling that she wasn't telling him everything. Was it possible that Frank had left something that might incriminate Dede Chamberlain, and that was why she'd risked everything to find it? Or that Dede had been after the necklace all along?

As he turned onto the road to Landusky, he checked his rearview mirror. The large brown car they'd passed earlier was a dozen car lengths behind them, but no other vehicle was in sight.

Lantry tried to relax. They were safe. No one would think to look for them in Landusky.

"THIS IS WHERE we're going?" Dede asked, both surprised and apprehensive as she spotted the handful of old buildings clinging precariously to the side of the mountain, half-buried in the deep snow.

"It's pretty much a ghost town now," Lantry said. "The town was named after Pike Landusky. He and another man discovered the gold here back in the late 1860s. Landusky was some character, I guess."

Lantry chuckled to himself. "As the story goes, one time he was taken captive by an Indian war party. Landusky, who should have been afraid for his life, attacked one of the braves—allegedly with a frying pan. The Indians, thinking he must be crazy, gave him two ponies to appease the demon and left him alone from then on."

"So what happened to him?" she asked, seeing how much Lantry was enjoying the story.

"Pike Landusky got on the wrong side of Kid Curry. The Curry brothers ranched about five miles to the south of here. Kid Curry killed him after an altercation in the local saloon. Landusky was buried nine feet deep—instead of six—to make sure he didn't come back."

Dede smiled, thinking Lantry would have fit into that Old West. She wondered, though, whether he would have been a Pike Landusky or a Kid Curry.

He drove through what was left of Landusky's wild town and took a side road that was even more narrow and lined with banks of snow. Then, shifting into four-wheel drive low, busted up through the pines on what appeared to be nothing more than a trail.

A large log structure appeared as they topped the hill. Lantry brought the pickup to a stop.

"We can stay here for a while," he said, cutting the engine. "It's all right. The place belongs to one of my brothers. He's having it built for his wife's birthday, but it's a surprise—so no one in the family knows about it except me. I took care of the legal work for him."

"This brother..."

"Not Shane, the deputy sheriff. Dalton, the cowboy rancher."

"How many brothers do you have?" Dede asked as they got out and waded through the snow to the back-door.

Lantry fished the key out of its hiding place and opened the door. "There's five of us." He stepped in to turn on the lights, glad to see the electricity was still on. "It's kind of a mess because it's still under construction."

There were ladders and sawhorses, piles of lumber and tools, as well as sawdust and drop cloths.

"I guess I didn't realize your whole family had moved to Montana," Dede said, working her way through to the living room.

"It's a long story. Maybe I'll tell you about it some time." Lantry looked around. "The fireplace is finished, and at least one bedroom." He pointed to the loft. Apparently the interior decorator had finished up there, since she could see a large bed with a brocade spread and other furnishings.

"See if there's anything to eat in the kitchen," Lantry said. "I'll get the boxes out of the truck."

Dede wandered into the kitchen. Unlike the ranch-house they'd broken into, these cupboards were practically bare. But she found some food in the refrigerator that the construction workers must have left.

As she walked through the beautiful log lodge, she envied Dalton Corbett's wife. To have a man love you so much that he planned such a wonderful surprise…

Dede caught movement out of the corner of her eye. Through the dusty window, she saw Lantry standing outside by his pickup. He was on his cell phone.

Her heart dropped.

"WHERE THE HELL are you?" Shane demanded the instant he answered.

Lantry had stepped outside so Dede couldn't see or hear him use the cell phone. He knew he'd be able to get service because the town of Landusky was just down the mountain side. He had thought about telling her he planned to call his brother, but he feared it might make her run again. "We need to talk."

"What the hell is going on?" Shane asked, lowering his voice.

"I have Dede Chamberlain."

"When are you bringing her in?"

"I'm not." He waited until his brother quit swearing. "At least not for twenty-four hours."

"Twenty-four hours?"

"There's something I need to check out first."

Shane bit off each word into the phone. "Do you have any idea the spot you've put me in?"

"I'm sorry, but like I told you, I believe her."

"Damn it, Lantry, Dede Chamberlain isn't just wanted for escaping a mental hospital or two. Bodies are piling up. Frank Chamberlain, Tamara Fallon, the hospital guard, one of the patients…" A beat, then, "I'm waiting for you to sound surprised, damn it."

"She didn't kill anyone."

"And you know that *how?*"

"She loved Frank Chamberlain. She still does. And as for the guard and the patient, Dede told me that the guard stopped the van and told her to get out. He was going to kill her, Shane."

"The guard from the hospital? So you're telling me it was self-defense."

"Yes, only Dede never touched the guard's gun. If you check, you'll find that the guard is from Texas. He's an old friend of Frank Chamberlain's, Dede's ex, and he only recently got the job at the hospital up here."

"And what did she tell you happened after the driver told her to get out of the van?" Shane asked.

Lantry could hear the skepticism in his voice. Why did his brother always have to be a cop? "The other escapees saw what was going to happen. The guard opened the metal mesh door between him and them and Roberta went for the gun. She and the guard were shot in the scuffle. Violet ended up with the gun. Dede feared she'd be next and took off across the pasture and hid until she saw Violet hitchhiking up the road."

"At least that's Dede's story." Shane slammed a file cabinet drawer or something that sounded a lot like one. The noise reverberated through the phone. "Listen to me. You have to turn her over now, Lantry. Otherwise, you are looking at aiding and abetting. I don't think I have to tell you what kind of sentence that carries with it, since you're a damned lawyer."

"I need twenty-four hours. That's all I'm asking. By then I hope to have the proof I need and can file papers to keep Dede from going back to that hospital." He could hear his brother breathing hard on the other end of the line. "Shane, I know this woman didn't kill anyone."

"You don't know. You can't know her after spending only a few hours with her."

"Either way, I take full responsibility for what I'm doing."

Shane's chuckle held no humor. "Even you may not be able to use that high-priced law degree to get out of this one, Lantry. There is a state manhunt on now for Dede and Violet. Turn her over to me, and then you can work your legal magic to get her freed. In the meantime, I will do everything I can to help her."

"I know you would," Lantry said. "But I can't trust that the men after her won't get to her through one of the mental-hospital guards or some rogue deputy."

"You're talking just as crazy as she is," Shane snapped.

"Don't forget that someone took a potshot at me. Did either of the three escapees or the hospital guard have a high-powered rifle on them when you found them? I didn't think so. There's still a killer out there. Give me twenty-four hours to find out why this person wants Dede and me dead."

"Do you believe this woman because of that face of hers or those big blue eyes or because she's actually telling the truth?"

"You should know me better than that," Lantry snapped back. "Check out Claude, the driver of the mental hospital van. He has a friend named Ed. That's all I know. But I figure Ed can't be far behind him."

"When I find you, I'm going to kick your butt all the way back to Texas," Shane said.

"Twenty-four hours." He snapped the phone shut and

swore. He hoped the sheriff's department couldn't trace the call. He doubted it.

His brother was right about one thing: Dede had gotten under his skin. He just hoped to hell it wasn't for the reason that Shane thought.

SHANE HUNG UP, furious with his brother and yet more worried than angry. Lantry had no idea what he was dealing with.

He thought about Dede Chamberlain and could understand how someone could be taken in by her. But *Lantry?* The divorce lawyer had never even had a serious relationship. He dated but seldom, and he'd made it clear he'd never planned to marry. That was a given, but he'd also never gotten close enough to a woman to give a real relationship a fighting chance.

So what was different about Dede?

She was a woman in trouble. That alone was a siren call for any of the Corbett brothers, Shane thought with a groan. But sticking your neck out to save a woman was one thing. Lantry had crossed a line with this one.

Shane knew what had him so upset. It wasn't that every law officer in several counties was looking for Dede Chamberlain or even that she was wanted for questioning in three murders.

It was Lantry trusting this woman with his life.

Sheriff Carter Jackson looked up as Shane stepped into his office. They'd just come off a shift change, though Shane had no thought of going home. He had to find his brother before it was too late.

"I just spoke with Lantry," Shane said, shutting the door behind him.

"Okay," Carter said. "Let's hear it."

"Lantry found Dede Chamberlain. He has her."

"He's bringing her in, right?"

"He wants twenty-four hours. He says he's following some lead and will bring her in then."

The sheriff was shaking his head. "He needs to bring her in now. I assume you told him that. He knows about the murders?"

"He found the van."

"So those were his footprints we discovered." The sheriff let out a curse. "You said he's a lawyer, so he knows that he's now wanted for questioning along with aiding and abetting?"

Shane nodded solemnly. "I tried to talk some sense into him, but he's convinced that if he brings Dede in, she won't live long enough to make it back to the state hospital. Given what happened to the van driver and the other patient…"

"You know we can keep her safe here at the jail."

"I'm sorry, Sheriff, but, truthfully, I don't know that. Look what happened before. Don't get me wrong. I did everything I could to convince my brother to bring her in. But just between you and me, she might be safer with Lantry right now."

"But is your brother safe?" He shook his head. "Do you have any idea where he has taken her?"

"He can't take her to the ranch, because he knows I would arrest them both. I really don't know where he's gone, but I intend to find him." Hopefully before anything bad happened to him.

VIOLET CAME TO in the dark. Her eyes flew open, panic making her jerk and hit her head. She let out a frightened moan and for a moment thought she was a little girl again and that her grandmother had locked her in the old coal bin.

She shivered at the memory. The cobwebs and spiders. The smell of sour earth. The sound of mice chewing somewhere in the dank basement. She had fought so hard not to cry. To cry meant her grandmother would leave her in there longer.

Violet quickly quieted herself as she realized she wasn't in the old coal bin, and her grandmother was dead—if not gone.

She could hear the hum of the tires on the highway over the roar of the big car's engine, and she could smell the too-sweet scent of recently cleaned rental-car carpeting where she lay.

Still, it took her a few minutes before she could chase away thoughts of the coal bin. She rubbed her face into the carpet until it hurt, until she could no longer imagine the brush of cobwebs on her skin or hear the creak of her grandmother's shoe soles on the other side of the darkness.

As Violet slowed her mind to catch her erratic thoughts, she knew two things. She was still alive, apparently none the worse for wear except for a splitting headache, and she hadn't been dumped beside the road. Instead, he'd left her alive—and taken her with him in the trunk.

What worried her was why.

Had she been in his position, she would have made sure Violet Evans had breathed her last breath. But then, he didn't know her, did he, she thought with what passed for a smile beneath the duct tape.

Violet began to make plans for her escape. The first step was getting the duct tape off her wrists. That was made more difficult since her wrists were taped behind her back.

She felt around in the trunk, only to discover it was empty. What tools there were must be in some hidden compartment—probably underneath her. She searched the interior of the trunk with her cold fingers, finding rope and more duct tape. Definitely not a good sign. She kept searching until she found a rough spot on the metal frame of the trunk.

Meticulously she began to work at the duct tape, letting her mind drift.

Ed had made a mistake keeping her alive. One he would live to regret.

DEDE WAS WAITING for him when Lantry came back into the house with the two boxes from the pickup.

When she'd seen him on his cell phone, she'd thought about taking off again, but soon it would be dark and the snow was even deeper up here in the mountains. The days up here, so close to the Canadian border, were short, and she was exhausted both mentally and physically, a part of her ready to concede. And yet another part of her was so angry and disappointed in Lantry that she wanted to stay and fight.

"Guess what," Lantry said as he closed the door behind him and set down the two boxes he'd brought in.

"I'm going back to jail. What a surprise since I saw you making the call."

His face clouded. "I *did* call Shane, but not to turn you in. I asked him to give me twenty-four hours. I didn't tell him where we are, and I sure as hell didn't sell you out."

Had she misjudged him again? "I thought—"

"I know what you thought. When are you going to start trusting me?"

"Maybe when you start trusting me," she snapped back.

"Damn it, Dede," he said closing his fingers over her upper arm and dragging her closer. "I've gone out on a limb for you." He shook his head. "By now there's an APB out on me as well as you. What more can I do to prove that I'm in this with you?"

He kissed her hard on the mouth, a punishing kiss that took her breath away. Then he practically flung her away from him, swearing under his breath.

"I'm sorry," he said as he dragged off his Stetson. "I shouldn't have done that."

The kiss was all her idea this time. Not that she gave it any thought before she went up on tiptoes and pressed her mouth to his. Just like the first time, his mustache tickled, but only for an instant before he dragged her to him, encircling her with his strong arms.

Her lips parted, opening for him, and she felt the tip of his tongue sweep over her lower lip. It had been so long since she'd felt desire, felt it run like a fire through her veins, felt it blaze across her skin.

She would have been shocked had she thought about how badly she wanted this man, but at that moment all reason had left her. Her body ached with a need for this cowboy, and Dede threw all caution to the wind as he swept her up and carried her to the loft.

He took her to the bed and set her down to look into her eyes. "Dede?"

She knew what he was asking. Reaching down, she grabbed the hem of the sweater he'd taken for her at the

Thompson's ranchhouse and pulled it over her head, baring her breasts.

Lantry groaned and pulled her to him, his kiss as hot as her blood. She breathed in the scent of him as his hands cupped her behind.

She wrapped her arms around his neck and pulled him down with her onto the cool fabric of the comforter. Her fingers worked at the snaps on his Western shirt, needing to feel his flesh against her own.

He wriggled out of his shirt, tossing it aside, his mouth coming back to hers. She felt his warm palm cup her breast; the rough pad of his thumb brushed the hard nub of her nipple, making her arch against him.

"Lantry," she cried on a breath, her fingers going to the buttons on her jeans, then to his, both of them needing and wanting this human touch.

She couldn't hold back the satisfied sound that came from her lips when they'd finally shed all their clothing and he took her in his arms. She touched his face and looked into his dark blue eyes, seeing her own desire reflected there as he made love to her.

The first time was fast and furious, both of them breathing hard, holding tight to each other.

LANTRY LAY SPENT on the strange bed, the naked, warm Dede in his arms. As he stared up at the ceiling, a smile on his lips, he tried to remember another time in his life when he'd felt like this. Never.

That alone should have scared the hell out of him. But he wasn't a man who scared easily. He'd ridden wild horses, wrestled his fair share of steers to the ground and even rode mean bulls. He'd known his share of women, drunk his share of good wine and even better booze, and had more than his share of successes in life.

But he'd never known such euphoria as he did at this moment. Or such peace. He pulled Dede a little closer, loving the feel of her skin on his own, breathing in the musky scent of the two of them entwined.

He felt her stir, her breath tickling his neck. "You asked how all the Corbetts ended up in Montana," he said quietly. "You still want to hear?"

She nodded and snuggled closer.

"Our mother died when we were young. Dad's recently remarried. That's how we all ended up in Montana. His wife, Kate, was from here. Trails West Ranch was her family's. My mother was born on the ranch. Her father was the ranch manager." He shrugged. "None of us planned to stay here, but then Dad found some letters my mom left. She wanted us to marry Montana girls. Mostly Dad wanted us close by. One of my brothers came up with this inane idea that we should make a marriage pact. Russell suggested drawing straws to see who would get married first."

Dede started laughing. "You would never have agreed to such a thing. Not you. Don't tell me that you—"

"I drew a damned straw just to shut them all up." The truth was, he'd gotten caught up in the moment, wanting to do this for their mother.

"And now all but you are married or engaged?" Dede asked in disbelief.

"I'm not sure how it happened. I guess it made us all more open to marriage." He realized Dede was staring at him.

"Except for you," she said, daring him to disagree.

"I still think marriage is a gamble," he said, cupping her cheek in his large palm. "I've never even been tempted. Never met a woman who made me want to risk it." He looked into her big blue eyes. But then, he'd never met anyone like Dede Chamberlain, had he? "Until—"

She pulled away, drawing the sheet around her as she got out of bed. "Don't, Lantry," she said, her back to him.

"Don't tell you how I'm feeling?"

"No." She turned to scowl at him. "I don't trust your feelings. Not right now. It's too soon." She glanced toward the living room. "We don't know what's in that box down there, and I think we're both afraid to look."

He wanted to pour his heart out to her, but he knew she was right. And for a while he'd forgotten that she was still in love with her ex-husband.

Also there was that damned box with the boat in it— and whatever might or might not be inside.

Even if there was no explosive device inside that boat, Lantry wasn't fool enough to think that whatever was in there couldn't blow up. He and Dede might never make this mess right again.

Dede looked as worried as he felt. Still, he couldn't help the way he felt about her. He didn't want this to end, damn it. And he was scared that whatever was in that box was going to destroy the two of them.

"If we survive this—"

"*When* we survive this," he said, grabbing hold of the edge of the sheet and jerking it to free her wonderful naked body. He reached for her hand and pulled her back into bed, back to him, and then he made love to her slowly, deliberately, passionately as snow began to fall outside and the light began to fade to black.

It wasn't until later, when they lay in the bed listening to the snow pelting the window, that Lantry knew they couldn't put it off any longer.

It was time to find out what the hell Frank Chamberlain had put into that boat. Something so valuable that it had cost him his life and, just having it, could cost them theirs, as well.

## Chapter Eleven

Lantry kissed Dede on the top of the head. Then, releasing her, he swung his legs over the side of the bed and dressed.

He could see the cold darkness of the evening through the curtainless windows downstairs. Earlier, when he'd gone out to call his brother, he'd heard a car go by. He'd waited to make sure it hadn't stopped. It hadn't.

Now he felt exposed. This is what it felt like being on the run.

Downstairs, he moved the two boxes into the living room, then built a fire in the fireplace with the scrap wood lying around.

Once the fire caught, he turned to the boxes, praying that whatever Frank had hidden in the boat would help them out of this mess.

He didn't even want to think about the laws the two of them had broken or the trouble they were in. The only way out was to find out the truth, expose the men involved and put an end to this. Then he would deal with the legal problems they would be facing.

At least if he could prove the danger Dede had been in, he believed he could clear her. That was his main concern as he pulled the box over in front of the fireplace and stopped to listen.

He could hear Dede in the shower. As he listened closer, he heard her singing. He got up and walked down the hall to stand outside the bathroom door. She had a beautiful voice. He remembered something. A photograph that had fallen out of Frank's wallet during one of their meetings about the divorce proceedings.

Lantry had picked it up from the floor where it had dropped and handed it back to Frank, who'd seemed flustered. But not before he'd seen the woman in the snapshot. She'd been playing a guitar and singing. Lantry had only gotten a glimpse of her. A young woman, college-aged, with long reddish-blond hair and big blue eyes.

With a jolt, he realized the photograph had been of Dede. What made his heart ache was the realization that Frank Chamberlain had hung on to a photo of the woman he was divorcing. Frank had never stopped loving Dede.

And Dede had never stopped loving him.

Stepping away from the door, Lantry went back to the box waiting for him. The present Frank had given him. Now more than ever, Lantry wanted to know what was inside. Taking out his pocket knife, he began to open the box.

He heard the shower shut off, the singing stop. He pulled back the cardboard flaps.

As he removed the packing material on top, Lantry was taken aback by the sight of what appeared to be a small replica of a wooden boat from the 1930s or 1940s.

It lay in a nest of packing material, the mahogany

wood lightly varnished and glowing warmly. The boat was perfect in every detail.

Looking up, he saw Dede come into the room. She stopped and hugged herself as she watched him lift out the boat.

"It's beautiful," he said in awe as he ran his fingers along the smoothly lacquered mahogany.

Dede nodded but said nothing.

Lantry held the boat up to the light. As he did, he heard something shift inside the hull. He felt his heart kick up a beat.

He glanced at Dede. Her eyes had filled with tears. Frank had let her down in so many ways. Would he let her down even more when they discovered what was inside the boat?

But as he inspected the boat, he could find no way to open it to get inside. "Dede, is there a secret compartment or door to get inside the hull?"

She seemed to hesitate, then came over and knelt down on the floor next to him. Her fingers trembled as she touched the slick surface of the boat, running her fingertips along the gunnels. She brushed over one of the tiny cleats, and a side panel in the boat popped open to reveal a compartment inside.

Lantry heard her let out a small sigh as she drew back her hand and looked over at him. He could almost see her hold her breath as he reached inside to work out a small padded bundle the size of his fist.

Glancing at Dede, he took a breath, then carefully began to unwrap it. Just as he'd feared. A nest of diamonds and gold appeared.

As he picked up one end, the diamond necklace unwound itself to snake downward in a long, glittering rope.

"So that was it," Dede said as their gazes met. "A simple case of greed." She stood, dusting off her pants as she went to warm herself in front of the fire. "I guess that explains why Ed and Claude are after us. Just as I feared. Frank double-crossed them and involved us."

It certainly looked that way. He could see that Dede was upset. Like him, she'd been hoping Frank had left a letter or document explaining what he'd done to her and why. Something that could be used to free her from the mental hospital, free her from Frank and the past.

Instead, all Frank had left was proof of his involvement in the Fallon burglary.

This explained what Ed and Claude were after. It didn't seem enough. Frank had lost his life for this. How could he have divorced and committed his wife for something this cold to the touch? That didn't jibe with the photograph Frank had kept in his wallet and Lantry's belief that the man had loved his wife.

While the necklace proved that Frank was involved in the burglary of the home of Dr. Eric and Tamara Fallon, it provided no insight into why Frank had given up everything for this. He'd been a wealthy man. What was another million or so dollars?

Apparently enough that, like Dede said, he'd double-crossed his partners in crime and ultimately lost everything.

Lantry started to put down the necklace, sickened by the thought of what Frank had done, when the stones caught the light of the fire. He froze.

ED HAD PARKED down the road in a wide spot that had been plowed for snowmobile trailers. He could see where the trucks and trailers had parked, where the snowmobiles had been unloaded and run through the woods, where the riders had shared a few beers and some smokes before leaving.

The parking area was empty now except for a few cigarette butts and a six-pack of crushed beer cans.

Ed had settled in to wait for darkness, dozing off for a while to wake to the gunmetal-gray sky. He knew at once that something had awakened him and looked around, thinking it was a snowmobiler.

The car moved, and he remembered with a start that he still had Violet Evans locked in his trunk.

He got out of the car and stepped back to the trunk, standing in the growing darkness of the winter night. The sky reflected the steel blue onto the snow, casting the snow-covered land in an eerie light.

As he stood outside his frost-coated rental car, Ed had never felt more alone—even with Violet just inches away in the trunk. Frank was gone. So was Claude. The thought wrenched at his heart. Frank had gotten what he deserved, but not Claude.

Emptiness and loneliness filled him, amplified by the desolate frozen landscape.

One clear thought worked its way through his grief. He should have killed Violet. He couldn't remember now why he'd kept her alive. The vehicle coming up the road. That's why he hadn't taken the time to end it right there in the middle of the highway. He'd always planned on disposing of her body. He just wished that he had killed her when he'd had the chance earlier rather than wait.

The cold made his movements slow and clumsy, his mind seemingly just as sluggish. He shuddered from the cold, stirring himself into action. Finish this.

In the pale cold light he bent down and inserted the key into the trunk lock, then listened. Violet hadn't moved for some time now. No sound emerged from inside. Maybe she'd done him a favor and succumbed to asphyxiation.

He hadn't even thought about whether there was enough air in the trunk for her. With the tape across her mouth...

He turned the key. The trunk lid yawned open, and he had to squint, leaning in to see her in the tomblike, shadow-filled hole.

The blow took him completely by surprise. She seemed to spring out, leaping at him, the thick roll of duct tape catching the eerie winter light before it connected with his skull, stunning him.

He fumbled for his gun, pulled it from his shoulder holster, but she got in another hard blow with the duct-tape roll before he could even backhand her with the pistol.

He stumbled back, tripped over an icy rut and went down hard, knocking the air out of him. He managed to hang on to the weapon—he just couldn't get it aimed at her before she took off into the trees on one of the snowmobile trails.

In the dim light, snow seemed to hang in the air, tiny crystals that danced around him as he struggled to his feet, torn between the pain from the fall and the raging anger caused by his injured pride and failure to kill Violet Evans.

She'd disappeared into the trees. He considered only a moment about going after her. He couldn't shoot her anyway. The report of the gunshot would echo across the mountain and alert Corbett.

Too bad Claude wasn't here. He'd go after her. Claude, though, had been better at killing. He didn't mind the mess.

Ed swore under his breath as he slammed the trunk and headed back toward the open driver's side door. He was still furious. He liked things neatly tied up.

Maybe she would trip in the woods and break something and not be able to get back up, and freeze to death and they wouldn't find her body until spring.

That thought made him feel a little better as he slid behind the wheel of the car with a groan. He'd been shot and now hurt all over from the fall. Anger and frustration coursed through him, warming him. He stared out into the night, daring her to come back for more.

She didn't.

And after a few minutes, the cold crept back. He started the car and turned on the heater. The night wasn't as dark as nights in Texas because of the blanket of snow on everything.

And to make matters worse, it was snowing more heavily now. At least it would make his approach more quiet, he thought as he drove back up the road a short way and pulled over.

He could see lights behind the dirty windows of the new cabin being built high up on the mountainside. He killed the engine and climbed out into the falling snow. The quiet was almost his undoing. He ached for Houston, the noise, the confusion of buildings and people.

He checked his weapon, then started up the mountain, following the tracks the pickup had left on the narrow road. It was time.

VIOLET HADN'T GONE FAR when she'd fallen, tumbling down into a small, snow-filled gully. She lay there, staring up at the sky, angry and scared.

She didn't think he'd come after her. But then again

she couldn't be sure of that. She pushed to her feet and heard the car drive off. He was leaving?

She listened, the sound of the car's big engine the only one on the mountainside.

He didn't go far before he pulled over. Then there was only the falling snow and silence.

Violet retraced her footsteps back to the empty snow-mobile parking lot. Her head hurt, and she couldn't remember the last time she'd slept or eaten. It made her irritable.

"Forget about him. You have bigger fish to fry," her grandmother said beside her.

This time Violet didn't mind her grandmother being here. She didn't like being alone on this mountainside. It felt too quiet, too isolated and alone.

Also, she'd had a lot of time to think in the trunk without her grandmother's constant nagging. Her grandmother had never liked dark, cramped places so hadn't shown up until now.

"Someone put you in those places when you were a girl," Violet said with sudden insight. Her grandmother suddenly didn't seem as large next to her. "*Your* mother? Is that who did it to you? Why you did it to me when my mother wasn't around?"

"Are you going to stand around here and freeze to death or take care of business? Your mother—"

"Hated you, you evil old harpy." Violet could see her grandmother clearly now. The stooped shoulders, the drooping skin of her neck, the harsh, bitter line of her thin lips. But it was the eyes, dark and small as raisins, that had always glinted with malice.

Only now Violet saw something else behind the malice—misery and pain. The two fed off each other.

"Where are you going?"

Violet didn't answer. Nor did she look back. She walked up the road, leaving her dead grandmother standing in the ruts, snow falling all around her.

DEDE TURNED AND SAW Lantry's expression. Her heart began to pound. "What is it?" she asked as she stepped back over to him.

She'd been so disappointed in Frank that she hadn't wanted to touch the necklace. It disgusted her. She thought she'd known her husband. The stolen diamond necklace proved she never had.

"Lantry?"

He held the necklace up. The stones flashing in the firelight. "It's a fake."

*"What?"*

He handed the necklace to her. It felt heavy and cold.

"It's not even a good copy." His gaze came up to meet hers.

She felt as stunned as he looked as she studied the necklace in her hands and saw what he meant. "But I don't understand. Why would Frank hide worthless jewelry in the boat?"

Lantry was shaking his head as if equally perplexed by this turn of events. "Why get himself killed for this, unless he didn't realize he didn't have the real thing?"

"Frank wouldn't have been fooled. Not if this was the way he'd made his fortune to begin with. But why hide this in the boat and give it to you? It makes no sense."

"Or does it?" Lantry said.

Her eyes widened as they both seemed to come to the same conclusion. "Inside jobs?"

He nodded. "The homeowners had to be in on it.

Which meant Frank was working with the people he robbed, stealing the phony jewelry, letting the home-owners collect the insurance and keep the real jewelry, paying Frank off with some of the insurance money."

Dede stared down at the necklace as a thought hit her. "But why would Frank keep this?"

"It's proof that the homeowner was in on the bur-glary," Lantry said. "These were wealthy people he was helping steal from the insurance companies. Is it pos-sible he was blackmailing them later? He had the du-plicate jewelry to prove they were in on the thefts."

Dede stared at the necklace, again feeling sick. "Quite an operation. But the last burglary was Tamara Fallon, his former assistant from the old days. Surely he wasn't planning to blackmail her." She felt Lantry staring at her and looked up to meet his eyes.

"Dede, didn't you say that Frank changed when Ed and Claude and Frank's former assistant, Tammy, turned up? Isn't it possible that Frank kept these par-ticular duplicates to keep them from ever involving him again? I know it's a long shot, but if you were right and Frank really did want to change…"

She smiled at him, touched that he would try to put a good spin on this horrible situation.

"He had Tammy right where he wanted her as long as he had the duplicates stolen from her house," Lantry was saying. "It would prove she was in on the burglary, and if she really was in the middle of an ugly divorce and was trying to get as much money out—"

"But why would Ed and Claude go to so much trou-ble to try to get the duplicates back? Unless they think the necklace is the real thing. Isn't it possible that if

Frank double-crossed Tammy, she double-crossed Ed and Claude?"

"Stranger things have happened. It might explain why Frank's dead and the police think they've found Tamara Fallon's body in a canal outside Houston."

Earlier, she'd heard a sound and thought it was the pop of the logs burning in the fireplace. But this time, she knew with certainty that the sound she heard hadn't just come from the fire—but from the back of the cabin.

As she turned, she saw a shadow fall across the floor. "Lantry—"

It was all she got out before the man stepped into the room and she saw the glint of the weapon in his hand.

He motioned to the necklace still entwined in her fingers. "I'll take that."

## Chapter Twelve

All Lantry saw at first was the gun aimed at Dede's heart—and froze. The man holding the weapon was short and stocky, and Lantry had the feeling he'd seen him before.

· "That's it, Mr. Corbett," the man said. "Don't do anything rash, or I'll have to shoot her."

"Let me guess. Ed, right?" Dede didn't sound afraid, and that amped up Lantry's fear for her twofold.

Ed gave a slight bow of his head in response. "I'll take that necklace now."

"You killed Frank for *this?*" Dede demanded, holding up the necklace. Lantry could hear the fury just under the surface. "You killed my husband for *this?*"

Ed shifted nervously as he watched Dede wind the necklace tighter around her fingers. "If you want to blame someone for Frank's death, you only have to look as far as that mirror on the wall."

Dede froze. "You're blaming me because *you* killed Frank?"

"Easy, Dede," Lantry warned, but he suspected she wasn't listening. He could see the rage etched on her face. She closed her hand into a fist around the necklace.

"If he hadn't been so busy trying to protect you, he'd

still be alive," Ed said, his own tone laced with anger. "I didn't want to kill Frank. But he forgot his loyalties. He betrayed us because of you."

Dede had her head cocked to one side, a stance Lantry had seen before. He didn't have to see the fire in her eyes to know that any moment she might launch herself at the man—to hell with the fact that he had a gun on her.

"He didn't betray you. He just didn't want any part of you or this burglary," she said, biting off each word.

"You don't know anything about Frank. He was one of us. He knew the cost of betrayal. He got greedy and wanted all the money for himself."

Dede opened her fist and let the necklace dangle from her fingers. "You think this was about money?"

"That necklace is worth almost two million dollars." His gaze flicked to Lantry. "Not chump change to some of us."

Just as they'd suspected, Ed didn't know the necklace was a worthless duplicate. Lantry thought it might be better to keep it that way.

Before Dede could spill the beans, Lantry jumped in. "There's no reason for bloodshed, Ed. You should have come to me right away. I'm a reasonable man. We could have made a deal for the necklace. It would have saved you a lot of time and effort. You wouldn't have had to kill Frank."

Ed seemed to relax a little, though he shifted his gaze to Dede every few seconds as if afraid of what she might do next. He wasn't the only one.

"We'd heard stories about you," Ed said. "We weren't sure you would be agreeable. But then, every man has his price, doesn't he?"

"Exactly. You could have cut me in. Much less messy that way."

Ed smiled. "A man who thinks like I do. I can appreciate that."

"Maybe it's not too late," Lantry said.

Ed laughed. "Under the circumstances, I'm not sure that's in my best interest."

Ed had killed Frank and probably Tamara Fallon. Clearly, the man had nothing to lose.

DEDE HAD BEEN so furious she'd almost blown it. As her blood pressure dropped a little, she realized what Lantry had right away.

Ed thought the necklace was the real thing.

She blinked, feeling lightheaded. She couldn't help but think of Frank when she looked at this man. He'd killed her husband, and for what? A pile of worthless glass and metal.

She had wanted to scratch the man's eyes out and take her chances with the gun in his hand.

Irrational thinking. She was thankful that Lantry had kept his senses. Ed seemed amused by Lantry, although she could tell he was watching her out of the corner of his eye, not sure what she might do next.

Dede shivered and realized Ed had left the back door open when he'd come in. That first sound she'd heard must have been him breaking the door lock.

She glanced toward the open doorway and the darkness beyond. Something moved through the falling snow behind him.

Someone else was out there.

"I'll take that necklace now. Nice and easy," Ed was saying.

"Why should we give it to you, knowing you plan to kill us either way?" Lantry asked.

"Like you said, there's no reason for more bloodshed," Ed said with a smile, lying through his teeth.

"What was it you had on Frank?" Dede asked.

Ed seemed surprised by the question. "Didn't he tell you?" He laughed. "No, of course, he didn't. He was ashamed." Ed's smile died abruptly. "Ashamed of his own brother."

*"Brother?"* Dede had barely gotten the word out when a figure materialized out of the snow and darkness behind Ed.

Dede felt a start as the person stepped into the dim light. Violet's face was bruised badly on one side of her face, her eye swollen and discolored. She carried something in her hands.

Dede didn't see what it was until she raised her arms and swung the large chunk of firewood at the back of Ed's head.

Ed must have sensed someone behind him or seen Dede's surprised expression. He started to turn, swinging around, leading with the gun.

Dede threw the necklace at him in a high arc. She saw the indecision on his face. The fear that someone was behind him and the irresistible need to catch what he thought was an almost two-million-dollar diamond necklace.

Greed would have won out but he was half-turned, the gun already coming around to point at whatever was behind him. Ed twisted back, reaching with his free hand for the necklace as the chunk of firewood clutched in Violet's hands made contact with his skull.

Dede heard the thwack and the gunshot, both seeming simultaneous. Before she could move, Lantry grabbed her, taking her down to the floor, covering her with his body as a second shot was fired. She heard a cry, then the sound of a body hitting the floor.

It all happened in a heartbeat. Lantry was on his feet, Dede scrambling up after him.

The deafening sound of the gunshots echoed like cannon booms inside the cabin. Violet's cry of pain and the sound of Ed's body hitting the floor were followed by the thud of the chunk of firewood landing next to him.

Dede looked toward the doorway to find Ed lying at Violet's feet and Violet clutching her chest, her fingers blooming red with blood. Violet's gaze met her own as the older woman slowly dropped to her knees and fell forward beside Ed.

Lantry lunged for Ed, snatching the gun from his hand—but there was no need. Dede could see death in the dull glaze of his eyes. She shook off her inertia and rushed to Violet's side.

The woman had saved her life. Again.

"Violet? Violet, can you hear me?" Dede looked over at Lantry. "We have to get her to the hospital."

THE AMBULANCE AND sheriff's deputies met them twenty miles out of Landusky. Dede sat in the back of the patrol car watching the falling snow as Violet was loaded onto a stretcher.

She could hear Lantry arguing with his brother outside the car.

"Damn it, Lantry, you don't know how lucky you are that you're not on *your* way to the jail," Shane said. "I fought like hell to get you released on your own recognizance pending further investigation into this case."

"You can't let them send Dede back to that mental hospital. She doesn't belong there. I'm telling you that all of this was her ex-husband's doing."

"She pulled a gun on a deputy and took you hostage at gunpoint."

"I'll say I went of my own free will."

Shane swore again. "Lantry, I'll see that she's protected, twenty-four seven, but I can tell you right now, she's got to go back to the hospital for a mental evaluation."

"I'll pay to have someone come here and do the evaluation," Lantry argued. "Help me with this, Shane. This woman is innocent. She's been through hell. If she hadn't come to Montana to warn me—"

"I'll see what I can do, all right?" Shane said, raising his voice over the sound of an ambulance taking off for Whitehorse.

Lantry climbed into the front of the patrol car and turned to look through the steel mesh at her.

"I hate to see you at odds with your brother," she said quietly.

He smiled and her heart took off at a gallop. "Shane and I are fine. It's you I'm worried about."

"Your brother's right. I'll be safe in jail. Both Ed and Claude are dead." Ed had confessed to killing Frank. Violet would back up her story about what happened in the van. There was that matter with the gun and the deputy, but even if she had to spend some time behind bars, she was just grateful that it was over and said as much to Lantry.

"It won't be over until you're cleared and free," he said with conviction. "You've been through enough."

His brother climbed behind the wheel and took off after the ambulance. Lantry fell silent. Dede watched the snowy landscape glide past as flakes fell like feathers from the ice-black sky overhead.

LANTRY SAT IN HIS brother's office, legs stretched out, his eyes dull from lack of sleep.

As Shane returned from down the hall with Dede, he stood up. Dede looked as awful as he felt. He drew her into his arms.

"Lantry, if you'll wait down the hall," Shane said to his brother after a moment. Lantry let go of Dede but didn't move.

"I'll be fine," she said.

He nodded and reluctantly left the room, closing the door behind him.

"I need to ask you some questions," Shane said. "I understand you hired a private investigator to follow your then-husband."

Dede nodded. "Jonathan O'Reilly."

"A private investigator by that name was found murdered the same week as your husband and Tamara Fallon. His office had been ransacked, all files and computers destroyed," Shane said.

Dede looked sick. "You don't think—"

"No, we don't believe you had anything to do with the murders, given the evidence we've uncovered."

"What kind of evidence?"

"You said Ed told you that Frank was his brother, right?" Shane asked.

"I'm sure he meant they'd been like brothers," Dede said.

"We ran the mental-hospital driver's fingerprints and

were able to ID him from an old arrest record," Shane continued. "He was using an assumed name for employment at the hospital. His real name is Claude Ingram. Ed was his brother."

"Brothers?" Dede couldn't believe this.

"There's more," Shane said. "I checked into Frank Chamberlain's background, assuming he must have been from the same small Idaho town since you'd said they'd apparently known each other since childhood." Shane glanced at Dede. She nodded. "No Frank Chamberlain."

She felt herself pale.

"Both Claude and Ed were born in Idaho, a little town called Ashton. They had two other siblings. A sister and a brother."

Dede felt a chill even in the small, cramped room.

"Franklin John Ingram—"

Dede let out a gasp.

"—and Tamara Sue Ingram."

"Tammy was Frank's *sister?*" She stared at him for a moment, then shook her head. "That can't be possible. I thought Frank and Tamara…"

"Apparently they were in business together—both in security alarm systems and the burglaries of the clients' jewels," Shane said. "We're still waiting on DNA results, but from the identification found near the body, the woman found in the river was Tamara Fallon."

Dede shivered, remembering the photos of Tammy the PI had shown her. A slim, pretty woman with long blond hair pulled back in a ponytail and high cheekbones.

"No wonder Frank couldn't say no to them," Dede said. "Some family the Ingrams turned out to be. Is it any wonder Frank wanted to get away from them? Obviously he'd changed his name, thought he'd escaped them." She felt sick. "And now they are all dead."

AFTER SHANE HAD TAKEN their statements separately, he got the call from the judge. He quickly realized just how small a town Whitehorse was and how things worked here.

Shane hung up and looked across the desk at Dede and Lantry. "Seems some strings have been pulled."

Dede would be remanded into Grayson Corbett's custody, fitted with a house-arrest device that would monitor her movements within a quarter-mile of the ranchhouse.

"How is Violet?" she asked Shane before she and Lantry left the sheriff's department.

"Looks like she's going to make it."

"Can I see her? She saved my life…and Lantry's."

Shane shook his head. "Only her mother has been allowed to see her. I can pass a message on to her mother for you."

"Just tell Violet thank you, all right? What she did was very brave." Or some might say crazy. Dede wondered why she'd done it. Why hadn't she just taken off and tried to save herself?

Kate Corbett put Dede up in the main house's guest suite and made her feel at home. Lantry was busy doing legal maneuvering, trying to keep them both out of jail, so she saw little of him that first day.

She couldn't believe it was almost Christmas Day. Trails West Ranch was decorated beautifully, and she knew that Kate had added several packages under the tree with Dede's name on them.

Dede wandered around the big house, feeling lost. She knew she was still in shock and dealing with everything that had happened. It saddened her how little she'd known about a man she'd married, and hated that Lantry might be right about marriage.

She'd loved Frank, planned to have his children. Now she was thankful she hadn't become pregnant.

Dede looked up to see a UPS truck pull up out front. A moment later Kate came into the room carrying a large package.

Kate had just gotten back from her knitting class in town and seemed more excited than usual. "I just found out that my daughters-in-law are all expecting! I'm going to have to learn to knit much faster if I hope to get baby buntings made before the grandbabies are all born."

Now Kate held out the package. "It's for you. It's from Lantry."

"Why would Lantry—"

"Open it," Kate said.

Dede tore open the box to find a beautiful guitar inside. Carefully she took it out. How had Lantry known? She felt tears rush to her eyes.

"You play?" Kate asked in confusion.

"I used to." Back before Frank, back before all of this. Her fingers ached to strum the strings, to make the music that used to fill her heart with such joy. "If you don't mind, I think I'll take it back to my room for now."

Kate nodded, looking concerned. "Is there anything I can do?"

Dede smiled and touched the woman's arm. Kate Corbett had been so kind to her. "Thank you, but I just need time to process everything that's happened. I feel that I got Lantry into this, and I—"

"Lantry and his profession got Lantry into this," Kate said, not unkindly. "Lantry took your husband's case. I would imagine he will always regret that." She smiled. "Except that it brought you into his life," she added quickly. "Otherwise, you two might never have met. I've seen the change in my stepson. Lantry had planned to go back to Texas right after Christmas, back to being a divorce lawyer. He won't do that now, you'll see. You've had a profound effect on him."

Dede smiled at that. "I almost got him killed. Have you heard anything on Violet Evans?"

"She's being moved to a private mental hospital close by right after the wedding Christmas Day," Kate said. "Arlene is marrying Hank Monroe tomorrow. Arlene got special permission for her daughter to attend the wedding."

As she carried the guitar Lantry had given her down to her room, Dede thought about what Kate had said. They'd all been changed by what had happened. Would Lantry really give up his career because of it?

Once in her room, Dede ran her fingers lovingly across the guitar strings. She hadn't played in so long. Slowly, she picked up the guitar, her fingers remembering the music as she began to play.

LANTRY HAD A LOT on his mind. In a word: Dede. At first he'd been so busy trying to get her cleared that he hadn't had time to think about the future. Her mental evaluation had gone well. Now, if he could just work his legal magic, Dede would be free to return to Texas after Christmas.

The duplicate necklace and both his and Dede's statements, along with evidence that continued to come in on the Ingram siblings, had forced a judge in Texas to take another look at Dede's commitment to the mental hospital.

Just after the holidays, a local judge would rule on the other charges against Dede.

There would be nothing keeping Dede in Montana after that. Nothing keeping him, either, for that matter.

He had come so close to being disbarred. It surprised him that he wasn't more upset about that. But he realized he had no interest in returning to his law practice in Texas. Or returning to Texas at all.

He could sell his practice, walk away with a nice chunk of change and then what?

He knew he was at a crossroads, but not one where he'd ever been before. For the first time in his life, he didn't know what he was going to do tomorrow or the next day.

He thought about his father's offer. "There's some good grazing land that will be coming up for sale soon to the south. If you were interested in staying, I sure could use your help."

"Dad, I…I'm not sure what I'm going to do," he'd said truthfully.

"This case has changed your mind about being a divorce lawyer?"

Lantry had chuckled. "You could say that."

"Or is it the woman?"

"A lot of both," he'd found himself admitting.

"Are you in love with her?"

Lantry had looked at his father, realizing this talk was Kate's doing, since it was so unlike his father to ask such a question. "Dede's still in love with her ex-husband."

"Oh." His father had looked uncomfortable. "Kate seems to think Dede's in love with you. Kate's seldom wrong about these things."

Lantry had laughed. "And she told you to talk to me."

His father had laughed as well. "She might have suggested I mention that land I was thinking about buying. Said there was a beautiful spot down that way for a house." Grayson had shrugged, unapologetic for trying. "You're a cowboy, son. It's in your blood."

That it was, Lantry thought as he drove toward the ranch, anxious to see Dede.

THE HOUSE WAS QUIET, Juanita in the kitchen, Kate in her study, knitting. Dede felt restless and more anxious by the hour. Not about going to jail, for she knew Lantry would move heaven and earth so that didn't happen.

No, it was about leaving Montana—and Lantry.

They hadn't been together since the cabin in Landusky. She had seen Lantry struggling when he was around her.

"He's in love with you," Kate told her that morning when she caught Dede watching Lantry leave the house.

Dede had laughed and shook her head. "I'm sorry, but you're wrong."

Kate had smiled a knowing smile. "He doesn't know how to handle it, since he's never felt like this before. Trust me. He's in love with you. Look how hard he's working to get you cleared of all the charges. Right now he's trying to get that stupid house-arrest device off your ankle before Christmas day."

Now Dede stood at the window, remembering Kate's

words. Lantry had definitely spent every waking hour since her arrest trying to get her freed. But she suspected he liked the work because it kept him from having to deal with his feelings, deal with her.

"Lantry thinks you're still in love with your ex-husband," Kate had said.

"The man I fell in love with didn't really exist," Dede had told her. "It's hard to explain how I feel about Frank. Empty. Sad. Disappointed. Sorry. I suppose a part of me still loves the man Frank could have been, the man he wanted to be."

Kate had smiled and hugged her. "You and I have more in common than you might think. I loved a man when I was young. He let me down. It is only now that I realize he never was the man I wanted or needed him to be. But I mourned for years for what that love could have been. As women it isn't easy to let go of those dreams, is it?"

"No, it isn't," Dede said to herself now. Just as it wasn't going to be easy to leave this place, to leave Kate and the rest of the family who had welcomed her so lovingly. Or to leave Lantry.

Just as it wouldn't be easy to spend Christmas here with all of them, knowing she would be leaving as soon as the holidays were over.

Since her father's death, Dede had pretty much ignored Christmas other than to go to church on Christmas Eve.

Kate had insisted Dede stay through the holidays even if Lantry was able to get her exonerated. Kate had been right about one thing: there was nothing waiting for Dede in Texas.

She pressed her fingers against the cool glass of the

window as she looked out over the ranch. A Chinook had blown in, the warm wind melting off the snow. The weatherman had promised a white Christmas, though, warning of another storm coming in tonight.

Lantry hadn't managed to get her freed of the house-arrest device on her ankle, but he had asked that she be given a larger area to roam.

She watched one of the mares running around the corral as if enjoying the feel of the warm wind. Dede thought about telling Kate she was going to walk down to the corral, but didn't want to disturb her when she was concentrating so hard on her knitting.

The wind was warm and smelled of spring—an illusion, since winter had only begun. Growing up in Wyoming, Dede remembered days like this that teased and tempted.

The sun was low, the daylight fading fast. She wondered when Lantry would be home. Late, she was sure. As she walked, Dede listened to the wind in the large pines. The Christmas lights swung to and fro on the branches.

The mare came right over to her. Dede reached in her pocket and took out the apple she'd gotten from Juanita and offered it to the horse.

"You're sure pretty," she said to the horse as the mare chomped the apple then snuffled her hand and pocket to see if there were any more.

Dede felt a sliver of trepidation at the thought of someday enjoying riding again, but Kate had told her this mare was gentle, and as she rubbed its neck she thought the mare wanted to go as badly as she did.

"How about I see if I can round up some tack?" she

told the mare. "The best I can do is a ride around the corral, but if you're up for it, so am I." The mare whinnied.

Dede headed for the barn, the mare trailing along beside her inside the corral.

It was dark in the big old barn. Dede felt around for a light, snapped it on. Inside the cavernous barn, she could still hear the howl of the wind. It was cooler in here, cold compared to the warm wind and waning sunlight outside.

She walked through the barn toward the stalls and found the tack room. She didn't hurry and knew part of it was fear.

It had been different riding the two horses she'd borrowed to escape. Greater fears had driven her.

She didn't have to ride ever again. She heard the mare whinny at the corral fence at the other end of the barn.

Dede laughed as she dragged out a halter and horse blanket and was checking out the array of saddles when she heard the barn door open and close. The wind? Or had Lantry returned and come looking for her?

Her heart did a little flip.

She listened. *Must just have been the wind,* she thought, disappointed. Dede reached for one of the saddles.

The barn lights went out.

## Chapter Thirteen

Lantry was almost to the ranch when his cell phone vibrated in his jacket pocket. He realized as he reached for the phone that he was hoping it was Dede. He knew he'd been avoiding her. Giving her space, is what he'd told himself.

Sending her the guitar had been one of those spur-of-the-moment decisions. Now that he'd done it, though, he was excited to hear her play.

Just the thought of talking to her made his heart beat a little faster and—

It wasn't Dede, but Shane.

"Hey," he said into the phone, reining in his disappointment as he stopped at the top of a hill to take the call, fearing it was about Dede's case and knowing he was going to want all his concentration on that—not driving.

"I have some news I thought you'd want to hear right away," Shane said, tension in his voice that set Lantry on edge.

"That body found in the canal in Texas wasn't Tamara Fallon's."

Lantry let that sink in. "I thought the police found ID—"

"Given what we know now, the Houston police think

she might have tried to fake her death so she could get away with the diamond necklace."

There was more. Lantry could feel it.

"A woman matching Tamara Fallon's description flew into Billings last night," Shane said. "Lantry, the Houston police told me that her husband, Dr. Eric Fallon, said his wife was obsessed with one of her brother's wives, and since Frank was the only one who was married…"

That disquiet was now full-blown worry. "You're saying Tamara Fallon flew to Montana because of Dede?"

"Dr. Fallon seems to think that Tamara blames Dede for Frank turning his back on her and his brothers."

Lantry glanced toward the Little Rockies in the distance. "I'm almost back to the ranch. I've got to go." He snapped off the phone and hit the gas. Everyone had planned to be away from the ranch house today except for Dede, Kate and Juanita.

As he topped the next rise in the road, he saw the smoke.

"Hey!" Dede called out. "Mind turning the lights back on?" No lights. No answer. "Hello?" She hated that her voice broke. The barn had taken on a weighty silence, and she realized she wasn't alone anymore.

But why didn't whoever had turned out the lights say something? The Corbett brothers joked and kidded around with each other, but they weren't big practical jokers, and this wasn't funny.

She looked around for something to use as a weapon, telling herself she was just being silly. She couldn't trust her emotions after everything she'd been through. Especially after falling for Lantry Corbett.

That thought stopped her cold for a moment. She'd fallen in love with him. Why had it taken until this moment to admit that?

*"Hello?"* she called again, praying someone would answer as she spotted a pitchfork stuck in a hay bale in one of the stalls.

She took a step in the growing darkness of the barn toward the pitchfork, then another, trying not to make a sound as she listened. She could hear nothing over the howl of the wind outside.

The barn had filled with deep shadows. She caught the scent of perfume just an instant before the figure stepped out of an adjacent stall in front of her—blocking her way out.

A flashlight beam snapped on, blinding her. She flinched, heard a chuckle, then the beam dropped to the barn floor.

Tamara Fallon had changed her hair color. She was no longer a blonde. Her hair was short and dark. But the face was the same one Dede had seen in the photographs the private investigator had shown her.

"Frank told me you were pretty," Tamara said. "In a sweet way." She made *sweet* sound like a dirty word.

Dede could see the resemblance, though slight between the siblings. She was too startled to speak, and while Tamara wasn't brandishing anything more deadly than a flashlight, she sensed that the woman was dangerous.

"What's wrong? Thought I was dead?" The woman's laugh was sharp as a blade.

"I'm just surprised to see you here," Dede said truthfully. Surprised and fearful.

"Did you know that Frank and I were fraternal twins?" Tamara shook her head. "I didn't think so. Your private investigator died before he could tell you that, huh? There's no stronger bond than the bond between twins."

"I've heard that," Dede said, reasoning that antagonizing this woman would be a mistake. No one knew Dede had gone down to the barn, and she wasn't sure when it would be discovered that she was missing, since she was able to go at least as far as the barn.

She wondered if Tamara knew about the house-arrest tracking device strapped to her ankle. Dede's jeans covered it. The alarm would go off at the sheriff's department if she went only a few yards farther than the back of the barn.

Tamara hadn't threatened her. Not yet, anyway. But Dede had already decided that she would have to find a way to step out of her specified area—and soon. Something about the woman's demeanor warned her that Tamara's visit wasn't a friendly one.

"So you probably wonder what I'm doing in Montana," Tamara said, glancing around the barn. "Aren't you the least bit curious?"

Dede could tell that the woman was watching her out of the corner of her eye. "Not really. I should get back to the house. Everyone will be looking for me."

Tamara laughed. "Not likely, since there was a fire behind the house and both women are out there right now fighting it in that awful wind. Wouldn't it be a shame if the blaze burned all the way down here to the barn?"

Dede's heart fell at the thought of Kate and Juanita being in danger because of her. As she caught the smell of smoke, she glanced toward the end of the barn. The mare was still standing there, waiting. Behind the horse, the horizon was an odd color, almost pink in the darkening sky. The snowstorm. It was probably already snowing in the Little Rockies.

If she could make a break for it, run to the end of the barn and out into the corral—

Dede felt the full weight of the woman's gaze. "My brothers are dead because of you."

The mare had picked up the scent of the smoke and was moving nervously. Dede shifted on her feet, saw Tamara tense.

Dede knew she had to do something. Now. "You blame *me* for your brothers' deaths?" she demanded, taking a step toward the woman.

Tamara reacted instinctively by taking a step back. The move gave Dede a little more room for when the time came to run.

"Your *brothers* tried to kill me," Dede said.

Tamara was clearly taken aback by this confrontational manner of Dede's. She had obviously expected Dede to cower in fear. Not that Dede wasn't shaking in her boots. She just couldn't let Tamara see that fear.

But there was also an underlying anger. Because of this woman who professed such a bond with her brother, Frank was dead. She said as much to the woman.

"He'd be alive if he hadn't married you and betrayed his own family," Tamara shot back. "You turned him against us. You poisoned his mind. Frank would never have—"

"Double-crossed you otherwise?" Dede demanded.

"The police have the duplicate necklace. They know about the other burglaries. They'll soon figure out who masterminded all of it—including killing Frank and sending your other brothers after a worthless necklace and to their deaths."

Tamara looked livid. Spittle came out of her mouth when she finally was able to speak. "You bitch."

Dede knew the woman would go for her throat. She'd been ready. As Tamara charged, she stepped to the side, managing to trip her up. Tamara stumbled. Dede didn't look back as she ran toward the end of the barn.

She just hoped this monitoring device worked.

But even if it alerted the sheriff's department, it would take someone a while to get out to the ranch, and Dede was all out of a plan to escape as she heard Tamara shout for her to stop.

Dede had almost reached the end of the barn when the wood of one of the stall supports splintered in front of her as a popping sound echoed through the large old barn. Another pop.

Dede felt a sharp pain in her side, felt her feet stumble. Something was wrong. Her hand went to her side and came away covered in blood.

THE PICKUP ROARED into the ranch yard. Lantry was out of it before the truck came to a stop. He ran toward where his stepmother and Juanita were dousing the last of the flames.

The dried grasses of fall had made perfect tinder for the flames that skittered across the back of the house chased by the wind.

But the two women had managed to narrow the blaze and now had it almost out.

"Lantry," Kate cried over the wind when she saw him. She had one of the fire extinguishers kept at the back door. Juanita was manning the garden hose. "We can't find Dede. I think she's down at the barn."

He could hear a horse whinnying. It had smelled the smoke.

"Go find her," Kate ordered.

He took off at a run as an unsettling thought lodged itself in his gut. Dede had grown up on a ranch. The moment she smelled the smoke, she would have come running. Wildfires were always a fear.

As he neared the barn, he saw the horse in the corral. It ran in a tight nervous circle. There was no way Dede wouldn't have heard the horse if she was in the barn.

He burst into the barn, surprised to find it dark inside. Reaching for the switch, he snapped on the lights and blinked.

"Dede!"

"Down here" came a female voice he didn't recognize.

"Lantry, no, she has a gun!"

The chilling sound of Dede's words rattled through him. He took a step, then another in the direction her voice had come from.

"Tamara?" he said as he neared the back end of the barn. "I heard you were in town."

"Good news travels fast," she shot back with a laugh that turned his blood to ice.

"Are you all right, Dede?" he asked, trying to keep the panic out of his voice.

"She's bleeding like a stuck pig," Tamara answered. "But she's still alive. Why don't you join us?"

That was exactly what he planned to do. He wasn't

about to let Dede spend another second alone with the woman.

As he drew closer, he saw a pair of jeans-clad legs protruding from the end stall.

"That's close enough," Tamara said and peered around the end of the stall nearer Dede's feet.

It wasn't near close enough, so he kept walking.

"Are you hard of hearing?" Tamara asked. "I said that was close enough."

He kept coming. So far he hadn't seen the weapon Tamara had used to shoot Dede. The stall walls were tall enough that she'd have a hell of a hard time shooting him over one of them. She'd have to step out and take aim. That meant he would have a few seconds before she fired.

"I said stop!" Tamara's voice rose, shrill even in the echo.

He was almost to her, coming fast. He knew he couldn't give her time to think. She had to fear him. If she had time to think, she would threaten Dede—the only thing that could hold him back. Instead, he had to make her fear for her own life if he reached her. He had to get her to turn the gun on him.

Tamara stepped out of the stall, leading with the barrel of the pistol just as he'd hoped she would. He was so close now that she didn't have enough time to aim. The gun made a popping sound. Wood splintered on the stall door next to him.

She tried to fire again, but she'd forgotten momentarily about Dede. Dede kicked Tamara's feet out from under her. A grunt escaped the woman's lips as she hit the ground, going down hard.

The gun popped again. Dust sifted down from the

barn ceiling. But by then, Lantry was on her, twisting the weapon from her fingers and pointing the barrel at Tamara as he dropped beside Dede.

"Are you all right?" he cried, seeing her lying in the straw bed of the stall holding her side, her angelic face pinched with pain.

She nodded and smiled. "I am now."

He started to pull out his cell phone to call his brother, but before he could, he heard sirens. He looked up confusion at Dede.

She pointed to her ankle monitor. The light was flashing. She'd managed to set it off.

"Nice work," Lantry said. As the barn filled with uniformed officers, he handed over Tamara Ingram Fallon's weapon and lifted Dede into his arms. "I'm not waiting for an ambulance," he said to his brother. "I'm taking her myself."

## Chapter Fourteen

Dede woke Christmas morning to find Lantry sleeping in a chair next to her bed.

"Good morning, sleepyhead," he said, opening his eyes.

She couldn't believe this cowboy. After the doctor told him that her gunshot wound wasn't serious, he'd hired a nurse and brought her back to the ranch.

"It's Christmas. I'm not having you spend it in a hospital," he'd told her.

"How are you feeling?" he asked now.

After waking up to find him next to her bed? Wonderful. "A little sore, but other than that, pretty good."

He smiled. He really did have a great smile. "Ready for Christmas?" He sounded like a kid, anxious to see what Santa Claus had left him under the tree.

"Ready," Dede whispered as Lantry carried her into the living room. All the family was gathered around the tree.

Dede smelled hot apple cider. It mingled with the scent of evergreen. Outside it was one of those amazing Montana days. All blue sky and sunshine, making last night's fresh snowfall glitter like diamonds.

For just a moment she couldn't help but think of

Frank. She felt nothing of the old pain, only a twinge of sadness. Her heart didn't ache. It felt like a helium balloon allowed to fly free again, she thought as she looked over at Lantry.

All around her there was laughter mingling with the sound of happy chatter. *These Corbetts,* Dede thought, shaking her head. *What a big, boisterous family.* The kind she'd always dreamed of being a part of.

She wiped at a tear, caught Lantry looking over at her with concern.

"Are you sure you're up to this?" he whispered, leaning close.

"I wouldn't miss this for the world." She smiled at him and hastily brushed away the moisture at the corner of her eye.

For a moment she thought he was going to kiss her.

The room seemed to have gone quiet, everything stopping in midmotion. All she could hear was her heart in her chest banging like a drum as she looked into Lantry's blue eyes and remembered the tickle of his mustache, the feel of his lips on hers.

"Better open this one," someone said, handing her a present. The room came alive again as Lantry leaned back, the moment lost.

Dede watched as the family tore into the presents spilling out from around the tree. There were ohhs and ahhs and laughter and hugs as the pile of paper and ribbons grew.

Kate had been kind enough to do some shopping for Dede since she couldn't leave the ranch with her monitoring device. The older woman smiled over at her now as family members opened the presents she'd bought from Dede. Kate had great taste, and Dede smiled back her thanks.

"Well, is that it?" Grayson asked as the frenzy slowed down. The family was sprawled around the tree, many sporting their presents of new slippers or sweaters. "Then let's have breakfast."

Everyone started getting up to head into the large dining room. The talk turned to Juanita's Christmas Day breakfast. It sounded like quite a spread.

Lantry didn't move until everyone else had left but he and Dede. "That's not quite it," he said as he got to his feet and went to the tree. From deep in the thick green boughs he took out a small velvet box.

Dede felt her heart set off at a gallop as Lantry came back over to the chair where she sat and knelt down in front of her. She was already shaking her head.

"Dede, there are some things I have to say. I used to figure if two people were stupid enough to get married, then they deserved whatever happened to them."

"Like me and Frank."

He shook his head. "Frank loved you. I believe that. He wouldn't have changed his name and tried to make a new life with you if he hadn't. You made him want to be a better person. It wasn't your fault that his family had such a hold over him."

"That whole 'blood is thicker than water' thing?"

He nodded. "I can't go back to what I used to do. I'm not cynical enough about love and marriage anymore. It's not a requirement for being a divorce lawyer, but it helps."

She let out a nervous laugh. For a while she'd been so afraid to dream that Lantry might feel the same way about her that she felt about him.

He pulled her close. "I'd never known what falling in love felt like. I had no idea the crazy thoughts that come into your head. It's no wonder people get married. Wait, I'm not saying this right."

He took her hand. Behind him, the lights of the Christmas tree glittered brightly. Somewhere in the house, "Silent Night" was playing. The room seemed magical, something out of a fairy tale.

"Lantry, what are you doing?" she asked, scared.

"I'm trying to ask you to marry me," he said, his voice breaking. "This is just our first Christmas together. But I want to spend the rest of them with you. I love you, Dede. I want to marry you."

She couldn't believe this. *"Marriage?"* Had he really said the M word?

"I'm as surprised as you are. I never thought this day would come. But then, I'd never met anyone like you. I can't imagine a life without you in it."

"Aren't you worried about the odds of us making it?" she had to ask, fearing this couldn't be real.

He shook his head. "You and I are going to be in that fifty percent who spend our lives together and die within days of each other when we are old because we can't stand to live without the other."

She couldn't help but smile. "That sounds awfully romantic, cowboy."

He grinned and placed the small velvet box in the palm of her hand. "I know it's too soon. I know you're going to need time. But I can't let you just walk out of my life."

"This is happening too fast," she said, unable to trust this moment. Hadn't her heart wanted this? Ached for this from the moment she'd fallen in love with this man?

"I know. That's why I'm suggesting a long engagement. Not for me," he added quickly, with a laugh. "If you'd have me, I'd marry you this afternoon right here in front of this Christmas tree."

She touched his handsome face. "This is so not like you."

"I know, but, Dede, I want to be that couple who wears out their wedding bands from years of marriage. I want that with you. I believe you and I can have that kind of marriage, or I wouldn't ask you. Just say you'll think about it and that you won't go back to Texas."

She raised an eyebrow. "Are you saying you're staying on here at the ranch?"

"My father is expanding the ranch. He's offered me a job and some land south of here for a house."

Dede wanted to pinch herself. Being here on the Trails West Ranch had reminded her how much she'd missed the ranch she'd grown up on. How much she'd missed this country and the lifestyle. She might even get over her fear of horses—with Lantry's help.

With his love, she knew there was nothing she couldn't do.

"DON'T MAKE UP your mind right now," Lantry said, his heart in his throat. He knew it was too early. He also knew she'd been hurt too badly by her first marriage. She would be afraid to trust.

But he couldn't just let her walk out of his life.

She looked down at the box in her palm.

"You can open it if you'd like. Or you can wait until you're ready." He wanted her to open it. Hell, he wanted her to accept his proposal and wear the ring.

Slowly, she opened the box and let out a small gasp.

"The ring belonged to my grandmother. She and my grandfather were married sixty-three years. I figured if it worked for them…" He shrugged.

Dede leaned down and kissed him. "It is *perfect*."

"Does that mean you'll marry me?"

"One day, I will, yes."

# Epilogue

The weddings of the last of the two Corbett brothers were huge affairs, with everyone in three counties invited.

There was dancing and Mexican food and a celebration that lasted for several days. Weeks later, everyone was still talking about how pretty the brides had been and how handsome those Corbett brothers were.

Lantry looked up to see his father framed in the doorway. "Dad?"

Grayson seemed to hesitate before he stepped into the room. "I suppose you'll be going back to Texas now that the wedding is over and you're back from your honeymoon."

So that explained his father's serious look.

"Actually," Lantry said, smiling at his father, "I've decided not to go back to being a divorce lawyer. I figure I'd better stay around my family given how much trouble this family gets into."

His father registered surprise. "I just assumed since Dede is from Texas…"

"Well, you know she grew up on a ranch in Wyoming. So this country up here feels more like home to her than Texas ever did."

His father grinned. "I couldn't be more pleased. I think I mentioned that there's a nice section to the south that would be a perfect place for a house. But in the meantime, no reason for you two not to stay in one of the cabins close by."

Lantry laughed. His father had gotten what he wanted, what their mother had wanted. The Corbett family had all settled in Montana on the Trails West Ranch. Not only would Grayson have his family close by, he now had five daughters-in-law—all strong-willed and independent—and grandbabies on the way.

"So tell me, Dad. Was there ever really any letters from our mother?"

Grayson smiled. "You were always such a skeptic. I suppose you were destined to be a lawyer—at least for a while." He reached into his inside jacket pocket and pulled out a yellowed envelope. "This one is for you, son."

Lantry saw his name printed on the front in a small, neat hand. His heart dipped and rose as he took the letter from the mother he could barely remember.

"I just gave your brothers theirs," Grayson said. "They wanted to wait until you all were married and had your letters before they opened them. I'll leave you to it," he said and left him alone.

Lantry turned the envelope over in his fingers. He had one clear memory of his mother he'd held on to all these years. It was of her leaning into his crib and touching his cheek as she sang softly.

He carefully opened the envelope and slipped out the single sheet of paper.

*To my dearest Lantry,*

And suddenly he could hear her sweet voice, feel

the brush of her fingers across his cheek, the memory coming alive again as his heart swelled and his eyes filled with tears.

For a few minutes he had his mother back.

He just wished she'd lived long enough to see this day. Her wish had come true. All five of her sons were happily married to cowgirls—or at least women who were fast becoming Montana cowgirls.

Carefully, he put the letter back in the envelope and went to find his wife. His wife. He smiled at the memory of Dede in her wedding dress standing next to him before the altar. Some day she would sing to their babies.

He headed out the door of the main ranchhouse. He knew he'd find her down at the corrals with the new mare. What she didn't know was that the horse was her wedding present, and one day she would ride again.

When he saw her leaning on the corral fence, his heart filled with so much joy and love he thought he might explode. A man didn't deserve to be this happy.

As he watched her, the sun in her hair, lighting her blue eyes, he remembered something his father had once told him. A horse always knows its way home. So does a cowboy.

\* \* \* \* \*

**Joanna Wayne** began her professional writing career in 1994. Now, more than fifty published books later, Joanna has gained a worldwide following with her cutting-edge romantic suspense and Texas family series such as Sons of Troy Ledger and the Big D Dads series. Connect with her at joannawayne.com or write her at PO Box 852, Montgomery, TX 77356.

Be sure to look for more books by Joanna Wayne in Harlequin Intrigue—the ultimate destination for edge-of-your-seat intrigue and fearless romance. There are six new Harlequin Intrigue titles available every month. Check one out today!

# MIRACLE AT COLTS RUN CROSS

## Joanna Wayne

To mothers everywhere who know what it means to love a child more than life itself.

And to every woman who's ever found that special man whose love is worth fighting for.

Here's to Christmas, miracles and love.

# Chapter One

Becky Ridgely grabbed her denim jacket from the hook and swung out the back door. A light mist made the air seem much cooler than the predicted fifty-degree high for the day. The gust of wind that caught her off guard didn't help, but she'd had to escape the house or sink even deeper into the blue funk that had a killer grip on her mood.

In a matter of weeks, her divorce from Nick would be final. Their marriage that had begun with a fiery blast of passion and excitement she'd thought would never cool had dissolved into a pile of ashes.

Nonetheless, Nick Ridgely, star receiver for the Dallas Cowboys, was in her living room on the Sunday before Christmas, as large as life on the new big-screen TV and claiming the attention of her entire family. She could understand it of their twin sons. At eight years of age, Nick was David and Derrick's hero. She'd never take that away from them.

But you'd think the rest of the family could show a little sensitivity for her feelings. But no, even her sister and her mother were glued to the set as if winning were paramount to gaining world peace or at least finding a cure for cancer.

Did no one but her get that this was just a stupid game?

Most definitely Nick didn't. For more than half of every year, he put everything he had into football. His time. His energy. His enthusiasm. His dedication. She and the boys were saddled with the leftovers. Some women settled for that. She couldn't, which is why she'd left him and moved back to the family ranch.

Her family liked Nick. Everyone did. And he was a good husband and father in many ways. He didn't drink too much. He had never done drugs, not even in college when all their friends were trying it.

He disdained the use of steroids and would never use the shortcut to improve performance. He didn't cheat on her, though several gossip magazines had connected him to Brianna Campbell, slut starlet, since they had been separated.

But his one serious fault was the wedge that had driven them apart. Once preparation for football season started, he shut her out of his life so completely that she could have been invisible. Oh, he pretended to listen to her or the boys at times, but it was surface only.

His always-ready excuse was that his mind was on the upcoming season or game. The message was that it mattered more than they did. She'd lived with the rejection as long as she could tolerate it, and then she left.

"Mom."

She turned at the panicked voice of her son Derrick. He'd pushed through the back door and was standing on the top step, his face a ghostly white.

She raced to him. "What's the matter, sweetheart?"

"Dad's hurt."

"He probably just had the breath knocked out of him," she said.

"No, it's bad, Mom. Really bad. He's not moving."

She put her arm around Derrick's shoulder as they hurried back to the family room, where the earlier cheers had turned deathly silent.

The screen defied her to denounce Derrick's fears. Nick was on his back, his helmet off and lying at a cock-eyed angle beside him. Several trainers leaned over him. A half dozen of his teammates were clustered behind them, concern sketched into their faces.

Becky took a deep breath as reality sank in and panic rocked her equilibrium. "What happened?"

"He went up for the ball and got tackled below the waist," Bart said.

Before her brother could say more, the network flashed the replay. A cold shudder climbed her spine as she watched Nick get flipped in midair. He slammed to the ground at an angle that seemed to drive his head and the back of his neck into the hard turf.

His eyes were open, but he had yet to move his arms or legs. Players from the other team joined the circle of players that had formed around him. A few had bowed in prayer. They all looked worried.

"Those guys know what it means to take a hit like that," her brother Langston said. "No player likes to see another one get seriously hurt."

"Yet they go at each other like raging animals." The frustration had flown from Becky's mouth before she could stop it. The stares of her family bore into her, no doubt mistaking her exasperation for a lack of empathy. But they hadn't lived with Nick's obsession for pushing his mind and body to the limit week after week.

"I only meant that it's almost inevitable that players get hurt considering the intensity of the game."

The family grew silent. The announcer droned on and on about Nick's not moving as the trainers strapped him to a backboard and attached a C-collar to support his neck.

David scooted close to the TV and put his hand on the corner of the screen. "Come on, Dad. You'll be all right. You gotta be all right."

"I got hurt bad the first time I played in a real game," Derrick said. "I wanted to cry, but I didn't 'cause the other players make fun of you if you do."

Becky had never wanted her sons to play football, but had given in to their pleadings this year when they turned eight. Nick had always just expected they'd play and spent half the time he was with them practicing the basic skills of the game. It was yet another bone of contention between them.

They showed the replay again while Nick was taken from the field. All of the announcers were in on the act now, concentrating on the grisly possible outcomes from such an injury.

"The fans would love it if Nick could wave a farewell but he still hasn't moved his arms or legs."

"It doesn't look good. It would be terrible to see the career of a player with Nick Ridgely's talent end like this."

"Did you hear that?" Derrick said. "The announcer said Daddy might not ever play football again."

Becky grabbed the remote and muted the sound. "They don't know. They're not doctors. Most likely Daddy has a bad sprain."

"Your father's taken lots of blows and he's never let one get the best of him yet," her brother Bart said, trying as Becky had to calm the boys.

"We better get up there and check on him," David said. "He might need us."

"You have school tomorrow," Becky said, quickly squashing that idea.

"We can miss," the boys protested in unison.

"It's only half a day," Derrick said. "A bunch of kids won't even be there. Ellen Michaels left Saturday to go visit her grandmother in Alabama for Christmas."

"You have practice for the church Christmas pageant right after school lets out. Mrs. Evans is counting on you."

Becky knew that missing school in the morning wouldn't be a problem. They would have been out all week had they not lost so many days during hurricane season.

They'd been lucky and hadn't received anything but strong winds and excessive rain from two separate storms that had come ashore to the west of them, but if the school board erred, it was always on the side of caution.

Still, if Nick was seriously hurt, the hospital would be no place for the boys. And if he wasn't, he'd be too preoccupied with getting back in the game to notice.

"You can call Daddy later when he's feeling better."

"But you're going to go to Dallas, aren't you, Momma? Daddy's gonna need somebody there with him."

"I can fly you up in the Cessna," Langston said, offering his private jet. He'd done that before when Nick had been hurt, once even all the way to Green Bay.

But that was when she and Nick were at least making a stab at the marriage. Things had become really strained between them since the divorce proceedings had officially begun. She doubted he'd want her there now.

"Thanks," she said, "but I'm sure Nick's in good hands."

"Maybe you should hold off on that decision until after you've talked to him," her mother said.

"Right," Bart said. "They'll know a lot more after he's X-rayed." The others in the room nodded in agreement.

Becky left the room when the game got back underway. Anxiety had turned to acid in her stomach, and she felt nauseous as she climbed the stairs and went to her private quarters on the second floor of the big house.

Too bad she couldn't cut off her emotions the way a divorce cut off a marriage, but love had a way of hanging on long after it served any useful purpose. Nick would always be the father of her children, but hopefully one day her love for him would be just a memory.

But she wouldn't go to Nick, not unless he asked her to, and she was almost certain that wasn't going to happen. They'd both crossed a line when the divorce papers had been filed. From now on, the only bond between them was their sons.

BECKY CALLED THE hospital twice during the hours immediately following Nick's injury. Once he'd still been in the emergency room. The second time he'd been having X-rays. The only real information she'd received was that he had regained movement in his arms and legs.

Her anxiety level had eased considerably with that bit of news, as had everyone else's in the family. The boys still wanted to talk to him, but she'd waited until they were getting ready for bed before trying to reach him again.

Hopefully by now the doctors would have finished with the required tests and Nick would feel like talking to them. Regardless, Nick would play down the pain when talking to her and especially when talking to the boys.

That was his way. Say the right things. Keep his true feelings and worries inside him. It was a considerate trait in a father. It was a cop-out for a husband.

And bitterness stunk in a wife. It was time she accepted things the way they were and moved past the resentment.

"Can you connect me to the room of Nick Ridgely?" she asked when the hospital operator answered.

"He's only taking calls from family members at this time. I've been told to tell all other callers that he is resting comfortably and has recovered full movement in his arms and legs."

Becky had expected that. No doubt the hospital was being bombarded with calls from reporters. "This is his wife."

"Please wait while I put you through to his room, Mrs. Ridgely."

A female voice answered, likely a nurse. "Nick Ridgely's room. If this is a reporter, shame on you for disturbing him."

"This is Becky Ridgely. I'm calling to check on my husband."

"Oops, sorry. It's just that the reporters keep getting through. You don't know how persistent they can be."

Actually, she did. "Is Nick able to talk?"

"He can, but the doctor wants him to stay quiet. I can give him a message."

"I was hoping he could say a word to his sons. They're really worried about him, and I'm not sure they'll sleep well unless he tells them he's okay."

"He isn't okay. His arms are burning like crazy."

This was definitely not a nurse. "To whom am I speaking?"

"Brianna Campbell."

The name hit like a quick slap to the face. He could have waited until the divorce was final to play hot bachelor. If not for her, then for David and Derrick.

"Do you want to leave a message?"

"Yes, tell Nick he can…" She took a quick breath and swallowed her anger as David returned from the bathroom where he'd been brushing his teeth. "No message." Saved from sounding like a jealous wench by the timely appearance of her son.

"Okay, I'll just tell Nick you called, Mrs. Ridgely."

She heard Nick's garbled protest in the background.

"Wait. He's insisting I hand him the phone."

Nice of him to bother.

"Becky."

Her name was slurred—no doubt from pain meds. Derrick had joined them as well now, and both boys had climbed into their twin beds.

"The boys are worried about you."

"Yeah. I knew they would be. I was just waiting to call until I was thinking and talking a bit straighter. Were they watching the game?"

"They always watch your games, Nick."

"Good boys. I miss them."

So he always said, but she wasn't going there with him right now. "How are you?"

"I have the feeling back in my arms and legs. They burned like they were on fire for a bit, but they're better now. The E.R. doc said that was the neurons firing back up so I figure that's a good sign."

"Is there a diagnosis?"

"They think I have a spinal cord contusion. They make it sound serious, but you know doctors. They like complications and two-dollar terms no one else can understand. I'll be fine."

He didn't sound it. He was talking so slowly she could have read the newspaper between sentences. "Do you feel like saying good-night to David and Derrick?"

"Sure. Put them on. I need some cheering up."

*That's what she thought Brianna was for.* She put the boys on speakerphone so they could both talk at once. Nick made light of the injury, like she'd known he would, and started joking with the boys as if this was just a regular Sunday night post-game chat.

He loved his sons. He even loved her in his own way. It just wasn't enough. She backed from the room as an ache the size of Texas settled in her heart.

Morning came early at Jack's Bluff Ranch, and the sun was still below the horizon when Becky climbed from her bed. She'd had very little sleep, and her emotions were running on empty. Still she managed a smile as she padded into her sons' room to get them up and ready for school.

"Okay, sleepyheads, time to rock and roll."

"Already?" Derrick groaned and buried his head in his pillow.

David rubbed his eyes with his fists and yawned widely as he kicked off his covers. "How come you always say time to rock and roll when we're just going to school?"

"Tradition. That's what your grandma used to say to me."

"Grandma said that?"

"Yes, she did. "Now up and at 'em. She said that, too. And wear something warm. It's about twenty degrees colder than yesterday."

"I wish it would snow," Derrick said as he rummaged through the top drawer of his chest and came up with a red-and-white-striped rugby shirt.

"It never snows in Colts Run Cross," David said.

"Not never, but rarely," Becky agreed. But a cold front did occasionally reach this far south. Today the high would only be in the mid-forties with a chance of thundershowers.

"Have you talked to Daddy this morning?" Derrick asked.

"No, and I don't think we should bother him with phone calls this early. Now get dressed, and I'll see you at breakfast."

Juanita was already at work in the kitchen and had been for over a half hour. Becky had heard the family cook drive up. She'd heard every sound since about 3:00 a.m. when she'd woken to a ridiculous nightmare about Nick's getting hit so hard his helmet had flown off—with his head inside it.

Crazy, but anxiety had always sabotaged her dreams with weird and frightening images. Some people smoked cigarettes or drank or got hives when they were worried. She had nightmares. Over the last ten years, Nick had starred in about ninety-nine percent of them.

Juanita was sliding thick slices of bacon into a large skillet when Becky strode into the kitchen in her pink sweats and fuzzy slippers and poured herself a bracing cup of hot coffee.

The usually jovial Juanita stopped the task and stared soulfully at Becky. "I'm sorry to hear about Nick."

"Thanks." She hoped she would let it go at that.

"I brought the newspaper in. Nick's picture is on the front page."

The front page and no doubt all the morning newscasts, as well. Nick would be the main topic of conversation at half the breakfast tables in Texas this morning.

"The article said he may be out for the rest of the season," Juanita said.

"The rest of the season could be only a game or two depending on whether or not Dallas wins its play-off games, but I don't think anyone knows how long Nick will be on injured reserve."

"I'm sure the boys are upset."

"They talked to him last night, and he assured them he was fine. So I'd appreciate if you didn't mention the article in the paper. They need to go to school and concentrate on their studies."

"Kids at school will talk," Juanita said. "Maybe it would be best if you show them the article and prepare them."

Becky sighed. "You're right. I should have thought of that myself."

Juanita had been with them so long that she seemed like an extension of the family. She fit right in with the

Collingsworth clan, none of whom had ever strayed far from Colts Run Cross.

And if Juanita had been helpful before, she'd been a godsend since Becky's mother, Lenora, had started filling in as CEO for Becky's grandfather Jeremiah after his stroke. Thankfully he was back in the office a few days a week now, and Lenora was completing some projects she'd started and easing her way out of the job that would eventually go to Langston. As Jeremiah said, he had oil in his blood.

Jack's Bluff was the second largest ranch in Texas. Becky's brothers Bart and Matt managed the ranch, and both had their own houses on the spread where they lived with their wives.

Her youngest brother, Zach, had recently surprised them all by falling madly in love with a new neighbor, marrying and also taking his first real job. He was now a deputy, in training for the county's new special crimes unit. He and his wife, Kali, lived on her horse ranch.

And though her oldest brother, Langston, lived with his family in Houston, close to Collingsworth Oil, where he served as president for the company, he had a weekend cabin on the ranch.

Her younger sister, Jaime, who'd never married or apparently given any thought to settling down or taking a serious job, lived in the big house with Becky and the boys, along with Becky's mother, Lenora, and Jeremiah, their grandfather. Jeremiah was currently recovering from a lingering case of the flu that hadn't been deterred by this year's flu shot.

Commune might have been a better term for the conglomeration of inhabitants. Becky hadn't planned to stay forever when she'd left Nick and returned to the ranch, but the ranch had a way of reclaiming its own.

The boys missed their father, but they were happy here. More important, they were safe from the kinds of problems that plagued kids growing up in the city.

Becky took her coffee and walked to the den. Almost impulsively, she reached for the remote and flipped on the TV. She was caught off guard as a picture of Nick with David and Derrick flashed across the screen.

Anger rose in her throat. How dare they put her boys' pictures on TV without her permission? Both she and Nick had always been determined to keep them out of the limelight.

"Nick Ridgely's estranged wife, Becky, is one of the Collingsworths of Collingsworth Oil and Jack's Bluff Ranch. His twin sons, Derrick and David, live on the ranch with their mother. There's been no word from them on Nick's potentially career-ending injury."

She heard the back door open and Bart's voice as he called to Juanita about the terrific odors coming from the kitchen. Becky switched off the TV quickly and joined them in the kitchen. It would be nice to make it through breakfast without a mention of Nick, but she knew that was too much to hope for.

The next best thing was to head her family off at the pass and keep them from upsetting Derrick and David with new doubts about their father's condition. Nick had left things on a positive note, and she planned to keep them there.

The phone rang, and she inwardly grimaced. Where there's a way, there would be a reporter with questions. And once they started, there would be no letup.

Whether she liked it or not, she and her family, especially her sons, were about to be caught in the brutal glare of the public eye.

BULL STARED IN THE mirror as he yanked on his jeans. "Hell of a looker you are to be living like this," he muttered to himself. Without bothering to zip his pants, he padded barefoot across the littered floor of the tiny bedroom and down the short hall to the bathroom.

After he finished in the john, he stumbled sleepily to the kitchen, pushed last night's leftovers out of his way and started a pot of coffee. This was a piss-poor way to live but still better than that crummy halfway house he'd been stuck in until last week.

And the price was right. Free, unless you counted the food he donated to the roaches and rats that homesteaded here. The cabin had been in his family for years, but he was only passing through until he came up with a plan to get enough money to start over in Mexico.

His parole officer expected him to get a job. Yeah, right. Everyone was just jumping for joy at the chance to hire a man fresh out of prison for stabbing a pregnant woman while in the throes of road rage. No matter that she deserved it.

He stamped his feet to get his blood moving and fight the chill. The cabin was without any heat except what he could get from turning on the oven, and he didn't have the propane to waste on that. The only reason he had electricity was because he'd worked for the power company in his earlier life just long enough to learn how to connect to the current and steal the watts he needed.

Once the coffee was brewing, he started the daily search for the remote. If he didn't know better, he'd swear the rats hid it every night while he was sleeping. This time it turned up under the blanket he'd huddled under to watch the late show last night.

The TV came to life just as the local station broke in with a news flash. He turned up the volume to get the full story. It was all about Nick Ridgely. Apparently he'd gotten seriously injured in Sunday's game. Like who gave a damn about Nick Ridgely?

They showed a picture of him with his sons. Cute kids. But then they would be. Nick was married to Becky Collingsworth. He still had sordid dreams about her in those short little skirts and sweaters that showed off her perky breasts.

But the bitch had never given him the time of day. The announcer referred to her as Nick's estranged wife. Apparently she'd dumped him. Or maybe he'd dumped her. Either way they were both fixed for life, lived like Texas royalty with money to burn while he lived in this dump. The little money he'd stashed away before prison was nearly gone.

No cash. No job. Nothing but a parole officer who kept him pinned down like a tiger in a cage.

Bull's muscles tightened as perverted possibilities skittered through his mind. He went back to the kitchen for coffee, took a long sip and cursed himself silently for even considering doing something that could land him right back in prison.

Still the thoughts persisted and started taking definite shape as the image of Nick Ridgely's twin sons seared into his mind.

# Chapter Two

"Too bad about your dad."

"Yeah, man. Tough."

Derrick joined the boys entering the school after recess. "I talked to him last night. He'll be back and better than ever."

"That's not what they said on TV this morning."

David pushed into the line beside them. "Yeah, but they don't know. My mother said they're just making news."

"Well, my daddy said neck injuries are the worst kind. Anyway, I'm sorry he got hurt,"

"Me, too," Butch Kelly added. "I'd be scared to death if it was my dad."

"It's not like he's crippled or anything," David said. "He just took a hit."

Janie Thomas squeezed in beside Derrick. "They put your picture on TV, too. My big sister thinks you're cute."

"Yeah, David, you're cute," Derrick mocked, making his voice sound like a girl.

"You look just like me, you clown. If I'm cute, you are, too."

David followed Derrick to their lockers. They were

side by side because they were assigned in alphabetical order. He shrugged out of his jacket and took off the Dallas Cowboys cap his dad had gotten signed by all his teammates. Derrick had one, too. His was white. David's was blue. He wore it everywhere he went.

"Are you worried about Daddy?" Derrick asked.

"I am now," David admitted. "Do you think he might really be hurt too bad to ever play again?"

"I don't know. I think we should ask Uncle Langston to fly us to Dallas to check on him."

"Momma said we couldn't go."

"She said we couldn't miss school, but he could fly us up there at noon, and we could be home by bedtime, like he did when he took us to watch Daddy play the Giants back in October."

David shrugged. "Yeah. Maybe, but I bet Momma's still going to say no."

"We ought to call Uncle Langston. He might talk her into it."

"We'd miss practicing for the pageant."

"So what?" Derrick scoffed. "How much practice does it take to be a shepherd?"

"I'm the little drummer boy."

"Big deal. You just follow the music. I say we call him. The worse thing he can do is say no."

"The office won't let us use the phone unless it's an emergency."

"Our daddy might be hurt bad," Derrick said. "That's an emergency."

"You're right. Let's go call Uncle Langston now. Maybe he'll check us out early, and we won't have to do math."

"I like that plan. I hate multiplication. It's stupid to

do all that work when you can just punch it in the calculator and get the answer right away."

The boys went straight to the office. The good news was that Mrs. Gravits, who worked behind the desk, let them use the phone to call their uncle. The bad news was that Langston wasn't in.

They left a message with his secretary saying they really needed to fly to Dallas today.

BECKY DROVE UP to the church ten minutes before the scheduled time for practice to end. Several mothers were already waiting, parked in the back lot nearest the educational building. Her friend Mary Jo McFee waved from her car. Becky waved back.

Normally she would have walked over and spent the ten minutes of waiting time chatting, but she knew that conversation today with anyone would mean answering questions about Nick, and she wasn't up to that.

As it was, the phone at the big house had rung almost constantly since breakfast, and Matt had wranglers guarding the gate to keep the media vultures off ranch property. A couple of photographers had almost gotten to the house before they were turned back.

Becky leaned back and tried to relax before she faced her energetic sons, who'd no doubt have new questions of their own about their father. Five minutes later, a couple of girls came out of the church. Mary Jo's daughter was one of them.

A couple of boys came next, and less than a minute later, the rest of the kids came pouring out the door. Some ran to waiting cars; the ones who lived nearby started walking away in small groups.

Two boys climbed on the low retaining wall between

the church and the parking lot. A couple of girls pulled books from their book bags and started reading. But there was no sign of David and Derrick.

Becky waited as a steady group of cars arrived to pick up the waiting children. Her cell phone rang just as the last kid left in a black pickup truck.

She checked the ID and decided not to answer when she didn't recognize the caller. Probably yet another reporter, though she had no idea how they kept getting her cell phone number.

She dropped the phone into the compartment between the front seats, her impatience growing thin. Any other day, her sons would have been the first ones out.

The slight irritation turned to mild apprehension when Rachel Evans, the church's part-time youth coordinator, stepped out the door and started walking toward the only other car in the parking lot. Rachel was in charge of the practice and never left until all the children had been picked up.

Rachel noticed Becky and changed direction, walking toward her white Mercedes. Becky lowered her window.

"I'm sorry to hear about Nick," Rachel said. "I guess the boys were too upset to come for practice, not that I blame them."

Becky's apprehension swelled. "Weren't they here?"

"No. Some of the boys said they were flying to Dallas to see their father."

"There must be some mistake. The boys were supposed to be here. Why did their friends think they were going to Dallas?"

"They said that their uncle Langston had picked them

up and was taking them in his private jet. In fact, Eddie Mason said he saw them getting into their uncle's car."

Langston would never pick up the boys at school without letting her know, much less fly them to Dallas. But maybe he'd tried to get in touch with her and kept getting a busy signal. Maybe he'd left a message and she hadn't gotten it. Maybe...

Rachel was staring at her, probably thinking she was a very incompetent mother not to know where her sons were. "I'll give Langston a call."

Rachel nodded. "I'm sure you'll find this is all just some kind of miscommunication. It frequently happens when everyone is stressed."

Becky nodded as Rachel walked away, no doubt in a hurry to pick up her own toddler daughter from day care. Becky's pulse rate was climbing steadily as she picked up her phone and punched in Langston's private number. She'd about given up hope of his answering when she heard his hello.

"Where are you, Langston?"

"In the office. Why? What's up?"

"It's the boys. Are they with you?"

"No, why would you think they were?"

"I'm at the church to pick them up from pageant practice, but they're not here."

"Maybe they caught a ride home with someone else."

"No, I just talked to Rachel Evans. She said they never showed up."

"Maybe they forgot about practice and got on the school bus."

"If they had, they would have been home before I left to pick them up. Rachel Evans said that some of the boys at practice mentioned that you were flying David and Derrick to Dallas."

"No. I had a message from David asking me to fly them up there, but I only got it about twenty minutes ago. I was in a meeting all day."

The apprehension took full hold now, and Becky started shaking so hard she could barely hold on to the phone. "If you didn't pick them up, who did?"

"Not mother. She's still here at the office. Did you talk to Bart and Matt—or even Zach?"

"No, but they never pick up the boys unless I ask them to. I'm scared, Langston."

"Try to stay calm, Becky. I'm sure they're fine and this is all a harmless mix-up. Call the ranch. See if they're there."

"And if they're not?"

"Then call Zach. Have him meet you at the church, and don't do anything until he gets there. In the meantime, let me know if you hear anything."

Hot tears welled in the back of Becky's eyes, but she willed them to stay there.

Becky called the big house first, just in case the boys had caught a ride back to the ranch. Juanita was the only one there, and just as Becky had feared, the boys weren't home. She hung up quickly and then punched in Zach's number. He was a deputy now, he'd know what to do. He didn't pick up, but she left a frantic message for him to return her call at once.

Her phone rang again, the jangle of it crackling along her frazzled nerves. This time it was Nick. He was the last person she wanted to talk to now. Still, she took the call.

"Becky, it's Nick," he said, identifying himself as if

she wouldn't recognize his voice after a decade of marriage. "Where are the boys?"

She heard the panic in his voice and knew he'd heard. "Did Langston call you?"

"I haven't talked to Langston, but this is very important, Becky. Do you know where the boys are? Are they with you?"

Her blood turned to ice. "What's going on, Nick?"

"Are the boys with you?" he asked again with new urgency in his voice.

"No. I'm at the church. I came to pick them up after their practice for the Christmas pageant, but they're not here. They never showed up."

Nick let loose with a string of muttered curses. "Are you by yourself?"

"Yes, but if you have anything to say, just…"

"I got a phone call a few minutes ago. It was from a man claiming he has the boys with him."

"Who?"

"I don't know. All he said was that he'd call back and that I'd best be ready to deal. I think they've been abducted."

No. Her sons couldn't be kidnapped. This couldn't be happening. She couldn't think, couldn't function. Couldn't breathe.

"We have to find them, Nick."

"We will. Just don't fall apart on me, Becky. We can't make any mistakes."

But she was falling apart, more with every agonizing heartbeat. "They'll be afraid. He might…" God, she couldn't let her mind go there or she'd never get through this. "We have to get them back at once. If it takes every penny either of us has, I don't care. I just want David and Derrick back."

"I'm leaving the hospital now. I'll meet you at Jack's Bluff as soon as I can get there."

"Langston can fly up and get you."

"I can get a chartered flight even quicker. Now go home and stay there in case the man calls you."

She swallowed hard. "I'll call Zach."

"I don't want the sheriff's department in on this, Becky. Not them or any other law enforcement agency, at least until after we talk."

"Don't be ridiculous, Nick. Zach can put out an AMBER Alert and have everyone in the state looking for this madman. And for the record, you don't get to call all the shots, even if it is your fault they're missing."

"Don't start with the blame, Becky, not now." His voice broke. He was hurting and probably as scared as she was.

But this was his fault. He was the one in the news, his name and face all over the TV and every newspaper in the state. And it was him the abductor had called for a ransom.

"The caller said that if we go to the cops, he'll…"

Nick stopped, leaving the sentence unfinished, though the meaning was crystal clear even in Becky's traumatized mind. Nausea hit with a vengeance. She dropped the phone, stepped out of the car and threw up in the parking lot. Weak and unnerved, she finally leaned against the car and gulped in a steadying breath of brisk air.

She would find out who took the twins, and whatever it took, she'd get them back. And heaven help Nick Ridgely if he got in her way.

NICK SHIFTED AGAIN, trying to find a way to get comfortable in the four-man helicopter he'd hired to fly him directly to the ranch's helipad. Pain shot through his neck and shoulders with each vibration, but no matter how bad it got, he wouldn't go back on the pain meds. He needed his mind perfectly clear to deal with the situation.

Becky had been quick to hurl the blame at him for the twins' abduction. He couldn't fault her for that. She'd always been determined to protect David and Derrick from the notoriety his career had brought him. She wanted them to have a normal life with solid values. She wanted them safe from the kind of sick person who had them now.

According to the attending physician who'd protested his leaving the hospital, his career could be over. Strapped with the fears of the moment, even that seemed inconsequential.

The pilot landed the helicopter approximately one hundred yards from the big house. Nick grabbed his quickly packed duffel bag, thanked the pilot and jumped out. He walked quickly, breaking into a jog as he neared the house.

He'd come by helicopter before. Then the boys had been watching, and the minute the chopper landed they'd raced to greet him. Their absence now sucked the breath from his lungs. By the time he reached the house, Bart and Matt were standing on the porch, their faces more drawn than he'd ever seen them.

He hoped Becky had kept this from the police, but he knew she wouldn't keep it from her family. Nor would he have wanted that. The Collingsworth brothers, the fearsome four as he'd called them when he'd first started dating Becky, were a powerful squad, and he'd be glad to have them on his side.

He put out his hand to shake Matt's as he stepped on the wide front porch, and then his gaze settled on Becky. She was standing just inside the door, her silhouette backlit by the huge, rustic chandelier that dominated the foyer. She looked far more fragile than the last time he'd seen her, the day she'd told him she was through with being his wife.

He ached to take her in his arms, needed that closeness now more than he'd ever needed it before. Her words of blame shot through his mind, and he held back. Rejection from her might annihilate the tenuous hold he had on his own emotions.

"Glad you made it so quickly," Matt said, his voice level and his handshake firm, though the drawn look to his face and the jut of his jaw were clear indicators of his apprehension.

Bart clapped Nick's shoulder. "Have you heard any more from the abductor?"

"Not a word."

"The family's waiting inside," Matt said. "We should join them."

Nick nodded. Becky had left the door by the time they entered. He followed Bart and Matt into the huge den. The family Collingsworth had gathered en masse—except for Langston's daughter, Gina, and the ill Jeremiah—filling the comfortable sofas and chairs.

Becky was standing near the hearth, and the heat from the blaze in the fireplace flushed her face. Her arms were pulled tight across her chest as if she were holding herself together. She looked at him questioningly, and his stomach rolled with a million unfamiliar emotions.

"He hasn't called back," he said, answering her unspoken question.

She started to shake, and he went to her, steadying her in the crook of his arm until she regrouped and pulled away.

Zach stood. It was the first time Nick had seen him in his khaki deputy's uniform, and he was struck with the added maturity the attire provided.

Zach propped a booted foot on the hearth. "We need an action plan."

"I made a fresh pot of coffee," Bart's wife, Jaclyn, said. "I'll get it."

Langston's wife, Trish, handed their six-month-old son, Randy, off to his dad. "I'll help."

"This is what I've pieced together so far," Zach said. "Eddie Mason said that he saw the boys get into a car right after school let out, apparently when they were walking to the church."

"Has anyone talked to Eddie?" Langston asked.

"Not yet. At this point I'm following Nick's instructions to hold off, but I think it's imperative that we get a description of the car."

"I agree," Matt's wife, Shelly, said. "That information could be critical. So is speed in getting the search under way. That's one thing I definitely learned while with the CIA."

Nick's cell phone rang. The room grew deathly quiet. He checked the caller ID. Unavailable. His hands were clammy as he punched the button to take the call.

"Just listen. No questions."

His gut hardened to a painful knot. There was no mistaking the abductor's voice.

# Chapter Three

"Here's the deal. Five million in small denominations, unmarked, and a flight into Mexico on the Collingsworths' private jet."

All doable, though it surprised Nick for the man to mention the private jet. It made him wonder if the man could live in Colts Run Cross. "Before I agree to anything, I want to talk to my sons."

"No can do."

Nick's body flexed involuntarily. "Why not?"

"They're not with me at the moment."

Dread kicked inside him, but it had fury for company. "Either I talk to the boys and know they're safe, or there will be no deal of any kind."

"You're not calling the plays, Ridgely."

"Put the boys on the phone, or I call in the FBI right now." It was a bluff at this point, but he certainly hadn't ruled out that option. His threat was met with silence, a match for the still, breathless tension that surrounded him.

"Screw yourself." The man's voice reverberated with anger.

Nick waited. Angry or not, if the boys were alive and safe, the guy wouldn't blow this deal by refusing to let him talk to them—not if he was sane. And heaven help them if he wasn't. There would be no way of predicting the behavior of a crazy man.

Becky had moved to his side, standing so close she could probably hear the hammering of his heart. She didn't touch him, but somehow it made him stronger just to have her near.

"I'll call you back in a half hour." He broke the connection before Nick could respond.

Nick hadn't realized until that moment how tightly he'd been holding on to the phone, as if it were a tenuous tether to his sons. He walked to the window and stared out at the wintry view of bare branches mixed with the green needles of the towering pines, keenly aware that everyone in the room was watching and judging his actions.

Before his marriage had hit the rocks, he'd considered himself as an integral part of the close-knit Collingsworth clan. On the last few visits, the tensions between him and Becky had left him feeling as if he were hovering on the outer rim.

Today all he felt was relief that he was among people who loved his sons and whom he knew would put their lives on the line in a second to save them. Still, he was the father. The final responsibility rested with him.

Trish and Jaclyn returned with the coffee. He waited until they'd served it before he delivered the abductor's message—word for word—or as close as he could remember them. No one interrupted, not even Becky, though she seemed to grow more distraught at every syllable he uttered.

She dropped to the sofa next to her mother. Lenora

reached over and took her daughter's hands, cradling them in hers.

"I'm really uneasy with a no-cops policy," Langston said. "There's a lot of knowledge about situations like this that we're not tapping into. I could call Aidan Jefferies. This is out of his jurisdiction, but he's a hell of a homicide detective, and I know he's had experience with abductions as well."

"I think we should let the sheriff's department handle this," Zach said. "We can put out an AMBER Alert, question anyone who may have seen the boys get into the abductor's car and start investigating any child molesters presently living in the area."

Nick's insides coated in acid at the mention of child molesters, though he'd already thought the same. But his gut feeling led him in another direction. "It seems likely that the abduction was a spur-of-the-moment decision spawned by the media attention yesterday, maybe someone desperate for cash."

"That makes sense," Bart agreed. "The man probably saw the boys' picture on TV."

"No sane person would let a picture of Nick and the twins lead them to kidnapping," Matt said.

Nick shoved his hands into his pockets. "That's my concern and the reason I hate to blow off his demand that we not bring in the authorities. The guy could be a mental case tottering on the edge."

"How will the abductor know if you talk to the cops?" Jaime asked. "I mean as long as they don't come roaring out here in squad cars or show up at the door in uniform."

"If we bring in law enforcement, the kidnapping

could get leaked to the media," Nick said. "I don't think we can risk that—at least not yet."

Lenora leaned forward. "But surely it wouldn't hurt for Zach to do some unofficial investigating."

Nick was amazed at how well his mother-in-law was holding up under this. He knew how much she loved David and Derrick, yet she had a quiet strength about her that he envied. Thank God she was here for Becky since his wife didn't seem to want any comfort or reassurance from him.

"I could fly under the radar," Zach answered, "but we've got to agree on what we're doing here."

"I say pay him off, get the boys back and then we hunt the bastard down," Matt said.

"I'd like to see the FBI brought in," Langston countered. "I have connections. I can make a call right now and have someone come out here from the agency. But Nick and Becky are the ones with the deciding votes. I know I'd make the decisions if it was Gina or little Randy here." He kissed the top of his son's head.

"Where is Gina now?" Jaclyn asked. "Does she know about the abduction?"

"Not yet," Trish said. "She's spending the night in Houston with a girlfriend from her high school who's hosting a Christmas party tonight."

"With a protection service secretly watching her and the house she's in," Langston said. "I'm taking no chances until this crazed abductor is apprehended."

"I curse myself a hundred times an hour for not thinking to do that," Nick said.

Jaime walked over and placed a hand on Nick's arm. "Don't blame yourself for this. How could you possibly have foreseen something so bizarre?"

Jaime was Zach's twin sister. She was the party girl, but Nick had always suspected she had a lot more depth to her than she let on.

"Would you all just stop talking?" Becky said. Her voice broke, and her whole body began to shake. "My boys are missing, and I want them back. I want them home and in their beds. I want…" Her ranting and shudders dissolved into sobs.

Nick could stand it no longer. He crossed the room and dropped to the sofa beside her. He wound an arm around her shoulders, hoping she wouldn't push him away.

Her head fell to his chest. "Get them back, Nick. Just get them back."

"I will." It was a promise he'd keep or die trying.

Lenora got up from her seat on the other side of Becky. "I think we should give Nick and Becky some time alone."

"Sure," Zach said, "but remember that every second counts in a kidnapping."

Nick had never been more aware of anything in his life.

BECKY FELT AS IF she were suspended in time, stuck in the horrifying moment when Nick had first told her the boys had been abducted. She pulled away from Nick and tried desperately to regain a semblance of control as the others filed from the room. "I can't stand doing nothing, Nick. I need to know that someone is out there looking for David and Derrick."

"The abductor was adamant that we not go to the police."

"And in the meantime, what about my sons? What's happening to them?"

"The kidnapper wants money, Becky. He's made that clear almost from the second he took them. There's no reason for him to hurt them as long as we cooperate."

"Since when do you know so much about kidnappers? Since when do you know about anything except football?"

"Please don't do this, Becky. It won't help us to tear each other down."

His gaze sought out hers, and she turned away, unable to deal with his pain when hers was so intense.

"I know I'm not all that good with reading people," he said, "but I'm convinced this was a spur-of-the-moment decision with the kidnapper. My guess is he's desperate for money. And desperate men commit irrational acts when pushed against the wall. That's why I don't want to push. I just want to give him the money and bring the boys home."

"And you really think you can pull this off without David and Derrick getting hurt?"

"I think working without the cops is our best chance of doing that."

Nick's face was drawn into hard lines that made him look much older than his thirty-two years. It was odd that she'd never thought of him as aging, though she was keenly aware of it in herself. He was constantly in training, keeping up his speed, agility and strength with the rigorous exercise routine that had kept him at the top of his game.

His boyish good looks and charm had come to him naturally and required nothing but his presence to make them work. But even those were lost tonight in the torment that haunted his eyes.

"If he puts the boys on the phone, I want to talk to them," she said.

"I don't know how much time he'll give us with them."

"Then put the phone on speaker."

"He'll be able to tell and will probably think I have a cop listening in."

She knew he was right, and yet the frustration started swelling in her chest again until it felt like her heart might burst from the pressure. "Are you certain you don't know the abductor, Nick, or at least have some idea who he is?"

"Of course not. Why would you think that?"

Actually, she had no idea where that idea had come from, but now that she'd voiced it, it wasn't all that farfetched. The man had contacted Nick on his cell phone. He'd had to get that number from somewhere.

And he'd known where the boys went to school. She was certain the morning newscast hadn't mentioned that and was pretty sure that none of the others would have given out that type of information.

"Was the voice disguised?"

"I don't think so."

"Did you get any feel for the man's age?"

"No. He's not a kid, but beyond that, it's impossible to say. He tries to sound tough, but his tone wavers at times. So does the timbre, as if he's getting overly excited or nervous and doesn't want me to know it. That's another reason I think he really just wants to get the money and get out. If we convince him we'll cooperate with him fully, I think this could be over in a matter of hours."

She ached to believe he was right. "Okay, Nick. I'll agree to holding off on calling the police or the FBI until he calls again. But if we don't talk to the boys, or if he's hurt them in any way, the deal is off."

"That's all I'm asking, Becky."

His cell phone rang again. She tensed, and the quick intake of breath was choking. He shook his head, a signal that it wasn't the kidnapper. The disappointment laid a crushing weight on her chest.

"I can't talk now. I'll have to call you back later."

Probably Brianna. Becky dropped to the sofa and lowered her head, cradling it in her hands as a new wave of vertigo left her too off balance to stand.

*Just keep David and Derrick safe,* she prayed silently. If she was granted that, she'd never complain about anything again.

DAVID SUCKED THE ketchup from a greasy French fry before stuffing it into his mouth. He chewed and swallowed. Momma didn't like for him to talk with his mouth full. "I don't think you really are my daddy's friend," he said, as he dipped the next fry.

"See, that's where you're wrong. I talked to your daddy when I was outside unloading the two-by-fours from the top of my car. He's real eager to see you boys."

Derrick wiped a dab of mayonnaise from his chin and sat his half-eaten cheeseburger in the middle of the paper wrapper he'd spread out in front of him. "Then how come you didn't take us to Uncle Langston like you said you were going to do?"

"I told you, there was a little misunderstanding, but

you'll get to see your daddy soon enough, as long as he cooperates."

"What's that supposed to mean?" David drew a circle in his ketchup with his last fry. He always ate his fries first. Then he ate the meat off the burger. He hated buns.

"It means your Dad and I are working out a deal. He comes up with cash. You go home."

The fry slipped from David's finger and plopped into the puddle of ketchup. "Have we been kidnapped?"

"No, no. Nothing like that. This is just a business deal, and you're the collateral."

"How much cash are you trying to get from Daddy?"

"Just a little pocket money. Five million. Do you think you're worth that?"

David choked and had to spit out the fry he was eating. His allowance was only a dollar a week, and when he'd asked for that super skateboard with all the fancy stuff on it the last time they went to Houston, Momma had said it was too expensive. And that didn't cost even a hundred dollars.

He didn't figure anybody had five million dollars except the Queen of England and maybe that woman who wrote the Harry Potter books. He and Derrick were in big trouble. He looked at his twin brother and could tell he was thinking the same thing.

Derrick jumped up from the rickety chair. "I'm getting out of here right now." He sprinted across the room, heading for the back door.

The guy with the dirty denim jacket grabbed his arm and twisted it behind his back until Derrick yelped in pain.

David ran over and kicked the man in his shins. The guy let go of Derrick and grabbed David. "You kick me again, and I'll take a belt to you, you hear me, boy? You won't have an inch of flesh that's not bruised."

"Then don't you hurt my brother."

Surprisingly the guy laughed. "So you two stick together, eh." Then he stopped smiling and his face turned red. "Let's get one thing straight. I don't want to hurt either one of you, but you try anything funny and I'll lock you in the bathroom and leave you there until this deal is done, do you understand?"

"Sure, I understand," Derrick said. "You're a criminal."

"Right, so don't even think of trying to escape. Besides, even if you did escape, you'd be so lost no one would ever find you but the snakes and buzzards."

"You hurt us and my daddy and uncles will kill you," David said. He was trying hard to act like he wasn't afraid, but he was plenty scared. Not for him but for his brother. Derrick didn't like to listen to anybody, and he might do something stupid.

"I'm treating you good, now aren't I?" the man said. "I bought you hamburgers and fries just like you said you wanted."

"Yeah, but you told us we were coming here to meet Uncle Langston so he could fly us to Dallas."

"I lied. Now I'm going to let you talk to your dad, but you have to tell him how good I'm treating you. And that's all you say. Tell him you're fine and that you want to come home. That way he'll close the deal, and this will all be over."

David nodded. He wanted to talk to Daddy. He wanted that real bad. He didn't like being kidnapped, and he didn't like this cabin. He didn't even want to go to visit his dad at the hospital now. He just wanted to go back to Jack's Bluff. But if he made this man mad, he might never get back.

The man took the cell phone from his pocket and started punching the buttons, whistling the same tune he'd been whistling when he'd picked them up in the car. David put his arm around Derrick's shoulders. He'd do what the man said for now, but he'd find a way out of this. Fast. He wasn't missing Christmas.

THIRTY MINUTES LATER, there was still no return call. Nick paced the floor, the pain from his injury shooting up his back and settling like smoldering embers in his shoulders and neck. He welcomed the pain. It was familiar and deserved. He'd willingly taken the risks that playing ball in the NFL carried with it.

His boys didn't deserve this mess they were in and neither did Becky. She might have turned against him, but she'd always been a terrific mother. She was the mainstay for both his sons—steady, constant, yet filled with a love of life.

The same Becky he'd fallen so madly in love with from the first day he'd spotted her jogging across the campus in a pair of tight blue running shorts and showing off the best pair of legs he'd ever seen. He'd asked her out for beers and pizza that very night. To his utter amazement, she'd said yes.

The phone vibrated in his clammy hand an instant before its piercing ring shattered the ominous silence surrounding them. No ID information. His muscles tensed as he took the call.

"Nice that you're so available these days, Nick. Who'd have ever thought you could call a famous Dallas Cowboys receiver and get him on the first ring?"

His grip tightened on the phone. "Are my boys with you?"

"Still don't like talking to people like me, though, do you, Nick Ridgely? Your sons are standing next to me. You can have thirty seconds with each boy."

"Their mother wants to speak to them as well."

"Thirty seconds. You guys divvy it up any way you like. Maybe Brianna Campbell can take a turn, too."

Go to hell! The words hammered against Nick's skull, but never left his mouth. The rotten piece of scum held all the power, and he couldn't risk riling him.

"Daddy."

His heart stopped beating for excruciating moments and then slammed into his chest. "Hi, Derrick. Good to hear your voice."

Becky was at his side in an instant, her eyes begging him for reassurance. He nodded but held on to the phone.

"David and I got kidnapped. Momma's gonna be mad 'cause we got in the car with a stranger, but we thought he was Uncle Langston's friend."

"Mom's not mad, son. Are you okay? Has he hurt you?"

"Not really. He didn't buy the kind of hamburgers we like, though, and he doesn't have much of a TV. It gets lines in it all the time."

A sorry TV. Nick swallowed hard as relief rushed through him. If that was their biggest complaint, he'd called this right. The guy wasn't a child molester. Now Nick just had to get the bastard the money and get the boys back before the situation worsened.

"Momma wants to say hello."

Tears filled Becky's eyes as she reached for the phone. "Are you okay, sweetheart?"

Nick could only hear her side of the conversation, but he could hear the relief in her voice when she realized as he had that their sons were apparently unhurt.

"Daddy and I are taking care of everything. You'll be back with us soon." There was a short pause, and then she whispered "I love you" and was apparently handed off to David.

"No, David, I'm not mad. I just want you home with me. Daddy's fine. He's here at the ranch. You'll see both of us soon. Are you warm? Did you get enough to eat? Okay, you can talk to Daddy. I love you."

She handed Nick the phone. His time was almost up with the boys, but now that he knew they were safe, it was the abductor he wanted to talk to. The quicker they made the exchange of his sons for money, the less likely they'd have complications.

"Satisfied?" the man asked after letting Nick have only a sentence or two with David.

"For now, but I mean what I said that you'd best not hurt them."

"Yeah, big guy. I'm doing my part. Now it's time for you to do yours."

"I'm ready."

"I'll give you twenty-four hours to get the cash together. Let's see, that will make it at 4:00 p.m. tomorrow."

"I won't need that long."

"Let's leave it at that for now. And have the plane ready."

"Where do you want to meet?"

"I'll call you in the morning with the details. And, remember, no cops or you'll be very, very sorry."

"I'm doing this your way, but if you hurt my sons, I swear I'll track you down, tear your heart out and feed it to the livestock."

"Just get the money and the plane."

Nick held on to the phone after the connection was broken, staring into the flames and the crackling logs in the big stone fireplace. His boys were safe, but he wouldn't breathe easy until they were back on the ranch.

He told Becky what the abductor had said. She cringed even though there was basically nothing new in the kidnapper's demands.

"And that's all?" she asked. "We just hand over the money and he releases the boys?"

"Apparently."

"Then we don't need twenty-four hours. The bank knows I'm good for the funds even if I don't have that much in totally liquid assets. If that's not good enough, my brothers and mother will sign any documents the bank requires."

"I told him we'd have the ransom sooner, but I'll get the money," Nick said, his tone more adamant than he'd intended.

"This isn't about you, Nick, and I couldn't care less about some silly pride thing you seem to have going. I just want David and Derrick home—and safe."

"Don't you think that's what I want?"

She shrugged and walked away, stopping to stand near the blazing fire. She warmed her hands before turning to meet his gaze.

"I don't know what you want anymore, Nick. Maybe I never did."

"No, I guess maybe you didn't."

And that summed up their ten years of marriage. Nothing could compare with the torment of the abduction, but still knowing he was losing Becky cut straight to the heart. He might deserve this, but he didn't see how.

Bart stepped into the den. "Mother gave Juanita the week off so that she didn't have to explain to her about the kidnapping, but the ladies made sandwiches and warmed soup. Can I get you some?"

"I can't eat," Becky said, "but we've finished up in here. Tell mother I'm going to my room for a while— and that I really need to be alone."

"Sure."

Being alone was the last thing Nick needed. And oddly, the soup sounded good. "I'll join you. I just need a minute to wash up."

"You're holding your neck at a funny angle," Bart said. "You must still be in a lot of pain from that hit you took yesterday."

"Some, but don't talk about it. I figure if I ignore it, it will give up and go away." He didn't believe that for a second, but still he'd leave the pain meds in his duffel bag. He was in the middle of the biggest game of his life, and he had to be completely alert.

DERRICK LAY IN THE twin bed and stared into the blackness. It was so dark he couldn't even see David though he was just a few feet away. There was a window, but the weird guy who'd brought them here had nailed boards over it so they couldn't escape while he was sleeping.

This was all Derrick's fault. He should have known

Uncle Langston wouldn't send someone to get them who looked like this guy. But then he didn't look so different from some of the cowboys who worked at the ranch. Some of them had tattoos, too, and they were good wranglers and nice people. Uncle Nick and Uncle Matt said so.

Only the guy hadn't mentioned Uncle Langston until Derrick did. He just stopped the car and called them by name. Then Derrick had asked him if he was there to take them to the hangar where Uncle Langston kept his jet. He said yes and told them to get in. Derrick had hopped in first.

All his fault, so he had to come up with a plan to get them out of here before this crazy guy started twisting their arms behind their backs again. Grown men weren't supposed to hurt kids.

Christmas was Friday. Their pageant was Christmas Eve. He had to come up with an escape plan fast.

He was smart for a third grader. He made A's, well except in math. He figured math didn't really matter if you were going to be a football player. He'd never once seen his dad working multiplication problems.

They could blindside the kidnapper and knock him out with a skillet. He'd seen that once on a TV show. Or sneak into his room while he was asleep and tie him up with the sheets. Only he and David were locked in the bedroom, and if they tried to break the door down he'd hear them.

But they could…

He closed his eyes and then opened them suddenly as the plan appeared like magic in his mind. He climbed out of the bed in the dark and felt his way to David's bed, sliding his hands across the covers until his fingers brushed his brother's arm.

"David." He kept his voice low but shook him awake. "We don't have to worry about Daddy getting five million dollars. I know how we can escape."

## Chapter Four

As it turned out, getting five million dollars in cash on short notice was more of a problem than any of them had anticipated. Nick had the funds but not in liquid assets. Converting it to cash would incur time that they didn't have.

Finally, it had been Langston who'd arranged the transaction through the business account of Collingsworth Oil. Becky wasn't sure how Langston had explained his need for so much money in small denominations, but apparently he had, or else the bank didn't ask questions of their larger business accounts.

Becky and Nick were on their way into Houston to pick up the money from one of the main branches now. Nick was still in obvious pain from Sunday's injury, so Becky was at the wheel and fighting the noonday traffic. Nick was holding his head at a weird angle and massaging the back of his neck.

"Do you have something to take for the pain?" she asked.

"Back at the ranch, but I'm not taking anything that affects my judgment."

Becky took the freeway exit to the downtown area. The city was decorated for the holidays with huge wreaths on the fronts of buildings and storefronts and holiday displays in all the shop windows. The light changed to red, and she stopped near the corner where a Salvation Army worker was standing by her kettle and ringing a large red bell.

The spirit of the season came crashing down on Becky like blankets of gloom. Ever since the boys were old enough to tear wrapping paper from a present, Christmas had been her favorite time of year. She loved the carols and decorations, the boys' excitement and the traditions.

They always decorated the tree before dinner on Christmas Eve. The entire family took part, but David and Derrick had more fun than anyone even though they spent as much time sneaking fudge from the kitchen as they did hanging ornaments.

Then, as far back as Becky could remember, they'd had hot tamales and Texas chili on Christmas Eve before leaving for the community Christmas pageant at their church. It was the highlight of the evening with even the eggnog, hot chocolate and desserts that followed taking a backseat.

"Derrick has a speaking part in the Christmas pageant, and David plays his drum." She didn't know why she'd blurted that out except that the thought of Christmas without them was unbearable.

"They'll be there for it," Nick said. "The boys will be back with us by tonight."

She wanted desperately to believe that, but the cold, hard knots of doubt wouldn't let go. The light changed again, and she sped through the intersection, eager to get the money in hand.

"I'd like to be here for the pageant," Nick said. "And for Christmas morning, too."

The old resentment surged. "Don't you have a big game in Chicago on Saturday?" Even when he hadn't been cleared to dress out, he'd always traveled with the team.

"I'll miss the game," he said.

"Are you feeling guilty, Nick?"

"I just think it's important that I be here for Christmas this year. Can we just leave it at that?"

She spotted the bank ahead and determinedly forced her bitterness aside. She parked the car in a lot across the street from the bank. Nick paid the attendant while she grabbed the large valises they'd bought for the money and locked the car door. When they left the bank, an armed guard in street clothes would walk them to the car.

"I'll take those," Nick said, joining her and slipping the bags from her arm.

He slung the strap over his left shoulder and linked his right arm with hers. An incredible feeling of déjà vu swept over her. Walking arm in arm with Nick, the valise over his shoulder, a feeling of urgency burned inside both of them.

Like the night they'd rushed to the hospital for the twins to be born. Her water had broken and she'd been propelled into labor with strong contractions that came much faster than normal. Nick had flown into action, trying to be tough but clearly as frightened as she was. But he'd stayed with her every second.

The image of him holding both the boys in his arms minutes after they were born pushed its way into her mind. His smile. His wet eyes. The tenderness when he'd kissed her and thanked her for giving him the world. She shivered as the memories took hold.

Nick let his hand slip down to encase hers. "It's going to be okay, baby. This is all going to be okay."

But who was Nick to promise a happy ending?

DAVID WAS CURLED UP in a smelly old chair with stains all over it. He looked like he was asleep, but Derrick saw his eyes move every now and then and figured he was just faking it, probably thinking about Derrick's stupid plan.

It had sounded great in the dark. The kidnapper couldn't watch them every second. He had to go to the bathroom and when he did, they'd raise one of the windows, kick out the screen and make a run for it.

They were fast. Derrick had won the relay race at school field day last year, and David had come in second. The kidnapper wouldn't have a chance to catch them if they had a head start. Sure, they might get lost in the woods, but Derrick wasn't worried about that. Uncle Matt had taken them camping lots of times and taught them all about survival. They'd find their way back to the road and wave down a passing car. Super easy.

Problem was that while they were locked in the bedroom last night, the kidnapper had nailed wood over the rest of the windows. That had made Derrick really mad, but he wasn't giving up. He just needed a better plan. He'd seen all the *Home Alone* movies a bunch of times. If that kid could take care of himself, so could Derrick and David.

In fact he and David could do it better. There were two of them and only one jerky kidnapper. That's why he wasn't really all that afraid. He'd let them out of the bedroom this morning, but the house was sealed tight. The kidnapper had the key to the front door and the back door was nailed shut.

The guy was lying on the lumpy old sofa now, whistling that same weird tune he was always whistling and watching a movie on the old TV that kept fading in and out. It looked like it could be a hundred years old, except their neighbor Billy Mack had told him they didn't have television back then.

Derrick waited for the commercial. The guy always hollered for him to shut up if he talked during the show. An advertisement for Dodge trucks popped up on the screen.

"How come you live out here all by yourself?"

"'Cause I'm not filthy rich like your parents."

"You could get a job and make some money."

"Don't get smart with me, kid."

"I wasn't."

The picture on the screen started rolling, and the man went over to fiddle with the knobs again. When that didn't work, he took the screwdriver from his back pocket and made a few adjustments on the back of the set. The picture steadied. He went back to the sofa and dropped the screwdriver onto the table next to him, beneath a heavy lamp that had scratch marks all over it.

Derrick walked over and propped on the edge of the sofa. He picked up the screwdriver and ran his fingers along the tapered tip. "Did you kidnap us 'cause our daddy's a superstar?"

"Who told you he was a superstar?"

"Nobody, but he is. He's been to the Pro Bowl three times."

"Is that what it takes these days for a kid to like his old man? You gotta be a superstar?"

"No," Derrick said. "You just have to love your kids like you're supposed to. Didn't your daddy love you?"

"Yeah. So much he beat me every time he got drunk and yelled at me when he was sober. Now, shut up. My show's back on."

"What about your mom?" Derrick asked, ignoring the man's comments to shut up.

"What about her?"

"Did she take care of you?"

"Yeah, sure, sometimes. When she was around. Enough with the questions. I didn't need nobody when I was a kid and don't need nobody now."

"Then why don't you just let us go?"

The guy didn't answer. But Derrick knew he wasn't going to let them go until he had the money from their parents, and he didn't see how Momma and Daddy would get five million dollars.

Derrick got up and walked to the kitchen though there was nothing in there to eat. They'd finished off the last two burgers for breakfast this morning. That had been hours ago. He wondered what Juanita was cooking for lunch.

He opened the refrigerator and looked at the empty shelves. That's when he heard the yell, a high-pitched shriek that sounded as if someone had their arm torn off at the shoulder. Derrick took off for the living room and then stopped in the doorway staring at the blood pooling on the floor by the couch.

Now he was scared.

"Quick, grab the door key out of his pocket, and get your jacket. We gotta get out of here," David yelled.

Derrick didn't move. He just stared at the kidnapper. The man was sprawled out on the floor behind the television set, blood pouring from a cut on the back of his head. The lamp was lying on the floor next to him, its shade at a cockeyed angle. "What happened?"

"He was tinkering with the TV, and I snuck up on him and hit him with the lamp."

"Do you think he's dead?"

"I don't know. C'mon. We have to get out of here now."

Derrick leaned over the man. He'd seen a dead cow before, but he'd never seen a dead man. It creeped him out, but he reached into the front pocket of the man's trousers and retrieved his key ring.

Derrick wasn't sure which one opened the door, so he tossed the key ring to David. He still wasn't sure if the man was breathing, but he could hear his own heart. It sounded like a banging drum.

David had found the right key and had the door open when Derrick saw the man's hand move. He wasn't dead, just knocked out. And when he came to, he was going to be roaring mad. Time to haul it.

Derrick picked up the screwdriver and grabbed his jacket from the back of a chair. He didn't know why he needed the tool, but it seemed like a good idea to have it. He took off running as fast as he could, finally catching up with David at the edge of the woods. They kept running, tripping over roots and getting hung up in branches and vines.

Derrick's legs started to ache. His chest hurt, too. And he was thirsty. He was glad when David stopped and leaned against a tree trunk.

"Do you think he's chasing us?" Derrick asked when he'd caught his breath enough to talk.

"He thinks he's getting five million dollars for us," David said. "What do you think?"

"Yeah, but you hurt him bad."

"Nah. I knocked him out, but his legs will still work when he comes to. We have to keep moving and try to find a road."

"We should have stolen his cell phone," Derrick said. "Then we could have called Momma or Daddy or 911."

"Yeah, but we didn't. So we gotta keep on the move. I don't want to spend the night in the woods."

"We can do it if we have to." Derrick tried to sound brave since he hadn't done much toward helping them escape. "We've slept under the stars before when we were camping with Uncle Matt."

"We had food then," David said. "And lanterns."

And Uncle Matt, though neither of them mentioned that now. Derrick jumped at a sound like cracking twigs in the distance. And then they heard the man's voice calling their names.

"Keep up with me," David called, and he was off again with Derrick right behind him. "I don't want to have to really hurt that man."

# Chapter Five

The fragrant smell of pine filled the house, just as it had every day since last Saturday when Lenora's sons had helped her drape the mantel and staircase with the fresh cut greenery. Her much-handled nativity was carefully placed along the top of the piano, where they always gathered to sing carols after church on Christmas Eve.

Randolph, Lenora's deceased husband, had spent hours in his workshop, first cutting out and then coating each of the nativity figures with lead-free paint for Langston's first Christmas. The set had been a favorite of all her children from the time they were toddlers and first heard the story of the birth of the baby Jesus. David and Derrick had spent their share of time moving the figures around and playing with the miniature sheep, cattle and camels as well.

The house was almost the way it had always been mere days before Christmas—except that it was shrouded in anxiety and the season's joviality was hushed by the burden of heavy hearts. Only Jaime was making a stab at normalcy. She was sitting on the floor by the hearth, tape, scissors and rolls of shiny Christmas wrap at her elbow.

Christmas in the Collingsworth family had never

been a time for lavish spending. When her children had been growing up, Lenora and Randolph had insisted that the focus of the season be on love and sharing with those less fortunate.

It was a tradition that had stuck, and instead of rabid shopping that they could well afford, each member of the family always put a lot of thought and frequently a lot of time and effort into their gifts.

Lenora's treats for her family had been carefully selected and wrapped weeks ago, but today she couldn't remember anything she'd bought except the skateboards the boys had picked out and begged for on a recent Houston shopping trip.

The front door to the house opened, and Lenora hurried into the hallway. Hopefully this time it would be Becky and Nick returning with the ransom money and not some pushy reporter who'd managed to bypass the guards at the gate.

Earlier today, one had cut down part of the fence to get on the property. Jim Bob had spotted him and sent him packing quickly enough. Like Matt said, if all their wranglers were as dependable as Jim Bob, running the ranch would be play.

"The money's in hand," Nick called, holding up a large valise. "Now all we need is that phone call."

"Then you haven't heard from the abductor today?"

"Not a word," Becky said, the weight of the situation dragging her voice the way it pulled at her face and painted dark circles beneath her eyes.

"I'll fix you a plate," Lenora said. "Trish and Jaclyn made chicken pasta and a salad for lunch."

Becky shook her head. "None for me. We stopped for lunch in Houston."

"Which she ate two bites of," Nick said.

He was sick over the boys but obviously worried about Becky as well. He was a good man, cocky and fun loving and sometimes she thought he had a football for a heart, but her sons liked Nick and that said a lot about his character. Lenora had always been sure he and Becky would work out their differences and make their marriage work.

But Becky was stubborn, always had been, and once she made up her mind about something, she developed a severe case of tunnel vision that never let her see another side.

She was a loving mother, though, generous to a fault. And unlike Jaime, she was seemingly unaware of her beauty or the fact that men were instantly attracted to her, as much for her grace and intellect as her stunning looks.

But stubborn, nonetheless. She'd no doubt inherited that trait from her grandfather. Jeremiah was the most hardheaded man Lenora had ever seen in her life. She'd be hard pressed to explain why everyone loved him. They just did. So did she.

Lenora and Nick followed Becky into the den.

Becky stopped next to the stack of wrapped gifts. "What are you doing?"

Jaime stuck a large red bow to a package. "Wrapping presents."

"How can you?" Becky's voice shook with unchecked emotion. "How can you go on like nothing's wrong when David and Derrick are in the hands of some madman?"

Jaime pulled a strip of tape from the dispenser. "Because I won't let myself believe that they're not going to walk though that door tonight with you and Nick, safe and excited to be home. When they do, they'll expect presents to shake and try to guess what's inside."

"But what if you're wrong? What if they don't come home tonight? What if…" Becky exploded, kicking one of the presents. It skidded across the thick rug and onto the wooden floor before thudding against the wall.

Jaime jumped up, dropping the roll of ribbon she'd just picked up as she pulled her sister into her arms. "Oh, Becky, you have to have faith that the boys are safe. We all do. We *have* to believe."

Both sisters were in tears now, holding on to each other while the fire crackled in the huge stone fireplace and streams of red satin entangled their feet. Tears burned at the back of Lenora's eyes. Jaime never ceased to amaze her. She'd never loved either daughter more.

NICK BACKED OUT of the den and went to the kitchen to get a cup of coffee though he was already so jumpy he could barely sit in one place for over five minutes. That and the ache in his neck and shoulders had made the ride back to the ranch pure torture.

There was a plate of homemade peanut butter cookies next to the coffeepot. There were always homemade cookies at Jack's Bluff. Juanita kept the freezer stuffed with them.

He picked up one. Still warm. One of his sisters-in-law must have done the baking honors in Juanita's absence. Everyone wanted to help. Everyone needed to keep busy.

He'd married into one terrific family—and then he'd blown it. How had he ever let things between him and Becky get to this point?

Who was he fooling? He'd known from the very beginning he wasn't the man Becky thought he was. She'd seen in him what she wanted to see, loved a man who hadn't really existed. It had just been a matter of time before she saw him for the fake he really was.

If anything, he'd loved Becky too much. He still did. There wasn't a day he didn't miss having her in his life, not a night that he didn't long to have her in his bed and in his arms. He couldn't even imagine making love to another woman.

But he'd never expected to bring this kind of terror into all their lives. If he hadn't gotten hurt... If they hadn't shown the boys' picture on TV... If the boys hadn't had to go to school Monday to make up for those lost hurricane days instead of already being out for the holidays...

So many ifs, but the biggest one now was if he was doing the right thing in not going to the police or trying to bring the FBI in on this. He wanted to believe he was right, but the longer this took, the more the doubts tormented him. What if he was wrong and the man never called back?

He put the cookie to his lips, then pulled his hand away and dropped the morsel into the trash. His stomach was still struggling to digest the ham sandwich he'd forced down at lunch. He was filling a pottery mug with the strong coffee when his cell phone jangled.

The coffee spilled over his fingers as he set the cup down, stuck his hand into his pocket and gripped the phone. He answered without bothering to check the caller ID. "Hello."

"This is Dr. Cambridge's nurse. I'm calling for Nick Ridgely."

Damn. The doctor's office. They'd badger him about getting back to the hospital so that they could finish the tests. The head trainer for the team had already called him about the same thing twice today. He didn't have time for this.

"This is Nick Ridgely, but I'm expecting a very important call and can't tie up my phone right now."

"This is an important call, Mr. Ridgely. The doctor needs to speak with you. Hold on. He's right here."

The seconds Nick waited seemed interminable. His phone line needed to remain open.

"We didn't meet, but I'm one of the staff neurosurgeons at the hospital where you were treated Sunday night. My colleague Dr. Krause asked me to review your records."

"I understand, but I can't talk now. I'll have to call you back later."

The doctor kept talking. "You left the hospital in a hurry."

"There was a family emergency. I signed the AMA form."

"I understand that. Are you still in a lot of pain?"

"Some." To put it mildly. To put it more accurately, the pain was constant, but waiting for a call from the abductor was a thousand times worse.

"I can't stress enough how important it is for you to check back in the hospital, Mr. Ridgely. It's urgent that we get a CAT scan and an MRI."

"Yeah, right. I'll do that one day next week."

"I don't think you understand the seriousness or potential damage you may suffer from your injury."

"Okay, give it to me straight—and fast. What's the worse that can happen?"

"The X-rays indicate that you may have a unilateral locked facet. It's not a common injury even in football, but it happens when the neck is flexed and rotated at the same time. The risk is that the spine may be unstable and can slip. Any sudden movement or bending of your neck could leave you paralyzed."

Nick fought the urge to slam a fist into the wall. He couldn't deal with this now. He had a contusion or whatever the hell the E.R. doc had said the other night. He just needed time for it to heal and he'd be fine. If it was something worse, he'd surely know it.

"Thanks for calling, Dr. Cambridge. I'll come back in for the tests as soon as I can."

It wasn't until the conversation was over and the connection broken that he realized Becky was standing in the doorway to the kitchen watching him. He had no idea how much of the conversation she'd heard.

"What's wrong?" she asked.

He shook his head. "Nothing." He needed to play this cool for her sake, though he felt anything but.

"Who was on the phone?"

"Dr. Cambridge reminding me that he needs to check out my neck in a few days."

"That's all?"

"That's it."

"You're lying, Nick. I heard the apprehension in your voice when you were on the phone, and it's written all over your face now."

"It's no big deal, Becky. I may miss a game or two." He turned his back on her and stamped toward the back door, not bothering to grab a jacket. Had it been freezing he doubted he'd feel the cold. How could he when he was sinking into hell?

Paralysis. A devil of a diagnosis to hold over a man whose sons were in danger. It wasn't like he could just walk away from the kidnapping. He'd be careful. No sudden moves. That was the best he could do.

NICK HAD SHUT HER out again, just like always. Becky had seen his face when he was talking to the doctor. The news had been bad, but instead of sharing with her, he'd stalked out the back door to deal with his problems without her.

It shouldn't matter so much in light of all that was going on. It shouldn't but it did, maybe because of what they were going through.

He expected her to lean on him, but he was not about to let himself need any emotional support from her. Not about to admit that he was upset over some damn football injury that he admitted wasn't serious.

Maybe he found it easier to confide in Brianna.

Anger and bitterness pooled in Becky's stomach until she stormed out the back door and down the steps. When she spotted Nick walking toward the stables, she ran to catch up with him. He turned, saw that it was her footfalls he'd heard and kept walking.

He didn't stop until he reached the railed fence that surrounded the riding arena. He propped his elbows on the top rung and stared straight ahead as if there were something to see.

A gust of wind cut through Becky's thin cotton shirt, and she hugged her arms around her chest as she approached him. Her nerves were raw, her composure diminished to the point she had to hold on to the railing to keep steady. "What was that about?"

"I don't know what you're talking about."

"Your rushing off to brood over your injury instead of telling me what the doctor said."

"I'm not brooding."

"I think you are. All that talk of being here for Christmas with the boys was just your guilt talking, wasn't it? Well, if you think I'm worried about your career while my boys are missing, you're dead wrong."

"The thought never entered my mind. But just for the record, do you actually think I'm *not* going through hell every second David and Derrick are with that lunatic?"

"I don't know what you're feeling, Nick, but whatever it is, I'm sure football and your star performance is involved in it."

She stepped away, realizing she said too much. She let her temper and vulnerability get the better of her.

Nick grabbed her arm and held her, his gaze so intense his dark eyes seemed to be searing into hers. "I won't contest the divorce any longer, Becky. I'll sign whatever you say."

She shivered as he kicked at a clod of dirt before releasing her and walking away. The finality of their relationship had never felt so real. But it was what she wanted. Holding on to a corpse wouldn't bring it back to life.

The analogy sent new chills up her spine to eventually settle deep in her bones. She forced herself to follow Nick back to the house.

The boys' safety was all that mattered, and Nick and his cell phone were her one link to her sons. No matter how she and Nick felt about each other, they had to get through this together.

BULL MUTTERED A new series of curses with every step he made in the growing darkness. His head felt as if it were splitting open and his brains were draining into the huge knot that had formed around the cut on the back of his head.

The blood had matted in his hair, and when he touched the wound, it felt like the sticky mess that had passed for oatmeal in the penitentiary. It gagged him, and he'd thrown up once, though the nausea was probably more from the throbbing pain at the base of his skull than the repulsive feel of his bloody scalp.

He'd never expected Nick's sons would go violent on him. They had to get their nasty streak from their father. Big-shot NFL receiver. No wonder Becky had separated from him.

He stopped and leaned against a tree trunk, gasping for air and trying to get his bearings before he was the one lost in these stinking woods. The image of Becky fixed in his murky mind until he dissolved into a fit of coughing.

He had to find those boys. Nick would never pay off if he couldn't produce them. No money. No flight to Mexico.

Worse, if the kids got free, they'd be able to identify him and he'd end up back in prison. No way he could let that happen. He had to find the vicious little devils before they reached the highway and flagged down a passing motorist.

Just his luck they'd been too smart to head back down the dirt road near the cabin to the highway. If they had, he could have taken his car and easily caught them before they reached help.

But the prints of their tennis shoes had led straight into the woods. He'd been able to track them easily at first, before they'd reached higher, dryer ground. Half the time they'd wandered in larger and larger circles—which meant they couldn't be that far away now.

But it was getting darker, and he'd lost all sight of their trail a good half hour ago.

An owl hooted overhead, claiming his hunting grounds for the night. Well, the dumb bird would have to share it. Something slithered at his feet. It was too cold for snakes to be slinking though the pine straw, but still he tensed as he searched the ground.

He didn't see the escaping creature, but he saw something a whole lot better. A screwdriver. He picked it up and rolled the amber handle around in his hand. It was his, all right, at least it was the one he used to constantly tinker with that piece-of-crap TV.

Apparently the boys had taken it with them when they'd gone on the run. Which meant they'd been in this exact spot, likely minutes ago. His heart began to pound, bringing more pain but still urging him on. It was almost as if he could smell the boys now.

This time when he got them in hand, there would be no more Mr. Nice Guy. He wouldn't be made a fool of twice.

The twenty-four hours were up. Nick would be waiting for his call. He might be the rich, NFL superstar, but there wouldn't be one damn thing he could do but wait.

Besting Nick Ridgely was almost as good a prize as the cash.

## Chapter Six

The twenty-four hour mark came and went with no word from the abductor. By eight-thirty Tuesday night, Becky felt as if every breath took supreme effort and every heartbeat pumped new agony into her veins. Earlier the family den in the big house had been crackling with anticipation and conversation.

Even then every phrase and syllable had sounded forced, brave attempts to keep the mood positive. The family was all still present, but the silence now was like an icy spray that froze the oxygen in the still, heavy air.

They'd done everything the abductor had asked. The ransom was waiting. The plane was ready to go. Langston was planning to fly the plane himself, and Zach would go along as copilot.

But with each tick of the clock, the dread swelled. So did the doubts.

Following Nick's wishes to leave the cops out of this might have been a monumental mistake. Had they put out an instant AMBER Alert, the boys might be home tonight, sleeping in their own beds. No one was blaming him, but she was certain he was second-guessing himself though they'd barely spoken since her blow up this afternoon.

Nick walked to the hearth and propped both hands on the mantel, leaning close even though the earlier blaze had died to glowing embers. His face was drawn, his neck corded from muscles that looked taut enough to break.

Zach walked over to stand beside him. Blackie padded over to Becky and cocked his head to the side; the lab's dark, soulful eyes peered into hers. She patted his head absently, sure that he not only missed his masters but sensed the tension.

Zach put a hand on Nick's shoulder. "I can get the ball rolling with police involvement anytime you say. All you have to do is give me the word."

Nick nodded.

"Another option might be to hire a team of private investigators," Matt said.

"Or we could get a search party organized," Bart added. "There's not a man in the county who wouldn't be out there right now going door to door to see if anyone's seen David and Derrick or knows anything about the abduction."

"And then the media circus would take over," Langston said. "But maybe that would help flush this guy out. I just don't know."

"That's the problem," Nick said. "There's no way to know."

"Why doesn't he call?" Becky lamented out loud, saying what they all were thinking. "If he wants the money, why doesn't he call?" The terror tore at her throat and her voice.

Jaime came over and settled on the arm of her chair, slipping an arm around Becky's shoulders. "He's going to call, sis. He may be rethinking the exchange, but he's going to call."

"You don't know that. Those are just empty words."

Trish walked in with a plate of oatmeal cookies and a bowl of sliced apples. She set them on the coffee table and slid onto the sofa beside Langston.

"Becky and I have to talk," Nick said.

"We'll clear out," Jaime said, "and give you a little privacy."

"No." Becky stood and struggled for a grip on her composure. "All of you stay as long as you want. I need some fresh air. Nick and I can take a walk."

Nick nodded again. "I'm not discounting any of your advice, guys. And I'll tell you this, I don't know of a single person on earth I'd rather have in this with me than the Collingsworth clan. That includes the FBI or any police force in the world."

"But don't rule any of that out," Langston reminded him. "It's not either/or. You can have us and professionals."

Becky paused to give her mother's hand a squeeze as she passed her. "Keep praying," she whispered.

"Always."

This time Becky stopped for a jacket and took a flashlight from the rack by the back door. She didn't wait for Nick, but she heard the crinkle of leather as he pulled on his own jacket and followed her.

She noticed everything, the creaking of the top step when she put her foot on it, the rustle of the wind in the oak trees, the sting of cold air on her cheeks.

It was as if the totality of her being had been crammed into this moment and the decisions they were about to make. Her boys' safe return, their very lives might depend on what she and Nick did in the next few minutes and the next few hours. She wouldn't leave this all to him the way she had earlier.

Nick caught up with her hurried stride and fell in beside her. "I thought we'd hear from the abductor by now. I was sure he just wanted his hands on the money as soon as possible."

"And now you've changed your mind?" she asked, fighting her frustration.

"Not entirely. There's no reason for him not to call us if it's the ransom he wants. He may have met with complications."

"How complicated can it be to make a phone call?"

"He could be driving somewhere to use a public phone or to buy one with limited minutes from the convenience store. He'll want to make sure we can't use the phone to find him before he's ready to close the deal. Maybe he got caught in traffic."

"You think he's just driving around with our boys in the car? How is he keeping them quiet? He might have them drugged them or locked them up in the trunk. Maybe that's why he said they weren't available the first time he called."

Her voice climbed steadily higher. Worse, she wasn't even sure she was making sense, but terrifying possibilities were storming her mind.

"Maybe he's just enjoying his power to keep us on edge," he countered.

"More than he'd enjoy five million dollars in his hand?" No. If this were only about the money, he would have called. They could have delivered it to him tonight. He could be in Mexico. This could all be over.

"We can't just sit here and do nothing, Nick. He

might be taking the boys out of the country or taking them who knows where. The longer we wait, the more difficult it will be to track him down. And…"

The rest of the sentence was swallowed by the growing lump in her throat. Nick put a hand on her shoulder. Her chest constricted painfully at his touch. She needed his strength, needed him. Yet she couldn't let herself lean on him. Reluctantly, she pulled away.

"Does my touch bother you that much, Becky?"

Yes, in ways she couldn't deal with in this situation. "I'm just trying to get through this, Nick. I have to be strong."

"We're in this together."

"I can't very well ignore that, can I, Nick, since you're the one the abductor contacts—or doesn't contact. You're the one making the decisions." The bitterness crept into her voice. She wished it hadn't, but there was too much at risk here to worry about that now.

Nick's cell phone rang. Becky's heart jumped to her throat. Please let it be the abductor. *Please let him be ready to give her back her sons.*

Nick's hello was firm, in control. She held her breath then released a sharp, painful exhale when she heard the agitation in Nick's voice.

Something was wrong. Her legs went weak, but somehow she kept standing, her mind grasping for meaning in every word Nick spoke.

"HELLO, NICKY BOY. I guess you realize by now that there's been a slight delay in our plans."

The cocky bastard. He was enjoying their torment. Nick's teeth ground together and his muscles clenched. "You said five million in small bills and a flight out of the country. I'm ready to meet those demands, so let's get this over and done with."

"Not so fast, champ. The boys are asleep. You don't want me dragging them out in the middle of the night, do you? Besides, I have a couple of things I need to take care of before I tell America *adios*."

"I want my boys, and I want them now. Tell me where to meet you or I go to the cops."

"That would be a major mistake if you want to get them back alive."

"Let me talk to them."

"I told you they're sleeping. I'll have them call you in the morning. We'll talk specifics then. But there is one other thing. I've decided I need a hostage with me on the flight to Mexico. You know, someone to be sure you don't plan any tricks like aborting the flight once you have your sons. I'm thinking having Becky along would be a great insurance plan."

Nick's body went rigid. "My wife is not a bargaining tool."

"Why not? You've already replaced her with Brianna Campbell. You're surely not so selfish as to deny me the pleasure of her company on a short flight."

"Five million. Do you want it or not?"

"You do realize that you're not calling the shots here, Nick. I want Becky on that plane. If there's any funny stuff, she takes a bullet. That way I know you won't have an armed greeting party waiting for me when we land."

"You want a hostage, you can have me. That's my best offer."

"I'll sleep on it and let you know in the morning."

"Let me talk to the boys." The menacing click of the

phone as it disconnected swallowed his demand. Nick stood still, his back ramrod straight, numb to the pain from his injury.

"What's wrong?" Becky demanded.

"Change in plans," he said.

"What kind of change?"

"Let's go to the porch. I talk better when I'm sitting." And he needed a minute to digest the kidnapper's new demand. Not that he'd even consider letting Becky get on a plane with that lunatic, even if she agreed. Their divorce wasn't final yet. She was still his wife and the mother of his sons.

She was still his to protect.

A LITTLE MORE than a half hour later, Nick and Becky sat down at the big oak table in the dining room with the core members of the Collingsworth family around them. The somber mood was foreign to the familiar setting where Nick had joined in many family celebrations and marvelous Sunday brunches.

The room was virtually unchanged from the way it had looked the Sunday morning he and Becky had officially announced their engagement, though it had been almost totally destroyed in the explosion this past summer.

That day the entire family had almost lost their lives for the sin of befriending and trusting the wrong man. Had it not been for the quick thinking of Matt's wife, Shelly, they would have been obliterated, his sons along with them.

If there was any weakness in the Collingsworths, it was their willingness to see the best in people. They'd certainly done that with Nick. Tonight that trust felt like weights pressing into his chest. He'd insisted on laying out the game plan, on going with his instincts. He'd made critical mistakes.

He'd failed the people who needed him most. Not for the first time and the memories that admittance unleashed were attacking him full force.

Langston took the seat at the head of the table. Lenora sat at the other end. Becky sat between him and Zach on one side of the table. Jaime, Bart, Matt and his wife, Shelly, sat opposite them. Jeremiah was still keeping to his room and had not been apprised of the situation. Had the elderly gentleman with the temper of Attila the Hun and the determination of a bull known, Nick was certain he'd have been right there with them.

Becky had specifically requested Shelly's presence. Her CIA experience might be invaluable. The other wives had suggested they not be part of the decision-making process though they were there to help in any way they could. The solidarity of the Collingsworths in crisis was nothing short of astonishing.

Nick was fairly certain the room had never been this quiet before. It was as if all of them were holding their collective breaths waiting to hear what Becky had to say. She'd held up so well on the porch that Nick had feared she was slipping into shock.

That wasn't the case. She was stronger than he'd ever known. Courageous. Determined. And ready to fight. She was a hell of a woman. Always had been. Maybe her strength had been their downfall, though it was definitely helping to hold him together now.

Nick filled the family in with the basics of his latest conversation with the abductor, minus the information about his wanting Becky for a hostage. He hadn't even mentioned that to her. It wasn't an option, so there was no reason to bring it up for discussion.

The family listened without interrupting until he was through, but he could sense the dread imbedding more deeply in their souls as he talked.

"I obviously misjudged the situation," Nick said. "I should have listened to the rest of you in the first place."

"Not necessarily," Shelly offered, the tone of her voice indicating the observation was more than sympathy. "You sensed the man was desperate and acting on impulse after seeing the boys' picture on the news. First instincts are frequently right on target. But that same impulsiveness might also make him edgy after the fact, and he may fear he's walking into a trap, thus his hesitance to make the exchange."

"But wouldn't his being on the edge make him even more dangerous?" Jaime asked. "Wouldn't that be more reason to move on this quickly and with every weapon in the arsenal?"

Shelly nodded. "Especially since we can't accurately judge the man's mental condition. But at the same time, we don't want to do anything to cause him to hurt the boys."

"Which is what might happen if we let the media get hold of this," Becky said. "Nick and I have talked and made the decision that we can't take that risk."

"So what are you saying?" Zach asked. "That you don't want police involvement? If so, I think you're making a big mistake."

"No, we just want to keep this as quiet as possible. We're open to suggestions."

Zach nodded. "At the very least, we need an APB out to all the law enforcement officers in at least a three-state area to be on the lookout for David and Derrick. And we need to contact the border patrol."

"I'd say that's top priority," Matt said. "We can't let him take the boys into Mexico."

They were talking prevention, but for all they knew, the man could have crossed that border with David and Derrick hours ago. That, too, would be Nick's fault. No one said it, but they all knew it.

"With that much law enforcement involved, word of the abduction is going to leak to the media," Langston said.

"Not necessarily," Zach said. "At least not before we can track the boys down. Everyone takes crime involving kids seriously. Besides, I think it's a risk we have to take."

"And we need a description of that car that Eddie Mason saw them getting into," Lenora said.

"I've got you covered there," Zach said.

"Black Oldsmobile sedan. An old one, an eighties model he thought. Dent in back right fender with patch of rust showing through. No hubcaps."

"When did you talk to Eddie Mason?" Nick asked. "I thought we'd agreed you wouldn't."

"I didn't. There are more subtle ways to get information. I just mentioned to the crossing guard that someone had reported seeing a group of teenagers speeding though the area on Monday about the time school let out and asked if he'd seen it. When he said no, I asked if he'd noticed any unfamiliar cars in the area."

"Did he say he saw David and Derrick get into the Oldsmobile?"

"No, but he said the car had driven by the school a few times before the closing bell. That made him suspicious, and he was about to call in a report to the sheriff's department when the bell rang and the kids came pouring out."

"Then we don't know if that's the same car," Matt said.

"We wouldn't if he'd left it at that, but when I asked if he'd seen the car again, he said that when he got a break from the crossing duties he spotted the same car parked across the street from the church.

"Two boys climbed in and the driver pulled away, so he figured it was just a relative who didn't know the rule about where to pick up students."

"Did he say anything about the driver?"

"That he wasn't a teenager and he wasn't speeding, since he thought that's what I was investigating. Said the driver looked to be in his late twenties, maybe older, but he'd just gotten a glimpse of him."

"Thanks," Nick said. "At least we have that much to go on."

"I'd still like to call my contact at the FBI," Langston said, "and get his take on this."

"I agree," Shelly said.

"And so do Nick and I," Becky said. "We've made that decision."

Becky had suggested it first, and Nick had been in total agreement. He'd forced himself to believe things would never get this far, that if he followed the abductor's orders to the letter his boys would be home tonight. Now the terrifying possibilities he'd worked so hard to keep at bay filled his mind.

It had to be the same for Becky. He ached to reach out to her in spite of their run-in this afternoon, but he couldn't face a rebuff right now. This was all so damn hard, their years together counting for nothing.

Nick took a deep breath and exhaled slowly. They were passing the point of no return as far as following the abductor's orders, but he couldn't stall any longer. "Call your friend at the bureau, Langston."

"You've got it." Langston stood and left the room to make the call without waiting for the rest of the decisions to be made.

"What about Zach?" Bart asked. "What do you want him to do? I'd put as much faith in him as I would the bureau—not that I don't think you should use them, too."

"Let's see what Langston finds out and then decide about that," Nick said.

"What if he's already crossed the border into Mexico? Then what?"

A choking knot clogged Nick's throat when he saw the fright in Becky's haunted eyes.

"Alert the border patrol to be on the watch for the car and them," Nick said. "See if we need to hire our own people to make sure he doesn't get that far. Do whatever it takes."

"In the meantime, I'm taking a drive and looking for an old rusted, dented, navy Oldsmobile," Matt said. "Sitting here doing nothing is maddening."

"I'm with you," Bart said.

"I'll stick to my prayers," Lenora said. She walked over and put her arm around Becky. "You need some rest, sweetheart."

"I can't sleep, Mother."

"Then just come and lie down in my room for awhile.

Exhaustion won't help the boys or your decision-making abilities."

Jaime and Shelly left with them, leaving only Nick and Zach at the table.

Zach stood and walked to the window, staring into the darkness before turning back to Nick. "Are you sure you've told us everything?"

Nick hesitated, but he knew he could trust Zach. "The kidnapper wants to take Becky as hostage when Langston flies him to Mexico."

"That's interesting."

"Don't tell me you think that's a good idea."

"No, absolutely not. I just wonder if it's possible he knows Becky."

Nick trailed his fingers up and down his neck, keeping the pressure light. "What are you getting at?"

"Just that if he knows Becky, that would narrow the suspects down considerably."

"I'm not sure how. Half the people in Houston know Becky or at least know of her. The Collingsworths are too active in local charities and arts foundations for them not to have heard of her."

"Yes, but half the people in America know who you are."

"Good point. He did call Becky by name, but that doesn't really prove he's had contact with her."

"Are you sure he didn't say anything that might give us a hint as to where he is?"

"No."

"Does he have a Texas accent?"

"Definitely."

"How was the grammar?"

"I don't see how this is helping."

"It could give us an idea of his background."

"His language is rough around the edges. Some slang. Nothing particularly unusual."

"I hate to even bring this up, but I've checked the files of all the registered people guilty of sex crimes living in this and neighboring counties. There aren't many in our immediate area, and I've made routine calls on all of them without giving any indication that I was investigating a crime. None of them have the boys with them. Of course that doesn't guarantee they aren't involved."

"Thanks, Zach. I really appreciate your efforts."

"The boys may be my nephews, but I don't think I could love them more if they were my own. They're great kids."

"Yeah." They were Nick's own, yet Zach had probably seen more of them this last year than he had. That said a lot for his quality of fatherhood, a point that Becky had been stressing for years.

Zach walked over to Nick and delivered a manly punch to the forearm. "I know this is tough, but hang in there, buddy. The boys are counting on you."

Langston stepped back into the doorway. "The FBI is sending out an agent from Houston who specializes in abductions. He'll be here in a matter of hours. Nick and Becky should probably try to get some sleep in the meantime."

"Fast work," Zach commented. "Pays to have friends in high places."

"Pays to have friends period," Langston said.

And it paid to have the clout of the Collingsworths on your side. Nick had to hold on to the faith that it and Lenora's prayers would be enough.

"LOOK," DAVID SAID.

"At what?" Derrick stumbled though the brush, hurrying to catch up with his twin brother. He was tired of walking. They should have come to a road hours ago. He wished he had his compass or that he'd paid more attention when Uncle Zach had been teaching him about using the stars to find your way home if you got lost in the woods.

"Look, through those trees. Somebody must live there."

"Oh, man! Am I glad to see that!" He was beginning to think they were going to be stuck out here all night—or until the kidnapper found them, which would be a lot worse.

They kept walking until they got a better look at the place. "Do you think somebody lives there?" David asked. "I don't see any cars around."

"It looks kind of empty, all right. But if there's a mobile home there has to be a road for people to get here. We can follow it to the highway."

"Yeah, and if someone lives there but isn't home, there still might be food."

"And water," Derrick added. "I'm really thirsty."

"Let's check it out."

"Maybe they have a phone, and we can call Mom to come get us."

"Now, that's what I'm talking about." David took off at a dead run toward the mobile home with Derrick on his heels. Before he got there, he slid to a stop, grabbing Derrick's arm and almost making him fall.

"What's wrong?" Derrick asked.

"Suppose the kidnapper is in there waiting for us?"

"Why would he be? He didn't know we'd come this way."

"Still, he just might be in there. Or a friend of his might live there."

"We'll peek through the window before we go inside," Derrick said. He led the way, marching as if they were soldiers. When he got closer to the house, he sneaked to the side and rose up to the tips of his toes so he could see inside the window.

"Well?" David whispered.

"Gimme a minute. It's dark in there." But there was a stream of moonlight lighting the area right in front of the window. Derrick didn't see anybody, and the place was quiet.

"I think it's all clear," he said, still keeping his voice low just in case. "Let's grab a broken limb for a weapon, but I don't think we'll need it. If the kidnapper were here, he would have left the light on to lure us in. And if somebody else is here, they'll help us get home."

They grabbed the sticks and climbed the three steps to a porch so small it wouldn't have held them and Blackie.

David knocked. Nobody answered. "Hey, anybody in there?" Still no response. He tried the knob. "It's locked."

Derrick propped his weapon against the house. "Then I guess we'll have to break in."

"We could go to jail for that."

Derrick shook his head. "Naw. We've escaped from a kidnapper. They'll just be talking about how brave we are."

"How do we get in?"

"We can break out a window."

"I was just about to say that," David said.

"Sure you were."

"I was, 'cause see that big rock out by the road. We can hurl it through the glass."

"But you better let me throw it," Derrick said, "'cause I can chuck it harder than you can." He wasn't sure that was right, but if they got into trouble for breaking out the window, he should face it since he suggested they break in.

David got the rock and handed it to him. He threw it as hard as he could. The rock went right through the pane, and glass shattered and scattered all over the ground.

"I'll heft you up to my shoulders," Derrick said. "You can reach in and unlock the window."

David took off his jacket and wrapped it around his right hand and arm so he wouldn't get cut. David was good at thinking of stuff like that. Once he was on Derrick's shoulders, he knocked out the rest of the window and just climbed through. "I'll unlock the door for you," he called, then disappeared into the dark house.

By the time Derrick got back around to the front door, it was standing open and the lights were on. The mobile home smelled like wet, dirty socks but it had furniture. Old stuff.

"Let's check out the kitchen," David said.

Derrick was right behind him. The refrigerator was mostly empty except for a few slices of cheese. There were a bunch of bottles of water though. Derrick took one for himself and handed one to David. He swallowed half of his in one gulp.

"There's sodas, too," he said. He opened the door to the freezer. There were bunches of packages of meat.

"Ice cream sandwiches," he said, pulling out the box of frozen treats.

David crawled up on the countertop to reach the higher shelves. "Not much in here but canned stuff. Chili. Chicken noodle soup." He shoved the cans around to reach to the back of the shelf. "And two cans of spaghetti with franks like Dad made one time at his house. All we need is a can opener and a pan to warm it."

"Now you're talking." This was starting to feel like an adventure. "Spaghetti and ice-cream sandwiches for dessert?" Derrick took another long swig of his water as he opened another cabinet. "I found a pan."

"Yeah, I was so hungry I almost forgot about that. David jumped down from the counter. "But I think I'll have dessert first." He grabbed an ice cream sandwich and took off to search for the phone.

They both had dessert first, but David didn't find a phone. Derrick was still plenty hungry when the canned pasta and sauce was ready. They divided it up into two big bowls and took them to the small table.

"Tastes just like Dad's," David said.

"Yeah, but not as good as Grandma's or Juanita's."

"You think Blackie misses us?"

"Yeah," Derrick said. "I wish he was here. We could sic him on the kidnapper."

"We don't need that. We got away all by ourselves. I think my screwdriver idea fooled him into going the wrong way to look for us after we took off our shoes and walked in the creek so he'd lose our tracks."

"Yeah, but that water was really cold." Derrick finished his food. He'd planned to eat another ice cream sandwich, but he was too full. He might have a soda, though. He spied a rope on a nail on the wall. He walked over, picked it up and tied a slipknot like he did when he practiced calf roping. "Do you think we should sleep here tonight?"

"I don't think so. The kidnapper might show up and grab us in our sleep. We better keep walking and try to reach a highway. We could follow that road outside but stay in the woods in case the kidnapper comes driving down it looking for us."

"I hope we get home in time for the Christmas pageant," Derrick said. "We could tell everybody how we escaped."

"The girls will think we're superheroes."

"Cool."

Derrick swung the rope, lassoing the back of an empty chair. "We should probably get going. The ice cream would melt if we tried to take it with us, but we can take some soda and water in our jacket pockets. I think I'll take the rope, too."

He put his jacket back on, rolled the rope and tucked it away in the big inside pocket. He stuffed the rest of his pockets with water. "I look fat," he said.

"Did you hear that?"

Derrick listened, and there it was. Whistling. The same stupid song the kidnapper always whistled. The adventure wasn't fun anymore.

## Chapter Seven

The house was quiet, shrouded in a dismal dread that felt as if they'd been plucked from Jack's Bluff Ranch and dropped on a cold, dark planet. Lenora felt the desperation and ached for her dead husband the way she hadn't in a long, long time.

Not a day went by that she didn't miss him. Not the ferocious shredding of her heart kind of pain she had suffered the first months after his death. She couldn't have survived over two decades of that. Now it was a more a melancholy vacuum that even her marvelous family couldn't completely fill.

Lenora stood at the front door watching as the rear lights of Trish's car faded in the distance. She was taking Gina and her infant son, Randy, back to their cabin for the night so that the baby could sleep in his crib. Trish was a good mother and knew her baby and especially her teenage daughter needed a break from the fear and tension that saturated the big house.

Gina was taking this really hard, her usually high teenage spirits scraping the bottom. She'd spent most of the afternoon lying listless on the floor or out walking with Blackie. Lenora's granddaughter looked as woeful as the nine-month-old pup.

When Zach's wife, Kali, had gone back to their ranch to check on a new foal, she'd brought Blackie's brother Chideaux back to Jack's Bluff with her. In an emotional crunch, two loving dogs were always better than one, and both Lenora and Kali had insisted Gina take the dogs with her for the night.

Bart's wife, Jaclyn, had left with Trish. Nick had insisted she try to get a good night's sleep for the sake of their unborn daughter. The rest of the family was still inside, waiting. Endlessly waiting.

As if drawn into the darkness and the solitude of the Texas night, Lenora pushed out the front door, her footfalls sounding on the wooden planks of the porch. The night air was brisk but not cold. The temperature had climbed into the sixties this afternoon, not unusual for December in this part of Texas. The low tonight would only be in the upper forties.

Wherever the boys were, they would likely be warm enough. But were they safe? Did they have food? Were they afraid?

Lenora started toward the porch swing but then changed her direction, descending the steps instead. The noises and smells of the night wrapped around her like the arm of an old friend as she took the well-worn, moonlit path to the huge oak tree where she'd laid Randolph to rest so long ago.

She fell to her knees at the tombstone and rested her head against the smooth marker as salty tears pushed from her eyes.

"Oh, Randolph. I miss you so desperately. If you were here, you'd take control. You'd know how to get our precious grandsons back." Her tears fell harder as her words shifted to a prayer.

"I trust you, God. I always have. I try not to ask for much, but I'm pleading with you to watch over David and Derrick. I'll bear anything you lay on me without complaining, but please bring my grandsons home safely."

Minutes later, the sobs and tears subsided and soothing warmth seeped inside her. She felt as if Randolph had reached from the grave and cradled her in his arms, giving her new hope.

She stayed at the grave site until her knees ached from being pressed into the grassy earth. She had no clear concept of how much time had passed before she started back toward the house.

She saw only the shadow outlined in the moonlight near the house, but she knew it was Becky. She hurried toward her, wondering if Becky had come looking for her, hoping it was with good news.

Becky looked up as Lenora approached. "Mom, what are you doing out here all by yourself?"

Odd to hear it put that way when she'd felt anything but alone. She walked over and clasped Becky's hand. "I went for a walk. Are you okay?"

"No. I'm afraid."

"I know, sweetheart. You're doing all you can. You have to trust God with the rest."

"I wish I had the faith you do, but I don't."

And more reassurances that the boys were going to be fine would sound trite and placating to Becky. "When you talked to the boys they sounded fine," she said, going for evidence Becky couldn't deny. "There's no reason to think that's changed."

"Then why didn't the kidnapper let us talk to them the last time he called? And why doesn't he call again?"

"I don't know. Maybe he can't get to a phone he trusts. Maybe he fell asleep."

"I should have never listened to Nick. I should have had an AMBER Alert go out right away. I should have called in the FBI sooner. Nick doesn't know anything about dealing with kidnappers."

The bitterness in her voice cut straight to Lenora's heart. "Don't be so hard on Nick, Becky. No one could have known the kidnapper wouldn't call as he said. Nick loves the boys. You know that."

"I suppose—in his way."

"That's the only way any of us can love—in our own way. You need Nick in this, Becky, and he needs you."

"Why would he need me? Haven't you heard? He has Brianna Campbell."

"I don't believe anything they print in those gossip magazines, certainly not that."

"It's more than gossip. She answered the phone when I called his hospital room after the accident."

Lenora swallowed hard. She had never given up on Becky and Nick getting back together, not even when the divorce papers were filed. They'd loved each other so much once. How could they throw their marriage away when they had two precious sons who needed them both?

Divorce was right for some people. She accepted that—but not for Becky and Nick.

The conversation was interrupted by the sound of a car engine and the illumination from the headlights of an approaching car. An unfamiliar black sedan pulled up in the drive and stopped a few feet from where they were standing. A lone man climbed out and started toward them.

The FBI had apparently arrived.

DERRICK TWISTED HIS HANDS and tried to loosen the duct tape that bound his wrists behind his back. No luck. His ankles were bound, too. Same with David. Worse, the goon had put David in the bedroom and left Derrick on the lumpy sofa so they couldn't even talk to each other.

He and David tried to run away when they'd heard that stupid whistling. They would have made it, too, if David hadn't tripped while running for the back door. Derrick had come back to help him, and that's when the man had grabbed both of them and put a killer grip around their necks with his muscular arms.

They'd tried to fight him off, but he was too strong for them. He'd locked David in the bathroom at the mobile home and dragged Derrick to the kitchen, where he'd found the duct tape. Then he'd left them both tied up and locked in the bathroom while he'd gone back to his cabin for his grungy old car.

Now they were worse off than they'd been before they'd escaped. Derrick blamed himself for that. He should have been smart enough to just grab some food and water and clear out of that mobile home before the kidnapper had found them and brought them back to his cabin.

The kidnapper stomped on a giant roach crawling across the floor.

"I'm hungry," Derrick said. He wasn't, but he hoped the abductor would leave them alone again and go after food. That would give him some time to come up with a better escape plan, one where they wouldn't get caught.

"You think I care if you brats starve? You're lucky I didn't beat you to death for attacking me and running off."

"You beat us and you'll be sorry. My daddy is probably going to kill you anyway."

"I'm not scared of your daddy or your rich uncles, either."

If that was true, the guy was dumber than he looked. The only problem was that neither his daddy nor his uncles knew where to find them.

"Cut out the yakking," the kidnapper said. "I'm going to call your parents, and when I get them on the line, you tell them I'm treating you well."

"Why would I tell them that when you got me and David tied up?"

"'Cause I'm telling you to. And because if you don't, I'll take this belt off and stripe your behinds with it the same way my daddy used to do to me."

"Really? Your dad did that?"

"Every Saturday night when he got drunk. Sometimes in between, if I didn't jump fast enough to suit him."

Derrick didn't like the kidnapper, but still, he kind of felt sorry for him. He couldn't even imagine his dad beating up on him or David. "Do you have a brother?"

"Nope. My mother ran off right after I was born, and nobody else was stupid enough to marry my father."

The kidnapper kicked one of the empty beer cans he'd just drained and sent it flying over Derrick's head. It landed in the part of the room where the table and chairs and kitchen stuff were.

"How come you don't put your cans in the trash like other people?"

"How come you don't mind your own business?" He pulled his cell phone from his pocket and started punching buttons. A few seconds and a bunch of cussing later, he hurled the phone against the wall. It broke into what looked like at least a hundred pieces.

"What did you do that for? You said you were going to call Daddy."

"Friggin' phone's used up."

"They don't get used up. Mom uses hers all the time, and it still works."

"Miss Becky has enough money to buy a better phone than I do."

"Just take us home, why don't you?" Derrick said. "My parents will pay the ransom, and then you'll have money to buy all the phones you want."

"I'll get the ransom. Don't you worry about that."

But the guy looked plenty worried. And mad. "So what are you gonna do now?" Derrick asked.

"Get another phone. I'll be out for a while. Don't try anything stupid. I won't be near as forgiving next time."

He shoved his burly arms into his ripped denim jacket and stamped outside, the key clicking as he locked the door behind him. Derrick waited until he heard the car drive away before maneuvering himself into a sitting position and turning toward the locked bedroom door.

"David, are you okay in there?"

"I guess so. I heard a car start. Did the kidnapper leave?"

"Yeah."

"Good. I hope he never comes back."

"He'll be back. He just went to get a phone so he can call Daddy. Can you get the tape off your wrists?"

"Nope. I can barely wiggle my fingers."

"Same here."

"If we had something sharp to rub up against, we

could cut the tape off," David said. "You know, like a knife."

"Right," Derrick agreed. "Or any kind of jagged edge." He wiggled off the sofa and leaned against it for support until he got his balance. Once done, he started shuffling his way to the kitchen. "I'll check out the kitchen. You look around in there. But try not to fall. It might be hard to get back up."

"Okay, but there's not much in here."

Derrick should have better luck in the kitchen, but he'd have to work fast. One of the drawers was slightly ajar. He could see a knife inside it but didn't see any way he could pick it up.

A daddy longlegs scurried across the floor and crawled over his toes. He couldn't move his foot to kick it off. Another thing, the kidnapper had taken their shoes away from them so that if they escaped again, they'd have to run barefoot through the woods. Like that would stop them.

He needed a jagged edge, and he needed it fast.

SAM COTRELLA HAD BEEN with the FBI for ten years now. He'd never planned to become a resident expert in dealing with child abductions. It had just happened over time, starting with his first kidnapping case in Ohio over five years ago.

Most of his cases had turned out well. A few hadn't. Those were the ones that came back to haunt him at moments like this. They were also the reason he knew there was no time to waste even though it was almost midnight.

He settled in the family den with Nick and Becky Ridgely and tried to size up the situation as best he could as they filled him in on the details. Becky's brother Zach, a local deputy, and her sister-in-law Shelly, formerly a CIA agent, were in the room, as well.

The rest of the family had left the room at his suggestion. Nick and Becky could fill them in later, but too many people talking while he was getting specifics often confused the issue.

"The man Langston talked to said you'd worked abductions before," Nick said once he'd given the rundown on what had happened and how they'd handled the situation to this point.

"Several. You might remember the Graham case in Houston last year."

"I remember it," Becky said. "A fourth-grade girl was abducted by one of her father's employees."

Nick looked puzzled. "I don't remember that."

"You wouldn't," Becky quipped. "It was during football season."

The tension in the room swelled to new proportions. Sam knew from the basic information he'd been given before arriving that the missing twins' parents were separated. He'd worked in situations like that before, too. The strain between them would not make this any easier.

"Julie Graham was the daughter of a Houston CEO," Sam explained. "A disgruntled employee with a history of mental illness abducted her from the park near their house while the nanny was tending to a younger sibling."

Nick leaned in closer, his muscles taut. "How did you get her back?"

"The father turned over the money at the agreed-upon time and location, and once Julie was safe, we came down on him with a SWAT team we'd put in place. The abductor tried to shoot his way out and was killed in the exchange of gunfire."

"I don't want gunfire," Becky said. "I don't want to take any chances."

"We never *want* gunfire," Sam said. "But the girl was never in danger. We'll negotiate a plan of exchange that focuses on keeping the boys safe."

"There's not much to negotiate," Nick said. "I have the money. He can have it. All I want is my sons."

"So what exactly do you expect from the FBI?" Sam asked.

"I want you to find David and Derrick in case the kidnapper doesn't call."

"My gut feeling is that he will call," Sam said. "He wants the money. That's what this is about. Otherwise he wouldn't have made that phone call about the ransom so soon after the boys were in his possession."

"That seems reasonable," Becky agreed. "But Nick told him we have the money and he didn't seem in any hurry to get it. And he wouldn't let us talk to the boys."

That worried Sam, as well. There could be several explanations for not letting them communicate with their sons but most obvious was that the boys were in no condition to assure their parents they were safe. No use to point that out. Both Nick and Becky were well aware of the danger their sons were in.

His goal now was to convince them that they needed his guidance all the way.

"If you do exactly as the kidnapper wants, we may not be able to protect your sons. That's why we need to negotiate and why you need to let me veto any arrangements for the exchange that I don't think are feasible."

Becky pulled her bare feet into the chair with her and hugged her knees close to her chest. She looked a lot like a vulnerable little girl herself in that position. Sam could only imagine how hard this had been on her—and the worst might be yet to come.

"The kidnapper promised that we'd get David and Derrick back safely if we cooperated," Becky said. "I guess we were fools to believe him."

"You were frightened parents," Shelly countered. "That's why we need Agent Cotrella's expertise."

"I'm still not sure how this works," Nick said. "Are you saying we should tell him you're from the FBI and that he'll have to negotiate with you? I'll tell you up front that if that's the plan, I don't like it."

Sam swiveled the desk chair so that he was looking directly at Nick. "The abductor won't even know I'm here. I'll listen in on the calls and guide you through the conversation by feeding you information, but you'll do the talking."

"If we put the phone on speaker, he'll immediately suspect police or FBI involvement."

Sam nodded. In spite of his reluctance to call in the FBI, Nick had a good grasp of the situation. "I have a two-man tech team on the way," Sam said. "They'll put attachments on the phone that will allow me to listen in to your calls without the kidnapper suspecting anything."

"Can they trace a cell call from a prepaid phone?"

"Maybe not to the exact location, but they'll be able to identify the general area where the calls are originating."

"And this equipment will prevent the kidnapper from

having any inkling that his calls are being monitored?" Nick asked.

"He won't be able to detect any difference in the sound of his voice or yours."

"He's been calling Nick's cell phone," Becky said.

"We'll monitor both your cell phones and the house phone," Sam said. "He may change up in an attempt to keep you off guard. Now let's get down to the specifics of negotiation. Up to this point, you've let him make most of the decisions. It's time you threw in a few demands of your own."

Apprehension darkened Becky's blue eyes. "What kind of demands?"

"Make it clear to him that the plane will absolutely not leave the ground until the boys are back with you."

Nick bristled. "You're damn right it won't. The guy can't be so crazy he doesn't know that."

"Assume nothing. He may try to ensure his safe arrival in Mexico by taking one of the boys on the plane as his hostage."

"Surely, he wouldn't," Becky said.

"You'd think, but I had a case in Nebraska a couple of years ago where the kidnapper had abducted a sister and brother. He gave the parents the sister in exchange for the money and told him that once he was sure there were no tricks, he'd tell them where their son was."

"And did he?" Shelly asked.

"No. Once he had the money, he had no reason to cooperate. He left the boy with an accomplice, who decided to ask for more money. That's when the FBI was called in on the case."

"Do we still provide the plane and the pilots?" Nick asked. "As per his instructions?"

"You can provide the plane. The FBI will take care of the pilots."

"Fine by me," Nick said. "But the boys will be released to me. I'll have it no other way."

Sam nodded. Cool-in-the-clutch Ridgely. That's how one sportswriter had described him. Sam had an idea that calm resolve would be tested as never before by the time this was over. But Sam's job went better with optimism. He would ensure the focus stayed on bringing David and Derrick home alive.

For Christmas.

For a brief second Sam let his mind wander to his own kids at home snuggled in their beds with visions of Christmas morning dancing in their heads.

He'd do all he could to make certain this had a happy ending, but the longer this took, the more the possibility of failure increased. The twins had already been in the hands of the abductor for more than thirty hours.

NICK PACED THE small downstairs study that Sam Cotrella had chosen for his operations room. The guy seemed to know his stuff and didn't come off as too cocksure of himself. Nick liked that about him, the same way he liked those qualities in his teammates.

Teammates. That was another problem—minor when compared to his sons but nagging, nonetheless. They kept calling and trying to find out what in the hell was going on with him. They were baffled. A few were downright angry and had accused him of going soft and sabotaging their chances of making the play-offs.

The NFL was a business and multimillion-dollar receivers did not just up and walk out of a hospital without a doctor's clearance.

He'd stalled everyone off with feeble excuses. He was resting at home while the swelling went down and he got the pain under control. He'd miss Sunday's game but would be ready to work out with the team on Monday. Things were under control.

That was the biggest lie of all. It was 3:00 a.m. and still no word from the son of a bitch who had his sons. Things had never been more out of control. As for the rest of his life, that hell would just have to wait.

The house was quiet, but Nick doubted there was much sound sleeping going on. Every time he stepped into the kitchen for a cup of coffee, there was a new group of family members sitting around the table.

Growing up the way he had, he'd never even imagined there were families like the Collingsworths. They had their differences, but when trouble appeared, they stuck together like superglue.

He'd miss them when the divorce was over. Not the way he'd miss Becky. Not the way he already missed her, even with her lying a few feet away, sleeping restlessly on the brown tweed sofa.

His gaze fixed on her, and a potent ache clogged his throat, making it difficult to swallow. He walked over and covered her with the knitted throw that was lying near her feet. She snuggled into it the way she'd once snuggled against him on cold, wintry nights.

Before he'd let things deteriorate to the point she could barely stand to be near him.

A sharp pain started in his shoulder and crept into his back, growing worse when he tried to take a deep breath. He grimaced and started to the kitchen for a glass of water.

The piercing ring of his cell phone stopped him.

His body grew numb, his feet frozen to the floor as he waited for the agreed-on signal from Sam to take a call. It was late. Not even his teammates would call at this hour.

The caller ID said Marilyn Close. He looked to Sam, who'd walked up behind him. "I don't know anyone by that name."

"Take the call anyway. The kidnapper could be using a stolen phone."

Becky jumped to a sitting position and grabbed for the earphones that would let her listen in on the conversation if the call was from the abductor. Sam's were already in place. He took a deep breath and took the call.

And then the panic he'd worked to keep in check exploded inside him. The voice was the kidnapper's, but Nick was certain something was seriously wrong.

## Chapter Eight

"You're lucky those brats of yours are still breathing."

The abductor's voice slurred as if he were drunk or on drugs, his anger seeming to vibrate through the phone into Nick's brain.

"If you've hurt them, I'll kill you." The words left his mouth before he remembered Sam's orders that he was to wait for a nod or instructions before responding. Even if he had remembered, he doubted he could have held back.

"Your threats don't scare me, Nick Ridgely. Are you ready to pay up?"

Sam nodded.

"I have the money you asked for."

"All five million?"

"Yes, in fifties and twenties, just as you instructed. Now I want to talk to my sons."

"But you're not in control here, are you, big shot? So listen up and do exactly as I say."

Sam mouthed the words for him to insist.

"I'm not doing anything unless you let me talk to my boys," Nick said, keeping his voice dead level.

The abductor spewed a string of vile curses. "Then I'm through talking to you. Put Becky on the phone."

Nick's muscles clenched. His fury went nuclear and would have resulted in some curses of his own had Sam Cotrella not been there motioning Nick to give the phone to Becky.

Reluctantly he did so, exchanging the phone for her headphones as Sam made quick notes on the yellow pad he was holding in front of her.

She read his question into the phone with a control that surprised Nick. "Do I know you?"

"You did once. Back in your rah-rah days. Maybe we'll just have us a grand little reunion on that plane to Mexico."

Sam quickly scribbled the response. Becky read it into the receiver. "I don't know what you're talking about."

"I don't trust your husband. I want you on that plane with me when I flee the country—my insurance that I actually get to Mexico a free man with money in hand."

Nick mouthed the words "no way," but Sam was already scribbling a different answer on his pad.

Becky nodded. "Deal," she said. "But the plane won't take off until I know both boys are safe."

"That's the deal I offered."

"We can meet at the airport in Houston where my brother Langston keeps his private jet."

"No. I'll tell you where we meet. You have the plane ready to go. I'll call you and let you know when."

Sam scribbled. Becky read. "Why wait? What's wrong with now?"

"I got this high going on, baby. If you were here, we could be having a real good time. Guess that fun will just have to wait until we're on your brother's jet."

Nick grabbed a pen, wrote out his own instructions and pushed them in front of Sam.

*Becky is not getting on that plane with him.*

Sam waved him off and nodded to Becky to follow the instructions he'd just written.

"What time will you call?"

"When I'm good and ready. Have the money, a pilot and you. If there's anyone else present or if I even suspect you've called the cops in on this, the deal is off and the boys are corpses. You got that?"

"The boys can't just be left at the airport on their own. Nick will need to be there," she said.

"Fine, bring Nick. Maybe I'll get his autograph."

The man laughed as if this were all some big joke. If Nick could have gotten his hands on his throat right then, he could have strangled him without a second thought.

"Let me talk to my sons," Becky insisted again.

"They're not exactly with me right now, sweetheart. They're kind of tied up somewhere else, but don't you worry. They're just fine. But you should have taught those little brats some manners. If I wasn't so nice, they'd be in big trouble."

"Don't hurt them," she begged, this time speaking on her own. "We'll give you everything you ask. Just please don't hurt them."

But the kidnapper didn't hear her plea. He'd already broken the connection.

"We'll have to move fast on this," Sam said, already punching in numbers on his cell phone.

Nick wasn't giving in that easily. "I don't know what you're thinking, but Becky is not going anywhere with that scumbag."

"Of course not," Sam said. "All the people in that plane will be FBI. A dozen more agents will be on the ground either hidden from view or posing as airport crew. Now, can you get Zach in here? Shelly, too. I can use their help in taking care of a few things. While you're at it, get Langston as well so we can verify information about his aircraft."

"I want to be there when he releases David and Derrick," Becky said.

"We'll talk about it," Sam said as he started giving orders to whomever it was he'd called.

"I don't want you there," Nick said. He knew the statement had come out too much like an order the second he saw the rebellious expression on Becky's face.

"I didn't ask for your permission," she said.

"I know," he said, this time going for appeasement. "I just don't want to add to the risk."

Thankfully, she let the confrontation dissolve without an argument. The wheels were turning again. His sons, *their* sons could be home in a matter of hours. Nick wouldn't breathe easy until they were.

Then the rest of his life could come crashing down on top of him—one heartbreak at a time.

BULL DROPPED THE PHONE to the seat beside him as he crossed the bridge heading back to the dilapidated cabin where he'd left the boys. He'd planned on buying another prepaid model from a convenience store in Livingston, but luck and fast thinking had saved him the money.

He'd stopped at an all-night truck stop on Highway 59 where he knew he could buy a fifth of cheap whiskey and some joints from the night manager. Under the table so to speak, though everyone in these parts seemed to know where to go for after-hours booze or a quick fix.

The phone had been easy pickings from a broad who'd stopped for coffee and left her phone sitting next to her cup and cigarettes while she went to the bathroom. He'd palmed it on his way out. She'd probably have it disconnected before he used it again, but that was okay. He'd stop at a pay phone next time—one on his way to meet Nick Ridgely.

The fifth of cheap whiskey was almost gone now. He shouldn't have started it before he made the call, but his head had been still pounding from the blow he'd taken from the boys that morning, and he needed something to kill it. Once he'd started, he'd stayed with it.

Women, drugs and booze. That had always been his downfall. But in a few more hours he'd have plenty of money to buy all he wanted. Not cheap booze or tawdry women, either. He'd have the best that five million could buy.

The car's wheels hit the shoulder and skidded completely off the roadbed. He yanked it back to the middle of the narrow strip of asphalt.

*Slow down, buddy. Stay focused. Your next turn is coming up, and then it's just a few more miles back to the cabin.*

The car swerved again. He could barely keep his eyes open, but he had to keep driving. He didn't dare leave those Ridgely brats alone any longer than he had to. They were his ticket out of here.

Just him, the pilot and Becky. He couldn't wait to get his hands on her—and all over her. She probably wasn't as hot as she'd been in high school in that sexy little cheerleading outfit. Firm little tits pushing at the fabric. He couldn't count all the nights he'd gotten his rocks off thinking of those.

She'd ignored him then. She wouldn't have that option now.

His turn was just ahead. He put on his brakes and slowed almost to a stop before turning on yet another winding, narrow road, this one dirt and half washed-out and with potholes big enough to bury a man.

Then a few more miles and he'd make the last turn onto the red clay trail that meandered back to the old fishing cabin. The place had belonged to his grand-pappy back before the creek had dried up and become clogged with logs and trash.

His dad had brought him fishing out here a few times when he was a kid. The last time had been his seventh birthday, but he remembered it as if it was yesterday. His father had gotten the poles and bait from the car, then proceeded to get falling-down drunk.

His dad had hooked him with the jagged end of his fishing hook, then kicked him until he was black and blue for crying when he yanked it loose, tearing a bloody hole in his flesh as he did.

It was the first time he'd thought about killing his dad, years before he actually did it. That had been a long, long time ago, and no one had ever suspected him of murder.

Bull's eyes closed. A second later he slammed into a tree.

"THE LAST PHONE CALL was made from somewhere in the area of Livingston, Texas, from a phone belonging to Marilyn Close of Longview. I've got someone check-ing her out as we speak," Sam announced, once the entire family had gathered in the cozy kitchen. The room smelled of coffee and the spicy apricot coffee cake Lenora had just pulled from the oven.

"I bake and pray," she'd said. "My way of holding together."

He would never have called a family conference at 1:30 a.m., but apparently none of the Collingsworths had done much sleeping since the boys' abduction. Now that he had all four of Becky's brothers, plus a few of the women, in attendance, he was glad to have them aboard.

They not only worked as a seamless team but they were smart and all willing to do whatever it took to get David and Derrick home safely. Families like that didn't come along every day, especially when they were also one of the wealthiest families in Texas.

"It's likely the phone was stolen," he continued, "but at least we know the general area where the abductor must be holding the boys."

"I say we start combing that area for them at daybreak," Zach said.

"Can you take care of that while still keeping the kidnapping quiet?" Sam asked.

"Absolutely."

"Then go to it." Sam made a couple more notes on his pad.

Nick stirred a bit of cream into his coffee. "What about the fact that the man seems to know Becky? Shouldn't we be checking into that?"

"He didn't say how he knew me," Becky said. "He could have been lying."

"We can't assume he's lying," Nick insisted, "and if he does know you I don't see how he'll be fooled by an FBI agent who's impersonating you."

"You'd be surprised how easy that is to achieve," Sam said, "as long as we keep the agent at a distance until the boys are with you."

"Do we know who that agent will be?" Langston asked.

Sam nodded and sipped his coffee. "All taken care of. Her name's Evie Parker, and not only is she petite like Becky but she's a master with undercover disguises. She has her own collection of wigs in every color. When I talked to her, she said she could fool Becky's mother as long as she didn't have to stand too close. However, that might be a slight exaggeration."

"But she hasn't even seen me," Becky protested.

"She has your picture."

"How?"

"I snapped it with my cell phone and sent it to her. She's on her way here now, flying in from Dallas with our pilot. They'll land at the same place Langston keeps his private jet in case there's no time for us to get together before that. She'll get a car and drive out here from there if there's time."

Sam had a feeling there would be plenty of time and that this was not going to play out exactly as it was being scripted. Just a hunch, but his hunches had a history of being right more often than they were wrong. Agent's intuition.

That and the fact that the kidnapper had been drunk when he called. The guy was obviously losing control of the situation. The question was *why?* He hoped the answer had nothing to do with the physical condition of David and Derrick.

"He must have known Becky in high school," Jaime

said, "assuming rah-rah days refers to her being a cheer-leader. She wasn't one in college."

"Good thinking."

"What can we do to help?" Matt asked.

"I need copies of Becky's high school yearbooks. I'd like her to peruse them and see if any of the guys stir bad feelings."

"My yearbooks are packed away in the attic."

Matt stood up. "I'll bring them down."

"I'll go with Matt," Bart said. "There are lots of boxes in the attic. Finding the right one could take a while."

Becky stuck a fork into the slice of coffee cake her mother had set in front of her. "I'm not sure what you mean by bad feelings."

"Perhaps someone you had problems with. Maybe a guy who had a crush on you that you didn't share. Maybe someone who aggravated you or even seemed creepy to you. We're grasping at whatever we can find," Sam admitted.

"I don't remember anyone like that attending Colts Run Cross High."

"Sometimes pictures can jog a memory. Have you ever been stalked?"

Becky hesitated. "Not exactly."

Not the answer Sam was expecting. "I'll need more than that."

She laid the fork back down and reached for the mug of hot coffee, sipping slowly before answering. "Right after I started college I met this guy in my freshman psychology class who I could have sworn was follow-ing me around campus. He never asked me out—not that I would have gone. He had zero personality. But he always seemed to be around, staring at me from a distance. It freaked me out big-time."

"Did you say anything to him about your concerns?"

"I thought about it, but before it came to that, he dropped out of school. But the really weird thing is, a few weeks ago I saw a man who reminded me of him in Colts Run Cross."

Sam saw the clench of Nick's jaw. Unless Sam was misreading the signals, he was more tuned in to his wife than Sam would have expected under the circumstances. And he was definitely protective of her.

His guess was that Nick Ridgely was not the one who'd initiated the divorce, though he might have made some dumb mistake that caused Becky to give up on him. Men with hero status had temptation thrown at them left and right.

Sam waited for Becky to elaborate on the man who'd reminded her of the college stalker. She didn't. "Do you think it could have been the same man?"

"I don't think so. It was more the feeling I got when I noticed him staring at me than his appearance. Not the old cliché about undressing me with his eyes, but more like the one about spiders crawling across the skin."

"Did you only see him that once?"

"Yes, and then only for a few seconds. I'd stopped at Thompson's Grocery to pick up a few items, and he was checking out in front of me. I'm almost positive he's not from around here. I would have seen him before—or since."

"Definitely weird," Sam agreed. "I'll need a description of him and as many specifics about the psych class as you remember. I'll have someone check the school records and see if we can get a roster for that class. You may recognize his name if you see it printed."

"I can sit with her while she skims her yearbooks," Shelly offered. "I can jot down her description of the man she saw in the store and make notes on anyone else of interest."

"I'd appreciate that." It would relieve Sam to go over the exchange plans with the other agents who'd be involved. "And Nick, you and Becky should try to get a little rest as soon as she finishes taking a look at those yearbooks. I doubt we'll be hearing from the abductor again before morning. He's probably sleeping it off right now."

"Is that everything?" Becky asked.

"For now." But Sam would have felt a lot better about this if the kidnapper had let Nick or Becky talk to their sons. Not hearing their voices raised a whole new set of questions with possibilities none of them wanted to consider.

NICK WALKED TO THE family den and stared out the window as the dawning light of a new day dissolved the night.

Wednesday morning. Two days before Christmas. His heart twisted as if it were trying to wrench itself from his chest. Becky stirred from her position on the sofa but didn't open her eyes.

He'd tried to talk her into going to her room for at least a few hours, but she wouldn't venture that far from him and his phone. Not only did she want the chance to hear her sons' voices but she wanted to be there if the kidnapper asked to speak to her again. Had it been left up to her, she'd have willingly climbed on the plane with the kidnapper in exchange for David and Derrick's safety.

Except for Zach, he hadn't seen the rest of the family in the past few hours. Zach had to be running on empty, but he'd left a half hour ago to get started on trying to locate the kidnapper and the boys. Sam had the FBI on the mission, as well. To Nick, it sounded like trying to find a particular face in a game-day crowd of seventy thousand.

Still, Nick envied their chance to do something useful. He would rather be doing anything other than pacing and waiting for the damned phone to ring.

He walked to the bookcase and studied the rows of family photographs. He picked up one and held it closer so that he could make out the details in the dim morning light.

In it, the boys were no more than four. David was crawling through a pile of wrapped presents. Derrick was on tiptoe reaching to hang an ornament on the Collingsworth Christmas tree. One of the many Christmases Nick had missed due to being on the road for an upcoming game.

Not that they hadn't always celebrated again when he got home, but nonetheless, he'd missed the actual day the same way he'd missed lots of big moments in their lives. School plays. Derrick's first touchdown on the parks department youth team. David's first win in the local rodeo's youth barrel riding competition.

Becky had captured the moments for him on film. At the time that had seemed enough. No. Who was he kidding? At the time, he'd been so involved with his own life, with the drive to win and the excitement of the upcoming game that what happened back home barely scratched his consciousness.

"What time is it?"

Becky's sleep-husky voice cut through his thoughts. When he turned, he saw that she'd kicked off the blanket and was sitting up, raking her fingers through her disheveled hair with one hand and clenching a throw pillow with the other. Her torment was tangible, a heaviness that filled the air like thick, poisonous smoke.

Nick glanced at his watch. "Six-twenty."

"You'd think he'd call."

"He's probably still sleeping it off."

"If he'd only let us talk to the boys, if I just knew they were safe, that they aren't being mistreated or abused, I could handle this."

"Don't think those things," he pleaded, though the same fears were eating away at him. He ached to drop to the sofa beside her and cradle her in his arms. In spite of his words about not contesting the divorce, it wasn't what he wanted. He wanted things to be the way they were in the beginning—when she loved him as much as he loved her.

Mostly he wished he had a chance to make up for everything he'd missed with his sons. He dropped to the edge of the leather hassock, waiting until Becky let her gaze lock with his.

Finally the question torturing his heart found its way to his tongue. "Am I a terrible father, Becky?"

BECKY FOUGHT the urge to lash out at Nick, to hurl all her frustration and fear at him. But it would only be a temporary release, a cruel, punishing sting that would do neither of them any good.

She opted to choose her words carefully. "David and Derrick love you," she said honestly. "You're their hero."

"A hero, but I'm not much of a caretaker. I'm not there for them to do the little things other fathers do, like go to their ball games or help with their homework, at least not on a full-time basis."

Surely he didn't expect her to contradict that. Yet one look into his haunted eyes, and she couldn't add to his guilt and pain. What purpose could it possibly serve?

"You love them," she said, willing to let it drop at that.

"It's not enough, is it? Not for the boys and definitely not for you. I'm away too much. You said it yourself a thousand times."

She dropped the pillow and clasped her hands in her lap. "It was never just your physical absence, Nick. Even when we were together during the season, you weren't really there. You pulled away emotionally. I know it sounds crazy, but I felt betrayed, as if football were your lover."

Nick shrugged and looked away. "NFL football is demanding."

"So is life, Nick."

And she had never been able to simply turn off their marriage and life together the way he had. Never once had she become so immersed in anything that she didn't need to reach out and touch him, if not in person then by letting their souls touch in some meaningful way on the phone.

Not so with Nick. It was as if they existed on different planets during football season, and the expanse of space that separated them couldn't be bridged. Not even when they'd made love. That had probably hurt most of all.

"Things are going to change, Becky. When we get the boys back, things will change. That's a promise." He reached over and took her hands in his.

"I hope so, Nick, for your sake and the boys." But he'd made those promises before, always when his back was up against the wall. To give him credit, he'd probably even tried to change. But then football season would start, and he'd fall into the consuming drive to be the best receiver in the league all over again.

"I just want the boys home safely," she said. "I can't think beyond that."

"I know." Nick reached up and tangled his fingers in her hair, his thumb brushing her earlobe.

It would be so nice to wrap herself in his arms and have him hold her. Just hold her, but she couldn't let herself. Her mother would say she was stubborn. Too much like Jeremiah.

But it was more than stubbornness that made her keep Nick at arm's length when she ached for the comfort of his arms. It was survival.

She looked up as heavy footfalls trod down the hallway and stopped at the doorway. Sam was standing there.

"There's been a new development."

The slump of his shoulders told her the news would not be good.

# Chapter Nine

"We haven't been able to acquire the log from your freshman psychology class in college," Sam said, "but we ran a routine computer check on males who were in your high school at the same time you were there."

Becky sucked in a ragged breath. "Then I hope you found a more promising suspect than I did by looking at old yearbooks."

"We had some luck." Sam handed her a computer printout with two names followed by sketchy information obviously gleaned from police files. She scanned the data quickly.

The first one was Tim Gillespie, a male Caucasian who recently went bankrupt due to gambling debts he'd incurred along the Mississippi coast. The name was only vaguely familiar. She checked his age. "He would have been two years ahead of me. I don't actually remember him."

"Not surprising," Sam said. "According to what we have on him, he only lived in the area a few months."

"His family may have been migrant farm workers," Becky said. "We always had several of those who rotated in and out according to what crops were being harvested at the time."

"He's a long-shot suspect," Sam admitted. He tapped the second name. "What about Adam Leniestier? He's been arrested three times, always for some kind of get-rich-quick scam."

Adam she remembered well. "I dated him a few times my junior year," she said. "He was a con man even then, always a charmer and constantly trying to get someone to do his homework for him, but he was never in any real trouble."

"He's obviously progressed, but still guilty of nothing that's put him behind bars for any extended period of time."

Nick leaned closer to read over her shoulder. "Stealing credit cards from girlfriends and writing hot checks. That sounds worthy of a jail term to me."

"Not if he sweet-talks the girlfriends into withdrawing the complaint," Sam said.

Becky kept reading. "According to this, he did serve a few months for bilking FEMA out of money after Katrina."

"Right," Sam said. "He claimed he lost everything. Truth was he was living in New Jersey at the time."

"His dad still lives in Colts Run Cross," Becky said. "Mr. Leniestier goes to our church and works for the highway department, but Adam's mother divorced him right after high school and I haven't seen Adam since."

"Still, he sounds like the kind of man who might try to pull off a kidnapping." Nick slid the printout closer. "Except that it says here he's living in Denver now."

Becky considered the logistics. "If Adam got the idea for the kidnapping after seeing you get injured on Sunday, he'd have had to move fast."

Sam nodded and rubbed the tendons in his neck.

"We checked. There's no record of his taking a flight to Texas."

"He could have driven all night," Nick said, "or bought a ticket using a fake ID."

"Distinct possibilities," Sam agreed. "We're following up on him, but I don't think he's our man."

Becky got the impression Sam hadn't told them everything yet. "Is there another suspect?"

His eyes narrowed. "Do you recall a student in your class named Jake Hawkins?"

This time the name triggered disturbing memories. "I remember him."

"What can you tell us about him?"

"He moved to Colts Run Cross my senior year—too late to be included in the yearbooks. He seemed nice enough, but…"

"But what?" Nick asked when she hesitated, his voice hoarse and edgy.

"He never talked about his parents, but he moved in with his grandmother, Nancy Hawkins. She was a retired schoolteacher, the kind of teacher students loved to hate. Anyway, she died from a fall on her stairs right after Jake started living with her, and some of the kids claimed he murdered her."

"He was never arrested for that," Sam said.

"No. The police said it was an accident, but you know how rumors are. They just get started and take on a life of their own, especially since Jake wouldn't talk to anyone about the accident after that—not even at the funeral. I don't know where he went to live after his grandmother died."

Nick stepped away from Becky, but closer to Sam. "What do you have on him?"

"He spent three years in a state penitentiary for attacking a pregnant woman in a case of road rage on I-20 near Dallas. Apparently she rear-ended him, and he yanked her out of the car and stabbed her repeatedly with his pocketknife. The woman didn't die or lose the baby, but she spent a month in the hospital. Jake was paroled two months ago."

"Was he in the Huntsville facility?"

Sam nodded.

"So he's likely still nearby." Nick rammed his right fist into the palm of his left hand. "Damn. That's just the kind of lunatic who might kidnap two young boys on an impulse."

"Wouldn't his parole officer know where to find him?" Becky asked.

"Unfortunately, he's already broken the conditions of his parole by moving from his original address without letting anyone know where he was relocating."

"So he could be anywhere," Becky said.

"Yes, and unfortunately, there's more."

Her legs grew wobbly, and she dropped back to the sofa. More. Always more. "What now?"

"The prison psychologist was the only one who didn't recommend parole. He felt Jake was still capable of violence when provoked. He believed Jake to be emotionally unstable, prone to irrational rage and generally angry with the world."

Becky fought the burgeoning dread, but she had to face facts. "In other words, he's a dangerous sociopath."

"Find Jake Hawkins," Nick said. "I don't care what it takes. Just find him, or I will if I have to hire a whole damn army of men to track him down."

"We don't know that he's our guy," Sam reiterated.

"Find him anyway."

Given to irrational rage when provoked. And nothing would likely provoke him faster than finding out that they'd called in the FBI. And the longer this went on, the more likely he was to discover that fact.

Becky felt the stirrings of vertigo. Why didn't that damn phone ring?

"DERRICK."

Derrick jerked awake instantly at the sound of his name. His eyes darted about the room as he came to terms with where he was and why he couldn't move his hands.

He remembered turning the faucet with his head and running water over his wrists to try to loosen the tape. It hadn't worked. Neither had rubbing his wrists back and forth across the edge of the TV. He didn't remember falling asleep on the sofa, but he must have.

"Wake up, Derrick, and talk to me."

"I am awake." He held his breath expecting to hear the kidnapper yell at them to shut up. There was nothing. Surely the guy was still gone to get a phone. Maybe he wasn't coming back.

"What's going on out there?" David asked.

"Nothing." Derrick wiggled his way to a standing position and wished he could go to the bathroom. He needed to real bad. "Are you doing okay in there?"

"Kind of. Where's the kidnapper?"

"I don't see or hear him. I don't think he came back last night."

"Then I'm doing great. I have the tape off my wrists and almost off my feet."

"You're kidding, right?"

"No, I fell asleep, but then I woke up and started looking for something sharp. There's a nail sticking out of my headboard. I rubbed against it until I finally cut through the duct tape. Oh, jeez!"

"What's wrong?"

"The last of the tape came off my ankle. Felt like the skin was going to come off with it, but it's okay now."

Derrick heard a clunk that he figured was David sliding off the bed. He started working his way toward the door that separated them. He was glad he wasn't an inchworm that had to move this slowly all the time. He heard David rattling the doorknob.

David groaned and muttered a word their mother would have a fit if she'd heard him say. "I can't get out of here."

"I'm sure the kidnapper took the key with him." Even if he hadn't, Derrick couldn't have reached the padlock near the top of the door frame, and he sure couldn't climb on a chair with his feet bound.

Derrick had never seen a padlock on a bedroom door before, and he figured the guy had put it there just to lock them in.

"I'll have to break the door down," David said, "like the guy did in that movie we watched with Grandpa the other night."

"He had something to ram it with," Derrick said. And he hated to say it, but the actor was a lot bigger and stronger than David.

"There's an old Indian statue in here. It's made of iron, I think, like that dinner bell Bart hung on the back porch. I can hammer the door down with it, I bet."

Derrick backed out of the way as the statue crashed into the wood. The old wood cracked and splintered.

Not enough that he could see David through the hole, but a few more hits and he might be able to.

The statue crashed into the wood again, and this time there was an opening big enough he could have pushed his fist through it. The kidnapper would be super mad when he saw that. They'd best be long gone.

"Hurry," he called.

This time when the metal crashed against the door, the statue broke right through and ended up on Derrick's side. David grabbed the splintered wood and tore it away until he could climb right through.

"Grab a knife and cut me loose," Derrick said. "We have to get out of here before that stupid kidnapper gets back and goes ape."

"Yeah. We gotta move fast. He may be out kidnapping more kids."

"We'll escape and come back and save them."

"That would be cool. Then we'd really get our pictures in the newspaper."

"We might even get to be on TV."

David grabbed a kitchen knife from one of the drawers under the counter. Derrick turned so his brother could reach his wrists.

"Boy, this sure works better than a nail."

Derrick wiggled his fingers as the tape came loose, and David peeled it from his wrists. "I'll do my own ankles," he said, reaching for the handle of the knife.

"Good, 'cause I got to go to the bathroom."

In practically no time, Derrick's feet were free, as well.

He gave a whoop and kicked one of the beer cans that littered the floor the way he'd seen the kidnapper do. It crashed into the wall and clattered to the floor as Derrick rushed to the bathroom to take care of business.

David was at the refrigerator when Derrick made it back to the kitchen. "There's a couple bottles of water," he said as he grabbed one and twisted off the top. "I say we drink this one and save the other until later."

"Okay. You drink first. Is there anything else in there?"

"Beer."

"Mom would kill us if we drank that."

"There's ketchup and some bread. We can make a ketchup sandwich. I like those."

"For breakfast?"

"Better than oatmeal."

Derrick pulled an opened package of pretzels from the cabinet. That was all there was except for a couple of cans of tuna with easy-open tops, some crackers and a package of uncooked lima beans. He stuffed everything except the beans into the pockets of his jacket just in case they got lost again.

David was waiting at the door. "I wish we had our shoes."

"I just wish we had a key," Derrick said, suddenly realizing that they'd have to break down the front door as well to get out of the house. He grabbed the Indian statue from the floor and had it hefted above his head when he saw David pull the rope from his inside jacket pocket. He let the statue slip from his hands and crash to the floor.

"Do you want me to break the door?" David asked.

"Not yet. I'm thinking maybe we shouldn't escape."

"Are you loony? I'm escaping and right now." David

dropped the rope and grabbed the statue, grunting as he hoisted it over his head.

"If we run, we might just get lost again and the kidnapper could find us like before."

"And if we don't escape, we'll be stuck here with ketchup sandwiches for Christmas."

"Not if we're waiting for the kidnapper when he comes back. He thinks we're all tied up, so he won't be expecting anything." The plan kind of took shape as he talked. He liked it better all the time. "You could lasso him and pull him down, and I could hit him over the head with the statue and knock him out again. Then we could get the phone he went after and call Mom and Dad to come get us."

David held on to the statue. "What if I miss when I try to lasso him?"

"Then I'll still hit him and knock him out. I'll be behind the door. You can be perched on top of a chair, ready to throw the rope as he walks in."

"I don't know," David said.

"Well, I do. We'll outsmart him. You know, like *Home Alone*. That way we won't have to run around in the woods barefoot trying to find the way back to the highway."

"How are we going to tell Mom and Dad how to come get us when we don't even know where we are?"

"Then we'll call 911. They can find you anywhere. We'll be home in plenty of time for Christmas Eve."

David swung the rope. "Okay, but we have to get ready for action. The kidnapper might walk in that door any second."

Derrick's heart was beating fast. But they could do

it. He knew they could. And it would sure feel good to see Mom and Dad walk through that door together.

He just wished the together part would last forever. Divorce was like having a "parent-napper" steal your dad and keep him for most of every year.

THE TWO MEN stamped along side by side. They'd been hunting together for more than forty years, ever since they'd married sisters. Their wives loved holiday gatherings. Hermann and Bruce loved getting away from the hustle and bustle and occasionally even killing a buck.

They'd gotten a late start this morning. Too much whiskey last night. Sun was full up now, but there was still time to bag a big one if they were lucky.

"What the Sam Hill?"

Bruce shouldered his rifle and stared into the woods. "I don't see anything."

"Over there." Hermann pointed toward the half-washed-out dirt road they'd driven in on. The front of a black car was wrapped around a pine tree.

"Lucky bastard if he walked away from that."

Hermann trudged toward the wreck. "Don't look like it's been there too long. Not rusted out—well, except for that spot on the back fender, and that's an old dent."

Bruce was fifty pounds lighter than Hermann, mostly because the sister he'd married was a lousy cook. He overtook Hermann, reaching the car first. Hermann was only a step behind.

The driver was slouched over the steering wheel, not moving. Blood smeared the side window and was clotted in a clump of hair on the side of his head.

Hermann moved so as to get a better look. "This

must have happened in the last few hours. If the man's dead, I bet he's not even cold yet. Color's too good."

He eased the door open. The smell of cheap whiskey and marijuana hit him in the face.

"Guess that explains why he collided with the tree," Bruce said.

"Yep. Poor bastard didn't even get to finish his stash." Hermann pulled two joints from the man's shirt pocket and stuffed them into his own. "For later." He felt for a pulse. "Heart's ticking."

"He's just sleeping off a drug and booze stupor. Do you think we should call for an ambulance?"

"If we do, we'll get stuck out here for hours waiting for them to show up and then have to talk to some meddlesome country bumpkin sheriff," Hermann said. "And we'll have to deal with this codger if he wakes up. And he ain't gonna be in a good mood when he finds I lifted his doobies."

Bruce leaned in and put a hand on the man's back. The man groaned and jerked but didn't open his eyes. "We could call 911, just in case he's hurt worse than he looks."

"If you call, they'll have your name and number, so you're still gonna get involved whether you like it or not."

"Guess you're right. Gotta wonder what he was doing out here in the middle of nowhere, though."

"Probably getting away from a wife who's a dry-hole gusher just like we're married to."

"You're not telling me nothing I don't know. Mary Sue can talk the horns off a billy goat." Bruce slid his hand down the back of the seat and lifted the injured man's wallet from his pocket.

"What are you doing now?"

"I'm just checking to see if he has some ID on him." He opened the wallet and looked in the money sleeve. "Guy's broker than we are."

"Well, I'm not contributing to the cause," Hermann said, his eyes already peeled for game. "Are we going to hunt or not?"

"Wait, here's an ID. A driver's license, just issued two months ago to Jake Hawkins. Age thirty-two. Address in Huntsville, Texas."

"That's not more than forty-five minutes from here. He'll find his way home when he comes back to the real world."

"Hey, what's this buried in the back?" Bruce pulled out two hundred-dollar bills and unfolded them. "What do you know? The guy's not totally busted." He started to refold the bills, then stopped.

Hermann put his hand on his brother-in-law's shoulder. "Are you thinking what I'm thinking?"

"Damn straight, I am. He's just going to waste it on booze and drugs. In a way you could think of it like we're doing him a favor to take it."

"If you put it that way..." Hermann grinned, though he felt a bit uneasy. He'd never stolen money before—unless you counted cheating on your taxes.

"One for me and one for you." Bruce handed Hermann his hundred. "Now, this is what I call a successful hunting trip."

"And we haven't even spotted a whitetail."

They walked off, not bothering to shut the car door behind them. A jaybird jeered from a tree branch over their head. A rabbit scurried from one thick clump of underbrush, only to disappear into another one.

And an elegant buck with an impressive rack stepped into the clearing mere yards away. Hermann found him in the sight of his rifle and poised his finger on the trigger.

But the crack of gunfire did not come from his gun. He spun around in time to see Bruce fall to the ground in a pool of blood. And then the second bullet fired.

ODORS OF COFFEE, bacon, sausage, eggs, grits and biscuits wafted from the kitchen as Nick and Sam joined the Collingsworth family in the dining room. It held one table in the house large enough for all of them to fit around. The table was new, but was an almost-exact replica built by Matt and Bart to replace the one lost in the fire and explosion that had barely missed taking all their lives.

The Collingsworths had been through a lot together. It didn't surprise Nick at all that they would hang together in this.

Nick took the chair to the left of Becky while Zach's wife, Kali, squeezed into the chair on Becky's left.

"I talked to Zach on the drive over here," Kali said. "He's in the Point Blank area, showing Jake Hawkins's picture around and hoping someone there may know where to find him. But he's not mentioning the kidnapping," she added quickly. "He's saying the guy jumped parole, which is the truth."

"Good," Nick said. Not that they knew for certain Jake was behind the kidnapping, but he was definitely the most likely suspect that had surfaced.

"Did Zach get any sleep last night?" Becky asked.

"Not much, but Zach can go longer without sleep

than anyone I know. When I was in danger last winter, there were nights when he barely closed his eyes."

Matt forked a couple of sausage patties from the serving platter before passing it on. "Bart, Langston and I are cutting out of here in a few minutes. We're all taking our own trucks up to the Point Blank area."

"To do what?" Becky asked.

"Help Zach. There's a lot of back roads up there and not a lot of extra deputies. It was Sam's idea," Langston said. "And it definitely beats sitting around here doing nothing."

Jaime pushed away from the table. "Why just you guys? I can drive and ask questions. David and Derrick are my nephews, too."

"You'll never pass for a deputy tracking down a parole jumper," Nick said.

"Maybe not, but I'll come a lot closer to getting men to talk to me than you guys will. And I can look like a deputy if I want. I have a pair of khaki chinos and a boring jacket I can wear." She turned to Sam. "What do you say Mr. FBI agent? Would you buy that I'm a deputy?"

"Not unless you're wearing heat on your hip."

"I not only have a pistol but I'm an excellent marksman," she said.

"And so am I," Shelly said. "I'll go with you."

"Is that a good idea?" Lenora asked.

"Time is of the essence," Sam said.

He let it go at that, but as far as Nick was concerned the solemnity in his tone said a lot more. The boys had been missing almost two full days now, and they hadn't actually talked to them since shortly after the kidnapping. They had the ransom. It was the kidnapper who kept changing his tune.

Something was obviously wrong. And if he knew that, so did Becky and the rest of her family. They were walking that thin line between anxiety and outright panic.

Nick managed to get down a few bites of food. Becky didn't. She stared into space as if she couldn't even bear to look at the spoonful of scrambled egg she'd put on her plate.

Nick hated to see her hurting like this, hated that he hadn't protected their sons better. Hated that the only comfort he could offer were empty phrases.

His phone rang. The room grew deathly silent. Nick checked the caller ID. "Out of area."

Sam nodded, and Nick took the call even as he, Becky and Sam hurried back to the study.

He answered with his name. "Nick Ridgely."

"Good. You're just the man I want to talk to."

His coach. Not the man he wanted to talk to. Nick motioned for Sam and Becky to ignore the call. "I'm sorry I haven't gotten back to you, but I'm involved in a family emergency that I can't leave. It should be resolved soon, and I'll rush back to Dallas the minute it is and have the MRI and the CAT scan the neurologist ordered."

"This isn't like you, Nick. Why don't you level with me about what's going on?"

"Would it help if I said this was literally a matter of life and death?"

"It helps. I really need for you to say more."

"Look, I know I'm breaking the terms of my contract. You can fine me whatever you think is fair."

"I don't want to fine you. I want you to check back in the hospital. From what I hear from the doctor, you're not only in danger of never playing again but of risking paralysis."

"I think he's overreacting, but I'll have the tests run. Soon. Hopefully tomorrow."

Nick glanced at Becky. Damn. She was still wearing the earphones. He didn't want to get into this with her. Not now. "I can't talk now, Coach. I'll get back to you soon."

"Don't wait too long."

"No. I won't." Nick broke the connection before Becky heard more. She'd already heard too much.

She stared at him with a haunted look in her red and swollen eyes that ripped away the last of his tenuous control.

"Were you ever going to tell me the truth, Nick, or was all that talk about you changing just another broken promise?"

She was right. If he was ever going to change, the time was now. Only, there were some secrets he could never share.

## Chapter Ten

Paralyzed. It was a fear every wife of a professional football player lived with, but it had never seemed this frighteningly real. Becky clasped the back of a chair. The nervous adrenaline she'd lived with since the boys' disappearance dissolved, throwing her balance off kilter.

"You told me you were fine," she accused, "that all you needed was a few days' rest."

"You had enough to deal with without adding my troubles to the list."

"Your troubles? You make it sound as if we're talking about the common cold." She struggled for a deep breath to steady her emotions and clear her mind. "You should be in the hospital."

"No, I should be here. The tests can wait until the boys are safe."

"I don't get it," she said, trying to make sense of the incredible. "You were in the hospital from early Sunday evening until Monday noon. Surely that was enough time for them to do a CAT scan and an MRI."

"The machine was down, so that had to wait until morning. And then the team decided to fly in a neurologist from California who specializes in sports injuries resulting in severe trauma to the neck and spinal cord. He wanted to be there to supervise everything."

"So they did nothing for you that night?"

"They gave me pain medication, kept me comfortable, took X-rays. The usual."

"But no prognosis of any kind?"

"The E.R. doctor said I most likely had a central spinal cord contusion. That's not necessarily serious."

No, not serious at all. Only possible paralysis. "Don't gloss over this as if I'm worrying over nothing. I may be your wife in name only at this point, but I'm still your wife. I think I deserve to know exactly what the doctors told you in the hospital."

"In the first place, I'm not glossing over anything. I've set my priorities. Getting the boys back is number one on that list. In the second place, I've had MRIs and CAT scans before. The doctors order them if there's any doubt. It's called preventing malpractice suits. Their worries never amounted to anything before, and I don't expect them to this time. I know my body. I'm not in that much pain."

He nailed her with a penetrating stare. "And in the third place, you're my wife in name only because you chose for it to be that way. You stopped living with me. Stopped letting me touch or make love to you. You're the one who filed for divorce. I've fought it every damn step of the way." His voice had become strained, hoarse with emotion.

He was right on all counts, but he was the one who'd repeatedly shut her out of his life, just as he'd done again by keeping his medical condition from her—as if it were none of her concern.

Her heart twisted, and a raging need settled in her

chest. She didn't know how she felt anymore except that she couldn't bear to think of Nick's being seriously injured. "I don't want to argue with you, Nick. Just tell me what the doctors told you."

"Fair enough." He crossed the room and stepped into her space, so close she could feel his warm breath as he took her hand and pulled her into the chair she'd been using for support. "Sit down, and I'll explain what I know."

He pulled a chair up close to hers. "I took a bad hit. I'm not denying that."

"I know. I saw the replay." And the horror of watching him motionless for long, agonizing minutes was a feeling she'd never forget. "You must have been in terrible pain."

"I didn't feel anything. That's what made it so alarming for me and the trainers who rushed onto the field."

Even admitting that much was a first for Nick. He always had to be tougher than anyone else, thought any sign of weakness on the field was for rookies or sissies.

"When did the feeling return?"

"Not until I was at the hospital and through with the X-rays. I told you that on the phone when you called."

"Exactly what is a central spinal cord contusion?"

"If you want the medically correct description, you'll have to go to the doctor for that."

"I'll take layman's terms. I just want to know what you're up against."

"I'm up against a possibly deranged kidnapper."

"Nick…"

"Right. You want facts. Your way. As best I can understand it, a spinal cord contusion happens when something thumps the spine and a bruise occurs. If it improves, no problem."

"And if it worsens?"

"Then the circulation to the spinal cord is affected."

"And you could wind up paralyzed." She shuddered and clasped her hands tightly to keep them from shaking. She'd thought she could handle this, but the images of Nick as a paraplegic or worse were making her physically ill.

Nick took her balled-up hands in his. "It didn't worsen, Becky. I'm here with you. You can see that I'm fine."

"Then why is the doctor who called yesterday and your coach so concerned?"

"The doctor is concerned that the spine might still be unstable and that if it were to receive another blow, it could still slip and cause complications. But, he doesn't know my body like I do. I've taken thousands of hits. I'd know if this were more than a routine injury. I'll go in and have all the tests he wants when the boys are safe. For now, just trust me with this."

Hot, salty tears burned at the back of her eyes. Their marriage might be over, but Nick was the father of her sons. She'd never stopped loving him. That's not what the divorce was about.

Nick caught an escaping tear with a brush of his thumb on her cheek. "How did we get here, Becky? How did we get to the place where we can't touch or hold each other when faced with the most frightening time in our life? And I'm not talking about my injury."

How? She'd gone over and over those reasons both with him and in her own mind, but at this minute, they didn't seem all that important. They would matter again when all of this was over. When David and Derrick were safe. When Nick was back on the playing field going on with his life, that didn't include her.

But right now, she needed him so much it hurt. She slipped her arms around his neck and held on tight.

BULL HAD THE mother of all hangovers. It felt as if someone were hammering nails into his skull as he dragged the men's bodies into the woods. He hadn't intended to shoot them. He'd just gone nuts when he realized they were robbing him.

Blown a fuse the way he had on the highway that day when the pregnant woman had cut in too close and forced him into the guardrail. That's how it was with him. Something snapped and he went crazy. Drinking and drugs made it worse.

He'd made a big mistake getting drunk and high last night when the biggest deal of his life was in the making. Five million dollars ransom for a couple of bratty boys he wouldn't have given two cents for. He should have already made the exchange by now. Should be in Mexico drinking a margarita with a pretty *señorita*.

Instead he was sweating like a pig and trying to cover up a couple of stupid murders. The man was heavier than he looked, and Jake's arms ached from maneuvering the deadweight through the heavy underbrush. And after this he still had another one to go. Then he'd have to find a way to cover up the blood. It wouldn't do to have the bodies found before he was long gone.

He had one of the men's phones and a set of car keys. He wasn't sure where their vehicle was parked, but he doubted it was far from here. Their boots weren't muddy enough for them to have been out here long. Besides, with that little shower they must have gotten while he was out of it last night, their trail should be easy enough to follow.

Too bad it hadn't rained before those Collingsworth kids had escaped. He could have found the little snots in no time and saved himself a lot of trouble. But he didn't have to worry about them now. They were tied up and locked in. They weren't going anywhere without him.

All he needed was to make the call to Nick Ridgely and have them meet him at Lone Star Executive Airport in Conroe. But he'd have to move quickly. In fact, he should make that call right now and then just bury the phone with the bodies.

Once these corpses were found, this area would be crawling with cops. He damn sure wasn't going back to prison on double murder charges. A man could die behind bars for that.

Which meant if there were any complications before the exchange, he'd have to kill the Ridgely boys so that they couldn't identify him. And then he'd find his own way to Mexico. He'd be poor, but poor and on the run beat death row by a country mile.

EVIE PARKER ARRIVED just after 9:00 a.m. carrying a medium-size tan piece of luggage and a grim expression that fit the chilly undercurrent that hung over the big house like a dark shroud. She was petite with ash-blond hair, razor cut to hug the nape of her neck.

Becky was immediately impressed with her professionalism and her warmth. Those two traits didn't always go hand in hand. She wasn't sure about her ability to take Becky's place in the plane, however. Their size was similar. Their facial features weren't.

"What's with the paparazzi outside your gate?" Evie

asked once the introductions were over. "Did word of the kidnappings leak out?"

"They're here hounding Nick," Sam explained. "He's a star receiver for the Cowboys. He was injured in last Sunday's game."

"My brother-in-law Matt Collingsworth assigned a few Rangers to guard duty to keep the media hounds at bay," Nick said. "The cowboys didn't hassle you when you arrived, did they? I'd told them we were expecting you."

"They were very efficient. They checked my credentials and waved me right through."

Trish brought a plate of warmed coffee cake and a pot of coffee to the study as Sam caught Evie up to speed on the negotiation progress or lack thereof and on the attempts to identify and locate suspects.

Evie sipped the coffee. "Then you don't have a real lead as to Jake Hawkins's whereabouts?"

"Not yet," Sam acknowledged. Crumbs showered his shirt as he bit into a chunk of coffee cake. He brushed them to the floor with the palm of his hand. "But he's only a suspect at this point. We have nothing to tie him directly to the crime. All we know is that he has a criminal record and he went to the same high school as Becky."

"For a few months," Becky added.

"So our best bet would be to get a call from the kidnapper," Evie said.

"I couldn't agree more," Becky said. "But one other thing while we're on the subject. No matter who the kidnapper is, if it turns out he has seen me recently, I find it difficult to think he'll believe you're me."

Sam leaned back in his chair. "That's only because

you haven't seen Evie's disguise mastery at work. Once she's done, even Nick may have difficulty telling the two of you apart."

Becky motioned toward the suitcase. "And everything you need for that transformation is in there."

"No. Some will come from your closet and dressing room. I'll wear the outfit you choose and apply your makeup. My bag contains a couple of blond wigs that I matched to your picture and materials for altering my facial features."

"You can alter your facial features?"

"Nothing dramatic, but minor adjustments. I took lessons from a Hollywood makeup artist who's worked on a lot of major films. You'd be surprised how easy it is to acquire a specific look. But I don't think we'll have to do much altering this time. Makeup, hair and clothing will pretty much do it."

Becky still had her doubts. "I guess seeing is believing."

Nick pushed up the sleeve of his black T-shirt and glanced at his watch. "How long will this transformation take?"

"I like to have an hour, but I can work faster if I have to."

"I once saw her put on twenty pounds and some serious wrinkles in under twenty minutes," Sam said.

"Was the kidnapper fooled?"

"Yes, and she managed to take his gun away from him and apprehend him. He's still in jail."

Becky's cell phone rang, startling her and running clawing fingers over her nerves. She checked the ID. "It's a friend from Colts Run Cross," she said, letting it ring. She'd avoided taking most of her calls since the boys' disappearance. Eventually she'd have to return some of them but not yet. Making small talk under the circumstances would be torturous if not impossible.

Evie finished her coffee and set her empty cup on the desk next to Sam's. "Shall we get started, Becky?"

"I'm ready, but still a bit apprehensive about your taking my place on the plane."

Sam rubbed his chin thoughtfully, though his facial expression never changed. "Evie has to take your place, Becky. It's too risky for you to go with the kidnapper. I couldn't guarantee your safety."

"I'm not worried about *my* safety."

"I am," Nick said.

Not his call, but she wouldn't argue the point until she saw what Evie could do with a wig and some war paint. "I'll have the walkie-talkie with me." She held it up to make her point. "Let me know immediately if the kidnapper calls."

"Absolutely," Sam said. "Hang in there. We're making progress, whether it seems like it or not."

She wasn't fooled. He might keep up an optimistic front, but the ticking clock was wearing down all their confidence, his included.

Nick followed her to the door. When they reached it, he took her hand, tentatively as if expecting her to yank it away. "I know you're uneasy with this, Becky, but you can't get on that plane with that crackpot. Don't even toy with that idea."

She tried to pull away, not wanting to argue with him and knowing she could make no promises.

His grip tightened. "Be reasonable. The boys will need you here with them." He met her gaze, his own fears written in every line of his face. "So do I, and I can't face going through all this again while you're riding the wild blue yonder with a lunatic."

He was talking like a husband, as if the bonds between them were strong and loving. She wanted to trust that, but his need for her had always been short-lived, dissolving completely when football season claimed his mind, body and soul. Only now his season might have come to a permanent end and…

And she couldn't deal with any of this now. The stakes for her sons were too high. She took the stairs with Evie, praying with every step that her boys were safe.


NICK'S CELL PHONE rang at exactly 10:18 a.m. The caller ID said Hermann Grazier. He didn't recognize the name, but something deep inside him shouted that this was the call he'd been waiting for. This time he didn't wait for Sam's thumbs-up to answer.

"Nick Ridgely," he said, answering with his name as he frequently did.

"It's time for the show."

Adrenaline rushed Nick's system, speeding his heart until it felt as if it might burst from his chest. He pushed the button on the walkie-talkie to let Becky know the kidnapper had made contact.

"I'm ready," Nick said.

"Then listen and get this straight. One screwup on your part and you'll be burying your sons for Christmas."

Nick had never hated a man more. "Which airport?"

"Lone Star Executive in Conroe."

That would work. In fact, Langston had already mentioned it as a possibility. Langston would fly them by a helicopter—which was already waiting on the ranch helipad—to the small reliever airport northwest of Houston, where his plane and the FBI pilot by the name of Pete Halifax and two additional agents were waiting. Then it would be a very short hop to Conroe.

"We can meet you there in an hour."

"You do that. Have the money and the pilot on the plane with the engine running. When I show up, have Becky standing near the plane. I'll release the boys when I see her, but I'll be armed. One foul-up and I'll shoot to kill. I'll get at least one of the three before you get me. I might even get lucky and get them all.

"I'll call when I get there, and you can direct me to the waiting jet. Just remember. Double-cross me once I'm on that plane and bang bang, your sons' mother is dead."

Sam nodded at Nick for him to accept the conditions.

"Everything will be just as we agreed," Nick said. "Now, let me talk to my sons."

"I'd like to do that, Nick, I really would, but we have a little problem."

Nick's fists knotted. His stomach followed suit. "What kind of problem?"

"They're not exactly with me at the moment. They're much too annoying for me to hang out with all the time. You really should teach them some manners."

"Where are they?"

"Telling you that would kind of void my bargaining powers, don't you think?"

"I want to talk to them and know they're safe and that you actually still have them before I turn over the money."

"You'll know soon enough. Meet me at the airport, Nick. My rules. No cops. One hour."

Nick was reaching for Sam's rapidly scribbled note when the connection went dead.

"I'm calling him back," Sam said. "Demand he let you talk to David and Derrick."

One touch of the sophisticated machinery Sam was manning had the kidnapper's phone ringing. There was no answer.

Becky yanked off her earphones and dropped them to the desk. "We're doing what he said. I don't care what either of you think. They're my sons. He says they're safe, and I have to believe that."

Sam grimaced. "Not the best scenario but this is manageable. So, you heard the woman. Time for the games to begin. The boys should be home by dinner."

Nick could sense Becky's apprehension, though she'd become more animated than at any time since this had all begun. He hated that he wouldn't be with her for the ride to Conroe, but she'd be with Sam. He'd keep her safe.

They went over the plans again. Sam would call the shots outside the plane. Pete would be the one in control inside the plane. Pete would pretend to have a problem while preparing for takeoff. As soon as the kidnapper was distracted, the two agents hiding in the food compartment of the plane would rush out, and between the four of them, they'd disarm and apprehend their target.

It sounded simple, but Nick knew that just like a Sunday game plan, one mistake could turn victory to defeat. But unlike a football game, failure to succeed could be deadly.

"I'll get Langston," Becky said.

"Right," Nick agreed, "and tell your mother to rev up the Christmas plans. This is going to be the best Christmas in the history of all Collingsworth Christmases. And I don't plan to miss a second of it."

Nick put out a hand to Sam as Becky disappeared through the door. "If we get David and Derrick back safely, we'll owe it all to you. Now, just take care of my wife. I'm leaving her in your hands."

"I'll do my best. She's a terrific woman. You're a lucky man."

"Damn lucky."

But luck or not, he might end up losing her to a ridiculous divorce. He didn't know how to keep her. And he couldn't call in the FBI for that.

## Chapter Eleven

Becky felt miles removed from the action and frustrated with her inability to know what was going on. She was standing at a window in a cargo company facility that was owned by the family of one of Bart's fraternity brothers during his college days.

Nick had explained that with the paparazzi clamoring after him since his accident, she was merely trying to avoid unwanted attention and endless questions while waiting to board a chartered jet. Perhaps that was why the workers had pretty much ignored her except for offering a soft drink when she'd arrived.

She sipped the diet cola from the can and shifted for a better look at Langston's plane. She was too far away to see any movement around it except for two businessmen climbing into a jet belonging to a local charter service.

She checked her watch again. Ten minutes past the appointed time. Still no sign of the kidnapper or David and Derrick.

Nick was on the plane with Evie and Pete. She'd learned from Sam on the way here that Pete was a top-notch agent who'd been a fighter pilot in the navy before leaving the service to join the Bureau. Sam claimed that he, Evie and the two agents who were hidden away were the perfect team to apprehend the abductor.

Sam was inside the waiting area, just a few yards away from the plane, posing as a businessman waiting to catch a charter flight.

Her phone rang. She recognized the number as Sam's and murmured a breathless hello.

"I just heard from Pete. There's been no word as yet. Nick wanted me to let you know."

Frustration rolled in her stomach and ground along her nerve endings. "He should be here. We did everything he said."

Only, that wasn't quite true. He'd ordered them not to call in law enforcement. They'd gone to the FBI. "Maybe he knows he's being set up."

"That's extremely unlikely. Don't start panicking, Becky. We have what he wants. There's no reason not to be optimistic."

None except that her sons were nowhere in sight. Her cell phone beeped. "I'm getting another call."

"It's probably Nick, though he'll be calling on Evie's or Pete's phone. We're leaving Nick's open for the kidnapper."

"Okay. Keep your fingers crossed. Keep everything you have crossed." She broke that connection and took the incoming call.

"All systems are go, here. Are you okay?" Nick's voice was strained, though he was obviously striving for upbeat.

"No," she answered honestly. She checked her watch again. Time had never moved so slowly. "Maybe this isn't the right airport."

"It's the right airport. Lone Star Executive in Conroe, Texas. He was perfectly clear on that. Take deep breaths and try to stay calm."

"Not going to happen."

"You've been great so far, Becky. Don't fall apart when we're this close to having the worst behind us."

*If* the demented abductor showed up. There truly was no reason for him not to, yet the dread seemed to be swelling inside her like an angry virus that was consuming her lungs. "Let me know the second you hear something."

"Will do. And, Becky…" His voice became a raspy whisper that faded to silence.

"What is it?"

"When this is over, when the boys are safe, we need to talk about us."

Her heart seemed to burst to life only to immediately shrivel back inside the cocoon where she'd hidden it away over the last painful months. They were both vulnerable now. Afraid for their sons. Treading panic. Double jeopardy for him with his future in football so unsure.

But she couldn't bear to start thinking their marriage could work again only to have those hopes slashed the second he went back to the team. Filing for the divorce had been like cutting her heart from her body. She'd put up a front during the day only to cry herself to sleep on countless nights, aching to crawl into his arms one more time. But she needed more than he could give.

She took a deep breath, wishing it could steady her soul. "We'll see." She couldn't promise more than that.

"HERMANN GRAZIER is a construction worker who lives in Livingston, Texas. His wife is a schoolteacher at a public elementary school. They have two children, a boy aged twelve and a girl aged nine. No criminal record and no reason to think he is involved in the boys' abduction."

"Any explanation for how the kidnapper came in possession of Mr. Grazier's phone?" Nick paced the small plane as he carried on the conversation with Zach, his eyes constantly peering out the window for any sign of David and Derrick. Their arrival was officially— he glanced at his watch—forty-six minutes past due.

"Mrs. Grazier says he had the cell phone last night when they went out to dinner. She knows because he called his mother from the restaurant. She thinks she took it with him this morning, but when she tried to call him, there was no answer."

"Where is he supposed to be today?"

"Deer hunting with her sister's husband. Her sister's family drove over from Birmingham, Alabama, yesterday for the Christmas holidays. They take turns visiting each other's homes every year and the men always spend at least one day hunting."

"Tradition." Nick mumbled the word, then wondered why. He couldn't care less about Hermann Grazier's traditions, and he was sick to his soul of clues that went nowhere and negotiations that were ignored.

Damn. He'd preached staying calm to Becky, but he was losing it fast. "Where is he hunting?"

"His wife didn't know, but the phone call came from somewhere near Oakhurst, Texas, just a few miles east of the area where the last call was made from. There have been no calls made on the phone since the one made to you by the kidnapper. And if the phone is turned on at the present time, it's lost the connection with the network."

"So basically we know nothing."

"I'm working every angle I can, while I'm saddled with keeping the kidnapping a secret."

"It won't matter anyway if this exchange takes place." Nick almost choked on the *if*. This had to take place. Everything the kidnapper had asked for was ready and waiting. Accompanied by FBI agents, but he was certain the kidnapper didn't know that. If he had, he'd have never set up the meeting to start with.

"You still think we should have gone with the AMBER Alert and full-scale search, don't you, Zach?"

"What do I know? The boys will probably come hopping across the tarmac toward the plane any minute now. We'll all be celebrating back at the big house by dark."

It sounded good. But the clock was ticking. The drive from the Oakhurst area where the call originated to the airport in Conroe shouldn't have taken more than an hour tops. "Did you give the information you just gave me to Sam?"

"I did. He's the one who gave me Pete's number so I could call you. I knew you'd be keeping your line open."

"Have you talked to Becky?"

"I did, but I didn't mention anything about Hermann Grazier to her. She's a meltdown waiting to happen. I'm not sure how much more she can take."

Neither was Nick and that was slicing away at his control like the sharp edge of a machete. They needed action. They needed their sons' boisterous antics. Needed to hear their laughter ringing in their ears.

They needed one lousy break.

He finished the conversation and went back to pacing. After another hour had passed, even Evie and Pete had given up on trying to reassure him.

Two hours later the kidnapper had still not made contact. Nick walked away from the plane and called Becky. He needed to hear her voice. Most of all he needed her with him. He didn't have to go back on the plane. He could drive her home, and Sam could ride with Pete and Evie.

He made the call, but he was too late. Jaime had already come for her and was driving her back to the big house. He'd call her on the way home, though. It was time they pulled out all the stops.

Nick picked up his pace as he walked to the area where Sam was waiting. From out of the blue, something felt as if it had snapped in his back and white-hot pain shot up his spine. The doctor's warning echoed in his mind. He ignored it. The negotiations were a bust, but he couldn't give up. He had to find David and Derrick. For them. For Becky. For anything in life to ever matter again.

"I'VE LOOKED IN every pocket. He doesn't have a phone."

Derrick dropped the cold rag he was using to soak up the oozing blood from the kidnapper's shoulder. "He has to have a phone. That's what he went after."

"Well, he must have just bought whiskey instead."

The kidnapper mumbled something that sounded like more of the bad words he'd been shouting before David had stuffed a cotton washcloth into his mouth to gag him.

Derrick picked up the almost empty roll of duct tape and tossed it to the sofa. The kidnapper was on the floor, right where he'd fallen when David had lassoed him and yanked him down like a mean calf.

Derrick had done the real damage, though, popping him over the back of the head with the Indian statue. Well, mostly he'd caught his shoulder, but it had left him howling in pain while Derrick bound his wrists and ankles just the way the kidnapper had bound theirs yesterday.

Then, just to make sure he stayed put, they'd tied the end of the rope to the leg of the sofa. He'd have to drag that around with him if he moved. Pretty cool. Derrick couldn't wait to tell his friends how they'd tricked the grown bully.

"I bet Janie Thomas tries to kiss me at the Christmas pageant when I tell how we captured this jerk," Derrick said.

"Ugh."

"I won't let her, but I bet she'll want to."

"How come she'll want to kiss you? I'm the one who lassoed the kidnapper."

"Yeah, but you wouldn't pick her for your kick ball team in PE."

"She can't catch. Can't kick, either."

"But she's hot."

"You don't even know what hot means."

"Do so."

David scratched the itch where the tape had irritated his right ankle. "Forget Janie. What do we do now that there's no phone?"

"We'll have to try to find our way back to the main road."

"What if we just get lost again?"

"We won't," Derrick said. At least he hoped they wouldn't. It had been pretty scary out there roaming around lost, especially in the dark. "But this time we won't have anyone chasing us. The kidnapper will be right here waiting on the cops."

The kidnapper started flopping his body around. His face got so red that Derrick thought he might be choking. He pulled the rag from the guy's mouth.

The man spit on the floor and then started cursing them out again.

David got down on one knee and held the rag over the man's head. "If you don't quit saying all those bad words, I'll put the stopper back in."

The man spit again, this time aiming it at David. It missed, and it ended up dribbling off his own cheek. Served him right.

"Neither one of you have a lick of sense. If you did, you'd be bargaining with me for part of the five million your parents are paying to get you back."

"Yeah, right, like our parents have that kind of money."

"You're Collingsworths. Your family has more money than God. Just your daddy's bonus is probably in the millions."

"That can't be right," David said. "Mom said those skateboards we wanted were too expensive."

"And that we were too young for them," Derrick added, to be fair.

"She's just stingy," the kidnapper said. "Anyway I already called them. They're on their way here right now to bring me the money and take you back to the ranch. I say you get this tape off of me and we make a deal."

"I say you're crazy," David said.

"Yeah, why would we even believe you that our parents are on their way here?"

"Did you think I was just going to keep you brats around forever? That's the whole point of a kidnapping. They give me ransom money. I give them you, and then I walk away."

That part made sense. And if Momma and Daddy were on their way here, they'd be the crazy ones if they went off and got lost again trying to find their way to the main highway or to find help.

Derrick motioned to David to follow him outside.

"You could buy a lot of skateboards with your share of the money," the kidnapper called after them. "And I'd sneak it to you so that your parents would never know you were involved. You'd be the richest kids in school."

"No way! Janie Thomas is the richest kid in school. Her dad owns the grocery store."

"Well, at least give me a drink of water before you leave."

"We aren't leaving—not yet anyway. And there's not any water except that gross stuff that comes out of the tap." And Derrick and David were way too smart to drink that stuff.

"There's plenty of bottled water. You just have to know where to find it. There's some food, too. Untie me, and I'll tell you where it is. You help me get the ransom. I help you. It's the way the world works. Smart kids like you should know that."

They ignored him, stepped onto the porch and closed the door behind them. A clap of thunder rattled the windows of the cabin. The wind had picked up, and the clouds turned dark. It was going to rain again. They'd get soaked if they left now.

"Do you think he's telling the truth about our parents coming to get us?" David asked.

Derrick knocked a cricket from the rickety banister. "I don't know. He didn't come back with a phone, so I guess that means he could have used a pay phone to tell them where to bring the money."

"He left here in that old black car and came back in a new one." David walked down the steps and leaned against the vehicle. "What do you make of that?"

"I don't know. Maybe he stole it to make his getaway after he gets the money."

"Football players do make a lot of money, so maybe Daddy is going to pay the ransom." David hurried back to the porch as the first drops of rain splattered his head.

"I guess we could wait a little while and see if Momma and Daddy come. It's not like the kidnapper is going to do anything to us now."

"Right," David agreed. "No way we'd be stupid enough to cut him free, and if he tries anything, I have his pistol."

"Which we should probably keep with us at all times." Instead of on the table where they'd left it when they came out here. Lightning lit up the gray sky followed by booming thunder. The rain fell harder.

"If we go now, we'll get drenched anyway," Derrick decided out loud. "I don't want to be sick during the holiday break."

"Me, either. Let's go see if we can find that water. Or I'll have to start drinking the rain."

"Food would be good, too."

"Yeah. I can't wait to get home."

BECKY TRUDGED THE few steps, hating to step into the big house. Her family would try to console her, but they'd feel the same crushing sense of fear and defeat that had haunted her since she'd first realized that the kidnapper was not going to show.

Lenora opened the door. She pulled Becky into her arms and, though she was no doubt trying to be brave, her hot tears wet Becky's neck.

"Please, Mom. I know you mean to help, but I can't handle this now. I just need to be alone."

"I understand, sweetheart. But you can't give up. We'll find the boys. We'll all help, and we won't give up until David and Derrick are back here with us."

Words. Just words. The smell of chocolate chip cookies hit Becky's nostrils and sent her stomach into feverish rolls. She ran for the bathroom, making it just in time to fill the toilet with green bile and the little nourishment she'd been able to force down that day. When she could hold her head up without the bathroom spinning, she went to the sink and splashed her face with cold water.

Reaching the towel, her fingers brushed a crystal bowl filled with shimmering red and gold ornaments. The sight of the bright decoration sent her over the edge, and before she could stop herself, she'd swept the bowl to the tile floor in a crash of broken glass and a stampede of rolling iridescent balls.

She sank to the floor, her body gripped by mind-numbing shudders. A crimson stream trickled down her leg. She'd cut herself, but she didn't feel anything but the scream gurgling in her throat.

The bathroom filled with people. Someone's arms went around her shoulders. Someone's hands tended her wound. The bile rose up in her throat again, and a wave of nausea gripped and tightened her stomach.

"Leave me alone. Please, just leave me alone."

"I'm here now. I'll take over."

Nick's voice rose above the noise and confusion.

"Go away," she said.

He didn't. The others did.

Tears were streaming down Becky's face now, and her heart felt as if it had died inside her chest.

Nick's arms wrapped around her, and he lifted her as if she were a small child.

"It's okay, baby. You have every right to cry, throw fits, scream. You do whatever helps."

She closed her eyes tightly and buried her face in his chest as he carried her up the stairs. The fight slowly went out of her but not the heartbreak of knowing every second that passed was taking her sons further away from her.

Nick pushed into her bedroom, yanked back the pale yellow coverlet and laid her on the sheets. "You need some rest. Lenora's calling the doctor to see if he'll prescribe something to help you sleep."

"I don't need pills. I need David and Derrick to come home."

Nick sat down on the bed beside her. "I just talked to Zach. He's following our latest dictates and going full speed ahead now like you told him you wanted when the kidnapper didn't show. The sheriff's department has put out an AMBER Alert and is faxing pictures of the boys to every law enforcement office in the state. He and Sam will coordinate the investigation together from this point on."

"This is some kind of bitter reprisal against one of

us, Nick. It has to be someone who hates us and wants to get back at us the way Melvin Rogers did when he tried to blow up the big house with all of us in it."

"Melvin failed. So will this man."

"But this man has our sons." She started to shake again, the sobs beginning somewhere deep inside her and fighting their way to the surface.

Nick kicked out of his shoes and climbed into bed beside her. He wrapped around her spoon-style, his broad chest fitting against her back. Just like old times. Only nothing was like old times and would never be again. She grabbed quick, sobering breaths and then pulled away.

"Please just let me hold you, Becky. I can't do this alone. Neither can you."

She ached to slide back into his arms, but the cold bitterness of reality wouldn't let her. She turned to face him, clinging to the same stubborn pride that had kept her going even before the boys were abducted.

"I wasn't the one who tore us apart, Nick." She was being a shrew but this all hurt so much. She couldn't hold all her feelings inside and not choke on the anguish. The kidnapping. Knowing that Nick's need for her could never last. "You chose football over the boys and me. You chose being a star over being a husband and dad."

"It was never like that, Becky."

"Then how was it, Nick? Tell me how it was when you decided to treat me as if I were as invisible as the cheers you craved, because it felt like total rejection to me."

"It felt like survival to me, Becky."

Nick slid his feet to the floor and walked away from

the bed, stopping at the window and staring into the dismal, gray afternoon sky. She'd never be satisfied short of the truth, never be satisfied until she sent him back to the darkest corners of his miserable youth.

Not that he'd ever fully escaped it. Not that he could and therein lay the roots of all their problems. He'd tried desperately to move past his tainted history, had buried it so deep that not even the news media had discovered it.

But the shame was still inside him, taunting him and reminding him that he would never be good enough for Becky. That he'd never come close to measuring up to Collingsworth standards.

Her brothers could always be counted on to do what was right. They'd never turn their back on a woman in trouble. Simple truths they lived by. The basics that set them apart from the crowd.

Well, he wasn't a Collingsworth and never would be. He should just accept that and let Becky go on with the divorce and on with her life.

Becky sat up in bed, her eyes wide and accusing. "Just admit it, Nick. Say I wasn't enough woman for you. Say you deserved someone like Brianna Campbell to sport around and play celebrity with. Tell me there were dozens of Briannas. Damn it, just say something."

"Brianna? You think our problems have something to do with the likes of her?"

"She was in your hospital room when I called."

"I didn't invite her. She just showed up."

"But you have been dating her."

"A friend of hers is going out with one of our running backs. The four of us had dinner together one night. If that constitutes a date, then I'm guilty. But dinner is all it was." He shoved his hair back from his face and went back to stand at the head of the bed.

"I could have lots of women, Becky. It goes with the territory. I've never wanted anyone but you, not since the first night we…"

The first night they'd made love. The memories rushed his mind now, so intense his body reacted in unwanted ways. He concentrated on killing the tell-tale stirrings that would only make this worse. "There's never been anyone but you, Becky."

She shivered and wrapped her arms around her chest. "I almost wish there had been other women, Nick. They would have been easier to compete with than football."

He nodded, knowing she was right on some level even though it wasn't what she thought. "Football wasn't my mistress, Becky. It was my life, at least I thought that until faced with losing David and Derrick."

He wrapped his hands around the bedpost, wishing he had a football in them right now. Only he might never have one in them again, at least not as an NFL player. He was losing everything. How the hell could the truth hurt him anymore?

"I'm not who you think I am, Becky."

"What are you saying?"

"My father didn't die while fighting insurgents in the Middle East. My mother didn't die of cancer."

"I don't understand."

No, how could she? She knew only the fabricated version of his life, the fairy tale he'd concocted when he'd gone to live with the last foster family. His muscles bunched and throbbed as his thoughts hurdled into the past.

"My father attacked my mother in a drunken fit of

rage when I was six years old. It wasn't the first time he'd hit her, and I'm sure it wouldn't have been the last. Only this time I was going to protect her. I went to the kitchen and got our longest knife.

"But I wasn't fast enough. When he slammed his fist into her stomach, she stumbled into the knife I was holding. I was going to protect her. Instead I killed her."

Becky slid from the bed and stood beside him. Her face had turned pale but her shoulders were squared, her stare unrelenting. "Why didn't you tell me this before?"

"The same reason I never told anyone. I wanted to forget it had ever happened. I thought about telling you time and time again, but you're a Collingsworth. Your family reeks of perfection. I didn't want your pity or theirs. I never wanted anyone's pity. Football made sure I never got it."

"But that was all so long ago, Nick. You've proved yourself over and over since then. Besides, you were just a kid, and none of that was your fault."

"You'd think, but it doesn't work that way. Football was the only thing I ever truly excelled at. It made me feel like I was somebody. And once I'm on the field I can't settle for less than perfection. No matter what I know logically, it's like I'm driven, the same as when I played high school and then college ball. I have to be better than everyone else to be good enough."

"You should have told me. It would have helped me understand."

"I'm telling you now. I want a chance to make us work, Becky. Just a chance, that's all I'm asking. But a real chance where you live with me even when things get tough, and you don't go running back to the ranch."

She leaned into him, resting her head on his chest.

He circled her with his arms and buried his face in her sweet-smelling hair.

"Oh, Nick. I want to say yes, but…I need time," she whispered, finally pulling away.

It wasn't the answer he wanted. But it was probably better than he deserved.

Becky's phone rang. She grabbed for it and checked the caller ID. "It's Zach."

"HAVE YOU FOUND OUT something new?" Becky asked before Zach had opportunity to return her greeting.

"I'm not sure. Some kids on four-wheelers out riding in the area near where the phone call was made found a car with its front end wrapped around a tree. They called the information in to the local sheriff's department. Two deputies are there now."

"That's all? Just a wrecked car?"

"I think the car may be the one used to abduct David and Derrick."

A collision would explain why the kidnapper didn't show. But… "Where are the boys? Have you checked the local hospitals? Was there blood?"

"We're checking the hospitals now. There's no sign of blood in the car, but the vehicle fits the description of the one that picked up the boys on Monday, and deputies have found two pairs of kids' sneakers in the floor of the backseat."

"What size? What brand?"

She swallowed hard at Zach's answers. "The shoes have to be theirs, Zach. I'm coming out there."

"That's not necessary. You should stay home in case the kidnapper makes contact again. Besides, there are law enforcement personnel on the scene, and I'm heading there with Bart and Matt as we speak. I'll keep you abreast of any new information as soon as I get it."

"No. I'm coming out there." She might not be any help, but if her sons were in the area, then she wanted to be there, too. "I'll need exact directions."

"Okay, but let me talk to Nick first."

"I don't need his permission."

"I know that."

She handed the phone to Nick and went straight to her closet, stretching to her tiptoes to reach the plain overnight bag she'd bought this fall. She had no intention of coming home until this was settled and she had her sons.

She dropped the bag to the bed, then leaned over Nick's shoulder to see what he was writing on the notepad she kept on her nightstand.

"Directions to the wrecked car," he mouthed without taking the pen from the paper.

Hopefully that meant she'd get no argument from him. She left him on the phone with Zach and went to the bathroom to start packing the basic necessities. Her reflection in the mirror stopped her cold.

She looked ten years older than she had before the abduction. New wrinkles had made deep grooves around her puffy eyes. Her cheeks looked sallow, her lips drawn, the bottom one cracked. She'd always chewed on it when she was nervous. And she was worlds beyond nervous now.

A light rain splattered on the bathroom window. She'd best take boots and rain gear. But the boys didn't even have shoes. The thought sent her determined attitude plummeting back to the abyss of dread.

But if they'd found the kidnapper's car then the boys had to be nearby.

Maybe wet. Maybe hungry. But safe. She wouldn't allow herself to think of them any other way.

When she returned to the bedroom, Nick was studying his notes. "We can be there in approximately an hour," he said, as if their going together was something they'd already agreed on.

"You can't go, Nick. You have to stay here with Sam."

He shoved a stray lock of her hair behind her ear. "Sam can come along if he likes, but I've had it with waiting around for this lunatic. I'm going after David and Derrick. I wish to hell I'd done that in the first place."

"You have to think of your neck and spine, Nick. You should stay here tonight and rest."

"My neck and spine are nonissues in this."

"Not according to Dr. Cambridge or your coach."

"Let it go, Becky. I'll check with Sam and let him know what's up. Can you be ready to leave in fifteen minutes?"

"I can be ready in ten."

"Have your mother and Jaime pack some sandwiches and a couple of thermoses of coffee, enough for your brothers and anyone else involved in the search. This might turn into a long, cold, wet night."

He started to walk away, then stopped to touch her cheek and let his eyes lock with hers. His gaze was penetrating and questioning. "I won't let you down, Becky. I hope you can believe that."

Her breath caught. He'd bared his soul to her, and now his eyes were pleading with her for something in return. A look that told him things had changed between them. A promise that she could start fresh.

She wanted so badly to give it. Already she felt her walls crumbling. But she'd built up those expectations time and time again over the last ten years only to have them sink into pools of regret. Would they ever be able to get past the heartbreak?

"I LIED TO YOU," Bull said. "Your parents aren't coming out here to get you. Obviously they don't think you're worth the ransom. Now that I've seen what brats you are, I can see why."

"You better stop lying to us, or you're gonna be sorry."

Derrick knotted his little fists as if he thought one of them could actually cause Bull misery. His punch couldn't. His and his brother's stupid cowboy and Indian trick had. But they hadn't done as much to blow the deal as those two bodies in the woods were going to do.

Bull had been certain he could trick the boys into setting him free, but they were as smart and determined as they were devilish. They weren't going to buy into his schemes, and they weren't going to give him a chance to escape—not as long as David was pointing Bull's own gun at his head. The little imp would be just spunky enough to shoot him, too.

He couldn't break free as long as they were in the cabin. That's why he needed to get rid of them. If a couple of eight-year-old boys could cut their way out of tightly wound duct tape, then surely he could do the same and a lot quicker.

Time wasn't on his side. If he hadn't given in to the

rage and been so quick to pull that trigger, he could have still pulled this off.

But dead bodies brought cops, and the leaves he'd piled over them had surely washed away in the rain. That left him one option.

"So you kids gonna hang around here with me all night?"

"Nope," Derrick said. "We're leaving now, and when we come back, we're bringing our daddy and our uncles, and you will be sorry you ever kidnapped us."

He was sorry already, but they wouldn't be bringing anybody back. Once they were out of here, he'd free himself, then escape and track them down. He'd kill both of them before they had a chance to identify him. Luckily he had the hunters' rifles stuffed in the trunk of their Jeep. A pistol belonging to one of the men was still in the glove compartment.

He watched as they pulled on their jackets and got ready to leave. They were probably nice enough kids when they hadn't been kidnapped. Too bad they had to die so young.

# Chapter Twelve

Jaime started filling the everyday glasses with ice water. "I don't know why we even pretend to have meals. It's not as if anyone is going to take more than a few bites. Even Blackie's not eating."

"We need food," Lenora said, "especially Jaclyn. Pregnant women can't do without proper nutrition." And Lenora needed the routine of familiar activities that required no concentration. She could have prepared the soup and ham sandwiches they were having tonight in her sleep—if she were doing any sleeping.

She'd finally dozed off a couple hours ago only to be wakened by a nightmare starring the boys.

"Are we eating in the kitchen again?"

Lenora nodded. The kitchen had a warmth the dining room lacked except when the whole family crowded around the big oak table.

"How many place settings do we need?"

"One for everyone who's not out searching for David and Derrick—except Jeremiah." Fortunately Lenora's father-in-law was still taking his meals upstairs, though he was feeing much better today.

Pulling him into this would add another layer of strain on all of them—especially Jeremiah. He'd made a miraculous recovery from his massive stroke over a year and a half ago, but she certainly didn't want to risk another one.

"I thought Kali went back to her ranch," Jaime said.

"She did, but only to check on her horses. She said she wouldn't be long. And Jaclyn is watching Randy while Trish is horseback riding with Gina."

"I'm glad," Jaime said. "Gina really needed to get out of the house for a while. She had her own meltdown today when we got the news that the kidnapper didn't show."

"No one mentioned that to me."

"Because you have enough on your own plate, Mom." Jaime stopped to kiss Lenora's cheek as she sashayed by her with silverware.

So they were protecting her the way she was trying to protect them. Sometimes terrible things like this tore families apart. This one seemed to be pulling them all together. If it did that for Becky and Nick, it would be a blessing. But nothing would feel like a blessing until the boys were safe.

"I think we should all be out searching," Jaime said.

"I know you do. You've said that a dozen times over the last hour."

"We always pull together when something bad happens in this family. I don't see why it should be any different now."

"Zach thinks the situation is better left in the hands of law authority. Too many cooks spoil the broth."

"My nephews aren't broth. And all my brothers are out there helping. And so is Shelly."

"Shelly is ex-CIA. And she's in Zach's office in Colts Run Cross doing record checks at the moment. I'm sure you could go sit there and watch her."

"No, thanks. Watching the show is not my game."

And never had been. If Jaime was involved, she usually was the show. She had never been good at taking orders, and she had a way of claiming far too much attention from cops or any other men who happened to be around—even when she wasn't trying.

Lenora ladled hot tomato soup into a blue pottery bowl. "Zach has serious doubts that the kidnapper is still in the same place that he made the calls from. He thinks he may be regrouping to make another attempt at claiming the ransom."

"Well, if we don't hear something positive soon, I'm driving up there even if I'm just in the way. I can't stand sitting around here like a helpless female."

A spoon slipped from Jaime's hand and went clattering to the floor. She picked it up and tossed it into the sink. "I can't stand the thought of David and Derrick spending one more night with that crazed monster."

A loud thump behind her startled Lenora so badly she spilled soup from the ladle, bathing her fingers with the hot liquid.

"What the hell are David and Derrick doing with a crazed monster?"

Lenora turned just in time to see as well as hear Jeremiah's banging of his cane. "I didn't know you were coming down for dinner."

"Don't change the subject. What's this about David and Derrick?"

Jaime handed Lenora a towel to wipe the soup from her fingers and took over with the ladling. "Might as well come clean with him, Mom. It is what it is."

And put bluntly, it was a living nightmare. Lenora

collapsed into one of the kitchen chairs. "There's bad news," she said. "Sit down, and I'll tell you about it."

"I can listen standing up."

"Fine." It never did any good to argue with Jeremiah. "David and Derrick were kidnapped from school on Monday."

His wrinkles folded in on themselves, and his chin quivered. "Kidnapped?"

"Yes, while they were walking from the school to the church."

His face turned the color of chalk as he sank into the chair kitty-corner from hers. "Who took them? What does he want?"

She fed Jeremiah the details as succinctly and as calmly as she could, but there was no way to paint the picture that it didn't come out in shades of gray and black.

Jeremiah stopped her after practically every sentence with questions, but he was taking this much better than she'd expected. In fact, after the initial shock wore off, his face took on the defiant hardness he was famous for.

Once he'd exhausted her supply of information, he hammered his cane against the floor again. He hadn't been using the cane much of late, but apparently the flu had weakened him to the point he felt he needed it.

Odd, but tonight the sharp pounding Lenora used to dread seemed entirely appropriate. Welcome, even. A replacement for the scream of frustration she'd wanted to give all afternoon.

Jeremiah hammered again, the echo of it reverberating off the walls of the kitchen as the back door slammed indicating at least part of the family had returned.

"That kidnapper is messing with the wrong dadburned

family this time. He's swallowed himself a bitter pill there'll be no recovering from."

Lenora put a hand over his thin, heavily veined one. "I pray you're right."

"Of course I'm right. All the Collingsworth men are out there with their hackles up looking for him. Becky and Nick, too. The devil and Tom Walker couldn't stop them from getting David and Derrick back."

Jaime walked over and put her arms around Jeremiah's neck. "I like the way you think, Grandpa."

Trish joined them in the kitchen, balancing her young son on one hip. Gina, Jaclyn and Kali were a few steps behind her. They all stopped and stared at Jeremiah as if waiting for the proverbial second shoe to drop.

"Grandpa was just telling us how big a mistake the kidnapper made in going against the Collingsworths," Jaime announced.

"And I'm not talking just the adults," Jeremiah added. "I'd be willing to bet David and Derrick have given the man fits, too. Those boys have spunk. It's in their genes. No one should ever underestimate a Collingsworth."

Gina started the applause and the others joined in with the spontaneous approval of Jeremiah's much needed reassurance of faith in the family.

Lenora was thankful for it. As usual, Jeremiah was right. They would find the abductor, and he would pay. And in a perfect world they would get the boys back safely.

In this world that just might take the miracle she'd been praying for all along.

IT TOOK AN HOUR to reach the area where the car they believed to be the kidnapper's had been wrecked. The car was registered to Jake Hawkins, purchased for twelve hundred dollars on time from a sleazy used-car lot the week after he got out of prison. It smelled of whiskey and marijuana and mold.

The CSI team was still on the scene, working in the misty rain and gusty wind, searching for evidence to link the car to David and Derrick. They'd shown Becky the shoes, and she'd verified they belonged to her sons or at least were perfect matches for the ones they'd been wearing when they'd left for school on Monday.

After that, both she and Nick were forced to watch the process from her car. They couldn't see much, but it was as close as the detective in charge would let them get. It was clear he didn't see any reason for their hanging around.

Becky was losing patience, and her stress-and-fatigue-laced headache was not making things any easier. As far as she was concerned, a lot of people were standing around doing very little instead of searching for her sons. She'd complained about that every time anyone got close enough to listen. They all assured her they were doing their jobs.

But ever since they'd arrived, she'd had a feeling, almost a premonition, that the boys were nearby. She knew how saying it aloud would sound, so she'd kept it to herself, but she felt it. Their presence seemed almost as tangible as Nick's, who was sitting next to her.

Finally Zach pulled up and parked next to them. He got out of his truck and slid into the backseat of her car. "Rotten weather."

"Damn the weather. Is anyone looking for David and Derrick?" she demanded.

Zach took off his wet hat and set it on the seat beside him. "Half of Texas now that we've alerted them."

"I don't see any sign of that."

"It's difficult to see past your nose in this weather, but a half-dozen deputies and your other three brothers are all combing the area and have been for the last few hours. They're checking every house, cabin and mobile home they can find.

"And the state highway patrol is setting up a roadblock on the highway to stop and search all vehicles leaving this area."

"The kidnapper's car is wrapped around a tree. What good does it do to check vehicles?" She wasn't even trying to fight her frustration now.

Zach leaned forward and massaged her shoulders. "Take it easy, sis. Getting riled at the cops isn't going to help. The kidnapper is either still holed up in the area or he's already cleared out. If he's here, we'll find him. If he's left the area, we have to depend on law enforcement agencies around the state to track him down."

Becky pressed her fingers into her temples, where the throbbing ache was building to an explosive crescendo. "It's not enough."

Nick reached over and put a hand on her thigh. "You need to get some rest before you bite someone's head off."

"He's right," Zach said. "You can only go so long without sleep. Why don't the two of you drive into Huntsville and get a room? That way you can be nearby and still get some rest."

"In other words, you're telling me to do nothing." She started to get out of the car but was hit with a wave of vertigo. She was sick, exhausted and now dizzy. Maybe getting some rest did make sense.

"What about you, Zach?" Nick asked. "What are you doing the rest of the night?"

"I'll be out here a few more hours, checking for any houses or cabins we've missed. We're working from a grid. The major areas have been covered, but there are a few seldom used back roads we haven't hit yet."

"I'd like to join you. I'll need to drive Becky into town first. I don't want her driving these dark roads alone when she's as tired as she is tonight, but I can meet you after that."

"Are you sure that's what you want to do?"

"Positive."

"Then why don't I get one of the CSI guys to drive Becky into Huntsville and make sure she gets checked into a room. They'll be through out here shortly."

"There's no need for that. I can go wizz you two," she said.

"Would you listen to yourself?" Zach exclaimed. "You're so tired you can't talk straight. You've been living on raw nerves and strong coffee for almost thirty hours. I'm not trying to get rid of you, but if you don't get some rest, you'll end up in the hospital."

"Okay, but I don't like leaving."

"I'll go arrange for a ride for you." Zach opened the door and scooted out of the car without waiting for a response.

Nick took her hand in his and squeezed gently. "I'll go with you if you need me."

"You need your rest more than me, Nick. You're the one who's injured. You already should be in a hospital."

"When the boys are safe."

She knew it was useless to argue about this. "I'll be fine alone," she said. "You do what you need to do."

Zach returned a few moments later, the arrangements apparently made. "They're saving you a room at Whistler's Bed and Breakfast Inn. Steve Jordon will drop you off, and he says it's the most comfortable accommodations in this part of Texas."

Zach gave her a hug. So did Nick. And then he kissed her. A quick kiss, but it was the first time their lips had touched in months. She'd almost forgotten the taste of him. Sweet. Salty. Nick.

"I'll join you in the room in a few hours," he said. "Get some sleep."

"I'll try."

She closed her eyes and imagined the boys walking out of the woods and strolling toward the car. And then it was the four of them—Becky, Nick, David and Derrick running hand in hand through a soft summer rain.

ZACH GUNNED HIS ENGINE, spitting gravel as he drove away from the mobile home where the inhabitants had told them about a recent break-in. The single wide was set in a clearing at the end of a ribbon of dirt and mud that looked more like a pig trail than a road, but this area was full of those.

Most led to deserted cabins, many built years ago before some river Zach had never heard of dried up. At least that was the word from the local sheriff, a giant of a Texan with arms like a gorilla's and thighs as big around as Zach's waist. His disposition was all snarl and growl, and Zach suspected that his bite was just as bad.

Nick reached for his seat belt as Zach's truck rocked and rolled through a couple of mud holes big enough to drown a large dog. "Do you think it's possible that the kidnapper was the one who broke into those folk's mobile home Monday evening?"

"It's possible, but it's hard to believe a man who'd put as much thought into how he wanted the ransom paid and how he'd planned his escape would risk alerting the cops of his whereabouts for ice cream and sodas."

"But then ice cream, sodas and spaghetti do sound like David and Derrick," Nick said.

"That's why I told him we'd like to check the house for fingerprints. I think we can get a team on that first thing in the morning."

"I'd like to think it was the boys and that somehow they'd escaped the kidnapper and were on the run. But if that were the case, why would he have called this morning and set up the meeting at the Conroe airport?"

Zach turned on the defroster. "Maybe he thought he could pull it off even without the boys?"

"And then changed his mind?"

"I'm just thinking aloud," Zach admitted. "The most likely scenario is that he was hiding out in one of these old cabins until he wrecked his car. He probably intended to steal a vehicle and close the deal this morning."

"But something stopped him."

"And if we knew what that something was, we'd have a handle on things and a hell of a lot better chance of finding all three of them."

The rain was more of a deluge now, and Zach was starting to seriously feel the crunch of a long day. Fortunately they had almost covered every inch of their grid—or rather unfortunately since they hadn't located the kidnapper.

Zach came across another road, this one in even worse shape than the one they were currently on. He was pretty sure it hadn't made the grid. He turned down it anyway, though he half expected it to ramble around a few curves and then dead-end into an overgrown patch of mud, grass and brush.

He hit a spot where the water from the rains completely covered the road, and he had to creep through it. Lightning cut a jagged path through the dark clouds followed by rumbling thunder. The weather might be about to get a lot worse.

Nick put his head next to the side window. "Did you see that?"

"The lightning?"

"No, but when it lit the landscape, I saw a house— or what's left of one off to the right."

"How far off the road?"

"I couldn't tell. I just got a glimpse."

Zach slowed to a stop and yanked the gear into Reverse. He backed up until he was in about the same spot they'd been in when the lightning struck. Grabbing his rain gear and a high-beam flashlight from the backseat, he opened the door. He was half out of the truck before he decided to grab a second gun from beneath his seat.

Nick did the same, and as soon as the ponchos were over their heads, they tramped through the slosh, their boots sucked into the muddy goop with every step.

Nick found the cabin again with the beam from his flashlight. Rundown. Leaning. But there was a vehicle parked in front of it.

Zach's adrenaline level spiked. "Looks like someone might be around."

"If they are, they're either already in bed or sitting in the dark. Unless the storm knocked out the electricity."

Zach's hand rode the butt of his pistol as they approached.

"A Jeep Cherokee," Nick said once they were close enough to get a good look at the vehicle. "Isn't that what Hermann Grazier's wife said he was driving?"

"Exactly."

"Maybe Hermann and his brother-in-law found this old cabin and took refuge from the storm."

"Except that they should have been out of here long before the worst of the storm started. And this vehicle's obviously been parked here since before the rain made a lake of the driveway."

"Makes sense."

"That's why I make the big bucks." The comment was more habit than joke. Nothing about this situation was a laughing matter. If the hunters were inside, Zach was pretty damn sure they hadn't ended up here willingly.

He doubted they were. But Jake Hawkins just might be. Which meant the boys might be inside, as well.

"Take this," he said, passing the extra gun to Nick. "I know you know how to use it. I've seen you on the driving range at Jack's Bluff. Keep your eyes peeled, and use the car for cover in case someone inside heard us approach."

Nick took the gun. "You think this could be it, don't you?"

"Yes, if by 'it' you mean that this could be where Jake Hawkins has been hanging out."

"I'd give anything to walk though that door and find David and Derrick alive and well."

"I know, but don't count on it. The place looks empty. And about the gun, I guess I don't have to tell you not to shoot unless it's a matter of life and death—then make sure you're not the dead one."

"Got it.

The hood of the Cherokee was up and rain was pouring into the car's guts. Zach failed to come up with a rational explanation for that.

"Work your way around to where you can see the back of the cabin just in case someone tries to escape that way. And stay protected."

Nick followed the order without question, staying low and near the tree line. Zach sprayed the front of the house with light, eventually letting the beam pinpoint the entrance. Gun poised for action, he walked up and knuckle-rapped the door.

"Police. Open the door and keep your hands in view."

Of course there was no response. That would have been way too easy.

He knocked and yelled the order again, sure that this time he'd shouted over the wind and rain. Still nothing. Mentally and physically geared for an ambush, he tried the knob and the door swung open.

He flicked on the light, keeping his back to the wall and his trigger finger ready. There was no movement, but chaos painted a vivid picture that left no doubt in his mind that his nephews had been in this cabin with the kidnapper. They weren't here now—unless…

A shadow moved outside the open front door. He was not the only one around.

## Chapter Thirteen

"Back up. Don't shoot."

"Damn it, Nick. I told you to watch the back of the cabin."

"Nothing going on back there." And Nick had far too much at stake to be hanging around outside. "I'll cover. Let's search the house."

With each step, Nick's alarm rose. His sons weren't in this house, but they had been. David's Dallas Cowboys hat that had been signed by the whole team was on the kitchen table. Their two school bags were slung over the arm of a kitchen chair.

And everywhere he looked, the sights made him recoil in horror. Shreds of duct tape that Hawkins must have used to bind his sons. A rope. Boarded windows. A broken lamp. Empty beer cans everywhere. And blood splattered on the front door. His stomach pitched.

"This is were he held them while he did no telling what to them." His voice broke with his resolve and he buried his head in his shaking hands. "Right here, not a good two hours from the house, and I couldn't find them."

Zach put a hand on his shoulder. "Haven't found them *yet*. We're not through, not by a long shot."

But Jake Hawkins or whoever had his twin sons had fled the area, not in the hunter's car but likely in some other vehicle he'd stolen. For some reason Nick couldn't fathom, the man must have given up on getting the ransom. If that were the case, there would be no reason for him to let the boys go free so that they could identify him.

He'd refused to think that the boys could be dead, but now the possibility hardened to cement in his gut. They might have found them in time if he'd let Zach call the shots from the beginning.

But he hadn't. He'd held out for the ransom attempt. He'd only wanted to protect them, but he might have destroyed them the same way he'd done his mother. He could have saved her if he hadn't waited until it was too late.

Becky was right to want the divorce. He didn't measure up. Cheering crowds, raving sports announcers and a huge bank account couldn't change that.

He walked over and picked up the cap David had been so proud of.

"Don't touch anything else," Zach said. "We need to preserve the evidence. There should be enough fingerprints in this room alone to put Jake Hawkins away."

"Then you're convinced Jake Hawkins is the kidnapper?"

"I'd stake my claim to my part of the ranch on it."

That was as sure as a man could get.

"He could be on his way to Mexico now," Nick conceded. But if he'd killed or even hurt David and Derrick, Nick would find him or spend the rest of his life trying.

"Let's get out of here, Zach. I need to give Becky the news."

*THE RAIN WAS FALLING in sheets, and Becky's clothes were drenched, her skin numb from the wind and falling temperatures. "David! Derrick?"*

*Why wouldn't they come? She'd been calling them for hours and, now she was lost in this pitch-dark forest. A low-hanging limb from a tree smacked her in the face when she tried to pass. Blood trickled down her cheek and across her lips. The metallic taste of it burned her tongue.*

*"David! Derrick? Answer me. I know you're out there."*

*A bird swooped down on her in the darkness, and its talons tangled in her hair. She fought it off, then tripped and fell on her face on the soggy ground.*

*A giant tarantula crawled across her hand. She screamed and knocked it away.*

*"Are you looking for us, Mom? We're right here."*

*She jumped to her feet and ran to them. When she reached them they were gone.*

BECKY WOKE UP SHAKING. It took several seconds to realize that she was still in her car on the edge of the woods near Jake Hawkins's wrecked car. She rubbed her eyes and tried to clear the troubling remains of the nightmare from her mind.

She glanced at her watch. Eleven-fifty. She must have fallen asleep while waiting on the deputy who was supposed to drive her into Huntsville. The few minutes she was supposed to wait for a ride into Huntsville had lasted for two hours.

If anything, there were more cars here now than when she'd drifted off. But the action was no longer centered on Jake Hawkins's wrecked car. In fact, there was no one around it. The activity was in an area of bright lights shining through the trees off to her left.

She lowered her window. The rain had stopped. The wind had died down, as well. She opened the door, got out and started walking toward the lights and din of voices.

Someone grabbed her by the arm. She turned to find the young deputy she and Nick had talked to earlier.

"I'm sorry, Mrs. Ridgely, but you can't go back there. Crime scene. Secured area. You know how it is."

"Is there new evidence?"

"Yes, ma'am. One of the deputies had gone to take a—well, you know because there aren't any bathrooms around."

"I understand." She could use some decent facilities herself. "What did he find?"

"Two bodies."

"Two bodies." She swayed, and the ground started rising to meet her face.

The deputy steadied her. "It was those hunters who were missing. It was their bodies that were found. I'm sorry. I should have said that first. No excuse, but it's been a night."

She still wasn't sure she'd heard him right. "Did you say that someone killed Hermann Grazier?"

"Yes, ma'am. Killed him and his brother-in-law. Shot one of them in the back of the head, the other in the front. Real nasty."

"Jake Hawkins must have killed them."

"I'm not at liberty to divulge any information. If I did, it would just be supposition."

But who else would it be? Surely he hadn't killed

them for a phone. Only someone who'd gone totally mad would commit such an act.

The totally mad person who had her sons. The depths of her soul started to shake. She needed to get out of here.

"Would you tell Deputy Steve Jordon that I'm feeling much better now and that I'm going to drive myself back to Whistler's Inn in Huntsville? And if either my brother Deputy Zach Collingsworth or my husband Nick Ridgely shows up, you can give them that same information."

"I'll do it."

She'd call Nick when she got back to Huntsville, but not until then. He'd only insist she wait for him to drive her. She was fully capable of doing that herself now that she'd had some sleep and a new shock to steel her mind.

The deputy stayed at her side. "Do you know how to get back to the main road?"

"Probably not. Can you point me in the right direction?"

"Do you have a compass in your car?"

"There's one with the GPS system."

"Then keep turning to the west. I think it's about four turns before you reach Highway 190. That will take you right into Huntsville."

"Thanks." She hurried back to her car. Two people were dead. Nothing about this could be good. She turned the key in the ignition. "O, Holy Night" was playing on the radio. The clock said ten past midnight.

It was Christmas Eve.

THE FIRST THING Nick noticed when he and Zach returned to the spot where he'd left Becky was the action taking place in the nearby woods. The second was that Becky's car was missing. "I thought Steve Jordon was going to drive Becky back to the hotel in his squad car and leave her car for me."

"He was, but he may still be here. Judging from the lights and the crowd and that new strip of bright orange tape going up in the trees, I'd say they've uncovered some new evidence."

Which meant that Becky had probably given up on her ride and driven back alone. He pulled out his cell phone and was punching in her number when a young deputy stuck his head in the window Zach had just lowered.

"Mrs. Ridgely left about ten minutes ago, maybe less. She said to be sure and tell you that she got some sleep first and that she was wide awake. Said she was driving into Huntsville."

"Thanks," Nick said. "Did she seem all right?"

"Seemed as coherent as any of us, not that that's saying much."

Zach turned toward the site of the lights and action. "What's going on in the woods?"

"We found those two hunters who went missing— Hermann Grazier and Bruce Cotton. Well, to be more specific, we found their bodies."

They listened to the gory details. Zach interrupted with questions several times. Nick's mind had jumped ahead to terrifying conclusions. Number one was that Jake Hawkins was capable of murder.

"Never seen a man more eager to get back to prison." Zach stepped out of the car and tossed Nick his keys. "Why don't you take my truck and go join Becky? I have a feeling she needs your company and that you need hers."

Nick nodded. "What about you? You need some sleep."

"I'll get some, but I want to take a look at exactly what they found. Steve or one of the other deputies will give me a lift into town when we're done. I'll get my keys from you over breakfast in the morning."

"That'll work."

Nick drove away from the scene, glad the rain was over, and thinking of his sons.

Memories of the night the boys were born sprang to life as if it had been yesterday. He'd been overcome with emotion the first time he'd held them in his arms—David in the right one, Derrick in the left.

He was certain his life had changed forever at that point. He was a father, a husband, a second-year player in the NFL. Finally he'd be able to bury the past and lose the insecurities and guilt that drove him.

He'd been wrong, of course. If anything the secret life of Nick Ridgely pushed him even harder to prove himself after he'd become a father.

Now he might lose his career and his marriage. And if that weren't terror enough, his sons were with a sociopath who'd already killed today. And that was the best scenario.

He beat a fist against the steering wheel as he pulled onto the rain-slick road. His day of reckoning had come.

HOURS OF POURING RAIN had left the old rock and dirt roadbed formidable and the shoulders a slimy sledge. Becky crept along, afraid to drive faster than a crawl.

She'd made one turn. Now her eyes were peeled for the next crossroad.

She hadn't realized earlier how narrow the roads were or how isolated they felt. Nick had been driving then, and she'd been consumed with the prospect of seeing Jake Hawkins's car and determining for certain if the shoes inside belonged to her sons. That seemed days ago.

So did Nick's shocking confession of a past she'd never even suspected. Even now, she struggled to fuse the Nick she knew with that frightened little boy who'd been forced to deal with issues far beyond his years.

The Nick she knew was driven, cocky, sexy. She'd fallen so hard for him when they met that she'd have married him that very night. Nick had been the sane one, insisting that they take it slow.

Not that they had in the lovemaking department. They'd been dynamite together—until football season started the following fall.

Even then he'd been driven to be the best player on the team. She'd accepted his ambition without question, considered it a good thing. She'd been far too in love with the star of the Longhorns to ever find fault with him.

But never once in all the years they'd been together had she seen the haunting pain in his eyes that had been there today when he'd told her about his mother's death. Had he hidden his vulnerability that well all those years or had she just been too blind to see what was in his soul?

She'd been quick to blame Nick for their lack of emotional attachment, but now it seemed that she'd been as guilty as he was of not seeing beyond the superficial.

She'd never bothered to look beyond the facade of the man he appeared to be to see the person deep inside.

Now it all came down to the fact that neither of them had ever really known the other.

He wanted to change. Maybe she needed to do some soul searching and some changing, as well…when this was over. When their sons were safe.

Her car went into a skid as she rounded a sharp curve that sent her straining against her seat belt and the beams from her headlights jutting across a patch of dark woods. She tensed but managed to keep the vehicle from leaving the road.

Going even more slowly now, she caught a glimpse of movement on the edge of the illumination from her headlights. Her heart slammed against her chest as the earlier nightmare flashed across her consciousness.

She braked slowly and stared into the pitch blackness of the moonless night. She was overreacting. The movement had most likely been a deer or several of them. She'd hit a huge buck once driving back to the ranch after a function in Houston.

A heavy fog had drastically reduced visibility, and by the time she'd spotted the animal, it had been too late to stop. Just as she reached it, it had darted across the road. Her car had been totaled. Luckily she and her mother, who was dozing in the passenger seat, only suffered a few bruises.

Becky lowered the window. The night seemed eerily silent at first, and then she became aware of the cacophony of sounds made by the wind in the trees and myriad nocturnal creatures that flew through the branches and scurried through the grass.

Her finger was on the button to raise the window

when she saw movement again. Not a deer but a person. She was almost sure of it—unless her mind was playing cruel tricks on her. After the past few days, that was entirely possible.

She got out of the car, rounded the back of it and stepped from the road into slush. "David! Derrick!"

The feeling of déjà vu was incredibly strong and frighteningly ghostly. It was the earlier nightmare all over again, only she was fully awake. She shivered as she took a few steps toward the thick growth of trees just feet from the road.

"David. Derrick. It's Mom."

A gust of wind slapped her in the face and jolted her from the harrowing state of hypnotic absurdity she'd fallen into. The constant stress was driving her over the edge. Her sons were with a kidnapper, not wandering the forest like spooked fawns.

She turned to walk back to the car, then stopped. Someone was here. She could hear whistling.

# Chapter Fourteen

Footfalls sounded behind Becky. She spun around as a brawny arm locked her in a stranglehold.

"Jake Hawkins?"

"Yeah, but we're about to be real friendly, and my friends call me Bull."

Becky tried to break free of his hold, but a sharp prick at the base of her neck stopped her. He had a knife. One jerky move and her jugular would be sliced.

"Where are my sons?"

"Where I left them. Bleeding. Crying for their momma."

She fought the rush of panic and fury that shook her. She'd never hated another person, but she did now.

"Why? Why us? Why David and Derrick?" Her heart cried into her words. "We did everything just the way you said. We had the money. You didn't show up to get it."

"You called in the authorities."

"We didn't."

"Don't lie, you bitch. The cops swarmed my wrecked car like a hive of killer bees." He spit the words at her.

He knew. There was no use in lying. Less use to fight as long as the knife was at her throat. "We only called them after you didn't show up as planned. We thought you no longer wanted the money."

"Like you'd know about wanting money. You living the friggin' dream life of a princess. Texas royalty. You like that, don't you? You always did."

"I don't know what you're talking about."

"High school, Becky. I'm talking Colts Run Cross High School. You parading around the football field in that cheerleading outfit that barely covered your behind. Wearing that stretchy top so that your young tits taunted every guy who passed."

"That was years ago, Jake. I wore the uniform they gave us. I didn't mean to taunt anyone. I barely knew you."

His grip tightened, and he lifted the arm under her chin, pulling her head back until she was looking up into his snarling face. "You didn't want to know me. You acted like I was dried-up paint on the wall until you started your nasty rumors. You liked thinking of me as a murderer, but you didn't know the half of it."

"That's not true. I never thought you killed your grandmother. I didn't." Not until now.

"The woman nagged me all the time. Told me I was as worthless as my tramp mother. Said I was a curse to her."

Becky fought to swallow against the pressure on her neck. "I'm sorry, Jake. I am. I didn't know."

"You didn't know. You didn't care. And now I don't care, either, not about you or your bratty kids. Not about Nick Ridgely, either."

Her face was so close to his that even in the dark she could see the rage in his eyes. The same fury he must have felt when he'd pushed his grandmother down those stairs. When he'd pulled a pregnant woman from her car and stabbed her with a pocketknife. When he'd killed two men for no reason at all.

But she couldn't give up. They'd find her body, but would they ever find David and Derrick in time?

"Nick has the money, Jake. Let me call him, and he'll bring it to you," she pleaded. "All five million, in small bills, just like you said. You get the money, and you give us back our sons."

"Where's your phone?"

"In my handbag. I left it in the car. I'll get it and call him."

"Sure you would, right after you drove off and left me here."

"No. You can go to the car with me." Anything to give her a chance to get out of this alive.

"One call, Becky. One chance. If anything goes wrong, I'll kill you along with your sons and then wipe Nick Ridgely's face in your blood."

She would have gladly given him the money, only Nick didn't have it on him. It was back at Jack's Bluff. He'd be here in minutes if she called, but she had to keep him from walking into a trap.

"Nick will want to know where the boys are. He'll want to talk to them."

"Haggling won't work, Becky. You lost all the pawns in the game the second my knife touched your flesh."

Jake pulled her into the clearing and started to drag her toward her car. The lights from an approaching car stopped him. He yanked her back into the trees, the knife piercing her skin as he did. She felt only a quick sensation and then the hot, wet trickle of blood dripping from her neck.

A pickup truck pulled to a stop behind her car. The beams from its headlights sent a muted whisper of illumination through the trees. Jake's right hand stayed around her neck, but he pulled the knife away and exchanged it for a pistol.

"Make one sound and you're dead."

She had no doubt he meant the threat. But if she stayed silent and the driver of the truck walked toward them, he'd be the one who was dead, shot just as Hermann Grazier and Bruce Cotton had been.

A man stepped from the driver's side of the truck and walked to her car. Her heart jumped to her throat and sent agonizing stabs of dread through every fiber of her being.

The driver of the truck was Nick

NICK STARED INTO Becky's empty car. Her keys were in the ignition. Her purse was in the passenger seat. Her jacket had been slung to the backseat. He struggled for some positive spin to put on the situation, but there was none.

Trepidation gave way to full-scale alarm. He peered into the darkness on either side of the road and then went back to the truck for a flashlight. He shot the bright beam into the trees, searching for a sign of Becky, though he couldn't imagine any reason that she'd have ventured into the heavily forested area.

He fervently wished that he hadn't given the weapon back to Zach when they'd left the cabin where the kidnapper had been holed up with David and Derrick, but he'd had no idea that he'd need one tonight.

Muscles clenched and adrenaline pumping, he stepped off the road and toward the trees, shining the beam toward the ground to search for Becky's trail. He found it quickly, imprints of her boots carved into the muddy clay.

"Becky!"

No response. Yet he was sure she'd come this way. Or been lured this way. He called her name again, louder, panic adding a crusty crack to his voice.

Something rustled the grass to his left. He took off running toward the sound.

"Don't, Nick. It's Jake. He has a gun."

Too late. Nick saw Becky being thrown to the ground and Jake Hawkins's heavy foot stamp down on her stomach. The gun in his hand was pointed at her head.

"I want my five million, Nick Ridgely, and I want it now."

This was crazy. Becky surely hadn't come out here alone to meet the kidnapper. But she was here, a gun at her head. Nick had to think fast.

"The money's in my truck," he lied. "Let Becky go, and I'll get it for you."

"I don't like those rules. Let's try mine. You bring me the money, and I'll let your bitch live."

He obviously didn't want to risk coming out of the clearing for fear an armed deputy might come along as Nick had. That was Nick's only advantage.

"Drop the gun."

"You're not giving the orders."

"Then shoot me."

"Nick, don't." Becky was crying and straining against Jake's killer hold on her. "Just go."

"Drop the gun, Jake, or get the money yourself."

"Get the money or she dies."

"Where are my sons?"

"Dead."

Becky wailed as if her heart were spilling onto the ground.

A blinding fury roared through Nick's veins along with the sure realization that Jake had no intention of letting either of them walk away from this alive.

"Your sons didn't cooperate, so I killed them, the same way I'll kill Becky if I don't have that money in my hand in thirty seconds. One."

Nick's past flashed before his eyes in living color. The red blood as his mother had drooped against him. The plum-colored dress Becky had worn on their first date. The baby-blue blankets they'd wrapped David and Derrick in the night they were born.

"The money, Nick, or do I just pull this trigger now?"

So who would it be in tonight's game? Nick Ridgely who let everyone down? Or Nick Ridgely, star receiver for the Dallas Cowboys. Great hands. Lightning speed. Amazing timing.

Or Nick Ridgely, his own man?

Nick took one more step toward the car, then turned, diving into the air in that unexpected split second and coming down on top of Jake. His left hand cracked against Jake's right one, sending the pistol flying though the air.

Jake recovered quickly, planting a fist into Nick's injured neck at the top of his spine. Nick went down in excruciating pain, then stumbled back to his feet. He swung at Jake and missed as Jake hammered him with another right punch to the center of his back and a left jab to his collarbone.

He was hitting the right spots to make the most of Nick's injury. Delivering blow after blow. Nick stumbled away, trying to get his balance. He spotted Becky clawing in the pine straw for the gun. "Get out of here, Becky. Now!"

Jake was at him again, fists pounding into Nick's neck and spine as he jumped on his back and dug his knees into his side as if he were riding a wild bronco. The pain was so intense, Nick was afraid he'd pass out or that the doctor's fears would materialize and he'd fall into a paralyzed mass.

It would take that for him to give up and leave Becky with this madman. He fought back, finally slamming his backside into a tree with enough force to shake Jake loose and send him sprawling to the ground. Nick backed away to catch his breath and regroup. Jake came up with a knife, the blade extended. He swiped it across Nick's chest, drawing blood.

Becky was still on her hands and knees in the mud. "Take the car, Becky. Get out. Please get out of here."

Jake sliced into him again, this time across the right thigh. Nick grabbed a broken limb from the ground and poked it into Jake's face. Jake howled but never slowed down, coming at Nick and knocking him to the carpet of pine straw that was fast turning red with his blood.

He was losing feeling in his arms and legs. His vision was blurry. In spite of all Nick's vows, Jake Hawkins was going to win.

And then a blast of gunfire exploded, and Jake Hawkins finally quit coming at him.

"Nick. Nick."

"I'm sorry, Becky. I'm sorry I let you down."

"You didn't. Oh, Nick, say you're okay. Please tell me you can move."

His brain was too hazy to know for certain if he was

alive or dead and dreaming. He rolled over and spit out a mouthful of blood and what felt like a dozen teeth.

"I thought he'd killed you, Nick. I was so afraid."

Slowly the scene came into view. Becky was crying and pushing Jake's body off him. He pulled her into his arms with the last of his energy and lay in the mud with her tears running down his chest.

"Are you all right?" she whispered between sobs.

He wasn't all right. He might never be all right again. Neither would Becky. He'd failed them, and their sons were dead.

"I'll call an ambulance," she said.

"I think it's too late for that. He looks dead."

"I meant for you."

"Not yet." He couldn't bear to have her leave his arms.

They lay in the dark holding on to each other, her sobs open and honest, his tears a burn of moisture seeping from his eyes.

He didn't know how much time had passed before the flashing blue lights from a squad car lit the area. The cops Jake had been trying so hard to avoid. He managed to stand and help Becky to her feet. There wasn't a part of him that didn't ache.

"Nick. Becky."

The deputy was no surprise. You could count on a Collingsworth. "Out here, Zach."

Zach strode to them. "What the devil happened here?"

"I saw someone in the trees," Becky said, her voice shaking and drenched in heartbreak. "I thought it might be David and Derrick, that they could have escaped from the kidnapper and were on the run. It was Jake."

"And then Nick came along and shot him," Zach said, jumping to the erroneous conclusion. He offered Nick a high five. "Good work, man. I didn't even know you were carrying a gun."

"I wasn't. It was his."

Zach knelt and felt for Jake's pulse, making sure he was really dead. "I guess the boys were wrong. They thought they'd taken his only pistol. He must have stolen one from Hermann Grazier."

Nick shook his head to clear it. "What are you talking about?"

"Why don't I let your sons tell you?" Zach whistled and motioned to the car. The door opened, and David and Derrick jumped out and started running to them.

"Becky wasn't that far off," Zach said. "The boys escaped and came walking out of the woods to where the cops were stringing yellow tape a couple of minutes after Nick drove off."

Becky didn't wait to hear the rest of her brother's explanation. She was already rushing toward David and Derrick. The three of them literally collided, tangling in a boisterous three-way hug before they pulled her down on top of them.

Nick couldn't move that quickly, but he did pretty well for a guy with a few new contusions to add to his medical report. He fell gingerly into the tangle of arms, legs and unadulterated joy.

THE HOMECOMING for David and Derrick was everything anyone could have expected and more. Every light in the big house was on, and every single member of the Collingsworth family had been waiting on the front porch when they arrived.

The only lull in the celebration had occurred in the short period of time it had taken for Becky, Nick, David and Derrick to shower off the mud.

Now David and Derrick were holding court in front of the fireplace, drinking hot chocolate, munching on cookies and fudge explaining for at least the tenth time how they'd lassoed the kidnapper and used his own duct tape stunt to render him helpless and at their mercy.

It was three in the morning, and no one seemed to realize that they should all be in bed.

Nick was the only quiet one, and Becky was certain he was paying the price for tangling with Jake Hawkins. He looked as if it hurt to move, but he never complained. It wasn't his style, and just maybe that wasn't so bad.

Becky slipped unnoticed from the family room and went back to the kitchen for a glass of water. Lenora was standing by the range, wiping tears from her eyes with a Santa Claus towel.

"So this is where you disappeared to," Becky said.

"I needed some alone time to count my blessings."

Becky put her arms around her mother, enfolding her in a hug. "You always believed they'd come home safely, didn't you? I tried, but I never seem to have your faith."

"I've had years to work on it. And I believe in miracles."

"After tonight, I think we all do. But I was afraid, so very afraid. And not only for the boys. I think the divorce may be a mistake, Mom. I don't think all the problems with our marriage belong to Nick."

"Tell your husband that, Becky."

"Tell me what?"

Neither Becky nor Lenora had seen or heard Nick come into the kitchen. Now that they knew he was there,

Lenora slipped from Becky's embrace and left them alone.

Nick frowned. "If this is bad news, I don't want to hear it tonight. Let me have Christmas first. Give me the holiday with you and the boys before I have to come back down to earth."

Her moment of truth. She took a deep breath. "I love you, Nick. I don't know if I ever realized how much until I thought Jake Hawkins was going to beat you into a pulverized, paralyzed mess. But I knew it then, and I know it now. I admit our marriage needs work, but..."

Nick crossed the room, slowly, the pain evident in his every step. "Oh, Becky. I love you so much. I'll do whatever it takes not to lose you. I'll give up football and move back here to the ranch. I'll talk every night about feelings until you are sick of hearing me. I'll attend every school function the boys ever have, even spelling bees. Just say what you need from me to make this work, and I'll give it my best shot."

"That's just it, Nick. I don't want you to give up football for me. I don't want you to give up anything. Our problems are not all your fault. They never were. Both of us have to work on being honest with each other about our feelings. You can't hide behind your past. I can't hide behind my stubbornness."

He cradled her face in his bruised hands. "Are you saying you'll give us a chance?"

"As many chances as we need. I don't want to face life without you. I want to raise our sons together, have grandchildren, grow old in each other's arms. I want to love you for the rest of my life. I just want the marriage to be all that it can be."

He pulled her into his arms and then winced in pain.

She pulled away. "I'm sorry. I guess this isn't the night for you to crawl back in my bed."

"Just try to keep me out. But promise not to move—or breathe heavy." He kissed her lightly on the lips, a sweet promise of all that would come in the lifetime ahead.

"Merry Christmas, Mrs. Ridgely."

"Merry Christmas, Nick."

She wouldn't have thought there was a chance of it a few hours earlier, but Nick had called it right. This really would be the merriest Christmas of their lives.

# Epilogue

*Three months later*

"I've never seen you so excited or secretive, Nick. When are you going to tell me what is going on?"

"I've already told you. It's spring. We're going on a picnic on the beautiful Jack's Bluff Ranch."

"Yeah, Mom. It's a picnic. Don't you get it?"

Nick stopped the truck and opened his door so the boys and Blackie could pile out of the backseat of the double-cab Dodge.

"This is the new me," Nick said. "Can't get enough of family time."

"There's more going on here. I just haven't figured it out yet. You're smiling like you just won the Super Bowl."

"That's because I have the old Becky back." He slipped his arm along the back of the seat and tangled his fingers in one of her loose curls. "The Becky who makes love like a wild woman."

She punched him playfully. "It's just that you're so thrilled to be back in the saddle again."

"You got that right, lady. And such a nice saddle. You can take a Collingsworth off the ranch, but you can't make her give up those wild bronc-riding ways in the bedroom."

"I'm just a rancher's daughter at heart."

"And don't I know it."

She had to admit she loved the weekends on the ranch, like this one. It was good for the boys, too. But she was happy in Dallas, as well. She thought she could probably be happy anywhere now that she and Nick were getting along so well—both emotionally and physically.

It was as if they'd found each other all over again. And best of all, the problems with his injury were practically behind him. He'd gone back to the doctor yesterday, and he expected the doctors to give him full clearance to start getting ready for the upcoming season any day.

Nick had parked at the spot where the creek that crisscrossed the ranch bubbled musically over a bed of angular rocks. They'd come here on his first visit to the ranch and made wild, passionate love on a blanket in the grass. He'd called it their special corner of the ranch ever since. She liked the fact that they'd come back here today.

"Can we go swimming?" Derrick called, already racing to the water.

Becky climbed out of the truck. "No. It's not summer yet. The water's too cold."

"Then can we wade?"

"Cold feet won't kill them," Nick said.

"Okay, wade, but take off your shoes and socks and watch out for snakes."

"Ah, the joys of ranch life." Nick walked to the front of the truck and leaned against the hood.

"It's not so bad," she said.

"Not bad at all. I was just teasing you."

She started to pull the picnic basket from the back of the truck.

"Let's wait for the food," Nick said. "I need to talk to you about something."

His voice had grown serious. She felt a sudden tightening in her chest. "This isn't about the doctor's report, is it? Did you hear something today?"

"Actually, I did."

He'd gotten bad news. That's why he was smiling— to hide his anxiety. She'd said she wanted him to share all his feelings with her, but she wasn't sure she was up to this.

Becky walked to the front of the car and snuggled next to him. He circled his arms around her.

Finally she got up the courage to ask the dreaded question. "Was the verdict bad?"

"Could be worse. I have some mild ligamentous injuries that are healing. Nothing to keep me from playing again, though I might be at slightly more risk of future injuries."

She breathed a sigh of relief, though the possibility of his having a serious injury never went down easily. "So you can still play?"

"I can." He kissed the back of her neck. "I've decided that I'm not."

She turned to face him, unsure she'd heard him right. "You can't give up football. You love it. It's your life."

"It *used* to be my life. Not that I'm knocking it. I've had a great career. Football was my salvation, but I don't need it anymore, not the way I did. I want to move on to new challenges and I'd like to do that here."

"In Colts Run Cross?" She was having difficulty buying this.

"Here. On Jack's Bluff Ranch. On this spot where we're standing. Our hideaway. Don't you think it's the perfect place to build our dream house?"

"I love it, but…I don't see you as a rancher, Nick." ·

"Whew. Now, that's a relief. I have no intention of being a rancher. I've talked to the school board. They need a head coach for the Colts Run Cross high school football team. I'd like to take that job. Football has given me a lot. It's time I gave something back."

He nudged her chin so that she was looking into his gorgeous brown eyes. "It's taken me a while to get here, but this is what I want. I was hoping it's what you want, too."

"Pinch me, Nick. I'm sure I'm dreaming."

"How about I just kiss you instead?"

His lips took hers hungrily, the passion as consuming as it had been when she'd first fallen in love with him.

"I love you, Nick Ridgely."

"That's good, Becky, because there is something else I need from you to make me totally happy."

"Name it, Coach."

"A daughter."

With pleasure.

"Or two."

She could handle that.

"And another son."

Now he was pushing his luck.

"Maybe even another set of twins."

She covered his mouth with her lips, cutting off his words before he'd talked her into a whole football team.

\* \* \* \* \*

We hope you enjoyed reading

# ONE HOT FORTY-FIVE

by *USA TODAY* bestselling author

## B.J. DANIELS

and

# MIRACLE AT COLTS RUN CROSS

by *USA TODAY* bestselling author

## JOANNA WAYNE

If you liked these stories, then you will love
**Harlequin® Intrigue®** books.

You crave excitement! **Harlequin Intrigue**
stories deal in serious romantic suspense,
keeping you on the edge of your seat as
resourceful, true-to-life women and strong,
fearless men fight for survival.

"Maybe you don't understand the fine line between snooping and jail. Breaking and entering is—"

"I'm going with you." Donning a hat and gloves, Gillian turned to look at him.

Austin was smiling at her as if amused.

"What?" she said, suddenly feeling uncomfortable under his scrutiny. She knew it was silly. He'd seen her at her absolute worst.

"You just look so…cute," he said. "Clearly, breaking the law excites you."

She smiled in spite of herself. It had been a while since a man had complimented her. But it wasn't breaking the law that excited her.

She breathed in the freezing air. It stung her lungs, but made her feel more alive than she had in years. Fear drove her steps along with hope.

At the dark alley, Austin slowed. It was late enough that there were lights on in the houses.

"Come on," Austin said, and they started to turn down the alley.

A vehicle came around the corner, moving slowly. Gillian felt the headlights wash over them, and she let out a worried sound as she froze in midstep.

Her moment of panic didn't subside when she saw that it was a sheriff's department vehicle.

"Austin?" she whispered, not sure what to do.

He turned to her and pulled her into his arms. Her mouth opened in surprise, and the next thing she knew, he was kissing her. At first, she was too stunned to react. But after a moment, she put her arms around his neck and lost herself in the kiss.

As the headlights of the sheriff's car washed over them, she let out a small helpless moan as Austin deepened the kiss, drawing her even closer.

The sheriff's car went on past, and she felt a pang of regret. Slowly, Austin drew back a little. His gaze locked with hers, and for a moment they stood like that, their quickened warm breaths coming out in white clouds.

"Sorry."

She shook her head. She wasn't sorry. She felt…light-headed, happy, as if helium-filled. She thought she might drift off into the night if he let go of her.

"Are you okay?" he asked, looking worried.

She touched the tip of her tongue to her lower lip. "Great. Never better."

*Find out what happens next in*
*DELIVERANCE AT CARDWELL RANCH*
*by* New York Times *bestselling author B.J. Daniels,*
*available December 2014,*
*only from Harlequin Intrigue.*

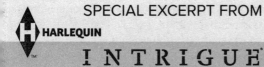
*When her search for a killer leads to danger and bull rider*
*Cannon Dalton, homicide detective Brittany Garner will*
*face her toughest case yet: catch her long-lost twin's killer,*
*and try not to fall for the man who might be her infant*
*niece's father…*

"The woman in Greenleaf Bar was you?"

"You don't remember?"

"Vaguely."

He struggled to put things in perspective. That had been a hell of a night. He'd stopped at the first bar he'd come to after leaving the rodeo. A blonde had sat down next to him. As best he remembered, he'd given her an earful about the rodeo, life and death as he'd become more and more inebriated.

She must have offered him a ride back to his hotel since his truck had still been at the bar when he'd gone looking for it the next morning. If Brit was telling the truth, the woman must have gone into the motel with him and they'd ended up doing the deed.

If so, he'd been a total jerk. She'd been as drunk as him and driven or she'd willingly taken a huge risk.

Hard to imagine the woman staring at him now ever

being that careless or impulsive.

"Is that your normal pattern, Mr. Dalton?" Brit asked. "Use a woman to satisfy your physical needs and then ride off to the next rodeo?"

"That's a little like the armadillo calling the squirrel roadkill, isn't it? I'm sure I didn't coerce you into my bed if I was so drunk I can't remember the experience."

"I can assure you that you're nowhere near that irresistible. I have never been in your bed."

"Whew. That's a relief. I'd have probably died of frostbite."

"This isn't a joking matter."

"I'm well aware. But I'm not the enemy here, so you can quit talking to me like I just climbed out from under a slimy rock. If you're not Kimmie's mother, who is?"

"My twin sister, Sylvie Hamm."

Twin sisters. That explained Brit's attitude. Probably considered her sister a victim of the drunken sex urges he didn't remember. It also explained why Brit Garner looked familiar.

"So why is it I'm not having this conversation with Sylvie?"

"She's dead."

*Find out what happens next in*
*MIDNIGHT RIDER*
*by Joanna Wayne,*
*available January 2015 wherever*
*Harlequin Intrigue® books and ebooks are sold.*